P9-DFW-404

Praise for the Merchant Princes series

The Merchants' War

"Charlie Stross's latest is a brilliant, amusing, and challenging piece of mestizo fiction—recklessly crossbreeding fantasy and SF tropes and using the resulting bonfire to say interesting things about culture, economics, politics, and really cool battles with chain mail and MP5s and horses and hang gliders. Very real people with very different backgrounds meet and collide and strike lovely sparks. This series is great and getting better all the time!"   —S. M. Stirling

"Twenty-first-century politics and high-fantasy intrigue make remarkably good bedfellows in Stross's The Merchant Princes."   —SciFi.com

"The action shifts rapidly among the three worlds in the fourth successive thriller in a fantastically thrilling series."
—*Booklist*

The Clan Corporate

"Charles Stross's [Merchant Princes] series continues strong with *The Clan Corporate*."   —*Analog*

"Stross provides a solid story with strong emphasis on the characters. Equally strong is the way that economic forces underpin the plot and the world-building. Readers who haven't picked up the first two volumes should definitely do so before starting on this one—they're well worth finding."   —*Asimov's Science Fiction*

TOR BOOKS BY CHARLES STROSS

THE
MERCHANTS'
WAR

BOOK FOUR OF THE MERCHANT PRINCES

CHARLES STROSS

TOR®
fantasy

A TOM DOHERTY ASSOCIATES BOOK
NEW YORK

This is a work of fiction. All the characters, organizations, and events por-
trayed in this novel are either products of the author's imagination or are
used fictitiously.

THE MERCHANTS' WAR

Copyright © 2007 by Charles Stross

All rights reserved.

Edited by David G. Hartwell

A Tor Book
Published by Tom Doherty Associates, LLC
175 Fifth Avenue
New York, NY 10010

www.tor-forge.com

Tor® is a registered trademark of Tom Doherty Associates, LLC.

ISBN 978-0-7653-5589-8

First Edition: October 2007
First Mass Market Edition: October 2008

Printed in the United States of America

0 9 8 7 6 5 4 3

For Gil, Jane, George, and Leo

the
MERCHANTS'
WAR

1

AFTER THE WEDDING PARTY

The wreckage still smoldered in the wan dawn light, sending a column of grayish-white smoke spiraling into the misty sky above Niejwein. Two mounted men surveyed it from a vantage point beside the palace gatehouse.

"What a mess."

"Unavoidable, I think. The best laid plans . . . have they found his majesty yet, your grace?"

The first speaker shrugged. His horse shuffled, blowing out noisily: the smell of smoke, or possibly the bodies, was making it nervous. "If he was inside the great hall we might never find identifiable remains. That could be a problem: I believe the blast must have far exceeded the plotters' intent. The soldiers found the Idiot, though—what was left of him. Near chopped in half by the rebels' guns."

It was not a cold morning, and the second speaker wore a heavy riding coat: nevertheless, he shivered. "If these are the spells the witch families play with, then I think we may conclude that his presumptive majesty struck not a moment too soon. The tinkers have become too accustomed to having the Crown at their convenience. This could well be our best opportunity to break their grip before they bring damnation to us all."

The first speaker stroked his beard. "That is the direction of my thoughts." He looked pensive. "I think it behooves us to offer our condolences and our support in his hour of need to his majesty; a little bird tells me that he is of like mind. Then we should look to our own security. His lordship of Greifhalt has a most efficient levy which I think will prove sufficient to our immediate needs, and for the honor of his grandfather he has to come to our aid. We can count on Lyssa, too, and Sudtmann. For your part . . . ?"

"Count me among your party, your grace. I think I can contribute—" He paused, thinking. "—two hundred? Yes, two hundred of horse certainly, and perhaps more once I've seen to the borders."

"That will be helpful, Otto. The more you can send, the better—as long as you do not neglect the essentials. We cannot afford to feed the scavengers, of whichever kind." The first speaker shook his head again, looking at the smoking rubble. Stooped figures picked their way through it, inspecting the battlefield for identifiable bodies, their movements as jerky as carrion birds. "But first, an appropriate demonstration of our loyalty is called for."

The Duke of Innsford nudged his horse forward; his companion, Otto, Baron Neuhalle, followed, and behind him—at a discreet distance—the duke's personal company followed suit. The scale of destruction only became apparent as Innsford rode down the slope towards what had been the Summer Palace of Niejwein. "It really does appear to have been visited by a dragon," he commented, keeping Neuhalle in view. "I can see why that story is spreading . . ."

"Oh yes. And it came to dinner with his late majesty and half the witch families' heads of household at his table for the feast," Neuhalle agreed. "They'll draw the right conclusion. But what a mess." He gestured at the wreck-age. "Rebuilding the palace will take years, once the im-mediate task of ensuring that his majesty's reign is long and untroubled by tinkers and demon-traffickers is com-pleted. And I do not believe that will be easy. The old fox will move fast—"

Neuhalle broke off, composing his face in an expres-sion of attentive politeness as he reined in his horse. "Otto Neuhalle, to pay his respects to his majesty," he called.

"Advance and be recognized." Neuhalle nudged his horse forward towards the guards officer supervising the salvage attempt. "Ah, my lord. If you would care to dis-mount, I will escort you to the royal party at once."

"Certainly." Neuhalle bowed his head and climbed heavily down, handing the reins to his secretary. "I have the honor of accompanying his grace, the Duke of Inns-ford. By your leave . . . ?"

The guards officer—a hetman, from his livery—looked past him, his eyes widening. "Your grace! Please accept my most humble apologies for the poor state of our hospitality." He bowed as elaborately as any courtier, his expression guarded as a merchant in the company of thieves: clearly he understood the political implications of a visit from the duke. "I shall request an audience at once."

"That will be satisfactory," Innsford agreed, conde-scending to grace the earth with his boot heels. "I trust the work proceeds apace?"

"Indeed." A lance of royal life guards came to attention behind the hetman, at the barked order of their sergeant: " 'Tis a grim business, though. If you would care to fol-low me?"

"Yes," said Innsford.

Neuhalle followed his patron and the hetman, ignoring the soldiers who walked to either side of him as if they were ghosts. "His majesty—the former prince, I mean—I trust he is well?"

"Yes, indeed." The hetman seemed disinclined to give much away.

"And is there any announcement of the blame for this outrage?" asked Innsford.

"Oh, yes." The hetman glanced over his shoulder nervously, as if trying to judge how much he could disclose. "His majesty is most certain of their identity."

Neuhalle's pulse raced. "We came to assure his majesty of our complete loyalty to his cause." Innsford cast him a fishy glance, but did not contradict him. "He can rely on our support in the face of this atrocious treason." Although the question of whose treason had flattened the palace was an interesting one, it was nothing like as interesting to Neuhalle as the question of whom the former crown prince was going to blame for it—for the explosion that had killed his father. After all, he couldn't admit to having done it himself, could he?

They rounded the walls of the west wing—still standing in the morning light, although the roof of the Queen's Ballroom had fallen in behind it—and passed a small huddle of Life Guards bearing imported repeating pistols at their belts. A white campaign pavilion squatted like a puffball on the lawn next to the wreckage of the west wing kitchens, and more soldiers marched around it in small groups or worked feverishly on a timber frame that was going up beside it. "Please, I beg you, wait here a while."

Innsford paused, leaning on his cane as if tired: Neuhalle moved closer to him, continuing the pretense that their escorts were as transparent as air while the hetman hurried towards the big tent, his progress punctuated interminably as he was passed from sentry to sentry. The guards were clearly taking no chances with their new monarch's life. "A bad night for the kingdom," he remarked quietly. "Long live the king."

"Indeed." Innsford looked almost amused. "And may his reign be long and peaceful." It was the right thing to say under the circumstances, indeed the only thing to say—their escort looked remarkably twitchy, in the shadow of the ruined palace—but Neuhalle had to force himself not to wince. The chances that King Egon's reign would be peaceful were slim, at best.

They didn't have long to reflect on the new order in peace. The guards hetman came loping back across the turf: "His grace the duke of Niejwein awaits you and bids me say that his majesty is in conference right now, but will see you presently," he managed, a long speech by his standards. "Come this way."

The big pavilion was set up for the prince's guests: royal companions and master of hounds at one side, and smaller rooms for the royal functions at the other. The middle was given over to an open space. The duke of Niejwein sat on a plain camp stool in the middle of the open area, surrounded by an ever-changing swarm of attendants: a thin-faced man of early middle years, he was, as Innsford might have remarked, *one of us*—a scion of the old nobility, the first fifty families whose longships had cleaved the Atlantic waves four centuries ago to stake their claims to the wild forested hills of the western lands. He was no friend of the merchant princes, the tinker nobles with their vast wealth and strange fashions, who over the past century had spread across the social map of the Gruinmarkt like a fungal blight across the bark of an ancient beech tree. Neuhalle felt a surge of optimism as he set eyes on the duke. "Your grace." He bowed, while his patron nodded and clasped hands with his peer.

"Be welcome, your grace. I had hoped to see you here. Rise, Otto. You are both welcome in this time of sorrow. I trust you have been apprised of the situation?" Niejwein's left eyebrow levered itself painfully upwards.

"In outline," Innsford conceded. "Otto was entertaining me in Oestgate when the courier reached us. We came at once." They had ridden since an hour before dawn from thirty miles down the coast, nearly killing half a dozen mounts with their urgency. "Gunpowder and treason." His lips quirked. "I scarcely credited it until I saw the wreckage."

"His majesty blames the tinkers for bringing this down upon our heads," Niejwein said bluntly.

"A falling out among thieves, perhaps?" Otto offered hopefully.

"Something like that." Niejwein nodded, a secretive expression on his face. "His Majesty is most keen to inquire of the surviving tinkers the reason why they slew his father using such vile tools. Indeed, he views it as a matter of overwhelming urgency to purge the body of the kingdom of their witchery."

"How many of the tinkers survived?" asked Innsford.

"Oh, most of them. Details are still emerging. But beside the death of his majesty's father and his majesty's younger brother—" Otto started at that point. "—it appears that his majesty is the only surviving heir for the time being." Niejwein nodded to himself. "The queen mother is missing. Of the tinkers, the heads of three of their families were present, some eighteen nobles in total, including the bitch they planned to whelp by the Idiot—" Otto startled again, then contained himself. "—and sixty sundry gentles of other houses. The tinkers not being without allies."

"But the main company of those families are untouched," Innsford stated.

"For the time being." Niejwein's cheek twitched. *Has he the palsy?* Otto wondered. "As I said, his majesty—" Niejwein stopped and rose to his feet, turning to face one of the side panels. A moment later he dropped to one knee: Otto scrambled to follow suit.

"Rise, gentlemen." Otto allowed himself to look up at his new monarch. The Pervert—*no, forget you ever heard that name, on pain of your neck,* he told himself—was every inch a prince: tall, hale of limb, fair of face, with a regal bearing and a knowing gleam in his eye. Otto, Baron Neuhalle, had known Egon since he was barely crawling. And he was absolutely terrified of him.

"Sire." Innsford looked suitably grave. "I came as soon as I heard the news, to pledge myself to you anew and offer whatever aid you desire in your time of need." Not grief, Otto noted.

Prince Egon—no, King Egon—smiled. "We appreciate the thought, and we thank your grace for your thoughtfulness. Your inclination to avoid any little misunderstandings is most creditable."

"Sire." Innsford nodded, suppressing any sign of unease.

Egon turned to Niejwein. "Is there any word of that jumped-up horse thief Lofstrom?" he asked offhandedly. Neuhalle kept his face still: to talk of Angbard, Duke Lofstrom, so crudely meant that the wind was blowing in exactly the direction Innsford had predicted. But then, it wasn't hard to guess that the new monarch—who had hated his grandmother and never seen eye-to-eye with his father—would react viciously towards the single biggest threat to his authority over the kingdom.

"No word as yet, sire." Niejwein paused. "I have sent out couriers," he added. "As soon as he is located he will be invited to present an explanation to you."

"And of my somewhat-absent chief of intelligence?"

"Nor him, sire. He was leading the party of the tinkers at the past evening's reception, though. I believe he may still be around here."

"Find proof of his death." Egon's tone was uncompromising. "Bring it to me, or bring *him*. And the same for the rest of the upstarts. I want them all rounded up and brought to the capital."

"Sire. If they resist . . . ?"

Egon glanced at Innsford. "Let us speak bluntly. The tinker vermin are as rich a target as they are a tough one, but they are not invulnerable and I *will* cut them down to size. Through magic and conspiracy, and by taking advantage of the good will of my forefathers, they've grown like a canker in my father's kingdom. But I intend to put a stop to them. One tenth of theirs, your grace, will be yours if you serve me well. Another tenth for our good servant Niejwein here. The rest to be apportioned appropriately, between the

Crown and its honest servants. Who will of course want to summon their families to attend the forthcoming coronation, and to take advantage of the security provided for them by the Royal Life Guards in this time of crisis."

Neuhalle shrank inwardly, aghast. *He wants hostages of us?* He found himself nodding involuntarily. To do aught else would be to brand himself as a rebel, and it seemed that Egon had no intention of being the bluntest scythe in the royal barn: but to start a reign with such an unambiguous display of mistrust boded ill for the future.

"We are your obedient servants," Innsford assured him.

"Good!" Egon smiled broadly. "I look forward to seeing your lady wife in the next week or two, before the campaign begins."

"Campaign—" Neuhalle bit his tongue, but the prince's eyes had already turned to him. And the prince was smiling prettily, as if all the fires of Hel didn't burn in the imagination concealed by that golden boy's face.

"Why, certainly there shall be a campaign," Egon assured him, beaming widely. "There will be no room for sedition in our reign! We shall raise the nobility to its traditional status again, reasserting those values that have run thin in the blood of recent years." He winked. "And to rid the kingdom of the proliferation of witches that have corrupted it is but one part of that program." He gestured idly at the wooden framework taking place on the lawn outside the pavilion. "It'll make for a good show at the coronation, eh?"

Neuhalle stared. What he had thought to be the framework of a temporary palace was, when seen from this angle, the platform and scaffold of a gallows scaled to hang at least a dozen at a time. "I'm sure your coronation will be a great day, sire," he murmured. "Absolutely, a day to remember."

A damp alleyway at night. Refuse in the gutters, the sickly-sweet stench of rotting potatoes overlaying a much nastier aroma of festering sewage. Stone walls, encrusted in lichen. The chink of metal on cobblestones, and a woman's high, clear voice echoing over it: "I don't believe this. Shit! *Ouch.*"

The woman had stumbled out of the shadows mere seconds ago, shaking her head and tucking away a small personal item. She wore a stained greatcoat over a black dress of rich fabric, intricate enough to belong on a stage play or in a royal court, but not here in a dank dead end: as she looked around, her forehead wrinkled in frustration, or pain, or both. "I could go back," she muttered to herself, then took a deep breath: "or not." She glanced up and down the alley apprehensively.

Another chink of metal on stone, and a cracked chuckle: "Well, lookee here! And what's a fine girl like you doing in a place like this?"

The woman turned to stare into the darkness where the voice had spoken from, clutching her coat around her.

Another chuckle. "Let's ask her, why don't we?"

The woman—Countess Helge voh Thorold d'Hjorth, to her vast and squabbling extended family, plain Miriam Beckstein to herself—took a step backwards then stopped, brought up against the crumbling brick wall. Figures solidified out of the shadows beyond the flickering gaslight glow from the end of the alleyway. Her gaze darted across them as she fumbled with the pockets of her coat.

"Heya, pretty lady, what have you got for a growing boy?"

"Show us your tits!"

Miriam counted three of them as her eyes adapted to the darkness. It helped that she'd just stepped over, across a gap thinner than an atom—or greater than 10^{1028} meters, depending how you measured it—from a lawn outside a burning palace, the night punctuated by the roar of cannon and the staccato cracking of the guards' pistols. *Three of them*, she realized, a sick tension in the pit of her stomach, *one of them's on the ground, crouching, or . . .* ?

The standing figure came closer and she saw that he

was skinny and short, not much more than a boy, bow-legged, his clothing ragged. At five foot six Miriam didn't think of herself as tall, but she could almost look down on the top of his head. Unfortunately this also gave her a good view of the knife clutched in his right hand.

Desperation and a silvery edge of suppressed rage broke her paralysis. "Fuck off!" She stepped forward, away from the wall, hands balling into fists in her black velvet gloves. "Right, that's it. I've had enough!"

The evening had started badly. She was already under house arrest in Niejwein, with a suspended sentence of death hanging over her head, and Miriam's great-uncle had casually informed her that she was to be married off to the king's youngest son—damaged goods, brain-damaged goods at that—and the betrothal would be announced that evening. Then, at the very court reception where she was due to be bought and sold like a prize heifer, something had gone so very badly off the rails that she still could barely believe it. There'd been blood flowing in rivers on the marble-floored corridors, brutal figures moving through the palace with guns in their hands: and she'd cut and run, only to find herself here: facing a back-alley mugging or worse on the streets of New London, shadowy ragmen lurching out of the muck and stench to menace her with their demands—

The man with the knife looked surprised for a moment. Then he darted forward, as if to punch her. Miriam felt a light blow across her ribs as he danced back. "Oof!" He was skinny, and short, and she outreached him, and his face was a frozen picture of surprise as she grabbed his arm, yanked him closer, stomped down on his foot, and then jerked her knee up inside his thigh. *Just like teacher said,* she thought, remembering the self-defense class she'd taken—what, two years? three years?—ago. Her assailant made a short, whimpering gasp, then dropped like a log, rolling on the ground in pain. Miriam looked past him, hunting for his friends.

The one standing behind him took one look at her as if

he'd seen a ghost, then turned tail and fled. "Doan' leave me!" wailed the third in a thick accent, waving spidery arms at the ground: there was a rattling noise. Miriam stared. *He's got no legs,* she realized as he pawed at the ground with hands like oars, scooting away on a crude cart. *Why did the other one run*—she put a hand to her chest. There was a rip in her stolen coat. *That's funny.* She frowned, stuck a finger through the hole, and felt the matching rip in the outer fabric of her dress where the knife had slid across the boned front. "Damn!" She looked down. The little guy with the knife lay at her feet, twitching and gasping for breath. The knife lay beside him in the gutter: the blade was about three inches long and wickedly sharp. "You little shit!" She hauled up her skirts and kicked him in the ribs with all her might. Then she knelt down and took the knife.

The red haze of fury began to clear. She looked at the moaning figure on the cobblestones and shuddered, then stepped round him and quickly walked to the end of the alleyway. Cold sweat slicked her spine, and her heart pounded so hard it seemed about to burst. *I could have been killed,* she thought dizzily, tugging her coat into place with jerky motions, her hands shaking with the adrenaline aftershock. It wasn't the first time, but it never failed to horrify her afterwards. She moved unconsciously towards the street lights, panicky-tense and alert for any sign that knife-boy's friends had stopped running and were coming back for her. *He tried to stab me!* She felt sick to the pit of her stomach, and her usual post-world-walking headache had intensified unbearably, thumping in time with her pulse. *I've got to get help,* she realized. *Got to find Erasmus.*

Miriam had grown up in Boston, in the United States of America, in a world where things made sense. Random spavined beggars in alleyways didn't try to gut you like a fish. There was no king-emperor in New York—New London, as they called it over here, in this world—no zeppelins, either. She'd had a job as an investigative journalist working for a leading tech business magazine, and a mother who she knew had adopted her when she was a baby, and a solid sense of her own identity. But it had all gone out of the window nine months ago, when she'd discovered that she was a long-lost relative of the Clan, a tight-knit body of world-walkers from another, far more primitive world.

The Medicis of their timeline, the Clan traded between worlds, parallel universes Miriam had heard them called. Which was bad news because the Gruinmarkt, where they came from, hadn't progressed much past a high-medieval civilization of marcher kingdoms up and down the eastern seaboard; in the world of the United States, the Clan was the main heroin connection for New England. Miriam's ingrained habit of sticking her nose into any business that took her interest—especially when it was explicitly forbidden—had landed her in a metric shitload of trouble with the Clan. And things had gotten even worse with the shockingly unexpected fight at the Summer Palace in Niejwein. Miriam had ducked out (with the aid of a furtively acquired world-walking locket) and ended up here, in New London. In another world that made little sense to her—but where she did, at least, speak the language passably well.

I've got to find Erasmus, she told herself, holding onto the thought as if it was a charm to ward off panic. The twisting road at the end of the alleyway was at least lit by rusting gas lamps. There was nobody in sight, so she put on a burst of speed, until she rounded a curve to see a main road ahead, more lights, closed shop fronts, a passing streetcar grinding its wheels on the corner with a shower of sparks from the overhead pickups. *Whoa.* She slowed, eyebrows furrowed, shoulders tensing as if there was a target pasted right above her spine at the base of her neck. *I can't go anywhere like this . . . !*

She stopped at the end of the side street, panting as she took stock. *I've got no money,* she realized. Which was not good, but there was worse: *I'm dressed like . . . like*

what? Clothing wasn't cheap in New Britain; that had
been a surprise for her the first time she came here. People didn't wear fancy dress or strange countercultural outfits, or rags—unless they could afford no better. If she'd
had the right locket to reach New York, her own world,
she might have passed for an opera buff or a refugee from
a Goth nightclub: but here in New London she'd stick out
like a sore thumb. And she did not want to stand out. To
mark herself out for special attention might attract the attention of the police, and the word had a different (and
much more sinister) meaning here. *I need somewhere to
blend in quick, or get a change. Contact Erasmus.* But
Erasmus was what, two hundred miles away, in Boston?
What was that place he mentioned? She racked her
brains. *Woman called Bishop. Some place, satirist, Hogarth, that's it. Hogarth House, Hogarth*—

A cab was clattering along the nearly-empty high street.
Miriam took a step forward and extended her right hand,
trying to hold it steadily. The cabbie reined in his horse
and peered down at her. "Yuss?"

Miriam drew herself up. "I want to go to Hogarth, Hogarth Villas," she said. "Immediately."

The cabby's reaction wasn't what she expected: a low
chuckle. "Oh yuss indeedy, your ladyship. Hop right in
and I'll take you right there in a jiffy, I will!" *Huh?*
Miriam almost hesitated for a moment. But he obviously
knew the place. *What's so funny about it?* She nodded,
then grabbed hold of the rail and pulled herself up. The
cabbie made no move to help her in, other than to look
down at her incuriously. But if he had any opinion of her
odd outfit he kept it to himself, for which she was grateful.
As soon as she was on the foot plate, he twitched the reins.

I'm going to have to pay him, Miriam thought, furiously
racking her brains for ideas as the cab rattled across the
stone pavements. *What with?* She fumbled in her greatcoat's pockets. One of them disgorged a foul-smelling
cheesecloth bag full of loose tobacco. The other contained
nothing but a loose button. *Oh, great.* They were turning

past Highgate now, down in what corresponded to the East Village in her world. Not an upmarket neighborhood in New London, but there were worse places to be—like inside a thief-taker's lockup for trying to cheat a cabbie of his fare. What was the woman's name, Bishop? Margaret Bishop? *I'm going to have to ask her to pay for me.* Miriam tensed up. *Or I could world-walk back to the other side, wait a couple of hours, and*—but her headache was already telling her no. If she crossed back to the Gruinmarkt she'd be good for nothing for at least three hours, and knowing her luck she'd come out somewhere much worse than an alley full of muggers. For the time being, returning to the other side was unthinkable. *Damn it, why did James have to give me the wrong locket?*

The journey seemed interminable, divided into a million segments by the plodding clatter of hooves. Probably a yellow cab in her own familiar New York would have gotten across town no faster—there was less traffic here—but her growing sense of unease was driving her frantic, and the lack of acceleration made her grind her teeth. *That's what's wrong with this world,* she realized, *there's no acceleration. You can go fast by train or airship, but you never get that surging sense of purpose—*

The traffic thickened, steam cars rattling and chuffing past the cab. The lights were brighter, some of the street lights running on electricity now: and then there was a wide curving boulevard and a big row of town houses with iron railings out front, and a busy rank of cabs outside it, and people bustling around. "Hogarth Villas coming up, mam, Gin Lane on your left, Beer Alley to your right." The cabbie bent down and leered at her between his legs. "That'll be sixpence ha'penny."

"The doorman will pay," Miriam said tensely, mentally crossing her fingers.

"Is that so?" The leer vanished, replaced by an expression of contempt. "Tell it to the rozzers!" He straightened up: "I know your type." A rattle of chain and a leather weather shield began to unroll over the front of the cab, blocking off escape. "I'll get me fee out of you one way or the other, it's up to you how you pays."

"Hey!" Miriam waved at a caped figure standing by the gate, pushing the side of the leather screen aside. "You! I need to see Lady Bishop! Now!"

The caped figure turned towards her and stepped up towards the cab. The cabbie up top swore: "Bugger off!"

"What did you say?" Miriam quailed. The man in the cape was about six feet six tall, built like a brick outhouse, and his eyes were warm as bullets.

"I need to see Lady Bishop," Miriam repeated, trying to keep a deadly quaver out of her voice. "I have no money and it's urgent," she hissed. "I was told she was here."

"I see." Bullet-eyes tracked upwards towards the cabbie. "How much?"

"Sixpence, guv, that's all I need," the cabbie whined.

Bullet-eyes considered for a moment. Then a hand with fingers as thick as a baby's forearm extended upwards. A flash of silver. "You. Come with me."

The weather screen was yanked upwards: Miriam lost no time clambering down hastily. Bullet-eyes gestured towards a set of steps leading down one side of the nearest town house. "That way."

"That—" Miriam was already halfway to the steps before several other details of the row of houses sank in. Lights on and laughter and music coming from the ground-floor windows: lights out and nothing audible coming from upstairs. The front doors gaped wide open. Men on the pavement outside, dressed for a good time by New London styles. Women visible through the open French doors in outfits that bared their knees—*oh*, she thought, feeling herself flush. *So that's what's going on. Damn Erasmus for not telling me!* Halfway down the steps, which led to a cellar window and a narrower, grubbier, doorway, another thought struck her: a brothel would be a good place for Erasmus's friends to meet up. Lots of people could come and go at all hours and nobody would think it strange if they took measures to avoid being identified.

Even her current fancy dress probably wasn't exceptional. Erasmus Burgeson, almost the first person she'd met on her arrival in New Britain, was connected to the Leveler underground, radical democrats in a country that had never had an American revolution, where the divine right of kings was still the unquestionable way the world was run. Which meant—

The door was snatched open in front of her. Miriam looked round. Bullet-eyes was right behind her, not threatening, but impossible to avoid. "I need to see—"

"Shut it." He was implacable. "Go in." It was a scullery, stone sinks full of dishwater and a couple of maids up to their elbows in it, a primitive clanking dishwasher hissing ominously and belching steam in the background: "through there, that way." He steered her towards a door at the back that opened onto a narrow, gloomy servant's corridor and a spiral staircase. "Upstairs."

Another passage. Miriam registered the distant sound of creaking bedsprings and groaning, chatter and laughter and a piano banging away on the other side of a thin plasterboard wall. Her chest was tight: it felt hard to breathe in here. "Is it much further?" she asked.

"Stop." Bullet-eyes grabbed a door handle and shoved, glanced inside. "You can wait here. Tell me again what you came for."

Miriam tensed and looked at him. She'd seen dozens of men like this before, hard men, self-disciplined, capable of just about anything—her heart sagged. "Erasmus Burgeson told me I should come here and talk to Lady Bishop next time I was in town," she managed to explain. "I wasn't planning on being here quite this early, without warning." She sagged against the door-frame, abruptly exhausted. "I'm in trouble."

"Has it followed you?" His voice was even, quiet, and it made the hair on the back of her neck stand on end as if someone had stepped over her open grave.

"No," she managed, "not here. I lost it on the way."

"Inside. I'll be back." She stumbled into the room. He

flicked a switch and a dim incandescent bulb glimmered
into light. "I may be some time." The door closed behind
her. The room was a servant's bedroom, barely longer
than the narrow bed that occupied half of it. There was a
window, but it opened onto a shaft of brickwork, another
darkened window barely visible opposite. *Click.* Miriam
spun round, a fraction of a second too late to see the lock
mechanism latch home.

"Shit," she moaned quietly, "shit!" She sat down on the
bed and rested her head in her hands, her energy and will
to resist fading frighteningly fast. It had been a long and
terrible day, and even standing up felt like a battle. *What
have I done?* Erasmus was nuts, or playing a sick joke on
her, sending her to a brothel to talk to the madam: although, on further thought, it didn't seem particularly
strange compared to the rest of this eventful day. She'd
been dragged out of her house arrest, shanghaied into a
forced wedding, just missed being blown up by a bomb,
seen the king and the prince she'd been engaged to
gunned down (and who knew what the hell was going to
happen in the Gruinmarkt now?) and run into an old
heartthrob (and what the hell was he doing there, working
for the DEA?). Then she'd fled for her life, been attacked
by muggers, menaced by a cabbie who thought she was a
prostitute, and finally locked up in another goddamned
prison cell, this time in a brothel. *I'm going to go mad,*
she thought dizzily, lying down on the lumpy mattress. *I
can't take much more of this.* But instead, she fell asleep.
And that was how they found her when they came for her,
an hour after midnight.

It was shaping up to be a night to remember for all the
wrong reasons, Mike decided. The flat metallic banging
of musketry outside blended with the screams of
wounded men and the sullen roar of the burning palace to
form a hideous cacophony, punctuated by the occasional
crack of modern smokeless-powder firearms and shouted

orders. *This is worse than that mess down in Colombia, that mountain village. What was it called?*

He inched carefully out from behind the broken wall. The stench of burnt gunpowder and charred wood lent an acrid taste to the nighttime air. About four meters from the wall, the indistinct shapes of a row of trees loomed out of the darkness. He turned his head, looking around cautiously.

That nameless village on a forested mountainside in Colombia: he'd been there as part of a DEA training team, working with the Colombian army to weed out cocaine plantations in the hilly back country. What he hadn't realized at first was that the cocaine plantations belonged to the other government—the Maoist guerrillas working to overthrow the authorities controlled vast swathes of territory, had battalions of expressionless men in green with machine guns and rifles. It wasn't a police raid, it was more like an army spearhead advancing into hostile territory. And then the shooting started . . .

He twitched back into focus, scanning the area for threats. The palace behind him was burning merrily, flames reaching through holes in the steeply pitched roof. Doors and windows had been blown out: some were half-blocked by improvised barricades where the defenders were trying to hold out. It was full dark, and they were trying to fight a battle against attackers who were shooting from outside the circle of light. The noises were getting louder, Mike noted. More banging of muskets, the hollow shotgun-like thump of a blunderbuss, then yells and a distant drumming of hooves, the sound of many horses running. He turned to face the darkness, closed his eyes for ten long seconds to let them adjust, then rose to a crouch and dashed towards the tree line, zigzagging madly and praying he'd make it without putting a foot in a rabbit hole or catching a tree root.

At least I got Miriam out of there. He dived past a tree, ducked under a low branch, and crouched down again to scan for watchers. *Wonder if she'll call.* It was just too weird: he'd known she'd be here, hell, that was the whole reason they'd inserted him, to see if he could make contact—but actually seeing her in the midst of all this weird medieval squalor, dolled up like an extra from a historical drama, brought it all home to him. She was part of the Clan: she was a world-walker, one of the narcoterrorist dynasty that was running drugs up and down the eastern seaboard. And she wanted out!

But he'd blown it. *You're going to make her an offer she can't refuse,* said the colonel, and instead he'd come out with the truth, limp-dicked and apologetic, and as good as told her to go to ground. *Phone me in a week or so,* he'd told her. *Yeah, right.* And all because he'd seen it coming, like a slow-motion train wreck: Miriam was about as unlikely to cooperate with Smith as anyone he could imagine. And he couldn't stomach the idea of them turning her into a mule, like the guy in the cellar with the collar-bomb and the handcuffs, terrified that Mike was going to execute him.

Something moved in the brush behind him. Mike spun round, gun raised.

"Sir!" The hissed voice was familiar: Mike lowered his pistol immediately.

"That you, Hastert?"

The shadow in front of him nodded. "O'Neil's twenty yards that way. Go to him now." Bulky night-vision goggles half-covered Hastert's face, in surreal contrast to his baggy trousers and chain mail vest. He'd acquired a gun from somewhere, some kind of machine pistol with a bulky silencer attached.

"Okay, I'm going, I'm going." Mike scuttled away, his pulse hammering with the adrenaline aftershock. Hastert and O'Neil were part of the forward support team in Zone Blue, specialists yanked out of Delta Force to handle the sharp end of the Family Trade Organization's intel operation on the ground in the parallel universe the criminals came from. Dangerous men, but it was their job to get him out of this alive. *I could have told her to come with me,* he told himself. Could have lied, offered her witness protection. *Hell, she asked for it! We could have gotten her out.*

But Miriam's potential value to Colonel Smith lay in her connection to the Clan hierarchy; and everything had gone to pieces. "They've got my mom," she'd said conversationally, right after he'd shot the soldier who was trying to murder her. And the royal they'd been trying to marry her off to against her wishes was dead—what the hell was going on? "O'Neil?" he whispered.

"Over here, sir. Keep down."

O'Neil was crouched behind a deadfall. "What's going on?"

"Looks like they're making whoopee." His grin was a ghostly crescent in the darkness. "Don't you worry, we'll get you out of here."

A moment of rustling and crunching, and Sergeant Hastert appeared. "Sitrep, Pete."

"Sam's on point." O'Neil gestured farther into the trees, where the ground fell away from the low hill on which the palace had stood. "He's seen no sign of anybody in the woods. Bad news is, the aggressor faction have got sentries out and they're covering the approaches from the road. There's maybe thirty of them and they've got riders—we're cut off."

"Get him back here, then."

O'Neil vanished into the darkness. "How bad is it?" asked Mike.

"Could be worse: nobody's shooting at us." Hastert turned to look at him. "But we'd better be out of here by dawn. Did you get what you wanted?"

"Yes and no." Mike hunkered down. "Everything we thought we knew about what was going on here is out of date. I got to talk to my contact, but she's in deep shit herself—didn't have much time, they were trying to kill her—"

A noise like a door the size of a mountain slamming shut a hundred meters away rocked Mike back on his heels.

"Down!" Hastert lurched against him, shoving Mike's face down on a matted bed of branches. Moments later, debris thudded off the branches above their heads, spattering down on the summer-dry soil. "Get moving, we're too close."

The next hour passed in a nightmarish crawl through the dark forest, heading always away from the boom and crash of gunfire and the shouts of the combatants. The royal palace, although nominally within the city of Niejwein, was surrounded by a walled garden the size of a large park—large enough that the palace itself was out of easy gunshot range of its neighbors. But in the chaos of the apparent coup, the shooters seemed to be inside the compound. Stray shots periodically came tearing through the treetops, so that Mike needed no urging to keep his head close to the dirt.

After an interminable crawl, Hastert tapped him on he shoulder. "Stop here, wait till I get back." He vanished into the darkness as silently as a ghost. Mike shivered violently. *Trouble?* he wondered. There was nothing he could do; on this part of the mission he was baggage, as much as Miriam would have been if he'd tried to extract her from whatever the hell that weird scene back at the palace had been about. *I can't believe I shot that guy without warning.*

Mike reran the scene in his mind's eye; the perp—even now, he couldn't drop the law enforcement outlook—with the knife, trying to stab the woman in the black gown, the stink of burning wood, snarling fear, taking the time to aim carefully, waiting for a clear shot as the woman shoved back hard against her assailant . . . then the shock of recognition. *It's her!* Despite the longer, intricately coiled hair, the drawn expression, the bruise on her cheek, and the rich Victorian widow's weeds, it was like nothing had changed since that ambiguous last dinner at Wang's, just off Kendall Square. The shock of recognition was still with him: the realization that, all along, the world he moved in was smaller than he'd realized, that during the whole fruitless search for

the east coast phantom network he'd been dating a woman
who could have—if she herself had known what she was—
put him right on top of it. *If.* Getting involved hadn't been
good for her. *They've got Mom.* And something about
an arranged marriage. The smell of raw sewage running
through the gutters in the middle of the unpaved road—

"Wake up." A hand touched his shoulder.

"I'm awake." Mike looked round. Hastert crouched beside him.

"There's an open area about fifty yards wide before
the wall, which is eight feet high. Just the other side of
the wall there's a road. O'Neil's setting up a distraction. We
have"—Hastert glanced at his watch—"six minutes to
get to the edge of the apron and wait. Then we have thirty
seconds to get over the wall and across the road. Take the
second alley on the left, proceed down it for twenty yards
then take the right turn, fourth door on the left is transit
house gamma. You ready?"

Mike nodded. "Guess so."

"Then let's get going."

TRANSLATED TRANSCRIPT BEGINS:

"Shit. He didn't."

"I'm afraid so."

(Sigh.) "That means we're down by what, two?
Three? Seats on the council. And the king. This is an absolute disaster. Who else have we lost?"

(Pause.) "Of our party, most of them. The dowager
Hildegarde is yammering her head off, but she survived,
as did her daughter. James Lee, we rescued. He's con-
cussed but will live—"

"Small mercies. Damn her for—damn her!"

"It's not your fault, your grace, or hers, that this had
to happen at the worst time."

(Sigh.) "Continue."

"We lost Wilem, Maris, Erik, three juniors of Hjorth-
Arnesen's cadet branch, and four others of middling rank.

We lost her majesty the queen mother, and the cadet branch of the royal family in the person of Prince Creon. He's a confirmed kill, by the way. About thirty retainers and outer family members, but that's by the by. The main losses are the royal family—except for the crown prince—and Henryk, Wilem, Maris, Erik, and others."

(Long pause.)

"Shit."

"We've taken worse—"

"No, it's not that. It's the little shit. The Pervert. What's he up to?"

"Holed up with Niejwein on the back lawn, scheming about something. Everyone with half a clue is rushing over to offer their firstborn to him."

"Has he sent up any smoke signals yet?"

"No."

"Damn. That confirms it, he's got what he wants and we're going to get the blame. He's hated us all along, since he learned about Creon's latency, and if he's listening to that snake Niejwein . . ."

"Your grace?"

(Sigh.) "I know, I'm rambling. What's your analysis?"

"I think we're in the shit, sir. I think—" (pause)—he's going to try to roll us over. All of us. Niejwein and Sudtmann and that crowd have been feeling their oats and they will take this opportunity once and for all to put us in our place. And the Pervert will use us as a lever to consolidate his power over them. He doesn't trust anyone, sir, and the rumors—"

"I don't care if he shags goats or rapes virgins, what I care about is *us*. Sky Father, this is a fifty-year setback!" (Inaudible muttering.) "Yes, yes, I already thought of that. Oliver, I know we see eye to eye over very little—"

"Your grace is overstating matters—"

"Permit an old man his moment of humor in the chaos: if you please? Good. I believe we do see eye to eye on the fundamentals. This is a war to the knife. We have a rogue king on the throne and even after we remove him from it we shall have civil war for the next decade—not family against family, but Clan against all. Do you agree?"

(Pause.) "Damn you."

"Indeed: I am damned."

(Pause.) "What do you propose to do?"

"Whatever I can. First, we must take our own to safety—then we must prepare to defend our possessions. Identify our allies, I should add. But if we can no longer count on being able to run our caravans up the coast in safety we must look for alternatives."

"The upstart bitch's plan."

"Be careful what you call my late niece, sir."

"I—" (Pause.) "—Please accept my apologies, your grace. You did not inform me of your bereavement. I had assumed she was rescued."

"She was not. She's not among those confirmed to be dead, but after the palace burned . . ." (Pause.) "I had high hopes for her."

"But her plan! Come now. You can't really believe it will work?"

(Sigh.) "No. I don't believe it will work. But I believe we should try it, in any event, with whatever energy we can divert from our defenses. Because if our ability to traffic in this realm is disrupted for any length of time, what other options do we have?"

(END TRANSLATION TRANSCRIPT)

2

FIRST LIGHT

narrow spiral staircase wormed upwards through the guts of a building, its grimy windowpanes opening onto a space that might once have been an alleyway but was now enclosed on all four sides by building extensions, so that it formed a wholly enclosed shaft at the bottom of which a pile of noisome debris had accumulated over the years. Other windows also opened onto the tiny courtyard; windows that provided ventilation and light to rooms that could not be seen from any street, or reached other than by the twisting staircase, which was concealed at ground level by a false partition in the back of a scullery closet. Almost a quarter of the rooms in the building were concealed in this fashion from the outside world. And in a garret at the top of the secret stairwell, a middle-aged woman sat working at a desk.

Bent over her wooden writing box, she systematically read her way through a thick stack of papers. Periodically she reached over to one side to pick up a pen and scrawl cryptic marginalia upon them. Less frequently, her brow furrowing, she would pick up a clean sheet of writing paper and dash off a sharp inquiry to one of her correspondents. Somewhat less frequently, she would consign a report—too hot to handle—to the glowing coals in the fireplace. The underground postal service that moved this mail was slow and expensive and prone to disruption: it might strike an ignorant observer as odd that Margaret, Lady Bishop would treat its fruits so casually. But to be caught in possession of much of this material would guarantee the holder a date with the hangman. Every use of the Movement's post was a gamble with a postman's life: and so she took pains to file the most important matters only in her memory, where they would not—if she had any say on the matter—be exposed to the enemy.

The darkness outside the window was complete and the stack of files before her was visibly shrinking when there came a knock at the door. "Come in," she called sharply: there was no possibility of a surprise police raid here, not without gunshots and explosions to telegraph their arrival.

The door opened and the rough-looking fellow outside cleared his throat. "Got a problem downstairs. Woman at the door, asking for you by name. Says *Burgeson* sent her."

"Was she followed?" Lady Bishop asked sharply.

"She said not, and I had a couple of the lads go 'ave a word with the hack what brought her. Nothing to fear on that account."

"Good." Lady Bishop breathed slightly easier. "Who is she? What does she want?"

"Figured we'd best leave that for you. She's not one such as I'd recognize, and she's dressed odd, like: Mal took her for a madwoman at first, but when she used your name and mentioned Burgeson I figured she was too dangerous to let go. So we stashed her in the cellar while we made arrangements."

"Right. Right." Lady Bishop nodded to herself, her face grim. "Is the Miller prepared?"

"Oh, aye."

"Then I suppose you'd better bring her up here and we can get to the bottom of this, Ed. I shall start with an interview—to give the poor woman a chance to excuse herself. But when you come, bring Mal. In case we have to send her down."

She spent the minutes before Ed's return with the prisoner methodically prioritizing her remaining correspondence. Then she carefully moved the manila paper folders to a desk drawer, closed and locked her writing case, and tried to compose herself. In truth, Lady Bishop hated interrogations. However necessary it might be for the pursuit of the declaration, the process invariably left her feeling soiled.

The rap at the door, when it came, was loud and confident. "Enter," she called. Edmund opened the door; behind him waited a woman, and behind her, the shadow of Mal the doorman. "Come in," she added, and pointed to a rough stool on the opposite side of her desk: "and sit down."

The woman was indeed oddly dressed. *Is she an actress?* Margaret wondered. It seemed unlikely. And her outfit, while outlandish, was in any case both too well tailored and too dirty for a stage costume. Then Lady Bishop took a good look at the woman's face, and paused. The bruise on her cheek told a story: and so, when the woman opened her mouth, did the startling perfection of her dentistry.

"Are you Lady Bishop?"

Margaret, Lady Bishop stared at the woman for a moment, then nodded. "I am." She had the most peculiar feeling that the woman on the stool opposite her was studying her right back, showing a degree of self-assurance she'd have expected from a judge, not a prisoner. *Titled? Or a lord's by-blow?*

"I'm Miriam Beckstein," said the woman. "I believe

Erasmus has told you something about me." She swallowed. "I don't know how much he's told you, but there's been a change in the situation."

Lady Bishop froze, surprise stabbing at her. *You're the* Beckstein *woman?* She turned to look at her assistants: "Ed, Mal, wait outside."

Ed looked perturbed. "Are you sure, ma'am?"

She gave him a hard stare: "you don't need to hear this." *Why in Christ's name didn't you say it was her in the first place?* She wanted to add, but not at risk of tipping off the prisoner about her place in the scheme of things.

Ed backed out of the room hastily and pulled the door shut. Margaret turned back to her unexpected visitor. "I'm sorry; we weren't expecting you, so nobody told them to be on the lookout. Do you know who struck you?"

Beckstein looked startled for a moment, then raised a hand to her cheek. "This? Oh, it's nothing to do with your men." A distant expression crossed her face: "The man who hit me died earlier this evening. Before I continue— did Erasmus tell you where I come from?"

Lady Bishop considered feigning ignorance for a moment. "He said something about a different version of our world. Sounded like nonsense at first, but then the trinkets started showing up." Her expression hardened. "If you think we can be bought and sold for glass beads—"

"I wouldn't dream of it!" Beckstein paused. "But, uh, I needed to know. What he'd told you. The thing is, I ran into some trouble. I was able to escape, but I came here because it was all I could do—I got away with only the clothes on my back. I need to get back to Boston and contact some people to let them know I'm alright before they, before I can get everything back under control. I was hoping . . ." She ran out of words.

Lady Bishop watched her intently. *Do you really think I'm that naive?* she asked silently, permitting herself a moment's cold anger. *Did you really think you could simply march in and demand assistance?* Then a second thought struck her: *or maybe you don't know who you're dealing with . . . ?*

"Did Erasmus tell you anything about me? Or who I am associated with?" she asked.

Beckstein blinked. "He implied—oh." Her eyes widened. "Oh shit."

Lady Bishop stifled a sigh of exasperation. Indelicacy on top of naivety? A very odd mixture indeed.

The Beckstein woman stared at her. "Erasmus didn't tell me enough . . ."

Margaret made up her mind. "I can see that," she said, which was true enough—just not the absolution it might be mistaken for. *Either you're really down on your luck and you thought I might be an easy touch, or perhaps you're really ignorant and in trouble. Which is it?* "Tell me who you think I am," she coaxed, "and I'll tell you if you're right or wrong."

"Okay," said Beckstein. Margaret made a mental note—*what does that word mean?*—then nodded encouragement. "I think you're a member of the Levelers' first circle. Probably involved in strategy and planning. And Erasmus was thinking about brokering a much higher-level arrangement between you and my, my, the people I represent. Represented." She swallowed. "Are you going to kill me?" she asked, only a faint quaver in her voice.

"If you were entirely right in every particular, then I would absolutely have to kill you." Margaret smiled to take the sting out of her words before she continued. "Luckily you're just wrong enough to be safe. But," she paused, to give herself time to prepare her next words carefully: "I don't think you're telling me the entire truth. And given your suspicions about my vocation, don't you think that might not be very clever? I want the truth, Miss Beckstein. And nothing but the truth."

"I"—Beckstein swallowed. Her eyes flickered from side to side, as if seeking a way out: Margaret realized that she was shaking. "I'm not sure. Whether you'd believe me, and whether it would be a good thing if you did."

This was getting harder to deal with by the minute, Margaret realized. The woman was clearly close to the end of her tether. She'd put a good face on things at first, but there was more to this than met the eye. "I've seen Erasmus," said Margaret. "He told me about the medicine you procured for him." She watched the Beckstein woman closely: "and he showed me the disc-playing machine. The, ah, *DVD player.* One miracle might be an accident, but two suggest an interesting pattern. You needn't worry about me mistaking you for a madwoman.

"But you must tell me exactly what has happened to you. Right now, at once, with no dissembling. Otherwise I will not be able to save you . . ."

BAM.

Judith Herz tensed unconsciously, steeling herself for the explosion, and crossed her fingers as the four SWAT team officers swung the battering ram back for a second knock. Not that tensing would do any good if there was a bomb in the self-storage room . . .

"Are you sure this is safe?" asked Rich Wall, fingering his mobile phone like it was a lucky charm.

Herz took a deep breath. "No," she snapped. *What do you expect me to say?* "According to Mike Fleming, the asshole who sent us on this wild goose chase has a hard-on for claymore mines. That's why—"she gestured at the chalk marks on the cinder block wall the officers were attacking, the heaps of dust from the drills, the fiber-optic camera on its dolly off to one side"—we're going in through the wall."

BAM.

A cloud of dust billowed out. There was a rattle of debris falling from the impact site on the wall. They'd started by drilling a quarter-inch hole, then sent a fiber-optic scope through with the delicacy of doctors conducting keyhole cardiac bypass surgery. The black plastic-coated hose had

snaked around, bringing grainy gray images to the monitor screen on the console like images from a long-sealed
Egyptian royal tomb. The dust lay heavy in the lockup
room, as if it hadn't been visited for months or years.
Something indistinct and bulky, probably a large oil tank,
hulked a couple of feet beyond the hole, blocking the line
of sight to the door to the lockup. The caretaker had
kicked up a fuss when she'd told him they were going to
punch through the wall from the other side—after uncer-
emoniously ejecting the occupants' property—until she'd
shown him her FBI card and the warrant the FEMA Sixth
Circuit court had signed in their emergency *in camera*
session. (Which the court had granted in a shot, the moment the bench saw the gamma ray spike the roving
search truck had registered as it quartered the city, looking for a sleeping horror.) Then he'd clammed up and
gone into his cubicle to phone the landlord.

"I think we're gonna need that jack," called one of the
cops with the ram. His colleagues laid the heavy metal
shaft down while two more cops in orange high-visibility
jackets and respirators moved to shovel the rubble aside.
"Should be through in a couple more minutes."

Judith glanced at Rich, who grinned humorlessly.
"This is your last chance to take a hike," she suggested.

"Naah." Rich glanced down. He was fidgeting with his
phone, as if it was a lucky charm. "Let's face it, I wouldn't
get far enough to clear the blast zone, would I?"

Judith suppressed a smile: "That's true." *Go on, whistle
in the dark.* She shivered involuntarily. The guys with the
battering ram didn't know what they were here for: all
they knew was that the woman from the FBI headquarters
staff wanted into the storage room, and wanted in bad.
She'd done the old stony stare and dropped an elliptical
hint about Mideast terrorists and fertilizer bombs, enough
to keep them on their toes but not enough to make them
phone their families and tell them to leave town *now*. But
Rich knew what they were looking for, and so did Bob,

who was suiting up in the NIRT truck in the back parking lot along with the rest of his team, and Eric Smith, back in Maryland in a meeting room in Crypto City. "You could always step outside for a last cigarette."

"I'm trying to give up. Last cigarettes, that is." Rich shuffled from foot to foot as two of the cops grunted and manhandled a construction site jack into place beside the blue chalk X on the wall, where it was buckling ominously outwards.

"Okay, one more try," called one of the cops—Sergeant McSweeny, Herz thought—as the ram team picked up their pole and began to work up their momentum.

BAM. This time there was a clatter of rubble falling as overstressed bricks gave way. The dust cleared and she saw there was a hole in the wall where the ram had struck, an opening into the heart of darkness. The battering ram team shuffled backwards out of the way of the two guys with shovels, who now hefted sledgehammers and went to work on the edges of the hole, widening it. "There's your new doorway," said one of the ram crew, wincing and rubbing his upper arm: "kinda short on brass fittings and hinges, but we can do you a deal on gravel for your yard."

"Ri-ight," drawled Rich. Judith glared at him, keeping her face frozen. *That's right, I'm a woman in black from a secret government agency,* she thought. *I've got no sense of humor and you better not get in my way.* Even if the black outfit was a wind cheater with a big FBI logo, and a pair of 501s.

The cop recoiled slightly. "Hey, what's up with you guys?"

"You have no need to know." Judith relented slightly. "Seriously. You won't read about this in the newspapers, but you've done a good job here today." She winced slightly as another sledgehammer blow spalled chips off the edge of the hole in the wall. Which was growing now, to the point where a greased anorexic supermodel might be able to wriggle through. A large slab of wall fell inward, doubling the size of the hole. "Ah, showtime. If you guys could get the jack into position and then clear the area I think we will take it from here." *If only Mike Fleming was about. This is his fault,* she thought venomously.

Ten minutes later the big orange jack was screwed tight against the top of the opening, keeping the cinder blocks above the hole from collapsing. The SWAT team was outside in the parking lot, packing their kit up and shooting random wild-assed guesses about what the hell it was they'd been called in to do, and why: Judith glanced at the wristwatch-shaped gadget strapped to her left wrist and nodded. It was still clean, showing background count of about thirty becquerels per second. A tad high for suburban Boston, but nothing that couldn't be accounted for by the fly ash mixed into the cinder blocks. The idea of wearing a Geiger counter like a wristwatch still gave her the cold shudders when she thought about it, but that wasn't so often these days, not after three weeks of it— and besides, it was better than the alternative.

A big gray truck was backing in to the lot tail-first. Rich waved directions to the driver, as if he needed them: the truck halted with a chuff of air brakes, five feet short of the open door to the small warehouse unit. The tailgate rattled up to reveal a scene right out of *The X-Files*—half a dozen men and women in bright orange inflatable space suits with oxygen tanks and black rubber gloves, wheeling carts loaded with laboratory instruments. They queued up in front of the tail lift. "Is the area clear?" Judith's earpieces crackled.

She glanced around. "Witnesses out." The SWAT team was already rolling up the highway a quarter of a mile away. They were far enough away that if things went really badly they might even survive.

"Okay, we're coming in." That was Dr. Lucius Rand, tall and thin, graying at the temples, seconded to the Family Trade Organization from his parent organization. Just like Judith, like Mike Fleming, like everyone else in FTO— only in his case, the parent organization was Pantex. He was in his late fifties. Rumor had it he'd studied at Ted Taylor's knee; Edward Teller had supervised his Ph.D. The tailgate lift ground into operation, space-suited figures descending to planet Earth.

"We haven't checked for booby traps yet," she warned.

"Well, what are you waiting for?" Rand sounded impatient.

Judith nodded to Rich as she pulled on a pair of disposable plastic shoe protectors: "Let's go inside."

The hole in the wall was about two feet wide and three feet high, a jagged gash. She switched on her torch—a tiny pocket LED lantern, more powerful than a big cop-style Maglite—and swept the floor. There were no wires. *Good.* She ducked through the hole, coughing slightly. Her Geiger watch still ticked over normally. *Better.* She stood up and looked around.

The room was maybe twenty feet long and eight feet wide, with a ten-foot ceiling. Naked unpainted cinder block walls, a galvanized tin ceiling, and a concrete floor completed the scene. There was a big rolling door at one end and dust everywhere. But what caught her attention was the sheer size of the cylinder that, standing on concrete blocks, dominated the room. "Sweet baby Jesus," she whispered. It was at least ten feet long, and had to be a good four feet in diameter. There was barely room to walk around the behemoth. She shone her torch along the cylinder, expecting to see—"what the hell?"

"Herz, report! What have you seen?"

"It's a cylinder," she said slowly. "About ten, twelve feet long, four, five feet in diameter. Supported on concrete blocks. One end is rounded; there's some kind of collar about three feet from the other end and four vanes sticking out, sort of like the fins on a bomb . . ." She trailed off. *Like the fins on a bomb,* she thought, dazed. *Jesus, this can't be here!* She shook herself and continued, "there's some kind of equipment trolley near the back end, and some wires going into the, the back of the bomb." She glanced down at her watch. The second hand was spinning round. It was a logarithmic counter, and it had jumped from tens of becquerels per second to tens of thousands as she crossed the threshold. Gamma emission from secondary activation isotopes created by neutron absorption, she heard the lecture replay in her mind's eye; Geiger counters can't detect neutrons until the flux is way too high for safety, but over time a neutron source will tend to activate surrounding materials. "I'm reading secondaries. I think we've got a hot one. I'm coming out now." A quick sweep across the screen door in front of the gadget's nose revealed no telltale trip wires. "No sign of booby traps."

"Acknowledged. Judith, I want you and Rich to go back into the van and wait while I do a preliminary site survey. Don't touch anything on your way out. I want you to know, you've done good." She realized she was shaking. *Don't touch anything. Right.* She clambered out through the hole in the wall, blinking against the daylight, and stood aside as two figures in bright orange isolation suits duckwalked past her. The cylinders hanging from their shoulders bounced under their rubber covers like hugely obese buttocks as they bent down to crawl through the hole. Two more suits waved her down with radiation detectors and stripped off her shoe protectors before pronouncing her clean and waving her into the truck.

The back of the NIRT truck was crowded with consoles and flashing panels of blinkenlights, battered laptops plastered with security inventory stickers, and coat rails for the bulky orange suits. This was a NIRT survey wagon, not the defuse-and-disarm trailer—those guys would be along in a while, as soon as Dr. Rand confirmed he needed them. Too many NIRT vehicles in one parking lot might attract the wrong kind of attention, especially in these days of Total Information Awareness and paranoia about security, not to mention closed-circuit cameras everywhere and journalists with web access spreading rumors. And rumors that NIRT were breaking into a lockup in Boston would be just the icing on a fifty-ton cake of

shit if Homeland Security had to take the fall for a botched
Family Trade operation. Rumors of any kind about NIRT
would likely trigger a public panic, a run on the Dow, and
a plague of boils inside the Beltway.

"Coffee?" asked Rich, picking up a vacuum flask.

"Yes, please." Judith yawned, suddenly becoming
aware that she felt tired. "I don't believe what I just saw. I
just hope it turns out to be some kind of sick prank." Low-
level lab samples of something radioactive stashed in an
aluminum cylinder knocked together in an auto body
shop, that would do it. *But it can't be,* she realized. *Nobody would be that crazy, just for a joke.* Charges of wast-
ing police time didn't even *begin* to cover it. And it
wasn't as if some prankster had tried to draw attention to
the lockup: quite the opposite, in fact.

"Like hell. That thing had fins like a fifty-six Caddy. I
swear I was expecting to see Slim Pickens riding it
down . . ." Don poured a dose of evil-looking coffee into
a cup and passed it to her. "Think it'll go off?"

"Not now," Judith said with a confidence she didn't
feel. "Dr. Strangelove and his merry men are going over
it with their stethoscopes." There was a chair in front of
one of the panels of blinkenlights and she sat down on it.
"But something about this whole setup feels wrong."

Her earphone bleeped, breaking her out of the introspec-
tive haze. "Yes?" she asked, keying the throat pickup.

"Judith, I think you'd better come back in. Don't
bother suiting up, it's safe for now, but there's bad news
along with the good."

"On my way." She put her coffee down. "Wait here,"
she told Rich, who nodded gratefully and took her place
in the swivel chair.

When she straightened up inside the warehouse she
found it bright and claustrophobic, the air heavy with masonry dirt and the dust of years of neglect. It reminded
her of a raid on a house in Queens she'd been in on, years
ago: one the mob had been using to store counterfeit

memory chips. Someone here had found the long-dead
light fitting and replaced the bulb. Seen in proper light,
the finned cylinder looked more like a badly made movie
prop than a bomb. Two figures in orange inflatable suits
hunched over the open tail of the gadget, while another
was busy taking a screwdriver to the fascia of the instrument cart that was wired into it. Dr. Rand stepped around
the rounded front of the cylinder: "Ah, Agent Herz. As I
said, I've got good news and bad news." There was an un-
healthy note of relish in his voice.

Judith gestured towards the far end of the lockup from
the NIRT team operatives working on the ass-end of the
bomb. "Tell me everything I need to know."

Rand followed her then surprised Judith by unzipping his
hood and throwing it back across his shoulders. He reached
down to his waist and turned off the hissing air supply. His
face was flushed and what there was of his hair hung in
damp locks alongside his face. "Hate these things," he said
conversationally. "It's not going to go off," he added.

"Well, that's a relief." She raised an eyebrow. "So, is
this the one?"

"That would be the bad news." Rand frowned. "Let me
give it to you from the top."

"Be my guest." Sarcasm was inappropriate, she realized, but the relief—

"I've met this puppy before," said Rand. "It's a B53-
Y2. We built a bunch of them in the sixties. It's a free-
fall bomb, designed to be hauled around by strategic
bomber, and it's not small—the physics package weighs
about six thousand pounds. It's an oralloy core, high-
purity weapons-grade uranium rather than plutonium, uses
lithium deuteride to supply the big bang. We originally
made a few hundred, but all but twenty-five were disman-
tled decades ago. It's basically the same as the warhead on
the old Titan-II, designed to level Leningrad in one go. The
good news is, it won't go off. The tritium booster looks to
be well past its sell-by date and the RDX is thoroughly

poisoned by neutron bombardment, so the best you'd get would be a fizzle." He looked pensive. "Of course, what I mean by a fizzle is relative. A B53 that's been properly maintained is good for about nine megatons—this one would probably top off at no more than a quarter megaton or so, maybe half a megaton."

"Half a—" Her knees went weak. She stumbled, caught herself leaning against the nose of the hydrogen bomb, and recoiled violently. *A quarter of a megaton?* The flash would be visible in New York City: the blast would blow out windows in Providence. "But—"

"Calm down, it's not going to happen. We've already made sure of that."

"Oh. Okay." *Jesus. If that's the good news—*

"Funny thing about the timer, though," Rand said meditatively. "Sloppy wiring, dry joints where they soldered it to . . . well, the battery ran down a long time ago. Judging by the dust it's been there for years."

"Timer?"

"Yes." Rand shook himself. "It was on a timer," he explained. "Should have gone off ages ago, taking Boston and most of Cambridge with it. Probably back during the Bush I or Reagan administrations, at a guess. Maybe even earlier."

"Holy, uh, wow."

"Yes, I can see why you might say that." Rand nodded. "And we are going to have real fun combing the inventory to find out how this puppy managed to wander off the reservation. That's not supposed to happen, although I can hazard some guesses . . ."

"Huh. Six—did you say it weighs six thousand pounds?" Herz stared at the nuclear weapons engineer.

"Well, of course it does; did you think air-dropped multimegaton hydrogen bombs were small enough to fit in a back pocket? Why do you think we ship them around in B-52s?"

"Uh." She took a deep breath. "And it's a, like, a single unit? You couldn't dismantle it easily?"

"No, I don't think so. We'll need to truck it away intact and examine it for—"

"Then we've messed up."

"What makes you say that?" Rand sounded offended.

"Because it's *too big*. A world-walker can't haul something any larger than they can lift. So it doesn't belong to the Clan."

"Oh," said Rand. He sounded at a loss for words.

"You can say that again." Judith turned to head back to the hole in the wall. "Listen, I've got to go, this isn't Family Trade business anymore, okay? Run it through the normal NIRT channels, I've got to go report to the colonel now. See you around." And with that, she ducked through the hole in the lockup wall, and headed back to the car park. Rich was waiting next to the truck. "Come on," he said, waving at her car.

"What's the story?"

"It's a nuke, but it's not our nuke," Herz said as she started the car.

"Oh."

"Yes. Come on, I've got to get back to the office and report to Eric."

"Shit."

"Language, please." Judith put the car in gear and crept out of the parking lot, leaving the gray NIRT van and the orange rubber-suited atomic bomb disposal specialists behind like a bad memory. "What a way to start the week." Somewhere out there in the city there was supposed to be another bomb. One that was activated four months earlier by Matt, when he defected from the Clan, as an insurance policy to hold over the Family Trade Organization's head. But Matt was dead, and Mike Fleming had failed to wheedle the location of the bomb out of him before he died—all they knew was, it was on a one-year countdown, and they had maybe two hundred days left to find it before they had to evacuate three or four million folks from Boston and Cambridge to avoid a disaster that would make 9/11 look like a parking violation.

* * *

Miriam had run through the emotional gamut in the past six hours, oscillating wildly between hope and terror, despair and optimism. Being taken out of the cellar room and escorted up to the top of this rickety pile of brick and lath by a pair of thugs, and ushered into a garret where a middle-aged woman with a kindly face and eyes like a hanging judge sat at a writing desk, and then being expected to give an account of herself, was more than Miriam was ready for. All she had to vouch for this woman was Erasmus Burgeson's word: and there was a lot more to the tubercular pawnbroker than met the eye. He had some very odd friends, and if he'd misread her when he suggested she visit this "Lady Bishop," then it was possible she'd just stuck her head in a noose. But on the other hand, Miriam was here right now, and there were precious few alternatives on offer.

"I'd quite understand if you thought I was mad," Miriam said, shivering slightly—it was not particularly warm in this drafty attic room. "I don't really understand everything that's going on myself. I mean, I thought I did, but obviously not." She felt her cheek twitch involuntarily.

Margaret Bishop leaned forward, her expression concerned. "Are you all right?" she asked.

Miriam twitched again. "No, I'm—" She took a deep breath. "A few bruises, that's all. And I'm lucky to be alive, people have been trying to kill me all evening." She took another deep breath. "Sorry . . ."

"Don't be." Lady Bishop rose to her feet and opened the door a crack. "Bring a pot of coffee, please. And biscotti. For two." She closed it again. "Would you like to tell me about it? Start from the beginning, if you please. Take your time." She sat down again. "I must apologize for the pressure, but I really need to know everything if I am to help you."

"You'd help me?" Miriam blinked.

"You've been very helpful to us in the past. We tend to

be suspicious, with good reason—but we look after our friends." Lady Bishop looked at her gravely. "But I need to know more about you before I make any promises. Do you understand?"

Miriam's vision blurred: for a moment she felt vertiginous, as if the stool she sat upon was half a mile high, balanced in a high wind. Relief combined with apprehension washed over her. *Not alone*—it was like waking suddenly from a nightmare. The world had been narrowing around her like a prison corridor for so long that the idea that there might be a way out, or even people who would help her willingly, seemed quite alien for a moment. Then the dizziness passed. "I'll tell you everything," she heard herself saying, in a voice hoarse with gratitude. "Just don't expect too much."

"Take your time." Lady Bishop sat back on her chair and waited while Miriam composed herself. "We've got all night."

"There are at least three worlds." Miriam squeezed her tired eyes shut as she tried to fumble her way towards an explanation. "I'm told there may be more, but nobody knows how to reach them. The people who *can* reach them . . . they're my relatives, apparently. It's a hereditary talent. It's what geneticists call a recessive trait, meaning you can't inherit it unless it was present in both sides of your family tree. It's difficult to do—painful if you do it too often, and you need a focus, a kind of knotwork design to look at to make it work—but it's made the families, the people who have the ability, rich. The world they live in is very backward, almost medieval: something went wrong, some blind alley in history a couple of thousand years ago, but they've risen into the nobility of the small feudal kingdoms that exist up and down the New England coastline.

"I'm . . . I'm an outsider. About fifty years ago the families started killing one another, there was a huge blood feud—what they called a civil war. My mother, who was pregnant at the time, was on the losing side of an ambush: she fled to the, the other of the three worlds we know about. Uh, I should have explained that the Clan families didn't know about this one at the time. There's a lost offshoot family of the Clan who ended up here more than a hundred years ago, who can travel from here to the Clan's world: they were the ones who kept the civil war going by periodically assassinating Clan leaders and pointing the evidence at the other families. The other world, the one I grew up in, is very different from either this one or the one the Clan comes from."

There was a knock on the door. Miriam paused while one of the guards came in and deposited a tray on the table where Lady Bishop had been working on her papers. The coffee pot was silver, and the smell drifting from it was delicious. "May I . . . ?"

"Certainly." Margaret Bishop poured coffee into two china mugs. "Help yourself to the biscotti." The guard departed quietly. "Tell me about your world."

"It's—" Miriam frowned. "It's a lot less different from yours than the Clan's world is, but it's still very different. As far as I can tell, they were the same until, um, 1745. There was an uprising in Scotland? A Prince Charles Stuart? In my world he marched on London and his uprising was defeated. Savagely. A few years later a smoldering war between Britain and France started—and while France eventually won a paper victory, there was no invasion of England. The wars between France and Britain continued for nearly eighty years, ending with the complete defeat of France and the British dominating the oceans."

Lady Bishop shook her head. "What is the state of the Americas in this world of yours?" she asked.

"There was a revolution . . . Why, is it important?"

"No, just fascinating. So, continue. Your world is very different, it seems, but from a more recent point of change?"

"Yes." Miriam took a mouthful of coffee. "Something went wrong here. I think it was something to do with the

French administration of England after the invasion, in the eighteenth century. In my world, a lot of the industrialization you've had here in the past hundred years happened in the late eighteenth and nineteenth centuries, in England. Over in this world it started late and it's still happening here, in New Britain. Things are further ahead in the United States, the nation on this continent where I come from. And in other countries in the other world. That doesn't mean things are necessarily better—they've got big problems, too. But no kings, at least not many: most countries got rid of them over the past century. And better science and technology. Cures for tuberculosis."

"How do your relatives, this Clan, account for their power? I'd have thought that if they live in a backward society it would be difficult to rise."

Miriam put her mug down. "They're smugglers," she said bluntly. "In their own world, they are the only people who can get messages across the continent in anything less than weeks. They use the U.S. postal service to accomplish miracles, in the terms of their own world. And they've got modern firearms and lots of toys, because in my world they smuggle illegal drugs: they can guarantee to get them past the Coast Guard and police and border patrols. They're immensely rich merchant princes. But they're trapped by the society they live in. The old nobility don't accept them, the peasants resent them, and the crown—" She shook her head, unable to continue.

"You said someone tried to kill you today. Which world did this happen in?"

"The Clan's," Miriam said automatically. She picked her mug up, took a sip, rolled it nervously between her palms. "I, when they discovered me, I needed to figure out a way to make some space for myself. I'm not used to having a big extended family who expect me to fit in. And there aren't enough of them. They wanted me to marry for political reasons. I tried to—hell, I made a big mistake. Tried to get political leverage, to make them leave me alone. Instead I nearly got myself killed. They left the, the political marriage as a compromise, a way out. Tonight was meant to be the official betrothal. Instead . . ."

She put the mug down. "The groom is dead," she said. "No, no need for condolences—I barely knew him. There was an attack on the betrothal party, and I only just managed to escape. And the United States government has found out about the Clan and discovered a way to get at the Clan's world."

Her eyes widened. "Hey, I wonder if Angbard knows?"

Mike's first hint that something had gone badly wrong was the scent of burning gunpowder on the night air.

He hunkered down behind a large, gnarled oak tree at the edge of the tree line and squinted into the darkness. Hastert and his men had night vision goggles, but they hadn't brought a spare pair for Mike and the moon wasn't an adequate substitute. The stone wall across the clear-cut lawn was a looming black silhouette against a slightly lighter darkness. The sounds drifting over the wall told their own story of pain and confusion and anger: it sounded like there was a riot going on in the distance, still punctuated with the flat bangs of black powder weapons and the bellowing of men like cattle funneled into the killing floor of an abattoir.

A shadowy figure moved across the empty space. Someone tapped Mike lightly on the shoulder, and he jerked half-upright. "Let's move," whispered Hastert. "After me." He rose lightly, and before Mike could say anything he faded into the gloom.

Mike forced himself to stand up. He'd been crouching for so long that his knees ached—and the nervous apprehension wasn't helping, either. *What have I gotten myself into?* It seemed to be the story of his life, these days. He shifted his weight from side to side, restoring the circulation in his legs, then took a step through the undergrowth around the big oak tree.

There was a sharp cracking noise, a moment's vibration as if a bowstring the size of a suspension bridge had just been released, and an excruciating pain lanced through his left leg, halfway between ankle and knee. He gasped with agony, too shocked to scream, and began to topple sideways. The serrated steel jaws buried in his leg were brought up sharply by the chain anchoring them to the oak tree, and dug their teeth into his shattered leg. Everything went black.

An indeterminate time later, Mike felt an urgent need to spit. His mouth hurt; he'd bitten his tongue and the sharp taste of blood filled his mouth. *Why am I lying down?* he wondered vaguely. *Bad thought*: In his mind's inner eye his leg lit up like a torch, broken and burning. He drew breath to scream, and a hand covered his mouth.

"O'Neil, get me a splint. Lower leg fracture, looks like tibia and fibula both. Fleming, I'm going to stick a morphine syrette in you. Don't worry, we'll get you out of here. Fuck me, that's a nasty piece of work." The hand moved away from his mouth. "Here, bite this if it helps." Something leathery pushed at his lips. Mike gritted his teeth and tried not to scream as the bones grated. "I'm going to have to get this fucker off you before we can splint your leg and get you out of here." A tiny sharpness bit into his leg near the searing agony. "How does it . . . eh. Got it. This is going to hurt—"

A sudden flare of pain arrived, worse than anything that had come before. Mike blacked out again.

The next time he woke up, the pain had subsided. *That's better,* he thought drowsily. It was comfortable, lying down on the ground: *must be the morphine.* Someone was tugging at his leg, lifting and moving it and tying stuff tightly around it. That was uncomfortable. Something told him he ought to be screaming his head off, but it was too much effort right now. "What is it?" he tried to ask aloud, but what came out was a drunken-sounding mumble.

"You stuck your foot in some kind of man trap. Spring-loaded, chained to the tree, scary piece of shit. It broke your leg and chewed up your calf muscles like a hungry great white. Fuck, why didn't nobody tell us these medievals had anti-personnel mines?" Hastert sounded distinctly peevish, in a someone's-going-to-get-hurt way. "Now we're going to have to carry you."

"Don't—" Mike tried to say. His mouth was dry: but he felt okay. *Just let me lie here for a couple of hours, I'll be fine,* he heard himself thinking, and tried to laugh at his own joke. The darkness was florid and full of patterns, retinal rod cells firing in aimless and fascinating fractals to distract him from the pain. *Medieval minefield, medieval minefield,* he repeated over and over to himself. Someone grunted and dragged his arm over their shoulder, then heaved him upright. His left leg touched ground and he felt light-headed, but then he was dangling in midair. *Shark bite. Hey, I'm shark bait.* He tried not to giggle. *Be serious. I'm in enemy territory. If they hear us . . .*

There was a wall. It was inconveniently high and rough, random stones crudely mortared together in a pile eight feet tall. He was floating beside it and someone was grunting, and then there was a rope sling around him. That was rough as it dragged him up the side of the wall, but Hastert and O'Neil were there to keep his leg from bumping into the masonry. And then he was lying on top of the wall, which was bumpy but wide enough to be secure, and on the other side of it he could see a dirt road and more walls in the darkness, and a couple of shadowy buildings.

His mangled leg itched.

Consciousness came in fits and starts. He was lying on the muddy grass at the base of the wall, staring up at the sky. The stars were very bright, although wisps of cloud scudding in from the north were blotting them out. Someone nearby was swearing quietly. He could hear other noises, a rattling stomping and yelling like a demonstration he'd once seen, and a hollow clapping noise that was oddly familiar, pop-pop, pop-pop—hooves, he realized. *What do horses mean?*

"Fuck." The figure bending over him sounded angry

and confused. "O'Neil, I'm going to have to call four-oh-four on Fleming. Cover—"

What's he doing with the knife? Mike wondered dizzily. The hoofbeats were getting louder and there was a roar: then a rattling bang of gunfire, very loud and curiously flat, not the crack of supersonic bullets but more like high caliber pistol shots, doors slamming in his ears. There was a scream, cut off: something heavy fell across him as an answering stutter of automatic fire cut loose, O'Neil with his AR-15. *Who's trying to kill whom, now?* A moment of ironic amusement threatened to swallow Mike, just as a second booming volley of musket fire crackled overhead. Then there was more shouting, and more automatic fire, stuttering in short bursts from concealment at the other end of the exposed stretch of wall: *we climbed the wall right into a crossfire!*

He tried to focus, but overhead the stars were graying out, one by one: shock, blood loss, and morphine conspired to put him under. But unlike the others, he was still alive when the Clan soldiers covering the escape of their leaders from the Thorold Palace reached the killing zone and paused to check the identity of the victims.

3

SECURITY BREACHES

ngbard's bad day started out deceptively, with a phone call that he had taken for a positive development at first. It was not until later, when events began to spin out of control, that he recognized it for what it was–the very worst disaster to befall the Clan during his tenure as chief of external security.

This week his grace was staying on the other side, in a secluded mansion in upstate New York that he had acquired from the estate of a deceased record producer who had invested most of the money his bands had earned in building his own unobtrusive shrine to Brother Eater. (Not that they used the Hungry God's true name in this benighted land, but the principle was the same.) The heavily wooded hundred-acre lot, discreet surveillance and security fittings, and the soundproofed basement rooms that had once served as a recording studio, all met with the duke's approval. So did the building's other-side location, a hilly bluff in the wilds of the Nordmarkt that had been effectively doppelgangered by a landslide until his men had tunneled into it to install the concealed exits, supply dumps, and booby-trapped passages that safety demanded.

Of course the location wasn't perfect in all respects—in Nordmarkt it was a good ten miles from the nearest highway, itself little more than an unpaved track, and in its own world it was a good fifty-minute drive outside Rochester—but it met with most of his requirements, including the most important one of all: that nobody outside his immediate circle of retainers knew where it was.

These were desperate times. The defection of the duke's former secretary, Matthias, had been a catastrophe for his personal security. He had been forced to immediately quarantine all his former possessions in the United States, the private jet along with the limousines and the houses: all out of reach for now, all contaminated by Matthias's insidiously helpful management. He had hold-outs, of course, the personal accounts held with offshore institutions that not even his secretary had known about—Duke Lofstrom had grown up during a time of bloody-handed paranoia, and never completely trusted anyone–but by his best estimate, it had cost him at least one hundred and twenty-six million dollars. And that was just how much it had cost *him,* as an individual. To the Clan as a whole, this disaster had cost upwards of two billion dollars. It was not beyond the realm of possibility that some of the more angry or desperate cousins might try to take their share out of his hide.

Events started with a phone call shortly after 11p.m. Or rather, they started with what passed for a phone call where the duke was concerned: although he received it on an old-fashioned handset, it arrived at the safe house by a circuitous route involving a very off-the-books patch into the local phone company exchange, dark fiber connections between anonymous Internet hosts, and finally an encrypted data call to a stolen mobile phone handset. Angbard, Duke Lofstrom, might write his personal correspondence with a fountain pen and leave the carrying of mobile phones to his subordinates, but his communications security was the best that the Clan's money could buy.

When the phone rang, the duke had just finished dining with the lords-comptrollers of the Post Office: the two silver-haired eminences who were responsible for the smooth running of the Clan's money-making affairs to the same degree that he was responsible for their collective security. The brandy had been poured, the last plates removed, and he had been looking forward to a convivial exploration of the possibilities for expansion in the new territories when there was a knock on the dining room side door.

"Excuse me," he nodded to his lordship, Baron Griben ven Hjalmar, causing him to pause in mid-flow: "Enter!"

It was Carlos, one of his security detail, looking apologetic. "The red telephone, my lord. It's ringing in your office."

"Ah." The duke glanced at his dining companions: "I must apologize, perforce, but this requires my immediate attention. I shall return presently."

"Surely, sir." Baron ven Hjalmar raised his glass: "By all means!" He smiled indulgently.

The duke rose and left the table without further ado. On his way out, Carlos took up the rear. "Who is it?" he asked as soon as the dining room door had closed behind them.

"The officer of the day in the Thorold Palace has just declared an emergency. The signal is Tango Mike. He crossed over to report in person. He's on the phone now."

The duke swore. "Who is he? On the duty roster?" The officer of the day was the Clan member entrusted with ensuring the security of Clan members in their area, and he would not cross over to the other world to make a report—effectively abandoning their post, if only for a few minutes—without a very good reason.

"I believe it's Oliver, Earl Hjorth."

The duke swore again. Then they were at his office door. He picked up the telephone before he sat down. "Put him through." His face fell unconsciously into an odd, pained expression: Oliver was a member of his half-sister's mother's coterie, an intermittent thorn in his side—but not one that he could remove without unpleasant consequences. What made it even worse was that Oliver was competent and energetic. If it wasn't for Hildegarde's malign influences, he might be quite useful ... "Good evening, Baron. I gather you have some news for me."

A quarter of an hour later, when he put the phone down, the duke's expression was, if anything, even more stony. He turned to stare at Carlos, who stood at parade rest by the door. "Please inform their lordships ven Hjalmar and Ijsselmeer that I deeply regret to inform them that there has been a development that requires—" He paused, allowing his head to droop. "Let me rephrase. Please inform them that an emergency has developed and I would appreciate their assistance, in their capacity as representatives of the Post Office board, in conducting a preliminary assessment of the necessary logistic support for execution of the crisis plan in the affected areas. Then bring them here." He sighed deeply, then looked up. "Go on."

"Sir." Carlos swerved through the door and was gone.

The duke half-smiled at the closing door. The fellow was probably scared out of his wits by whatever he'd overheard of the duke's conversation with Earl Hjorth. Who should, by now, be back in Niejwein, and organizing his end of the crisis plan. The duke shook his head again. "Why *now*?" He muttered to himself. Then he picked up the phone and dialed the digit 9. "Get me Mors. Yes, Mors Hjalmar. And Ivan ven Thorold. Teleconference, right now, I don't care if they're in bed or unavailable, tell them it's an emergency." He thought for a moment. "I want every member of the council who is in this world on the line within no more than one hour. Tell them it's an emergency meeting of the Clan council, on my word, by telephone." This was unprecedented; emergency meetings were themselves a real rarity, the last having been one he'd called at the behest of his niece barely six months ago. "And if they don't want to make time, tell them I'll be *very annoyed* with them."

Angbard hung up the phone and settled down to wait. A knock at the door: one of his men opened it. "Sir, their lordships—"

"Send them in. Then fetch a speakerphone." Angbard rose, and half-bowed to Hjalmar and Ijsselmeer. "I must apologize for the informality, but there has been an unfortunate development in the capital. If you would both please be seated, I will arrange for coffee in a minute."

Hjalmar found his voice first; diffidently—incongruously, too, for he was a big bear of a man—he asked: "is something the matter?"

Angbard grinned. "Of course something is the matter!" he agreed, almost jovially. "It's the crown prince!"

"What? Has Egon had an accident—"

"In a manner of speaking." Angbard sat down again, leaning back in his chair. "Egon has just murdered his own father and brother, not to mention Henryk and my niece Helge and a number of other cousins, at the occasion of his brother's betrothal. He's sent troops to lay siege to the Thorold Palace and he's issuing letters of attainder against us, promising our land to anyone who comes to his aid." Angbard's grin turned shark-like. "He's made his bid at last, gentlemen. The old high families have decided to cast their lot in with him, and we can't be having that. An example will have to be made. King Egon the Third is going to have one of the shortest reigns on record—and I'm calling this meeting because we need to establish who we're going to put on the throne once Egon is out of the way."

Hjalmar blanched. "You're talking about high treason!"

The old scar on Angbard's cheek twitched. "It's never treason if you win." His smile faded into a frown and he made a steeple of his fingers. "And I don't know about you gentlemen, but I see no alternative. Unless we are to hang—and I mean that entirely literally—we must grasp the reins of power directly. And the very first thing we must do is remove the usurper from the throne he's claimed."

Morning in Boston: a thick fog, stinking of coal dust and burned memories, swirled down the streets between the brown brick houses, blanketing the pavement and forming eddies in the wake of the streetcars. Behind a grimy window in a tenement flat on Holmes Alley a man coughed in his sleep, snorted, then twitched convulsively. The distant factory bells tolled dolorously as he rolled over, clutching the battered pillow around his head. It was an hour past dawn when a bell of a different kind broke through his torpor, tinkling in the hallway outside the kitchen.

The gaunt, half-bald man sat up and rubbed his eyes, which fastened on a cheap tin alarm clock that had stopped, its hands mockingly pointed at the three and the five on the dial. He focused on it blearily and swore, just as the doorbell tinkled again.

For someone so tall and thin, Erasmus Burgeson could move rapidly. In two spidery strides he was at the bedroom door, nightgown flapping around his ankles; three more strides and his feet were on the chilly stone slabs of the staircase down to the front door. Upon reaching which he rattled the chain and drew back the bolts, finally letting the door slide an inch ajar. "Who is it?" he demanded hoarsely as an incipient wheeze caught his ribs in its iron fist.

"Post Office electrograph for a Mister Burgeson?" piped a youthful voice. Erasmus looked down. It was, indeed, a Post Office messenger urchin, barefoot in the cold but wearing the official cap and gloves of that institution, and carrying a wax-sealed envelope. "Thruppence-ha'penny to pay?"

"Wait one." He turned and fumbled behind the door for his overcoat, in one pocket of which he always kept some change. Three and a half pence was highway robbery for an electrograph: the fee had gone up two whole pennies in the past year, a sure sign that the Crown was desperate for revenue. "Here you are."

The urchin shoved the envelope through the door and dashed off with his money, obviously eager to make his next delivery. Burgeson shut and bolted the door, then made his way back upstairs, this time plodding laboriously, a little wince crossing his face with each cold stone step. His feet were still warm and oversensitive from bed: with the fire embargo in effect on account of the smog, the chill of the stairs bit deep into his middle-aged bones.

At the top step he paused, finally giving in to the retching cough that had been building up. He inspected his handkerchief anxiously: there was no blood. *Good.* It was nearly two months, now, and the cough was just the normal wheezing of a mild asthmatic caught out by one of Boston's notorious yellow-gray smogs. Erasmus placed the electrograph envelope on the stand at the top of the staircase and shuffled into the kitchen. The cooking range was cold, but the new, gas-fired samovar was legal: he lit it off, then poured water into the chamber and, while it was heating, took the bottle of miracle medicine from the back of the cupboard and took two more of the strange cylindrical pills.

Miriam had given him the pills, three months ago, last time she'd visited. He'd barely dared believe her promises, but they seemed to be working. It was almost enough to shake his belief in the innate hostility of the universe. People caught the white death and they died coughing up their lungs in a bloody foam, and that was it. It happened less often these days, but it was still a terror that stalked the camps north of the Great Lakes—and there was no easy cure. Certainly nothing as simple as taking two tablets every morning for six months! And yet . . . *I wonder where she is?* Erasmus pondered, not for the first time: *probably busying herself trying to make another world a better place.*

The water was close to boiling. He spooned loose tea

into the brewing chamber then wandered over to the window, squinting against the smog-diffused daylight in hope of glimpsing one of the neighborhood clock towers. He'd have to wind and reset the alarm once he'd worked out by how long it had betrayed him. Still, nobody had jangled the bell-pull tied to the shop door handle while he was sleeping like a log. Business had boomed over the springtime and early summer, but things had fallen ominously quiet lately—nobody seemed to have the money to buy their possessions back out of hock, and indeed, nobody seemed to be buying much of anything. Even the local takers were slacking off on enforcing the vagrancy laws. Things seemed alright in the capital whenever his other business took him there to visit—*the rich man's cup spilleth over; the poor man gets to suck greedily on the hem of the tablecloth*—and the munitions factories were humming murderously along, but wages were being cut left and center as the fiscal crisis deepened and the banks called in their loans and the military buildup continued.

Finally the water began hissing and burbling up into the brewing chamber. Erasmus gave up on staring out the window and went in search of his favorite mug. A vague memory of having left it in the lounge drew him into the passage, between the bookcases stacked above head-height with tracts and treatises and rants, and as he passed the staircase he picked up the letter and carried it along. The mug he found sitting empty on top of a pyramid of antinomianist-utilitarian propaganda tracts and a tottering pile of sheet music.

Back in the kitchen, he spooned rough sugar into the mug. The samovar was still hissing like a bad-natured old cat, so he slit open the electrograph's seal while he was waiting for it to finish brewing. The letter within had been cast off a Post Office embosser, but the words had been composed elsewhere. YOUR SISTER IN GOOD HANDS DURING CONFINEMENT STOP MIDWIFE OPTIMISTIC STOP WHY NOT VISIT STOP BISHOP ENDS.

His eyebrows furrowed as he stared at the slip of paper, his morning tea quite forgotten. Nobody in the movement would entrust overtly coded messages to the government's postal service; the trick was to use electrographs for signaling and the movement's own machinery for substantive communications. But this wasn't a prearranged signal, which made it odd. He'd had a sister once, but she'd died when he was six years old: what this was telling him was that Lady Bishop wanted him to visit her in New London. He stared at it some more. It didn't contain her double cross marker—if she'd signed her first name to a signal it would mean *I've been captured*—and it did contain her negative marker—if a message contained an odd number of words that meant *I am at liberty*. But it wasn't a scheduled meeting: however he racked his brains he couldn't think of anything that might warrant such an urgent summons, or the disruption to his other duties.

Does this mean we have a breach? He put the treacherous message down on the kitchen table and turned off the gas, then poured boiling hot tea into his mug. *If Margaret's been taken, it's a catastrophe. And if she hasn't*—gears spun inside his mind, grinding through the long list of possibilities. Whatever the message meant, he needed to be on a train to the capital as soon as possible.

An hour later, Erasmus was dressed and ready to travel, disguised as himself (electrograph in wallet, along with ID papers). He carefully shut off the gas supply and, going downstairs, hung up the CLOSED DUE TO ILLNESS sign in the shop window. It needed no explanation to such folk as knew him, and in any case the Polis had been giving him a wide berth of late, ever since his relapse in their cells. *They probably think I'm out of the struggle for good,* he told himself, offering it as a faint prayer. If he could ever shed the attention he'd attracted, what use he could make of anonymity with his age and guile!

It took him some time to get to the new station besides

the Charles River, but once there he discovered that the mid-morning express had not yet departed, and seats in second class were still available. And that wasn't his only good fortune. As he walked along the pier past the streamlined engine he noticed that it had none of the normal driving wheels and pistons, but multiple millipede-like undercarriages and a royal coat of arms. Then he spotted the string of outrageously streamlined carriages strung out along the track behind it, and the way the gleaming tractor emitted a constant gassy whistling sound, like a promise from the far future. It was one of the new turbine-powered trains that had been all the talk of the traveling classes this summer. Erasmus shook his head. This was unexpected: he'd hoped to reach New London for dinner, but if what he'd heard about these machines were true he might arrive in time for late lunch.

His prognostications were correct. The train began to move as he settled down behind a newspaper, accelerating more like an electric streetcar than any locomotive he'd been on, and minutes later it was racing through the Massachusetts countryside as fast as an air packet.

Burgeson found the news depressing but compelling. **Continental Assembly Dismissed**! screamed the front page headline. **Budget Deadlock Unresolved.** The king had, it seemed, taken a right royal dislike to his Conservative enemies in the house, and their dastardly attempts to save their scrawny necks by raising tariffs to pay for the Poor Law rations at the expense of the Navy. Meanwhile, the rocketing price of Persian crude had triggered a run on oil futures and threatened to deepen the impending liquidity crisis further. Given a choice between a rock and a hard place—between the need to mobilize the cumbersome and expensive apparatus of continental defense in the face of French aggression, and the demands of an exhausted Treasury and the worries of bondholders—the king had gone for neither, but had instead dismissed the quarrelsome political mosquitoes who kept insisting that he make a choice between guns and butter. It would have

struck Erasmus as funny if he wasn't fully aware that it
meant thousands were going to starve to death in the
streets come winter, in Boston alone—and that was ignoring the thousands who would die at sea and on foreign
soil, because of the thrice-damned stupid assassination of
the young prince.

There were some benefits to rule by royal edict, Erasmus
decided. The movement was lying low, and the number of
skulls being crushed by truncheons was consequently
small right now, but with the dismissal of the congress,
everyone now knew exactly who to blame whenever anything bad happened. There was no more room for false
optimism, no more room for wishful thinking that the
Crown might take the side of the people against his servants. The movement's cautious testing of the waters of
public opinion (cautious because you never knew which
affable drinking companion might be an agent provoca-
teur sent to consign you to the timber camps, and in this
time of gathering wartime hysteria any number of ordi-
narily reasonable folks had been caught up in the most
bizarre excesses of anti-French and anti-Turkish hysteria)
suggested that, while the king's popularity rose whenever
he took decisive action, he could easily hemorrhage support by taking responsibility for the actions usually carried out by the home secretary in his name. No more
lying democracy: no more hope that if you could just
raise your thousand-pound landholder's bond you could
take your place on the electoral register, merging your
voice with the elite.

The journey went fast, and he'd only just started reading the small-print section near the back (proceedings of
divorce and blasphemy trials; obituaries of public offi-
cials and nobility; church appointments; stock prices)
when the train began to slow for the final haul into Queen
Josephina Station. Erasmus shook his head, relieved that
he hadn't finished the paper, and disembarked impatiently. He pushed through the turbulent bazaar of the station concourse as fast as he could, hailed a cab, and

directed it straight to a perfectly decent hotel just around
the corner from Hogarth Villas.

Half an hour later, after a tense walk-past to check for
signs that all was in order, he was relaxing in a parlor at
the back of the licensed brothel with a cup of tea and a
plate of deep-fried whitebait, and reflecting that whatever
else could be said about Lady Bishop's establishment, the
kitchen was up to scratch. As he put the teacup down, the
side door opened. He rose: "Margaret?"

"Sit down." There were bags under her eyes and her
back was stooped, as if from too many hours spent
cramped over a writing desk. She lowered herself into an
overpadded armchair gratefully and pulled a wry smile
from some hidden reservoir of affect: "How was your
journey?"

"Mixed. I made good time." His eyes traveled around
the pelmet rail taking in the decorative knick-knacks:
cheap framed prints of music hall divas and dolly-mops,
bone china pipe-stands, a pair of antique pistols. "The
news is—well, you'd know better than I." He turned his
head to look at her. "Is it urgent?"

"I don't know." Lady Bishop frowned. There was a discreet knock at the door, and a break in the conversation
while one of the girls came in with a tea tray for her.
When she left, Lady Bishop resumed: "You know Adam
is coming back?"

Erasmus jolted upright. "He's *what*? That's stupid! If
they catch him—" That didn't bear thinking about. *He's
coming back?* The very idea of it filled his mind with the
distant roar of remembered crowds. *Inconceivable—*

"He seems to think the risk is worth running, given the
nature of the current crisis, and you know what he's like.
He said he doesn't want to be away from the capital when
the engine of history puts on steam. He's landing late
next week, on a freighter from New Shetland that's putting into Fort Petrograd, and I want you to meet him and
make sure he has a safe journey back here. Willie's putting together the paperwork, but I want someone who he

knows to meet him, and you're the only one I could think
of who isn't holding a ring or breaking rocks."

He nodded, thoughtfully. "I can see that. It's been a
long time," he said, with a vertiginous sense of lost time.
*It must be close on twenty years since I last heard him
speak.* For a disturbing moment he felt the years fall
away. "He really thinks it's time?" He asked, still not sure
that it could be real.

"I'm not sure I agree with him . . . but, yes. Will you
do it?"

"Try and stop me!" He meant it, he realized. Years in
the camps, and everything that had gone with that . . . and
he still meant it. *Adam's coming back, at last.* And the na-
tions of men would tremble.

"We're setting up a safe house for him. And a meeting
of the Central Executive Committee, a month from now.
There will be presses to turn," she said warningly. "He'll
need a staff. Are you going to be fit for it?"

"My health—it's miraculous. I can't say as how I'll
ever have the energy of a sixteen-year-old again, but I'm
not an invalid anymore, Margaret." He thumped his chest
lightly. "And I've got lost time to make up for."

Lady Bishop nodded, then took a sip of her tea.

"There's another matter, I needed to speak with you
about," She said. "It's about your friend Miss Beckstein."

"Yes?" Erasmus leaned forward. "I haven't heard anything from her for nearly two months—"

"A woman claiming to be her turned up on my doorstep
three nights ago: we've spent the time since then questioning her. I have no way of identifying her positively,
and if her story is correct she's in serious trouble."

"I can tell you—" Erasmus paused. "What kind of
trouble?"

Margaret's frown deepened. "First, I want you to look
at this portrait." She pulled a small photograph from the
pocket of her shalwar suit. "Is this her?"

Erasmus stared at it for a moment. "Yes." It was slightly
blurred but even though she was looking away from the

camera, as if captured through the eye of a spy hole, he recognized her as Miriam. He looked more closely. Her costume was even more outlandish than when she'd first shown up on his doorstep, and either the lighting was poor or there was a bruise below one eye, but it was definitely her. "That's her, all right."

"Good."

He glanced up sharply. "You were expecting a Polis agent?"

"No." She reached for the picture and he let her take it. "I was expecting a Clan agent."

"A—" Erasmus stopped. He picked up his teacup again to disguise his nervousness. "Please explain," he said carefully. "Whatever I am permitted to know."

"Don't worry, you're not under restriction." Lady Bishop's frown momentarily quirked into a smile. "Unfortunately, if Miss Beckstein is telling the truth, it's very bad news indeed. It appears she fell into disfavor with her family of the first estate—to the point where they imprisoned her, and then attempted to marry her off. But the arranged marriage provoked a violent backlash from the swain's elder brother, and it seems she is now destitute and in search of a safe harbor. Her family doesn't even know if she's still alive, and she believes many of them are dead. Which leaves me with a very pressing dilemma, Erasmus. If this was subterfuge or skulduggery, some kind of plot to pressure us by her relatives, it would be easy enough to address. But under the circumstances, what should I do with her?"

Burgeson opened his mouth to speak, then froze. *Think very carefully, because your next words might condemn her.* "I, ah, that is to say—" He paused, feeling the chilly fingers of mortal responsibility grasp the scruff of his neck like a hangman's noose. "You invited me here to be her advocate," he accused.

Lady Bishop nodded. "Somebody has to do it."

The situation was clear enough. The movement existed from day to day in mortal peril, and had no room for deadweight. Prisons were a luxury that only governments could afford. *At least she invited me here to speak,* he realized. It was a generous gesture, taken at no small risk given the exigencies of communication discipline and the omnipresent threat of the royal security Polis. Despite the organization's long-standing policies, Lady Bishop was evidently looking for an excuse *not* to have Miriam liquidated. Heartened by this realization, Erasmus relaxed a little. "You said she turned up on your doorstep. Did she come here voluntarily?"

"Yes." Lady Bishop nodded again.

"Ah. Then that would imply that she views us as allies, or at least as possible saviors. Assuming she isn't working for the Polis and this isn't an ambush—but after three days I think that unlikely, don't you? If she is then, well, the ball is up for us both. But she's got a story and she's been sticking to it for three days . . . ? Under extraordinary pressure?"

"No pressure. At least, nothing but her own isolation."

Erasmus came to a decision. "She's been a major asset in the past, and I am sure that she isn't a government sympathizer. If we take her in, I'm certain we can make use of her special talents." He put his teacup down. "Killing her would be a—" *tragic* "—waste."

Lady Bishop stared at him for a few seconds, her expression still. Then she nodded yet again, thoughtfully. "I concur," she said briskly.

"Well, I confess I am relieved." He scratched his head, staring at the picture she still held.

"I value your opinions, Erasmus, you must know that. I needed a second on this matter; my first leaning was to find a use for her, but you know her best and if you had turned your thumb down—" she paused. "Is there a personal interest I should know about?"

He looked up. "Not really. I consider her a friend, and I find her company refreshing, but there's nothing more." *Nothing more,* he echoed ironically in the safety of his own head. "I incline towards leniency for all those who

are not agents of the state—I think it unchristian and in-
decent to mete out such punishment as I have been on the
receiving end of—but if I thought for an instant that she
was a threat to the movement I'd do the deed myself."
And that was the bald unvarnished truth—a successful
spy would condemn dozens, even hundreds, to the gallows and labor camps. But it was not the entire truth, for it
would be a harsh act to live with afterwards: conceivably
an impossible one.

Lady Bishop sipped her tea again. "Then I think you'll
be the best man for the job."

"What job?"

"Finding a use for her, of course. In your copious spare
time, when you're not off being Sir Adam's errand boy."

Erasmus blinked. "Excuse me?"

"I'd have thought it obvious." She put her teacup down.
"We can't keep her here. Her inexperience would render
her dangerous, her strange ideas and ways would be haz-
ardous and hard to conceal in the front of the house, and,
bluntly, I think she'd draw unwelcome attention to herself. If we're not to send her to the Miller, it's essential to
put her somewhere safe. You're the only person she
knows or trusts here, so you drew the short straw. Moreover, I suspect you know more about how to make use of
her unique ability than I do. So, unless you protest, I'm
going to assign her to you as an additional responsibility,
after you see to Adam's travel arrangements. Take her in
and establish how we can use her. What do you say?"

"I say—um." His head was spinning: Erasmus blinked
again. "That is to say, that makes sense, but—"

Lady Bishop clapped her hands together before he could
muster a coherent objection. "Excellent!" She smiled. "I'll
have Edward sort out documents and some suitable clothing for her, and you can take her back to Boston as soon
as possible. What do you say?"

"But—" *The servant's room is full of furniture in hock,
the second bedroom doesn't have room to swing a cat for
all the old clothing and books I've got stored in it, and the*

*old biddies up the street will wag their tongues so fast
their jaws explode*—"I think the word Miss Beckstein
would use is 'okay.' " He sighed. "This is going to be interesting."

His Majesty King Egon the Third had convened his special assizes in the grand hall of the Thorold Palace—still
smoking, and somewhat battered by his soldiers in their
enthusiasm to drive out the enemy—precisely thirty-six
hours after the explosion and subsequent attack on his father. "By parties of great treachery in league with the Tinker tribe," as the gebanes dispatched by royal messenger
to all his vassal lords put it: "Let all know that by decree
of this court in accordance with the doctrine of outlawry
the afore-named families are declared outwith the law,
and their chattels and holdings hereby escheat to the
Crown." The writs were flying by courier to all quarters
of the kingdom; now his majesty was dictating a codicil.

"This ague at the heart of our kingdom pains us grievously, but we are young and healthy enough that it shall
soon be overcome and the canker cut out," his majesty
said. "To this end, an half of all real properties and chattels recovered from the outlaw band is hereby granted to
whosoever shall yield those properties to the Crown." He
frowned: "is that clear enough do you suppose, Innsford?"

"Absolutely clear, my lord." His excellency the duke of
Innsford bobbed his head like a hungry duck plowing a
mill pond. "As clear as temple glass!" *Whether it is wise
is another matter,* he thought, but held his counsel. Egon
might be eager to rid himself of the tinker clan, and declaring them outlaw and promising half their estates to
whoever killed them was a good way to go about the job,
but in the long run it might come back to haunt him: other
kings had been overthrown by ambitious dukes, with cof-
fers filled and estates bloated by the spoils of a civil war
fought by proxy. Innsford harbored no such ambitions—

his old man's plans did not call for a desperate all-or-nothing gamble to take the throne—but others might think differently. Meanwhile, the scribe seated at the table behind him scratched on, his pen bobbing between ink pot and paper as he committed the King's speech to paper.

His majesty glanced up at the huge, clear windows overhead, frames occupied by flawless sheets of plate imported from the shadowlands by the tinkers. "May Sky Father adorn his tree with them." In the wan morning light his expression was almost hungry. Innsford nodded again. The king—a golden youth only a handful of years ago, now come into his full power as a young man, handsome as an eagle and strong as an ox—was not someone anyone would disagree with openly. He was fast to laugh, but his cruel streak was rarely far below the surface and his mind was both deceptively sharp and coldly untrusting. He kept his openness for a small coterie of friends, their loyalty honed beyond question by bleak years of complicity during the decade when his father had held him at arm's reach, suspicious of the brain rot inflicted on his younger brother Creon during a sly assassination attempt. The other courtiers (of whom there were no small number, Duke Innsford among them) would have a long wait until they earned his confidence.

And as Egon had demonstrated already, losing the royal confidence could be a fatal blunder.

Egon glanced at the scribe: "That's enough for now." He stood up, shifting his weight from foot to foot to restore the circulation that the hard wooden chair had slowed. "My lord Innsford, attend us, please. And you, my lord Carlsen, and you, Sir Markus."

The middle-aged duke rose to his feet and half-bowed, then followed as the young monarch walked towards the inner doors. Four bodyguards paced ahead of him, and two to the rear—the latter spending more time looking over their shoulders than observing their royal charge—with the courtiers Carlsen and Markus, and their attendant bodyguards, and Innsford's own retainers and guards taking up the tail end of the party. His majesty affected a scandalous disregard for propriety, dressing in exactly the same livery and chain mail jerkin as his escorts, distinguishable only by his chain of office—and even that was draped around his neck, almost completely hidden by his tunic. It was almost as if, the duke mused, his majesty was afraid of demonic assassins who might spring out of the thin air at any moment. *As if*. And now that the duke noticed it, even Egon's courtiers wore some variation on the royal livery . . .

"Markus, Carl, we go outside. I believe there is an orangery?"

"Certainly, sire." Carlsen—another overmuscled blond hopeful—looked slightly alarmed. "But snipers—"

"That's what our guards are for," Egon said dismissively. "The ones you don't see are more important than the ones you do. We are at greater risk in this ghastly haunted pile—from tinker witches sneaking back in from the shadowlands to slip a knife in my ribs—than in any garden. The less they know of our royal whereabouts, the happier I'll be."

"The land of shadows?" Innsford bit his tongue immediately, but surprise had caught him unawares: *does he really believe they come from the domain of the damned? How much* does *he know?*

The king glanced round and grinned at him lopsidedly, catching him unawares. It was a frighteningly intimate expression. "Where did *you* think they came from? They're the spawn of air and darkness. I've seen it myself: one moment they're there, the next . . ." He snapped his fingers. "They walk between worlds and return to this one loaded with eldritch treasure, weapons beyond the ken of our royal artificers and alchemists: they buy influence and insidiously but instinctively pollute the purity of our noble bloodlines with their changeling get!" His grin turned to a glare. "I learned of this from my grandmother, the old witch—luckily I did not inherit her bloodline, but my brother was another matter. Had Creon not been poisoned in his infancy there is no doubt that once he reached his majority I should shortly have met with an accident."

He paused for a minute while his guards opened the thick oak side door and checked the garden for threats. Then he turned and strode through into the light summer rain, his face upturned towards the sky.

The formal gardens in the grounds of the Thorold Palace had been a byword for splendor among the aristocracy of the Gruinmarkt for decades. The hugely rich clan of tinker families had spared no expense in building and furnishing their residence in the capital: individuals might dress to impress, but stone and rampart were the gowns of dynasties. Some might even think that Egon had brought his court to the captured palace because it was (in the aftermath of the fighting that had damaged the Summer Palace) the most fitting royal residence in the city of Niejwein. Rows of carefully cultivated trees marched alongside the high walls around the garden; rose beds, fantastically sculpted, blossomed before the windowed balconies fronting the noble house. A pool, surmounted by a grotesque fountain, squatted in the midst of a compass rose of gravel paths: beyond it, a low curved building glinted oddly through the falling rain. The walls were made of glass, huge slabs of it, unbelievably even in thickness and clear of hue, held in a framework of cast iron. Green vegetation shimmered beyond the windows, whole trees clearly visible like a glimpse into some fantastic tropical world. Egon strode towards it, not once glancing to either side, while his guards nervously paced alongside, eyes swiveling in every direction.

Innsford hurried to keep up with the royal personage. He cleared his throat: "Your Majesty, if the tinkers suspect you are making free with their former estate—

Egon rounded on him with a grimace. "It's not their estate," he snapped. "It's mine. And don't you forget it." He continued, moderating his tone, "Why do you think everyone around me dresses alike?" His ill-humor slipped away.

"Yes, they can send their assassins, but who is the assassin to shoot first? And besides, I will not stay here long."

They were at the orangery doors. "Where does your majesty wish his court to reside?" the duke inquired, almost casually.

"Right here." Egon flashed him a momentary grin. "While I play the King of Night and Mist." He glanced over his shoulder at Sir Markus. "I need a beater for the royal hunt. Would you fancy the title of general?"

Markus, a strapping fellow with an implausibly bushy mustache, thrust his chest out, beaming with pride: "Absolutely, sire! I am dizzy with delight at the prospect!"

"Good. Kindly make yourself scarce for a few minutes. You too, Carlsen, I'll have words with you both shortly but first I must speak in confidence with his grace."

The orangery doors were open and the guards completed their study: Egon stepped over the threshold, and the small gaggle of courtiers followed him. Innsford studied Markus sidelong. Some backwoods peer's eldest son, beholden to Egon for his drinking space at a royal table, ancestral holdings down at heel over the past five decades: more interested in breaking heads and carousing than the boring business of politicking that his father before him was so bad at. And Egon had just casually offered him a post from which he could reap the drippings from the royal trencher? Innsford blinked slowly, watching the two young bloods bounce away into the glazed pavilion, marveling loudly and crudely about its trappings. "A beater for the hunt should hold the title of general?" he asked.

"When you're hunting for armies, why yes, I believe that is the custom." His majesty's lips quirked slightly, in what might have been intended to be a smile. "If I am in the field at the head of an army, I am clearly looking to the defense of my realm, am I not? Such a grand undertaking will have, I hope, a salutary effect on any secret ambitions the father of my betrothed might hold towards

our lands. Leading an army against the tinkers will permit
me to burnish my honor, strive for glory, and ensure that
those who rally to my banner do so under my eyes so that
their claims to the spoils of victory be adjudicated immediately." *Oh, so you don't trust your vassals with sharp
implements out of your sight?* Innsford nodded gravely,
while Sir Markus beamed like an idiot. *A useful idiot,
come to think of it.* "And the tinker assassins will have little success in striking from the shadows if they do not
know, from one day to the next, where I make my bed."

The duke nodded thoughtfully. "I am pleased by your
majesty's perspicacity and foresight," he said carefully,
thinking: *Sky Father! He's sharp.* If Egon was going to go
into the field at the head of an army, he was going to slay
about six birds with one stone. Hunting down the tinker
Clan's holdings in the wild would compel them to confront
him on his own terms, while making it difficult for their assassins to stick a knife in his ribs. An army in being would
prevent the neighbors from getting any ideas about picking
off a province here or a holding there. Meanwhile, Egon
had rung a bell to make his backwoods vassal dogs salivate
at the thought of loot: now he would go into the field to
gather the leashes of the men they had released for service.
He could simultaneously claim the lion's share of the
spoils he'd promised, while maintaining the appearance of
generously disbursing loot to his followers. Handled carefully it would raise him to the stature of a true warrior
king—somebody only fools or the truly desperate would
scheme against—without the attendant risks of declaring
war on one of the neighboring kingdoms. *If it worked*—"I
see much in your plan to commend it." Innsford paused.
Egon had come to a halt in front of a bench at the center of
a circle of low, dark green trees. Small orange fruits glimmered among their shadowy branches. "But you did not
summon me here to tell me this."

"Indeed not." Egon inhaled deeply, closing his eyes for
a moment. Innsford sniffed, but his sinuses—chronically

congested, the aftermath of a broken nose in his youth—stubbornly refused to disclose the cause of Egon's blissful expression. The king opened his eyes: "I have some—problems. I believe you might be able to assist me in their resolution."

Ah. Here it comes. Innsford had lived through the reign of two kings before this young upstart: nevertheless, his stomach tingled and he felt a shiver of fear, as if a black cat walked across his future grave. "I am at your command, your majesty."

"While I am on campaign, I must look to the good cultivation of my earthly field." *Niejwein and territories,* Innsford translated. "I must also look to the good administration of my army. Who am I to trust, in the halls of power while I am elsewhere?" For a moment the royal gaze fell on Innsford, unblinking and cold as any snake. "His grace of Niejwein is under threat from the tinker knives if he stays in the capital whose name he bears: perhaps he would be safer were he to undertake a pilgrimage to the southern estates? His eldest son will be all too pleased to look to the household's duties in his father's absence, while his grace could earn my gratitude by looking to the good management of those provinces."

Innsford stiffened. *But Niejwein's your man!* he thought indignantly. Then he unpacked Egon's plan further. *Niejwein's too powerful, here. Send him away from his power base while keeping his son—inexperienced—as a hostage, and he can serve your ends safely. Is that what you plan?* "You have a task in mind for me." It was an admission, but denying any awareness of the deeper political realities would merely suggest to Egon that he was too stupid to be of any use. And Innsford had a nasty inkling that being pigeonholed as useless by King Egon was unlikely to be conducive to a peaceful and prosperous old age. Especially if one was of high enough birth to conceivably be a threat.

"Indeed." Egon smiled again, that disturbing smirk with a telltale narrowing of the eyes. "Laurens—the next

Duke of Niejwein, I should say—is none too bright himself. He'll need his hand holding and his back watching." The smirk faded. "The defense of Niejwein is no minor task, your grace, because I am certain the tinkers will attempt to retake the city. Their holdings are not well adapted to support a war of maneuver, and they are by instinct and upbringing cosmopolitans. Furthermore, Niejwein is the key to their necromantic trade with the land of shades. There are locations in this city that they need. I must assign an army to the defense of the capital, but I would be a thrice-damned fool to leave it in his grace of Niejwein's own hands. Will you take it?"

"I—" Innsford swallowed. "You surprise me."

"Not really!" Egon said lightly. "You know as well as I the value of a certain—reputation." His own reputation for bloody-handed fits of rage had served well enough at court to keep his enemies fearful. "Should you accept this task, then this palace will be yours—and your son Franz? He is well, I trust? I will be needing a page. Franz will accompany me and win glory on the battlefield, and in due course he will inherit the second finest palace in the land from his father's prudence in this matter."

Innsford stared. "I wo-would be delighted to accept your gracious offer," he forced out. *You're going to leave me in charge of this death trap while you take my son as your page?* The audacity was offensive, but as an act of positioning it was a masterstroke: rebel against the king and Egon would already hold his firstborn hostage. *But meanwhile . . .* thoughts whirled in his head. "You expect the tinkers to try to retake the city, my liege?" he asked: "Is there sound intelligence to this effect?"

"Oh, indeed." Egon's reply was equally casual in tone, and just as false. "I have my ways." He smirked again. "Well, truth be told, I have my spies." He chuckled dryly. "You understand more than you can politely say, my lord, so I shall say it for you: I trust no one. *No one.* But don't let that fool you. The rewards for being true and constant to my service will be great and in time you'll come round to my way of thinking, I'm sure. It is no blind ambition that desires my impression of your son: I have a nation to rid of witchcraft and nightmares, to make fit for men such as your son to live in. He will eventually play a privileged role at court; I would like to meet him sooner rather than later. But now—" He gestured at the orange grove around them. "—I have arrangements to make. There is a war to conduct, and once I have seen to my defense I must look to my arms." He took another deep breath. "If success smells half so sweet as this, I shall count myself a lucky man."

The bench seat stank of leather, old sweat, gunpowder, and a cloying reek of fear. It rattled and bounced beneath Mike, to the accompaniment of a metallic squeaking like damaged car shock absorbers. His leg ached abominably below the knee, and whenever he tried to move it into a less painful position it felt as if a pack of rabid weasels was chewing on it. His face pressed up against the rear cushion of the seat as the contraption swayed from side to side, bouncing over the deep ruts in the cobblestone surface of the road.

Despite the discomfort, he was calm: everything was distant, walled off from him by a barrier of placid equanimity, as if he was wrapped in cotton wool. *They'll kill me when they find out,* he told himself, but the thought held no fear. *Wow, whatever Hastert stuck me with is really smooth.*

Not that life was entirely a bed of roses. He winced at a particularly loud burst of gunfire rattling past the carriage window. One of the women on the other bench seat rattled off something in hochsprache: he couldn't follow it but she sounded scared. The old one tut-tutted. "Sit down, you'll only get your head blown off if you give them a target," she said in English.

More hochsprache: something about duty, Mike thought vaguely.

"No, you shouldn't . . ."

The distinctive sound of a charging handle being worked, followed by a gust of cold air.

Crack. The sound of a rifle firing less than a meter from his ear penetrated Mike's haze. He pushed back against the seat back, rolling onto his back just as a particularly violent pot-hole tried to swallow one of the carriage's rear wheels, and the shooter fired again: a hot brass cartridge case pinged off the back of the seat and landed on his hand. Curiously, it hurt.

"*Ow*—" He twitched, shaking the thing off, wincing repeatedly as the woman in the fur coat leaning out of the carriage window methodically squeezed off another three shots. *What's the word for . . . ?* "My leg, it hurts," he tried.

"Speak English, your accent's atrocious," said the old woman. "It won't fool anyone."

Mike stared at her. In the semi-darkness of the carriage her face seemed to hover in the darkness, disembodied. Outside the window, men shouted at each other. The carriage lurched sideways, then bounced forward, accelerating. The shooter withdrew her head and shoulders from the window. "That is all of them for now, I believe," she announced, with an accent of her own that could have passed for German. She glanced at Mike, mistrustfully, and adjusted her grip on the gun. The real moon, outside, scattered platinum highlights off her hair: for a moment he saw her face side-lit, young and striking, like a Russian princess in a story, pursued by wolves.

"Close the window, you don't want to make a target of yourself," said the old biddy from beneath the pile of rugs. "And I don't want to catch my death of cold." A cane appeared from somewhere under the heap, ascending until it battered against the carriage roof. "Shtoppan nicht, gehen'su halt!" She was old, but her lungs were good. She glanced at Mike. "So you're awake, are you?"

Answering seemed like too much of an effort, so Mike ignored her: it was much easier to simply close his eyes and try to keep his leg still. That way the weasels didn't seem to bite as hard.

A moment later, the cane poked him rudely in the ribs. "Answer when you're spoken to!" snapped the Russian princess. He opened his eyes again. The thing prodding his side wasn't a cane, and she might be pretty, but she was also clearly angry. *Is it something I did?* he wondered hazily. "Where am I?"

"In a carriage," said the old woman. "I'd have thought that was obvious." She snorted. "The question you meant to ask is, how did I end up in this carriage in particular?"

"Jah: and, how am I, it, to leave, alive?" The Russian princess gave his ribs a final warning poke, then withdrew into the opposite corner of the cramped cabin, next to the old woman. Mike tried to focus: as his eyes adjusted he saw that under her fur coat she was wearing a camouflage jacket. The rifle—he focused some more—was exotic, some sort of foreign bullpup design with a huge night vision scope bolted above its barrel. *Blonde bombshell with fur coat and assault rifle.* His gaze slid sideways to take in the older one, searching for reassurance: she smiled crookedly, one eyebrow raised, and he shuddered, déjà vu spiking through his guts as sharply as the pain from his damaged leg.

"That's enough, Olga," the old lady said sharply, never taking her eyes off Mike. "We've met, in case you'd forgotten."

Oh shit. The penny dropped: *that's the entire mission blown!* He stared at her in mortified disbelief, at a complete loss for words. His mind flashed back to events earlier in the evening, to a hurried snatch of conversation with Miriam, the way she'd stared at him in perplexity as if she couldn't quite fathom the meaning of his reappearance in her life: now he felt the same scene repeating, horribly skewed. "You were—" he paused. "Mrs. Beckstein. Well . . ." His lips were as dry as the day when Miriam had casually suggested they stop off on their way to the restaurant to say hello, *just for ten minutes, so you've met my mother*—"I'm surprised. I thought you'd adopted Miriam? What are you doing here?"

Olga, the Russian princess as he'd started thinking of her, glared at him malevolently: her rifle pointed at the floor, but he had no doubt she could bring it to bear on his head in an eyeblink. But Mrs. Beckstein surprised him. She began to smile, and then her smile widened, and she began to chuckle, louder and louder until she began to wheeze and subsided into a fit of coughing. "You really believed that? And you saw us together? What kind of cop are you?" Something else must have tweaked her funny bone because a moment later she was off again, lost in a paroxysm of thigh-slappingly disproportionate mirth. Or maybe it was just relief at being out of the fire-fight.

"I do not see the thing that is so funny," Olga said, almost plaintively.

"Ah, well, but he was such a nice young—" Mrs. Beckstein began coughing again. Olga looked concerned, but given a choice between keeping Mike under observation and trying to help the older woman—"Sorry, dear," she told Olga, when she got her voice back. "That's how Miriam described you." She nodded at Mike. "Before she changed her mind."

Mike closed his eyes again. *Jesus, Mary, and Joseph, is this a fuckup!* He winced: obviously demons were feeding his leg-weasels crystal meth. "He's called Mike," Mrs. Beckstein continued remorselessly, "Mike something-beginning-with-F, I've got it in my diary. And he works for the Drug Enforcement Agency. Or he used to work for the DEA. Do you still work for the DEA, Mike?"

He opened his eyes, unsure what to do: the painkillers were subsiding but he still felt unfocused, blurry about the edges. "I'm not supposed to talk—"

"You will *talk*, boy." Mrs. Beckstein glared at him, and he recoiled at the anger in her expression. "You can take your chances with me, or you can make your excuses to my half-brother's men, but you are going to talk sooner or later." She glanced at Olga. "Sometimes I can't believe my luck," she said dryly. She turned back to Mike, her expression harsh: "What have you done with my daughter?"

"I—" Mike stopped. Time seemed to slow. *My brother's men. Jesus, she's been one of them all along! How deep does this go*? He shuddered, his guts churning. Until now he'd known, understood in the abstract, that Miriam was involved with these alien gangsters, narcoterrorists from Middle Earth: even meeting Miriam, dressed up for a medieval wedding in the middle of an exploding castle, hadn't really shaken what he'd thought he knew. But Miriam's mother was a different matter entirely, a disabled middle-aged woman living quietly in a small house in New England suburbia—*they're everywhere!* He swallowed, choking back hysterical laughter. "I don't know where she went. She said she had a, one of the lockets, got it from a friend. Said she'd be in touch later. There was a perp in black, tried to stab her so I shot him—"

"Why?"

"Orders." He cleared his throat. "They told me, talk to her. Offer her whatever she . . . well, anything."

Mrs. Beckstein glanced at the Russian princess: evidently her expression meant something because a moment later she turned back to him. "You're colluding with Egon."

"Who?" His bewilderment must have been obvious, because a moment later she nodded.

"All right. So how did you get over here?"

Mike stared at her.

Mrs. Beckstein took a deep breath. "Olga. If Mr. Fleming here doesn't answer my questions, you have my permission to shoot him in the kneecap. At will."

"Which one?" asked the Russian princess.

"Whichever you want." Mrs. Beckstein sniffed. "Now, Mike. I want you to understand one thing, and one thing only—I'm concerned for my daughter's well-being. I'm especially concerned when an ex-boyfriend of hers with

a highly dubious employment record appears out of
nowhere at a—"she coughed "—joyous occasion, and all
hell breaks loose. And I am more concerned than you can
possibly begin to imagine that she has vanished in the
middle of the sound and the fury, because there is an official decree in force that says if she world-walks without
the permission of the Clan committee, her life is forfeit.
She is my daughter, and blood is thicker than water, and I
am going to *save her ass*. Call it atonement for earlier mis-
takes, if you like: I've not always been a terribly good
mother." She leaned closer. "Now, you may be able to help
me *save her ass*. If I think you might be useful to me, I can
protect you up, to a point. Or." She nodded at Olga. "Lady
Olga is a friend of Miriam's. She's concerned for her wel-
fare, too. Miriam has more friends than she realizes, you
see. Thousands and thousands of them . . . So the question
is: are we all agreed that we are friends of Miriam, and
that we intend to *save her ass*? Or—"she fixed Mike with
a vulture stare"—were you stringing her along?"

"No!" he exclaimed. "Whoa. *Ow.*" The weasels had
graduated from carnivore school and were working on
their diplomas in coyote impersonation. "What do you
want to know?"

"Let's start with, how you got over here."

"Same way Matthias got over to our—my—world." He
could almost see the lightbulbs going on over Olga's and
Mrs. Beckstein's heads. "Family Trade captured a couple
of world-walkers. Forced them to carry." He tried to shrug
himself into a more comfortable position, half-upright.

"Forced? How?" Olga stared at him. "And what is Family Trade?"

"Collar . . . bombs. They carry a cargo and come back,
Family Trade resets the timer. They don't come back, it
blows their head off. When they're not world-walking,
FTO keeps them in a high-rise jail."

Mrs. Beckstein interrupted. "Family Trade—this is some
spook agency, isn't it?"

"Yes. I'm—seconded—to it. Not my idea. Matt walked

into the Boston downtown office while Pete—my partner—
and I were on the desk. That's all."

"Ah." Mrs. Beckstein nodded to herself. "And they sent
you here because they worked out that Miriam was . . .
okay. I think I get it. Am I right?" She raised an eyebrow.

"Yes, mostly," he said hastily: Olga was still glaring at
him from her corner. "We don't have much intel on the
ground. Colonel Smith figured she'd be able to develop a
spy ring for us, in return for an exit opportunity. He wants
informants. I told him it was half-assed and premature,
but he ordered the insertion."

"He wants informants, does he?" Mrs. Beckstein
grinned. "What do you make of that, Olga?"

Olga's expression of alarm surprised Mike in its inten-
sity, cutting through the fog of drugs: "you can't be serious! That would be treason!"

"It's not treason if it's known to ClanSec in advance."
Mrs. Beckstein waved a hand in dismissal. "One man's spy
is another man's diplomatic back channel to the other side; it
just depends who's playing the game and for what stakes."
Her eyes narrowed as she looked at Mike. "Your colonel
wants information? Well, he shall have it, and you shall take
it to him. But in return, you're going to find my daughter."
A brief sideways nod: "you and Lady Olga, that is."

4

RUNNING DOG

The next day came too early for Erasmus. It was barely a quarter to eight when he checked out of the cheap traveler's hotel he'd stayed in overnight, and walked around to the rear entrance to Hogarth Villas. Lady Bishop's taciturn manservant Edward answered the door, then led him down a servants' passage and a staircase that led to a gloomy basement, illuminated by the dim light that filtered down to the bottom of an air shaft.

"Wait here," said Edward, disappearing round a corner. A moment later, he heard a rattle of keys, and low voices. Then:

"Erasmus!"

He smiled stiffly, embarrassed by his own reaction. "Miriam, it's good to see you again."

"I'd been hoping—" She took two steps towards him, and he found himself suddenly at arm's length; he'd advanced without noticing. "I'm not imagining things?"

"Everything will be alright." His voice sounded shaky in his own ears. "Come on, I'll explain as we go." He forced himself to look past her face, to make eye contact with Edward (who grimaced and shrugged, as if to say *you're welcome to her*): "Do you have any luggage?"

"It's here." Edward hefted a leather valise. Erasmus took it. "I'll be going now," said the servant, "you know the way out."

A moment later they were alone. He found himself staring at Miriam: she looked back at him with an odd expression, as if she'd never seen him before. *Is this all a terrible mistake?* He wondered: *is she going to be angry with me for sending her here?* "You came. For me?"

"As soon as I heard." He found it difficult to talk.

"Well, thank you. I was beginning to worry—" She shivered violently.

"My dear, this isn't the sort of establishment one drops in on unannounced." He noticed her clothing for the first time; someone had found her a more suitable outfit than the gown she'd worn in Lady Bishop's spy-hole picture, but it would never do—probably a castoff from one of the girls upstairs, threadbare and patched. "Hmm. When I asked them to find you something to wear I was expecting something a little less likely to attract attention."

Her cheeks colored slightly. "I'm getting sick of hand-me-downs. You've got a plan?"

"Follow me." It was easier than confronting his emotions—predominantly relief, at the moment, a huge and fragile sense that something precious hadn't been shattered, the toppling vase caught at the last moment—and it was nonsense, of course, a distraction from the serious business at hand. He climbed the stairs easily, with none of the agonizing tightness in his chest and the crackling in his lungs that would have plagued him two months ago. The parlor was empty, the fireplace unlit. He placed the valise on the table. "Let's see what we've got."

Her shadow fell across the bag as he opened it. "Ah, papers." He opened the leather-bound passport and held the first page up to the light. "That's a good forgery." He felt a flash of admiration for Margaret's facilities; if he hadn't known better he'd have been certain it was genuine. Below it was a bundle of other documents: birth certificate, residence permit for the eastern provinces, even a—his cheeks colored. "We appear to be married," he murmured.

"Let me see." She reached over and took the certificate. "Damn, I knew something had slipped my mind. Must have been all the champagne at the reception. Dated two days ago, too—what a way to spend a honeymoon." She sighed. "What is it about this month? Everyone seems to want to see me married."

"Lady Bishop probably thought it would be an excellent explanation for travel," he said, heart pounding and vision blurred. The sense of relief had gone, shattered: blown away by a sense of disquiet, the old ache like a pulled tooth that he'd lived with for far too long. The last time he'd seen Annie, alive or dead. "Or perhaps Ed wanted a little joke at our expense. If so, it's in very bad taste." He made to take it from her hand, but Miriam had other ideas.

"Wait up. She's right, if we're traveling together it's a good cover identity." She looked at him curiously. "We're supposed to travel together?"

Erasmus pulled himself together, with an effort. "I'm supposed to take you back to Boston and look after you. Find a way to make her—you—useful, Margaret told me. Personally, I don't know if that's possible or appropriate, but it gives her a respectable excuse to get you off her plate without sticking a knife in you first. What we do afterwards—"

"Okay, I get the idea." Miriam picked up the passport and stared at it, frowning. "Susan Burgeson. Right." She glanced at him. "I could be your long-lost sister or something if you've got trouble with the married couple idea."

He shrugged. *Compartmentalize.* "It's a cover identity. Nothing more."

She looked thoughtful. "Is Erasmus Burgeson a cover identity, too?"

God's wounds but she's sharp! "If it was, do you think I'd tell you?"

"You'd tell your wife," she said, teasingly—then immediately looked stricken. "Shit! I'm sorry, Erasmus! I'd—it completely slipped my mind. I'm sorry . . ."

"Don't be," he said tightly. "Not your fault."

"No, me and my—" She took his hand impulsively. "I tend to dig, by instinct. Listen, if you catch me doing it again and it's sensitive, just tell me to back off, all right?"

He took a deep breath. *It's not your fault.* "Certainly. I think I owe you that much."

"You owe—" She shook her head. "Enough of that. What else have we got?"

"Let's see." The bag turned out to contain a suit of clothes, not new but more respectable than those they'd already given Miriam. "If we're traveling together, you'd probably better change into these first. We'll look less conspicuous together."

"Okay." She paused. "Right here?"

"I'll wait outside."

He stood with his back to the parlor door for a few scant minutes that felt like hours. He spent some of those hours fantasizing about wringing Ed's neck—a necessary proxy, for the thought of challenging Lady Bishop over the matter was insupportable, but damn them! Why did they have to do that, of all things?

Miriam was a sharp knife, too sharp for her own good—sharp enough to cut both ways. Dealing with her as a contact and a supplier of contraband had been dicey, but not impossible. Living with her was an entirely different matter, but it wasn't exactly feasible to stick her in a tenement apartment and leave her to her own devices. *She'll figure everything out, sooner rather than later. And then what?* The precious vase was back teetering on the edge of the precipice, with no hand in place to catch it this time. And it was full of ashes.

There was a knock at the door. A moment later it

opened, as he turned round. "How do I look?" She took a step back.

"You look—" he paused to collect himself, "fine." The black walking suit was a little severe, but it suited her. However . . . "before we travel, I think we'd better find you a hairdresser."

"Really?" She frowned. "It's not particularly long—"

"Or a wig maker," he explained. "You're probably on the Polis watch list. But if you've got long blond or brown hair, a different name, and a husband, and the informants are all looking for a single woman with short black hair, that's a start. Details are cumulative: you can't just change one thing and expect to go unnoticed, you've got to change lots of different things about yourself simultaneously."

"Right. It'll have to be blond. Damn it, I always get split ends." She ran one hand through her hair. It was longer than he remembered. "There's other stuff I need to do. When I can figure out what . . ."

A moment he'd been dreading: at least, a small one. She didn't seem to be committed to killing herself just yet. "That will be a problem."

"Ah." She froze. "Yes, somehow I didn't think it was going to be easy."

"The—situation—you drew our attention to is troublesome. For the time being, I think it would be a very bad idea indeed for you to try to make contact with your Clan. Or with the other, ah, local faction. I can make inquiries on your behalf, discreet inquiries, if your relatives are still trying to run your company. But until we know how they will react to your reappearance, it would be best not to reappear. Do you agree?"

Miriam looked baffled for a moment: an achingly familiar bewilderment, the first bright moment of incomprehension that everyone felt the first time, as the doors to the logging camp swung to offer a glimpse into a colder, harsher world. "All I want is to go home."

He reached out and rested a hand on her shoulder, surprising himself: "Listen, home is wherever you are. You've got to learn to accept that, to let go, or sooner or later you're going to kill yourself. Are you listening? Margaret told me your story. Do you want to go back to the situation you just escaped from? Or do you want the Polis to find you instead? I nearly killed myself once, trying to go back. I don't want you to make the same mistake. I think the best way forward would be for you to come with me. It's not forever: it'll last as long as, as long as it needs to. Eventually, I'm sure, you'll be able to go back. But don't . . . don't try to take on too much, Miriam. Not until you're ready."

"I—" She reached up and removed his hand from her shoulder, but she didn't let go of it. "You're too kind!" Without warning she stepped right up to him and put her arms around him, and hugged him. Too surprised to move, he stood rooted to the spot, at a loss for words: after a while she stepped away. "I'm ready now," she said quietly. "Let's get out of here."

Everyone gets a run of bad news sooner or later, thought Eric Smith, *but this is ridiculous.*

"This is not making my day any easier," murmured Dr. James, leaning back in his chair as the door closed behind Agent Herz. He glanced sidelong at Eric. "Got any bright ideas, Colonel?"

Eric stared at the hard copy of Herz's report, sitting on the blotter in its low-contrast anti-photocopying print and SECRET codewords, and resisted the impulse to pound his head on his desk. It would look unprofessional—there were few stronger terms of opprobrium in Dr. Andrew James's buttoned-down vocabulary—and more important, it wouldn't achieve anything. But on the other hand, banging his head on the desk would probably be less painful than trying to deal with the self-compounding clusterfuck-in-progress that was, of late, what passed for the Family

Trade Organization's infant steps towards dealing with the transdimensionally mobile narcoterrorists they were hunting.

(And their goddamn stolen nukes.)

"Come on. What am I going to tell the vice president tonight?"

Eric took a deep breath. "From the top?"

"Whatever order you choose."

"Well, shall we get the small stuff out of the way first?"

"Start."

Eric shrugged. "I don't like to admit this, but the current operations we've got in train are all hosed. CLEANSWEEP has driven into a ditch and we're lucky we got anybody back at all—going by Agent Wall's observations, they got caught in the crossfire during some kind of red-on-red incident. We're lucky Rich was able to exfiltrate in good order, else we wouldn't even know that much. I think we can write off the alpha team and Agent Fleming, they're two days overdue and they've overrun their provisioning.

"On the plus side, Rich got out. We've continued to monitor the CLEANSWEEP team's dead letter drops from the OLIGARCH positions, and they look clean. The fact that nobody's visited or tried to stake them out suggests that the bad guys didn't take any of our men alive. So CLEANSWEEP isn't blown, and once we get more field-qualified linguists prepped we should be able to reactivate it—possibly in as little as three weeks. The real problem we've got is that we're multiply bottlenecked: bottlenecked on linguists, bottlenecked on logistics, bottlenecked on general intelligence. If we could find one of their safe houses we'd be in place to run COLDPLAY against them, but the trail's gone cold and there's a limit to how long I can hold on to an AFSOCOM team with no mission—they're needed in the middle east."

"Hmm." James rolled his pen between the finger and thumb of his left hand. His lips whitened, forming a tight, disapproving line that made the resemblance to Hugo

Weaving in *The Matrix* even stronger. Agent Smith, with a small lapel-pin crucifix and a Ph.D. from Harvard: "I might be able to shake something loose on one of those fronts presently. But VPOTUS isn't going to be happy about the lack of progress."

"Well, I'm not happy either!" Eric dug his fingers into the arms of his chair. His damaged carpal tunnels sent twinges of protest running up his arms. "If you think I enjoy losing agents and trained special forces teams . . . hell." He raised a hand and ran fingertips through his thinning hair. "I'm sorry. But this failure mode wasn't anticipated. Nobody expected them to blow up the fucking palace and start a civil war in the garden. Maybe we should have anticipated it, if we'd been better informed about their internal political situation, but they don't exactly have newspapers over there and even if they did, we'd have trouble reading them. We'd have to have been fucking mind readers to spot a bunch of plotters running a coup!"

"Language, Colonel, please."

"Shi—sorry." Eric shook his head, angry at his own loss of control. "I'm upset. We've now lost two high-clearance, high-value agents and an AFSOCCOM specops team and we've only really been up and running for fourteen weeks."

"I feel your pain," James said dryly. Eric stared at him, taken aback. "But I'm going to have to brief the vice president tonight on all the progress we haven't been making, and believe me, chewing on ground glass would be less painful," he added. "Now. I've heard from Herz. How's CLANCY going?"

"Badly." CLANCY was the ongoing investigation into the nuclear device that Source GREENSLEEVES claimed was planted somewhere in the Boston/Cambridge area, before he'd so inconveniently managed to get himself killed. "We hadn't found anything really noteworthy—a couple of meth labs, a walled-up cellar full of moonshine left over from the nineteen twenties, that sort of thing—until Judith turned up her anomaly yesterday. I was half-convinced GREENSLEEVES was lying to us, but now—well, I don't think we can afford to take that risk." He shivered. "Just who the he—heck stuck a B-53 bomb on blocks in a warehouse and set it to go off on a ten-year timer?"

"Is that a question?" Doctor James leaned back in his chair, steepling his fingertips again, and the piranha-like set of his lips quirked slightly. *Is he trying to smile?* wondered Eric.

"Only if I'm not treading on any classified toes," Smith said warily.

"It's not a healthy question to ask. So I suggest you don't ask me about it. Then I won't have to tell you any lies."

"Ah." Smith dry-swallowed.

"Even if I did know anything about it. Which I don't," James said, with a twitch of one eyebrow that spoke volumes.

"Right. Right." *Change the subject, quick.* The fact that they were sitting in a secure conference cell that was regularly swept for bugs didn't mean that nobody was listening in, or at least recording the session for posterity: all it meant was that nobody outside the charmed circle of the National Security infrastructure was eavesdropping. *But what kind of black operation would involve us nuking one of our own cities?* Smith filed the question away for later.

"Well, we're looking for a needle in a haystack. The original idea of taking the county planner's database and data mining it for suspicious activities is sound in principle, but it yields too many false positives in a city the size of this one. I mean, there are tens of thousands of business premises, many tens of thousands of homes with garages or large basements, and if only one percent of them flag as positives for things like lack of visible tenants or occupants, zero phone use but basic utility draw for heating, and so on, we're swamped. It might be a bomb installation, or it could equally well be Uncle Alfred's old house and he died six months ago and the estate's still in probate or something. Or it could be an overenthusiastic horticulturist trying to breed a better pot plant. On the other hand, hopefully the neutron scattering spectroscopes our NIRT liaisons are getting next week will allow us to make an exhaustive roving search. And we can cover for it easily, by telling the truth—we're testing a bomb detector for terrorist nukes. Everyone will assume we're worried about al-Qaeda, and if we actually do find GREENSLEEVES's gadget . . . well, do you suppose the VP would like to make hay with that?"

The raised eyebrow was back. "I suppose you have a point." James nodded slowly. "Yes, that would kill two terrorist threats with one stone." Eric relaxed slightly. "What else do you have for me?"

"Well, I'm not saying we're not going to get another break—I think it's only a matter of time—but I can't give you a time scale for quantum leaps. I think if we can reactivate CLEANSWEEP, or figure out some way around the bottleneck in our logistics chain we might be able to progress on CLANCY through other avenues. I mean, if we can get our hands on some useful intelligence about the Clan's nuclear capability that could open up some avenues of inquiry about where GREENSLEEVES got his hands on a gadget, and where it might be now. But for the time being, we're not really pursuing a specifically intelligence-led investigation. Getting back into the Gruinmarkt is, in my opinion, vital—and the more force we can project there, the better."

"I see." James made a brief note on his pad. "Well. I'm hoping we'll have a solution to the logistics issues shortly."

"More couriers? A target for COLDPLAY?"

"Something better." He looked smug.

Eric leaned forward. "Tell me. Whatever you can. Is this more of that harebrained physics stuff from Livermore?"

"Of course." Then something terrifying happened: Doctor James actually smiled. "I think it's time to bring you in the loop on the, as you put it, logistics side of things.

There's a cross-disciplinary team under Professor Armstrong from UCSD who've been working on a subject under, um, closed conditions. They haven't worked out everything that's going on yet, but they've made some fascinating progress that points to a physical explanation for their anomalous capability. I'm going to be flying out there tomorrow morning, and I was hoping you could join me."

Eric glanced at his desk. It'd mean another couple of nights away from Gillian and the boys, and more apologies and tense silences at home, but it needed to be done. "As long I can be back here by Friday—if nothing new comes up in the meantime—I should be able to fit it in." Briefly, he let his bitterness show: "it's not as if I'm needed for the post-CLEANSWEEP debrief, or to report CLANCY as closed out."

"Then you'll accompany me." Doctor James rose abruptly, his expression as warm as any killer robot's. "Now if you'll excuse me, I have an appointment it wouldn't do to be late to . . ."

BEGIN TRANSCRIPT:

"You called for me, sir."

"Indeed I did, indeed I did. I trust you've been keeping well. Any trouble getting here?"

"Only the—not really. Not given the prevailing afflictions. I was most surprised to be summoned, though. Under the circumstances."

"Well, you're here now. Have a seat. Make yourself comfortable, this may take some time—I must apologize in advance for any interruptions, I am somewhat busy at present."

"There is nothing to apologize for, sir."

"Ah, but there will be. I'm afraid I've got another delicate task for you. One that will require you to visit the new world and spend some considerable length of time working there on your own initiative."

"But, the fighting! Surely I'm of use there?"

(Clink of glassware.) "Glass of wine?"

"Ah—yes, thank you sir."

(More clinking of glassware.) "Your health, my lady."

"And yours, your grace. Sir. I don't understand. Is this more urgent than dealing with the pretender? As a need of immediacy?"

"Yes."

"Oh." (Pause.) "Then I'll do it, of course. Whatever mysterious task you have in mind."

"I wouldn't be so fast to accept. You may hear me out and deem it a conflict of loyalty."

"Conflict of—" (Pause.) "Oh."

"Yes. I am afraid you're not going to like this."

"It's about her grace, isn't it?"

"Partly. No, let me be honest: mostly. But, hmm, let me think . . . how clear are you on her current circumstances?"

(Tensely.) "She didn't tell me anything. Before—whatever."

"Indeed not, and I did not summon you to accuse you of any misdeeds. But. What is your understanding of what she did?"

(Pause.) "Lady Helge has many bad habits, but her incurable curiosity is by far the worst of them. I was led to believe that she stuck her nose into some business or other of Henryk's, and he slapped her down for it. Confinement to a supervised apartment under house arrest, no contact with anyone who might conspire with her, living on bread and water, that kind of thing. Is there more to it?"

"Yes, you could say that." (Sigh.) "You could hold me responsible, as well. I—placed certain evidence where I expected her to encounter it. It was in the context of a larger operation which you are not privy to. I expected her to rattle some cages and shake loose some useful fruit that were previously hanging out of reach. She has a tendency to stir things up, you will agree?"

"I'm afraid so . . ."

"The trouble is, she—well, she used unacceptable methods of inquiry: and worse, she allowed herself to be caught. Which indeed drew out certain conspirators at court, but not the ones I was looking for and not in the manner I had hoped. I trust this will go no further than your ears, but . . . she tampered with the Post."

"You're kidding!"

"I wish I was."

(Pause.) (Muttered expletive.)

"I didn't hear that, my lady."

"I'm sorry sir, my tongue must have stumbled . . . that's terrible! I can see why she didn't talk to me first, if that is what she was thinking of doing, but how *could* she?"

"I'm afraid that's not the important question right now. Why-ever and however, she did it and was caught. Henryk had no option but to act fast to secure her obedience, even though that cost us any use we could hope to have made of her in the original plan: as it is, he has been accused of undue leniency by certain elderly parties, and I have had to call in many favors to placate the postal commission—or in some cases, to buy their silence. She has not been charged with the offense, and will not be: instead, Henryk offered her a way out—if she would bring us a child in the direct line of succession. She was as reluctant as you can imagine, but agreed to his proposal in the end."

"I had no idea!"

"You weren't meant to: the groundwork was prepared in the deepest secrecy, and her marriage to Prince Creon announced—"

"Creon? The Idiot?"

"Please—sit down! Sit down at once, I say! . . . I'm not going to repeat myself!"

(Pause.) "I'm sorry, sir."

"No you're not. You're outraged, aren't you? It offends you because like all young women who've spent overmuch time in the other world you have absorbed some of their expectations, and the idea of an arranged marriage—no, let me be blunt, a forced marriage—is a personal affront to you. Am I right?"

(Sullen.) "Yes."

"Well, so it may be. And the idea of tampering with the Post does not also offend you?"

(Pause.) "But that's—that's—"

"Need I remind you of the normal punishment for tampering with the Post?"

"No." Heavily. "I understand."

"Are you sure? Let me be blunt: the countess Helge committed a serious crime, for which she might have been executed. She could not be trusted with the corvee anymore. Baron Henryk managed to make an alternative arrangement, by which the countess might be of sufficient use to us to justify sparing her, and might in time redeem the stain from her honor. As a punishment, I will concede that it was severe. But she was given the choice: and she accepted it of her own free will, albeit without grace."

"Huh! I can't imagine she'd have taken such an imposition lightly. But Creon of all people—"

"Creon's grandmother, the queen mother, was one of us. Creon, unlike his brother the pretender, was outer family. The progeny of Creon and Helge would have been outer family beyond doubt, and half likely world-walkers as well."

"But he's defective! How do we know they wouldn't have inherited the—"

"We know. We know why he was defective, too. He was poisoned as a child, not born that way. But it's irrelevant now. Creon—and the queen mother—died when the pretender made his move. I believe they, and Helge, were in fact the real targets of the attack."

"Surely, he's the legitimate heir in any case? He didn't need to do that!"

"You are too well meaning to make a politician, my

lady. If Helge had borne children to Creon, Egon would have good reason to fear for his life. Not necessarily from us, but there are factions with fewer scruples . . . and if Egon's reading of our consensus was that we wanted to place one of our own upon the throne, then his action was ruthless but entirely rational."

"So Creon is dead? And the queen mother? What about Helge?"

"Ah. Well, you see, that's why I wanted to talk to you. There are more important tasks for you to be about than preparing a doppelgangered ambush for the pretender to the throne."

(Pause.) "You've lost her. Haven't you?"

"I very much fear that you are right."

"Shit."

"I do not know that she is still alive. But she has not been confirmed dead; her body was not found in the wreckage. And there are other reasons to hope she survived. She was reported to be speaking to James Lee, the hostage, shortly before the attack: he passed her something small."

"Oh. You think she's in New Britain somewhere?"

"That would be the logical deduction. And were circumstances different I would expect her to report in within a day or two. But right now—well. She was told, in regrettably unequivocal terms, that if she world-walked without permission she would be killed. And we have systematically alienated her affections."

"Why, damn it, sir? I mean, what purpose did it serve?"

(Pause.) "As I indicated, I hoped she would— suitably motivated—lead me to something I wanted. But she is a dangerous weapon to wield, and in this case, she misfired. Then circumstances spun out of my independent control, and . . . you see how things are?"

(Long pause.) "What do you want me to do?" (Pause.) "I assume you want me to find her, wherever she's gone to ground, and bring her back?"

"You are one of the few people she is likely to trust. So that would be a logical deduction, would it not?"

(Suspiciously.) "What else?"

(Pause.) "I trust that you will do everything within your ability to find her and bring her back into the fold. To convince her, you may convey to her my assurances that she will face no retribution for having fled on this occasion—given the circumstances, it was entirely understandable. You may also remind her that Creon is dead, and the arrangement made on his behalf is therefore terminated. The events of the past week are swept away as if they never transpired." (Pause.) "You may also want to tell her that Baron Henryk was killed in the fighting. If she cooperates, she has my personal guarantee of her safety."

"That's not all, is it?"

(Long pause.) "No."

"Then . . . ?"

"I very much fear that Helge will not return willingly. She may want to go to ground on her own—or she might make overtures to the lost cousins. Worse, she might go back to her compulsive digging. She stumbled across a project that is not yet politically admissible: if she exposes it before the council, it could do immense damage. And worst of all, she might seek to obtain a copy of the primary knot and use it to return to her own Boston, then contact the authorities. They will believe her if she goes to them, and she is in a position to do even more damage than Matthias if she wants."

(Pause.) "You want me to kill her if she's turned traitor."

"I *don't* want you to kill her. However, it is absolutely vital that she be prevented from defecting to the new agency the Americans have set up. She could do us immense—immeasurable—damage if she did, and I would rather see her dead than turned into a weapon against us. Do you see now why I warned that you might see this as a conflict of loyalty?"

(Long pause.) "Oh yes, indeed, sir." (Pause.) "If I say no, what happens?"

"Then I will have to send someone else. I don't know who, yet—we are grievously shorthanded in this task, are we not? Likely it will be someone who doesn't know her well, and doesn't care whether she can be salvaged." (Pause.) "I am not sending you to kill her, I am sending you to salvage her if at all possible. But I will not send you unless you are prepared to do your duty to the Clan, should it be necessary. Do you swear to me that you will do so?"

"I—yes, your grace. My liege. I so swear: I will do everything in my power to return Lady Helge voh Thorold d'Hjorth to your custody, alive. And I will take any measure necessary to prevent her adding her number to our enemies. Any—" (Pause.) "—measure."

"Good. Your starting point is inconveniently located—she will have crossed over near the palace, from Niejwein—but I am sure you are equal to the task of hunting her down. You may draw any necessary resources from second security directorate funds; talk to the desk officer. Harald is running things today. You'll want a support team for the insertion, and a disguise."

"I have a working cover identity on the other side already, sir. Was there anything else I should know?"

"Oh yes, as a matter of fact there is. It nearly slipped my mind. Hmm."

"Sir?" (Pause.) "Your grace?"

"Ah. Definitely a problem." (Pause.) "The arrangement with Creon . . . before the betrothal, she was visited more than once by Doctor ven Hjalmar. At the behest of Baron Henryk, I thought, but when I made inquiries I discovered it had been suggested by none other than Patricia."

"Patricia? What's she doing suggesting—hey, isn't Ven Hjalmar the fertility specialist?"

"Yes, Brilliana, and the treatment he subjected the countess Helge to is absolutely unconscionable: but

I believe it was intended as insurance against the Idiot being unable to . . . you know. Be that as it may, he *did* it. Consequently, you have about twelve weeks to find Helge and bring her back. After that time . . . well, you know what happens to women who world-walk while they're pregnant, don't you?"

END TRANSCRIPT

5

TRAVELERS

It was a warm day in New London, beneath the overcast. A slow onshore breeze was blowing, but the air remained humid and close beneath a stifling inversion layer that trapped the sooty, smelly effusions of a hundred thousand oil-burning engines too close to the ground for the comfort of tired lungs.

Two figures walked up the street that led away from Hogarth Villas, arm in arm: a tall, stooped man, his hair prematurely graying, and a woman, her shoulder-length black hair bundled up beneath a wide-brimmed sun hat. The man carried a valise in his free hand. They were dressed respectably but boringly, his suit clean but slightly shiny at elbows and seat, her outfit clearly well worn.

"Where now?" Miriam asked as they reached the end of the row of brick villas and paused at the curb, waiting for a streetcar to jangle and buzz past with a whine of hot electric motors. "Are we going straight back to Boston, or do you have business to attend to first?"

"Come on." He stepped out into the street and crossed hastily.

She followed: "Well?"

"We need to take the Northside 'car, three miles or so downtown." He was staring at a wooden post with a streetcar timetable pasted to a board hanging from it. "Then a New Line car to St. Peter's Cross. I think there's a salon there." He glanced sidelong at her hair. "By the time we've got that out of the way—well, unless we find a mail express, I don't think we'll get back to Boston to-night, so I suggest we take a room in one of the station hotels and entrain at first light tomorrow."

"Right." She shrugged, slightly uncomfortably. "Erasmus, when I crossed over, I, um, I didn't bring any money . . ."

He glanced up and down the street, then reached into an inner pocket and withdrew a battered wallet. "One, two—all right. Five pounds." He curled the large banknotes between bony fingertips and slipped them into her hand. "Try not to spend it all at once."

Miriam swallowed. One pound—the larger unit of currency here—had what felt like the purchasing power of a couple of hundred dollars back home. "You're very generous."

He smiled at her. "I owe you."

"No, you—" She paused, trying to get a grip on the sense of embarrassed gratitude. "Are you still taking the tablets?"

"Yes. It's amazing." He shook his head. "But that's not what I meant. I still owe you for the last consignment you sold me." A shadow crossed his face. "You needn't worry about money for the time being. There are lockouts and beggars defying the poor laws on every other street corner. Nobody has money to spend. If I was truly dependent on my business for a living I would be as thin as a sheet of paper by now."

"There's no money?" She took his arm again. "What's the economy doing?"

"Nothing good. We're effectively at war, which means there's a blockade of our Atlantic trade and shipping raiders in the Pacific, so it's hit overseas trade badly. His majesty dismissed parliament and congress last month, you know. He's trying to run things directly, and the treasury's near empty: we'll likely as not be stopped at the Excise bench as we arrive in Boston, you know, just to see if there's a silver teapot hiding in this valise that could be better used to buy armor plate for the fleet."

"That's not good." Miriam blinked, feeling stupid. *How not good?* she wondered uneasily. "Is the currency deflating?"

"I'd have said yes, but prices are going up too. And unemployment." Burgeson smiled humorlessly. "This war crisis is simply too damned soon after the last one, and the harvest last year was a disaster, and the army is overstretched dealing with civil disorder—they mean local rebellions against the tax inspectorate—on the great plains and down south." It took Miriam a moment to remember that *down south* didn't mean the southern United States— it meant the former Portuguese and Spanish colonies that the New British crown had taken by force in the early nineteenth century, annexing to the empire around the time they'd been rebelling against their colonial masters across the ocean in the world she'd grown up in. "And the price of oil is going up. It's doubled since this time last year."

Miriam blinked again. The dust and the smelly urban air were getting to her eyes. That, and something about Burgeson's complaint sounded familiar . . . "How's the government coping?" she asked.

He chuckled. "It isn't: the king dismissed it. We're back into the days of *fiat reale,* like the way King Frederick the Second ran things during the civil war." He noticed her expression and did a double take. "Seventeen ninety-seven to eighteen hundred and four," he murmured. "I can find you a book on it if it interests you. Long and the short is, there was a war across the Atlantic and the states of Carolina, Virginia, and Columbia tried to rebel against the Crown, in collusion with the French. They nearly mustered a parliamentary majority for secession, too: invited in a French pretender to take their crown. So Frederick dissolved the traitor parliament and went through the plantation states with fire and the sword. He wasn't merciful, like your, ah, Mister Lincoln. Frederick was not stupid, though: he recognized the snares of unencumbered absolute power, and he reconvened the estates and allowed them to elect a new parliament—once he'd gibbeted the traitors every twenty feet along the road from Georgetown to New London."

"That's martial law, isn't it?"

"No, it's worse: it's the feudal skull showing through the mummified skin of our constitutional settlement." Erasmus stared into the near distance, then stuck his arm out in the direction of the street. A moment later a streetcar lumbered into view round the curve of the road, wheels grinding against the rails as it trundled to a halt next to the stop. "After you, ma'am."

Miriam climbed onto the streetcar's platform, waited while Erasmus paid, then climbed the stairs to the upper deck, her mind whirling. Things have been going downhill fast, she realized: war, a liquidity crisis, and martial law? Despite the muggy warmth of the day, she shivered. Looking around, she realized the streetcar was almost empty. The conductor's bell dinged and the 'car moved off slowly as Erasmus came up the stairs, his hair blowing in the breeze that came over the open top of the vehicle. Sparks crackled from the pickup on top of the chimney-like tower behind her. "I didn't realize things were so bad," she remarked.

"Oh, they're bad all right," he replied a little too loudly: "I'll be lucky to make my rent this month."

She gave him an old-fashioned look as he sat down beside her. "Afraid of eavesdroppers?" she muttered.

"Yes," he whispered, almost too quietly to hear.

Whoops. Miriam shut up and stared out the window as the city unrolled to either side. This city might be called New York, but the layout was bewildering; from the citadel and palaces of Manhattan Island—here called New London—to the suburbs sprawling across the mainland around it, Jersey City to Brookhaven, everything was different. There was no orderly grid, but an insane mishmash of looping and forking curlicues, as if village paths laid out by drunkards had grown together, merging at the edges: high streets and traffic circles and weird viaducts with houses built on top of them. Tenement blocks made of soot-stained brick, with not a single fire escape in sight. In the distance, blocky skyscrapers on the edge of the administrative district around the palace loomed on the skyline, but they weren't a patch on her New York, the New York of the Chrysler and the Empire State buildings and, not long ago, the twin towers. High above them a propeller aircraft droned slowly across the underside of the clouds, trailing a thin brown smear of exhaust. For a moment she felt very alone: a tourist in the third world who'd been told her ticket home was invalid. *I wanted to escape, didn't I? To cut loose and go where the Clan can't find me.* She pondered the irony of the change in her circumstances: it all seemed so long ago, now.

"Nearly there," remarked Burgeson, and she noticed his hand tightening on the back of the chair in front of them.

"Nearly where?"

"New Line crossing. Come on." He unfolded from the seat and rolled towards the staircase, pulling the bell chain on his way. Miriam scrambled to follow him.

There were more people here, and the buildings were higher, and the air smelled of coal smoke and damp even in the summer heat. Miriam followed Burgeson across the street, dodging a horse-drawn cart piled high with garbage and a chuffing steam taxi. A lot of the people hereabouts were badly dressed, their clothing worn and threadbare and their cheeks gaunt: a wheeled stall at one corner was doing a brisk trade, doling out cupfuls of stew or soup to a long queue of shuffling men and women. She hurried to keep up with Erasmus as he walked past the soup kitchen. *Stagflation, that's it*, she remembered vaguely. *The treasury's rolling the presses to print their way out of the fiscal crisis triggered by the war and the crop failure, but the real dynamic is deflationary, so wages and jobs are being squeezed even as prices are going up because the currency is devaluing* . . . she remembered the alleyway three nights before, the beggar threatening her with a knife, and abruptly felt sick at the implications. *They were starving,* she realized. *This is the capital. What's going on, out in the boonies?*

Erasmus stopped so suddenly that she nearly ran into his back. "Follow me," he muttered, then lurched into the road and stuck an arm out. "Cab!" he called, then stepped back sharply to avoid being run over by a steamer. "Get in," he told her, then climbed in behind. "St. Peter's Cross," he called forward to the driver: "An extra shilling if you can get us there fast!"

"Aye, well."

The driver nodded at him and kicked the throttle open. The cab lurched forward with a loud chuffing noise and a trail of steam as it accelerated, throwing Miriam backwards into the padded seat. Erasmus landed at the other side from her, facing. She grinned at him experimentally. "What's the hurry?"

"Company." Burgeson jerked his chin sideways. A strip of cobbled street rattled beneath the cab's wheels. "We're best off without them."

"We were followed?" A sudden sense of dread twisted her stomach. "Who by?"

"Can't tell." He reached out and slid the window behind the driver's head closed. "Probably just a double-cross boy or a thugster, but you can't be too sure. Worst case, a freelance thief taker trying to make his quota. Nobody you'd want to be nabbed by, that's for sure."

"In broad daylight?" she demanded.

He shrugged. "Times are hard."

Shit. She stared at him. His closed expression spoke volumes. "What am I going to do?" she asked. "My business. My house. They'll be under surveillance."

He raised an eyebrow. "I'm sure they will be."

"But what can I—"

"You can start by relaxing," he said. "And letting the salon dye your hair." His lips twitched in a brief smile. "Then, once we have checked into the hotel, if you'd honor me with your presence at dinner, you can tell me all about your recent travails. How does that sound?"

"That sounds—" *This is going to be tougher than I realized,* she thought faintly, as the cab lurched around a corner and pulled in opposite an imposing row of store windows near the base of a large stone building. "—acceptable."

Late afternoon in NYC, mid-morning in San Francisco. Colonel Smith had brought a laptop and a briefcase full of work with him on the Air Force Gulfstream, holing up at the back of the cabin while Dr. James worked the phones continuously up front. Dr. James had brought along a small coterie of administrative gofers from NSC, and two Secret Service bodyguards: the latter had sized Smith up immediately and, after confirming he was on their watch list, politely asked him to stay where they could keep their eyes on him. Which was fine by Eric. Every time he ventured down from one of the FTO aeries he got a sensation between his shoulder blades as if a sniper's crosshairs were crawling around there. Even Gillian had noticed him getting jumpy, staring at passing cars when they went places together—in the few snatched hours of domesticity that were all this job was leaving him. *Bastards,* he thought absently as he paged through the daily briefing roundup, looking for any sign that things weren't going as badly as he feared. *I hope this isn't a waste of time . . .*

Dr. James had been as infuriatingly unreadable as usual, saying nothing beyond the cryptic hints about some project at UC Berkeley. Lawrence Livermore Labs weren't exactly on campus in Berkeley—it wasn't even a daily commute—but that seemed to be where they were going. The gray Gulfstream executive jet touched down at San Francisco International and taxied towards a fenced-in compound where a couple of limos and two SUVs full of security contractors were waiting for them. "Take the second car," James had told Eric: "The driver will take you to Westgate badge office to check you in before bringing you to JAUNT BLUE." He nodded. "I've got prior clearance and an appointment before I join you."

"Okay." Eric swung his briefcase into the back of the Lincoln. "See you there," he added, but James had already turned on his heel and was heading for the other car.

It took more than an hour to drive out to the laboratory complex, during which time Eric ran and reran his best scenarios for the coming meeting, absent-mindedly working his gyroball exerciser. *James wouldn't be visiting in person if he didn't think it was important, which means he'll be reporting to the vice president. Progress. But what are they doing here?* He'd pulled the files on the only professor called Armstrong who was currently on faculty at UCSD: some kind of expert on quantum computing. Then he'd had Agent Delaney do a quick academic literature search. A year ago, Armstrong had coauthored a paper with a neurobiologist, conclusively demolishing the Penrose microtubule hypothesis, coming up with a proof that quantum noise would cause decoherence in any circuit relying on tubulin-bound GTP, whatever the hell that was. Then he'd written another paper, about quantum states in large protein molecules, before falling mysteriously silent—along with his research assistants and postdocs. The previous year they'd put their names on eighteen papers: this year, the total was just three, and those were merely citations as co-authors with other research groups.

Quantum computing. Neurobiology. Quantum states in large protein molecules. Eric shook his head over the densely written papers Delaney had copied for him. *Then Armstrong dropped off the map, and now James is taking me to see him.* He grinned humorlessly. *I wonder if this means what I think it means.* The gyroball whirred down as he shifted it to his left hand, twisting his wrist continually, trying to drive out the stiffness and shooting pains by constant exercise.

Security at the sprawling laboratory complex—more like a huge university campus than anything else—was pervasive but not heavy-handed at first. His driver, Agent Simms, smoothed the way as he checked in his mobile phone, laptop, and the hand exerciser with the security guards. "You ready to visit JAUNT BLUE now, sir?"

"Take me there."

Back in the car, it was another five-minute drive past endless rows of windowless buildings. Eric sat back, watching the chain-link fence and the site road unfold around him. One DoD site looked much like any other, but there were signs here for those who knew what to look for. Inner fences. Curious, long berms humped up beneath a carpet of sunburned grass, like state secrets casually swept out of the view of passing spy satellites by a giant security-obsessed housekeeper. Driving past some clearly disused buildings, Simms turned into a side road then pulled over in front of a gate. "Okay, sir, we walk from here. Building forty-seven."

"Right." Eric opened the door and got out, feeling the heat start to suck him dry. Late morning and it was already set to be a burning hot summer day. "Which way?"

"Over here." Simms walked over to one of the disused warehouse units. The walls were simple metal sidings and the doors and windows were missing, the building itself just a hollow shell.

"Here? But it's abandoned—"

"It's meant to look that way. Building forty-seven. If you'd follow me? Sir?"

The secret service agent was clearly sure of himself. *Someone's spent a lot on camouflage,* Eric told to himself, clutching his briefcase and following behind. *What's going on?* The inside of the warehouse was no more promising than the exterior. Huge ceiling panels were missing, evidently the holes where air conditioning units had been stripped out. The concrete loading bay at the rear of the building was dusty and decrepit, the doors missing. Simms walked over to the near side, where a rusty trailer was propped up on blocks. Eric glanced past him, and for the first time noticed something out of place—a black dome, about the size of his fist, fastened to the wall somewhere above head height. Closed circuit cameras? In an abandoned shed?

Simms climbed a ramshackle flight of steps and opened the door of the trailer. "This way, sir."

Eric relaxed, everything clicking into place. The camera, the abandoned trailer, the shadows thick and black under the trailer—it was all intended to deal with visitors from the Clan. "Okay, I'm coming." He climbed the steps and found himself in a small lobby behind Simms, who was waiting in front of an inner door with a peephole set in it. The door was made of steel and opened from the inside.

"Agent Simms, Colonel Smith of FTO, visiting JAUNT BLUE," Simms announced.

A speaker crackled. "Close the outer door now."

Eric reached back and pulled the door shut. The inner door buzzed for a moment, then whined open sideways to reveal the bare metal walls of a freight elevator. "Neat," he said admiringly as they descended towards the tunnels under the laboratory complex. "If you can't go up without being obvious, go down."

"This all used to be part of the high-energy physics group, back in the sixties," Simms said laconically. "They repurposed it this year. There are several entrances. Dr. James told me to show you in through the back door." A back door disguised as a derelict building, complete with

spy cameras and probably some kind of remotely controlled defense system: whatever James had going on down
here, he didn't welcome unexpected visitors.

The freight elevator ground to a halt and Eric did a
double-take. *Jesus, I've just fallen into* The Man from
U.N.C.L.E.*!* He glanced around at the rough-finished concrete walls, fluorescent lights, innumerable pipes and
conduits bolted overhead—and at the end of the passage,
a vast, brightly lit space.

"Badges, please." The Marine guards waiting in an al-
cove off one side of the corridor were armed, and not for
show. Smith extended the badge he'd been issued and
waited while one of the guards checked him off a list.
"You may proceed, sir."

"Where's Dr. James's group?" he asked Simms's receding back.

"Follow me, sir."

Smith followed, trying not to gape too obviously. He
was used to security procedures on Air Force bases and
some other types of sensitive installations, but he'd never
seen anything quite like this. The main tunnel was domed
overhead, rising to a peak about fifty feet up; it stretched
to infinity ahead and behind. There were no windows, but
more conduits and the boxy, roaring ducts of a huge air
conditioning system overhead. The concrete piles that
had once supported a mile-long linear accelerator were
still visible on the floor, but the linac itself had long since
been removed and replaced by beige office partitions surrounding a forlorn-looking clump of cubicles, and a line
of mobile office trailers that stretched along one wall like
a subterranean passenger train. The train didn't go on forever, though, and after they'd walked a couple of hundred
feet from the "back door" they reached the end of the column. Beyond it, the concrete tunnel stretched dizzyingly
towards a blank wall in the distance, empty but for a grid
of colored lines painted on the floor. *Lots of room for expansion,* he realized.

Simms gestured at the trailer on the edge of the empty floor space. "Dr. James uses Room 65 as his site office when he's visiting. I believe he's in a meeting until fifteen hundred, but he told me to tell you that Dr. Hu will be along to give you the dog and pony tour at eleven thirty. If you make yourself at home, I'll find Dr. Hu and get things started."

Eric paused at the door to the trailer. "Dr. James didn't exactly tell me what it is you people do out here," he said slowly. "Can you fill me in on what to expect?"

Simms frowned. "I think I ought to leave that to Dr. Hu," he said.

"Is Dr. Hu one of Professor Armstrong's team?"

Simms nodded. "I'll go get him."

"Okay." Eric climbed the step up to the site office trailer and went inside to wait.

BEGIN TRANSCRIPT

"You wanted to s-see me, sir?"

"Yes, yes I did. Have a seat, lad. Your parents: doing well, I hope?"

". . ."

"Calm down, there's a good fellow. Try to relax, I'm not going to bite your head off. I'm sure they'll be perfectly fine, current emergency notwithstanding. No, the pretender isn't about to go haring off into the Sennheur marches, and if he does, they'll have plenty of warning to evacuate. Now, where was I . . . ? Ah, yes. I wanted to ask you about your studies."

(Mumble.)

"Yes, I know. In the current situation, it's difficult. But I think it may be possible for you to go back there in the fall, if things work out well."

"But I'll be behind. I should be working right now, with my roommates—it's not like a regular school. They'll want to know where I was while they were working on our project."

(Snorts.) "Well, you'll just have to tell them you were called away by urgent family business. A dying relative, or something. Don't look at me like that: worse things happen in wartime. If you go back to your laboratory at all you will be luckier than many of our less talented children, Huw. But as it happens, I have a little research project for you that I think will smooth your way. One that you and your talking-shop friends will be able to get your teeth into, and that will be much more profitable in the long term."

"A research project? But you don't need someone like me—I mean, the kind of research your staff do, begging your pardons in advance, your grace, aren't exactly where my aptitude lies—"

"Correct. Which is why I want you for a different kind of research."

"I don't understand."

"On the contrary, I think you'll understand all too well." (Pause.) "Red or white?"

"Red, please." (Sound of glass being filled.) "Thank you very much."

"Show me your locket."

"My" (coughing) "locket? Uh, sure. Here—"

"Put it there. Yes, open. Don't focus on it. Now, this one. You can see the difference if you look at them—not too close, now! What do you think?"

"I'm—excuse me, it's easier to study them if you cover part of the design and compare sections. Less distracting."

"You sound as if you've done that before."

(Hurriedly): "No sir! But it's only logical. We've been using the Clan sigil for generations. Surely" (pause) "hey, I think the upper right arc of this one is different!"

"It is." (Sound of small items being cleared away.) "It came from our long-lost, lamentably living, cousins. The Lees. Who, it would appear, discovered the hard way that redesigning the knotwork can have catastrophic consequences."

(Pause.) "I'd heard they used a different design. But . . ." (Pause.) "Nobody thought to experiment? Ever?"

"Some of the Lee family did, generations ago. Either they failed to world-walk, or they didn't come back. After they lost a couple, their elders banned further experimentation. For our part, with no indication that other realms than the two we know of might exist, who would bother even trying? Especially as most of the simple variations don't work. Look at yourself, Sir Huw! The finest education we can buy you, a graduate student at MIT, and you, too, took the family talent for granted."

"I, I think—hell. I assumed that if it was possible to do something, it would already have been done, surely?"

"That's the assumption everyone who has given the subject a moment's thought comes up with. It tends to deter experimentation, doesn't it, if you believe an alley of inquiry has already been tried and found wanting? Even if the assumption is wrong."

"I—I feel dumb."

(Pause.) "You're not the only one of us who's kicking himself. There have been a number of unexplained disappearances over the centuries, and simple murder surely doesn't explain all of them—but the point is, nobody who succeeded came back to tell the tale. Which brings me to the matter at hand. When Helge reappeared with the family Lee in unwilling thrall, I had reason to send for the archivists. And to have my staff conduct certain preliminary tests. It appears that the Lee family design has never been tested in the United States of America. And our clan symbol doesn't work in New Britain. That is, it doesn't in the areas that correspond to the Gruinmarkt. The east coast. But that's all we know, Huw, and it worries me. In the United States, the authorities have made their most effective attack on our postal service for a hundred years. This would be a crisis in its own right, but on top of that we have the pretender to the throne raising the old aristocracy against us in Niejwein.

He can be contained eventually—we have means of communication and transport that will permit us to meet his army with crushing force whenever he moves—but that, too, would be crisis enough on its own. And I cannot afford to deal with any new surprises. So I want you—I have discussed this with members of the council—to set your very expensively acquired skills to work and do what our none-too-inquisitive ancestors failed to do."

"You want me to, to find out how the sigil works? Or . . . what?"

(Clink of glassware.) "When there was just one knot, life was simple. But we've got two, now, and three worlds. I want to know if there are more worlds out there. And more knots. I want to know why sometimes trying a design gives the world-walker a headache, and why sometimes the experimenter vanishes. I want to know, Sir Huw, so that I can map out the terrain of the battlefield we find ourselves on."

"Is it really that bad?"

(Pause.) "I don't know, boy. None of us know. That's the whole point. Can you do it? More importantly, what would you do?"

"Hmm." (Pause.) "Well, I'd start by documenting what we already know. Maps and times. Then there are a couple of avenues I would pursue. On the one hand, we have two knots. I can see if the clan knot is failing to work in New Britain because of a terrain anomaly. If, say, it leads to a world where the world-walker would emerge in the middle of a tree, or underwater, that would explain why nobody's been able to use it. And I'd do the same for the Lee family knotwork in the United States, of course. That's going to take a couple of world-walkers, some maps and surveying tools, and someone to report back if everything goes wrong. Next, well . . . once we've exhausted the possibilities, we've got two knots. I need to talk to a mathematician, see if we can work out the parameters of the knots and come up with a way of generating a family of relatives. Then we need to invent a protocol for testing new designs: not so much what to do if they don't work, but how to survive if they take us somewhere new. If this works, if there are more than two viable knots, we're going to lose world-walkers sooner or later. Aren't we?"

"I expect so."

"That's awfully cold-blooded, isn't it, sir?"

"Yes, boy, it is. In case it has slipped your attention, it is my job to be cold-blooded about such things. I would not authorize—I suspect my predecessors did not authorize—such research, if the situation was not so dangerous. The risk of losing world-walkers is too high and our numbers too few for gambling. Already there have been losses, couriers taken in transit by American government agents. You met the Countess Helge. Your opinion . . . ?"

"Helge? She's, she's—what happened to her? Shouldn't she be here, given her experience?"

"I am asking the questions, Sir Huw. What was your opinion of her?"

"Bright . . . inquisitive . . . fun, I think, in a scary way. Where is she?"

" 'Fun, in a scary way' . . . yes, that's true enough. But she scared too many cousins, Huw, cousins who lack your sense of *fun*. I did what I could to protect her. If she surfaces again, well, circumstances have changed, and it may be possible to distract her pursuers, as long as she is not involved in the regrettable business unfolding in New York. But for the time being, she is not available, and so I am turning to you."

"I'm, um, I'm at your disposal, sir. How would you like to proceed?"

"Write me a report. No more than three pages. Tell me what you're going to do, what resources you need, what people you need, and what you expect to learn

from it. I want your report no later than the day after tomorrow, and I want you to be ready to begin work the
day after that."

"Sir! That's rather—"

"What, you're going to tell me you've never written a grant proposal in a hurry? Please don't insult my
intelligence."

"I wouldn't dream of it, sir! But it's going to cost,
people and money—"

"Let me worry about that. You just tell me what you
need, and I'll make sure you get it."

"*Wow!* Thank you—"

"*Don't* thank me, boy. Not until it's over, and we're
still alive."

END TRANSCRIPT

Dr. Hu was alarmingly young and bouncy, a Vietnamese-
American postdoc with a ponytail, cargo pants, sandals,
and a flippant attitude that would have annoyed the hell
out of Eric if Hu had been working for him. Luckily Hu
was someone else's problem, and despite everything,
he'd been cleared by security to work on JAUNT BLUE.
Which probably means the Republic is doomed, Eric
thought mordantly. *Ah well, we work with what we're
given.*

"Hey man, the professor told me to give you the special tour. Where you wanna start? You been briefed or
they dropping you in it cold?"

Eric stared at him. "I'll take it cold."

"Suits me! Let's start with . . . hell. What do you know
about parallel universes?"

Eric shrugged. "Not a lot. Seen some episodes of *Slid-
ers.* Been catching up on some sci-fi books in my copious
free time." The writers they'd sounded out hadn't been
good for much more than random guesses, and without
priming them with classified information that was all they

could be expected to deliver. It had been a waste of time, in his opinion, but—"and then there's the day job."

"Heh. You bet, boss!" Hu laughed, a curious chittering noise. "Okay, we got parallel universes. There's some theoretical basis for it in string theory, I can give you some references if you like, but I can only tell you one thing for sure right now: we're not dealing with a Tegmark Level I multiverse—that's an infinite ergodic universe, one where the initial inflationary period gave rise to disjoint Hubble volumes realizing all possible initial conditions."

Eric crossed his arms and frowned. "So you've ruled that out." *Asshole? Or show-off?*

"Yup!" Hu seemed unaccountably pleased with himself. "We *can* get *there* from *here,* which rules out Level I, because in a Level I multiverse the parallel universes exist in the same spacetime, just a mind-bogglingly huge distance apart. Which means we're dealing with either a Level II, Level III, or Level IV multiverse. I'm in the cosmology pool—we've got an informal bet running—that it'll turn out to be a Level IV theory. Level II depends on a Linde chaotic inflationary cosmology, in which you get multiple branching universes connected by wormholes, but travel between universes in that kind of scheme involves singularities, and the phenomenon we're studying doesn't come with black holes attached."

Bumptious enthusiast, no social skills. Eric decided. He forced himself to nod, draw the guy out. "So you're saying this isn't a large scale cosmological phenomenon—then what is it?" Some of this stuff sounded half-familiar from his physics minor, but the rest was just weird.

"We're trying to work out what it is by a process of elimination." Hu thrust his hands in his pockets, looking distant. "The thing is, we have no theoretical framework. We've got a lot of beautiful theories but they don't account for what we're seeing: we're looking at an amazingly complex artifact and we don't understand how it works. It's like handing a nuclear reactor to a steam engineer in the nineteenth century. If you don't understand the physics behind it you might as well say it works by magic pixie dust as slow neutron-induced fission. Absent a theoretical understanding all we can do is poke it and see if it twitches. And coming up with the theory is, uh, proving difficult." He slowed down as he spoke, finishing on a thoughtful note.

Now's as good a time as any . . . "What's the black box you think you're trying to reverse-engineer?" Eric asked, hoping to draw Hu back on track.

"Ah!" Hu jerked as if a dozing puppeteer had just realized he'd slackened off on the strings: "That would be the cytology samples Dr. James provided two months ago. That's how we got started," he added. "Want to see them? Come down to the lab and see what's on the slab?"

Eric nodded, and followed Hu out through the door. *If this is the* Rocky Horror Picture Show, *all we're missing is the mad scientist.* Hu made a beeline towards the maze of brown cubicle-farm partitions at the edge of the floor, and dived into a niche. When Eric caught up, he found him sitting at a desk with a gigantic tube monitor on it, messing with something that looked like the bastard offspring of a computer mouse and a joystick. "Here!" he called excitedly.

Eric glanced round. The neighboring cubicles were empty: "Where is everybody?"

"Team meeting," Hu said dismissively. "Look. Let me show you the slides first, then we'll go see the real thing."

"Okay." Eric stood behind him. "Take it from the top."

Hu pulled up a picture and Eric blinked, taken aback for a moment. It was in shades of gray, somehow messy and biological looking. After a moment he nodded. "It's a cellular structure, isn't it?"

"Yeah! This slide was taken at 2,500 magnification on our scanning electron microscope. It's a slice from the lateral geniculate nucleus of our first test sample. See the layering here? Top two layers, the magnocellular levels? They do fast positional sensing in the visual system. Now let's zoom in a bit."

The image vanished, to be replaced by a much larger, slightly grainier picture in which individual cells were visible, blobs with tangled fibers converging on them like the branches of a dead umbrella, stripped of fabric.

"Here's an M-type gangliocyte. It's kind of big, isn't it? There are lots of dendrites going in, too. It takes signals from a whole bunch of rod and cone cells in the retina and processes them, subtracting noise. You with me so far?"

"Just about," Eric said dryly. Image convolution had been another component of his second degree, the classified one he'd sweated for back when he'd been attached to NRO. "So far this is normal, is it?"

"Normal for any dead dried human brain on a microscope slide." Hu giggled. It was beginning to grate on Eric's nerves.

"Next."

"Okay. This is where it gets interesting, when we look inside the gangliocyte."

"What—"it took Eric longer, this time, to orient himself: the picture was very grainy, a mess of weird loops and whorls, and something else—"the heck is that? Some kind of contamination—"

"Nope." Hu giggled again. This time he sounded slightly scared. "Ain't nothing like this in the textbooks."

"It's your black box, isn't it?"

"Hey, quick on the uptake! Yes, that's it. We went through three samples and twelve microscopy preparations before we figured out it wasn't an artifact. What do you think?"

Eric stared at the screen.

"What is it?"

A different voice said, "it's a Nobel Prize—or a nuclear war. Maybe both."

Eric glanced round in a hurry, to see Dr. James standing behind him. For a bureaucrat, he moved eerily quietly. "You think?"

"Cytology." James sounded bored. "These structures are

in every central nervous system tissue sample retrieved so far from targeted individuals. Also in their peripheral tissues, albeit in smaller quantities. At first the pathology screener thought he was looking at some kind of weird mitochondrial malfunction—the inner membrane isn't reticulated properly—but then further screening isolated some extremely disturbing DNA sequences, and very large fullerene macromolecules doped with traces of heavy elements, iron and vanadium."

"I'm not a biologist," said Eric. "You'll have to dumb it down."

"Continue the presentation, Dr. Hu," said James, turning away. *Show-off,* thought Eric.

Hu leaned back in his chair and swiveled round to face Eric. "Cells, every cell in your body, they aren't just blobs full of enzymes and DNA, they've got structures inside them, like organs, that do different things." He waved at the screen. "We can't live without them. Some of them started out as free-living bacteria, went symbiotic a long time ago. A very long time ago." Hu was staring at Dr. James's back. "Mitochondria, like this little puppy here—"he pointed at a lozenge-shaped blob on the screen"—they're the power stations that keep your cells running. This thing, the thing these JAUNT BLUE guys have, they're repurposed mitochondria. Someone's edited the mitochondrial DNA, added about two hundred enzymes we've never seen before. They look artificial, like it's a tinker-toy construction kit for goop-phase nanotechnology—well, to cut a long story short, they make buckeyballs. Carbon-sixty molecules, shaped like a soccer ball. And then they use them as a substrate to hold quantum dots—small molecules able to handle quantized charge units. Then they stick them on the inner lipid wall of the, what do you call them, the mechanosomes."

Eric shook his head. "You're telling me they're artificial. It's nanotechnology. Right?"

"No." Dr. James turned round again. "It's more complicated than that. Dr. Hu, would you mind demonstrating preparation fourteen to the colonel?"

Hu stared at Eric. "Prep fourteen is down for some fixes. Can I show him a sample in cell twelve, instead?"

"Whatever. I'll be in the office." James walked away.

Hu stood up: "If you follow me?"

He darted off past the row of cubicles, and Eric found himself hurrying to keep up. The underground tunnel looked mostly empty, but the sense of emptiness was an illusion: there was a lot of stuff down here. Hu led him past a bunch of stainless steel pipework connecting something that looked like a chrome-plated microbrewery to a bunch of liquid gas cylinders surrounded by warning barriers, then up a short flight of steps into another of the ubiquitous trailer offices. This one had been kitted out as a laboratory, with worktops stretching along the wall opposite the windows. Extractor hoods and laminar-flow workbenches hunched over assemblages of tubes and pumps that resembled a bonsai chemical plant. Someone had crudely sliced the end off the trailer and built a tunnel to connect it to the next one along, which seemed to be mostly full of industrial-size dish-washing machines to Smith's uneducated eye. A technician in a white bunny suit and mask was doing something in a cabinet at the far end of the room. The air conditioning was running at full blast, blowing a low-grade tropical storm out through the door: "Viola, the lab."

Eric winced: the horrible itch to correct Hu's behavior was unbearable. "It's *voilà*," he snapped waspishly. "I see no medium-sized stringed instruments here. And you'll have to tell me what everything is. I know that's a laminar-flow workbench, but the rest of this stuff isn't my field."

"Hey, stay cool, man! Um, where do you want me to start? This is where we work on the tissue cultures. Over there, that's the incubation lab. You see the far end behind the glass wall? We've got a full filtered air flow and a Class two environment; we're trying to get access to a Class four, but so far AMRIID isn't playing ball, so there's some stuff we don't dare try yet. But anyway, what we've got next door is a bunch of cell tissue cultures harvested from JAUNT BLUE carriers. We keep them alive and work on them through here. We're using a 2D field-effect transistor array from Infineon Technologies. They're developing it primarily as an artificial retina, but we're using it to send signals into the cell cultures. If we had some stem cells it'd be easier to work with, but, well, we have to work with what we've got."

"Right." The president's opinion on embryonic stem-cell research was well known; it had never struck Eric as being a strategic liability before now. He leaned towards the contraption behind the glass shield of the laminar-flow cabinet. "So inside that box, you've got some live nerve cells, and you've, you've what? You've got them to talk to a chip? Is that it?"

"Yup." Hu looked smug. "It'd be better if we had a live volunteer to work with—if we could insert microelectrodes into their optic nerve or geniculate nucleus—but as the action's happening at the intracellular level this at least lets us get a handle on what we're seeing."

Live volunteers? Eric stifled a twitch. The "unlawful combatant" designation James had managed to stick on Matthias and the other captured Clan members was one thing: performing medical experiments involving brain surgery on them was something else. Somehow he didn't see any of them volunteering of their own free will: was Hu really that stupid? Or just naive? Or had he not figured out how the JAUNT BLUE tissue cultures came to be in his hands in the first place? "What have you been able to do with the materials available to you?"

"It's amazing! Look, let me show you preparation twelve in action, okay? I need to get a fresh slide from Janet. Wait here."

Hu bustled off to the far end of the lab and waved at the person working behind the glass wall. While he was pre-occupied, Eric took inventory. *Okay, so James wants me to figure it out for myself. He wants a sanity check?* So far, so obvious. But the next bit was a little more challenging. *So there's evidence of extremely advanced biological engineering, inside the Clan members' heads. Quantum dots, fullerene stuff, nanotechnology, genetic engineering as well. Artificial organelles.* He shivered. *Are they still human? Or something else? And what can we do with this stuff?*

Hu was on his way back, clutching something about the size of a humane rat trap that gleamed with the dull finish of aluminum. "What's that?" asked Eric.

"Let me hook it up first. I've got to do this quickly." Hu flipped up part of the laminar-flow cabinet's hood and slid the device inside, then began plugging tubes into it. "It dies after about half an hour, and she's spent the whole morning getting it ready for you."

Hu fussed over his gadgets for a while, then plugged a couple of old-fashioned–looking coaxial cables into the aluminum box. "The test cell in here needs to be bathed in oxygenated Ringer's solution at body temperature. This here's a peristaltic pump and heater combination—" He launched into an intricate explanation that went right over Eric's head. "We should be able to see it on video here—"

He backed away from the cabinet and grabbed hold of the mouse hanging off of the computer next to it. The screen unblanked: a window in the middle of it showed a grainy gray grid, the rough-edged tracks of a silicon chip at high magnification. Odd, messy blobs dotted its surface, as if a microscopic vandal had sneezed on it. "Here's an NV51 test unit. One thousand twenty-four field effect transistors, individually addressable. The camera's calibrated so we can bring up any transistor by its coordinates. These cells are all live JAUNT BLUE cultures—at least they were alive half an hour ago."

"So what does it do?"

Hu shrugged. "This is preparation twelve, the first that actually did anything. Most of the later ones are still—

we're still debugging them, they're still under development. This one, at least, it's the demo. We got it to work reliably. Proof of concept: watch."

He leaned close to the screen, muttering to himself, then punched some numbers into the computer. The camera slewed sideways and zoomed slightly, centering on one of the snot-like blobs. "*Vio*—sorry. Here we go."

Hu hit a key. A moment later, Eric blinked. "Where did it go? Did you just evaporate it?"

"No, we only carry about fifty millivolts and a handful of microamps for a fiftieth of a second. Look, let me do it again. Over . . . yeah, this one."

Hu punched more figures into the keyboard. Hit the return key again. Another blob of snot vanished from the gray surface.

"What's this meant to show me?" Eric asked impatiently.

"Huh?" Hu gaped at him. "Uh, JAUNT BLUE? Hello, remember that code phrase? The, the folks who do that world-walking thing? This is how it works."

"Hang on. Wait." Eric scratched his head. "You didn't just vaporize that, that—" *Neuron*, he realized, understanding dawning. "Wow."

"We figured out that the mechanosomes respond to the intracellular cyclic-AMP signaling pathway," Hu offered timidly. "That's what preparation fourteen is about. They're also sensitive to dopamine. We're looking for modulators, now, but it's on track. If we could get the nerve cells to grow dendrites and connect, we hope eventually to be able to build a system that works—that can move stuff about. If we can get a neural stem-cell line going, we may even be able to mass-produce them—but that's years away. It's early days right now: all we can do is make an infected cell go bye-bye and sneak away into some other universe—explaining how that part of it works is what the quant group are working on. What do you think?"

Eric shook his head, suddenly struck by a weird sense of historical significance: it was like standing in that baseball court at the University of Chicago in 1942, when they finished adding graphite blocks to the heap in the middle of the court and Professor Fermi told his assistant to start twisting the control rod. *A Nobel Prize or a nuclear war? James isn't wrong about that.* "I'd give my left nut to know where this is all going to end," he said slowly. "You're doing good work. I just hope we don't all live to regret the consequences."

6

MANEUVERS

As forms of transport went, horse-drawn carriages tended to lack modern amenities—from cup holders and seat-back TV screens on down to shock absorbers and ventilation nozzles. On the other hand, they came with some fittings that took Mike by surprise. He gestured feebly at the raised seat cushion as he glanced at the geriatric gruppenfuhrer in the mound of rugs on the other side of the compartment: "If you think I'm going to use *that*—"

"You'll use it when you need to, boy." She cackled for a moment. The younger woman, Olga, rolled her eyes and sent him a look that seemed to say, *humor her*. "We'll not be stopping for bed and bath for at least a day."

"Damn," he said faintly. "What are you going to do?"

Iris said nothing for a moment, while one wheel crunched across a rut in the path with a bone-shaking crash that sent a wave of heat through his leg. She seemed to be considering the question. "We'll be pausing to

change teams in another hour or so. Don't want to flog
the horses; you never know when you'll need a fresh
team. Anyway, you can't stick your nose outside: you
wouldn't fool anyone. So the story is, you're unconscious
and injured and we need to get you across to a hospital in
upstate New York as soon as possible. If they're still using the old emergency routes—"she looked at Olga, who
nodded "—there should be a postal station we can divert
to tomorrow evening. If it's running, we'll ship you
across and you can be home in forty-eight hours. If it's
not running . . . well, we'll play it by ear; you've been hit
on the head and you're having trouble with language, or
something. Until we can get you out of here."

Mike tried to gather his thoughts. "I don't understand.
What do you expect me to do . . . ?"

Miriam's mother leaned forward, her expression intent. "I expect you to tell me your home address and zip
code." A small notepad and pencil appeared from somewhere under her blankets. "Yes?"

"But—"

She snorted. "You're working with spies, boy. Modern
spies with lots of gizmos for bugging phone conversations and tapping e-mail. First rule when going up against
the NSA: use no communications technology invented
in the last half-century. I want to be able to send you mail.
If you want to contact me, write a letter, stick it in an envelope, and put it in your trash can on top of the refuse
sacks."

"Aren't you scared I'll just pass everything to my superiors? Or they'll mount a watch on the trash?"

"No." Eyes twinkled in the darkness. "Because first,
you didn't make a move on my daughter when you had the
chance. And second, have you any idea how many warm
bodies it takes to mount a twenty-four/seven watch on a
trash can? One that's capable of grabbing a dumpster-
diving world-walker without killing them?"

"I've got to admit, I hadn't thought about it."

Olga cleared her throat. "It takes two watchers per team,

minimum. Five teams, each working just under thirty hours a week, in rotation. They'll need a blind, plus perimeter alarms, plus coordination with the refuse companies so they know when to expect a legitimate collection, and that's just the watchers. You need at least three spare bodies, too, in case of sickness or accidents. To be able to make a snatch, you need at least four per team. Do you have thirty agents ready to watch your back stoop, mister? Just in case her grace wishes to receive a letter from you, rather than sending a messenger to pay a local wino to pick it up?"

"Jeez, you sound like you've done this a lot."

Mrs. Beckstein rapped a knuckle on the wooden window frame of the carriage: "Fifty years ago there were three times as many world-walkers as there are now, and they didn't all die out because they forgot how to make babies."

"Huh?"

Olga glanced down. "Civil war," she said very quietly. "And now, your government."

"Civil—" Mike paused. *Didn't Matthias say something about internal feuds?* "Hold on. It killed *two thirds* of you?"

"You wouldn't believe how lethal a war between world-walkers can be, boy." Mrs. Beckstein frowned. "You should hope the Clan Council never decides they're at war with the United States."

"We'd wipe you out. Eventually." He realized he was gritting his teeth, from anger as much as from the pain in his leg: he tried to force himself to relax.

She nodded thoughtfully. "Yes, probably. But right now? You think you have a problem with terrorism? You have seen *nothing,* boy. And we are not religious fanatics, no. We just want to live our lives. But the logic of power—" she stopped.

"What do you want me to do?"

"I want my daughter out of this mess and home safe, Mr. Fleming. She had a sheltered upbringing: she's in danger and her own ignorance of it is her worst enemy. Second . . . when she came over she raised a shit storm among our relatives. In particular, she aired some very dirty family linens in public half a year ago. Called for a complete rethink of the Clan's business model, in fact: she pointed out that the emperor has no clothes, and that basing one's income on an enemy's weakness—in this case, the continuing illegality of certain substances, combined with the continuing difficulty your own organization and others face in stopping the trade—is foolish. This made her a lot of enemies at the time, but it set minds a-thinking. The current upheavals are largely a consequence of her upsetting that apple cart. The Clan will change in due course, and switch to a line of work more profitable than smuggling, but as long as she remains among them, her presence will act as a reminder of the source of the change to the conservative faction, and will provoke them, and that will make her a target. So I want her out of the game."

"Uh, I think I see where you're leading." Mike shook his head. "But she's missing . . . ?"

Iris snorted. "She won't stay missing for long—unless she's gotten herself killed."

"Oh." He thought for a moment. "That's not all, is it?"

She stared at him. "No, Mr. Fleming, that is *not* all, not by a long way. I mentioned a conservative faction. You won't be surprised to know that there exists a progressive faction, too, and current circumstances—the fighting you may have noticed—is about to tip the scales decisively in their favor. Your interests would be served by promoting the progressives to the detriment of the conservatives, believe me."

"And you're a progressive. Right?"

"I prefer to think of myself as a radical." She leaned against the seat back as the coach hit another rough patch on the dirt track. "Must be all the sixties influences. A real flower child, me."

"Ah." Verbal punctuation was easier than trying to hold his own against this intimidating old woman. "Okay, what do the progressives want?"

"You'd best start by trying to understand the conservatives if you want to get a handle on our affairs, boy. The Clan started out as the descendants of an itinerant tinker. They learned to world-walk, learned how to intermarry to preserve the family ability, and got rich. *Insanely* rich. Think of the de Medicis, or the Saudi royal family. That's what the Clan represents here, except that 'here' is dirt-poor, mired in the sixteenth or seventeenth century—near enough. It's not the same, never is, but there are enough points of similarity to make the model work. But the most important point is, they got rich by trade in light merchandise, by running a postal service. The postal service ships high-value goods, whatever they are, either reliably—for destinations in your world, without fear of interception—or fast—for destinations in this world, by FedEx across a continent ruled by horseback."

She pushed herself upright with her walking stick. "Put yourself in their shoes. They want nothing to change, because they feel threatened by change—their status is tenuous. A postal network is a packet-switched network, literally so. If world-walkers drift away from it, the bandwidth drops, and thus, its profitability. New ventures divert vital human capital. They're against exploration, because they're scrambling to stay on top of the dung heap."

"Sounds like—" Mike could think of a number of people it sounded like, uncomfortably close to home—*change the subject.* "What about the progressives?"

"We want change, simple as that. Miriam observed that we are mired in a business that scales in direct proportion to the number of world-walkers, like a service business. She suggested—and her uncovering another world provided the opportunity—that we switch to what she called a technology-transfer model, trading information between universes."

"How many are there?" he asked, side-tracked by fascination.

"At least three. We thought two, until a year ago. Now we know there are three, and we suspect there are many more. Yours is the most advanced we know of, but what might be lurking out there? We can trade, Mr. Fleming. We could be *very useful* to the United States of America. But first we need a . . . change of management? Yes, a change of management. We originated in a feudal realm, and our ability is hereditary: don't underestimate the effects of reproductive politics on the Clan's governance. Before we can change the way we do things, before we can end our unfortunate reliance on illegal trafficking, we need to break the grip of the conservative factions on the council, and to do that we need to entirely overturn our family and tribal foundations."

"Your family structures?"

"Yes." Olga pulled a face: Iris either ignored it, or pretended to do so. "You must be aware of the implications of artificial insemination. There's been a quiet argument going on within the Clan's council for a generation now, over whether it is our destiny to continue existing as braided matrilineal families in a patriarchal society, or to become . . . well, not a family organization anymore, but one open to anyone born with the ability, whatever their parentage."

Mike shut his eyes. *I think my brain just exploded,* he thought. "Who are the progressives?"

"Myself for one, to your very great good fortune. My half-brother for another, although he is as circumspect in public as befits the head of the Clan's external security organization—a seat of significant power on the council. There are others. You do not need to know who they are. If you're captured or tortured, what you don't know you can't give away."

"And the conservatives?"

"Miriam's great-uncle Henryk, if he's still alive. He

was the late king's spymaster in chief. My mother, Hildegarde, who is also Miriam's grandmother. Baron Oliver
Hjorth, about two thirds of the council . . . too many to
enumerate."

"Okay. So you want me to set up a covert channel between you—your faction—and, my agency? Or just me?"

"Just you, at first." Iris's cheek twitched. "You're injured. When you are back on your feet I will contact you.
You will excuse me, but I am afraid I will require certain
actions from you in order to demonstrate that you are
trustworthy. Tokens of trust, if you like."

I don't like the sound of this. "Such as . . . ?"

"That's for me to know and you to find out." She relented slightly: "I can't do business with you if I can't
trust you. But I won't ask you to do anything illegal—
unlike your superiors."

Mike shivered. *She's got my number.* "What makes you
think they'd issue illegal orders?"

"Come now, Mr. Fleming, how stupid do I look? How
did you get here? If your superiors could move more than
one or two people at a time they'd have sent a division.
They sent you because their transport capacity is tiny, probably because they're using captured—or renegade—world-
walkers. Probably the former, knowing this administration;
they don't trust anyone they haven't bought for cold cash."
Her expression shifted into one of outright distaste. "Honor
is a luxury when you reach the top of the dung heap.
Everybody wants it, but it's in short supply. That's even
more true in Washington, D.C. than over on this side, because aristocrats have at least to keep up the appearance of
it. Let me give you a tip to pass on to your bosses: if you
mistreat your Clan prisoners, their relatives will revenge
them. The political is taken *very* personally, here."

"That's—" he swallowed "—it may be true, but that's
not how things work right now. Not since 9/11."

"Then they're going to regret it." Her gaze was level.
"You *must* warn your superiors of this—the political is per-

sonal. If the conservatives think your government is mistreating their prisoners, they'll take revenge, horrible revenge. Timothy McVeigh and Mohamed Atta were rank amateurs compared to these people, and Clan security probably can't prevent an atrocity from happening if you provoke them. You need to warn your bosses, Mr. Fleming. They're playing with fire: or would you like to see a suicide bomber invite himself to the next White House reception?"

Whoops. Mike cringed at the images that sprang to mind. "They're that crazy?"

"They're not crazy!" Her vehemence startled him. "They just don't think about things the same way as you people. Your organization is trying to wage war on the Clan: all right, we understand that. But it is a point of honor to avenge blood debts, and that suicide bomber— that's the *least* of your worries." She paused for breath. When she continued, she was much less strident: "That's one of the things Miriam thought she could change, with her reform program. I tend to agree with her. That's one of the things we *need* to change—it's one of the reasons I reintroduced her to her relatives in the first place. I knew she'd react that way."

"But she's your daughter!" It was out before he could stop himself.

"Hah. I told you, but you didn't listen, did you? We don't work the way you think we do—and it's not just all about blood debts and honor. There's also a perpetual intergenerational conflict going on, mother against daughter, grandmother for grandchild. *My* mother is a pillar of the conservative faction: by raising Miriam where Hildegarde couldn't get her claws into her, I temporarily gained the upper hand. And—"she leaned forward again"—I would do anything to keep my granddaughter out of this mess."

"You don't have a granddaughter," Olga commented from the sidelines, "do you?"

Iris glanced sideways. "Miriam has not married a world-walker, so I do not have a granddaughter," she said coldly. "Is that understood?"

Olga swallowed. "Yes, my lady."

What was that about? The carriage bounced again, throwing Mike against the side of the seat and jarring his leg painfully. When he could focus again, he realized Iris had been talking for some time.

"—Stopping soon, and we will have to lock you in the carriage overnight. I hope you understand. When we get to the waypoint Olga will carry you across, put you somewhere safe, call for an ambulance, then leave. I hope you understand the need for this? Olga, if you would be so good . . ."

The Russian princess was holding a syringe. "No!" Mike tried to protest, but in his current state he was too weak to fight her off. And whatever was in the needle was strong enough that it stopped mattering very shortly afterwards.

Miriam had just been through two months under house arrest, preceded by three months in carefully cosseted isolation. Then she'd managed a fraught escape and then been imprisoned yet again, albeit for a matter of days. Walking the streets of New York again—even a strangely low-rise New York wrapped around the imperial palace and inner city of New London—felt like freedom. The sight of aircraft and streetcars and steam-powered automobiles and primitive flickering neon signs left her gaping at the sheer urban beauty of it all. As they moved closer to the center of the city the bustle of the crowds and the bright synthetic colors of the women's clothing caught her attention more than the gray-faced beggars in the suburbs. *I'm in civilization again,* she realized, half-dazed. *Even if I'm not part of it.* Erasmus paused, looking at a news vendor's stand displaying the stamp of the censor's office. "Buy me a newspaper, dear?" she asked, touching his arm.

Erasmus jerked slightly, then recovered. "Certainly. A copy of the *Register*, please."

"Aye, sorr. An' here you is."

He passed her the rolled-up news sheet as they moved up the high street. "What bit you?" he asked quietly.

"I've been out of touch for a long time. I just need to—" *I need to connect,* she thought, but before she could articulate it he nodded, grinning ironically.

"You were out of touch? Did your family have you on a tight leash?"

She shuddered. "I had nothing to read but a grammar book for two months. And that wasn't the worst of it." Now that she had company to talk to she could feel a mass of words bubbling up, ideas seeking torrential release.

"You'll have to tell me about it later. I was told there was a public salon here—ah, that's it. Your hair, Miriam. You can see to it yourself?"

He'd stopped again, opposite a diamond-paned window. Through it she could just about make out the seats and basins of a hairdresser: some things seemed to evolve towards convergence, however distinct they'd been at the start. "I think I can just about manage that." She tried to smile, but the knot of tension had gotten a toehold back and wouldn't let go. "This will probably take a couple of hours. Then I need to buy clothes. Why don't you just tell me where the hotel is, and I'll meet you there at six o'clock? How does that sound?"

"That sounds fine." He nodded, then pulled out a pocketbook and scribbled an address in it. "Here. Take care."

She smiled at him, and he ducked his head briefly, then turned his back. Miriam took a deep breath. A bell rattled on a chain as she pushed the door open; at the desk behind the window, a young woman looked up in surprise from the hardcover she'd been reading. "Can I help you?"

"I hope so." Miriam forced a smile. "I need a new hairstyle, and I need it now."

Six hours later, footsore and exhausted from the constant bombardment of strangeness that the city kept hurling at

her, Miriam clambered down from the back of a cab outside the Great Northern Hotel, clutching her parcels in
both hands. The new shoes pinched at toe and heel, and
she was sweating from the summer weather: but she was
more presentable than she'd have been in the shabby outfit they'd passed off on her at Hogarth Villas, and the
footman leapt to open the doors for her. "Thank you!"
She smiled tightly. "The front desk, I'm meeting my husband—"

"This way, ma'am."

Miriam was halfway to the desk when a newspaper rattled behind her. She glanced round to see Burgeson unfolding himself from a heavily padded chair. "Miriam! My
dear." He nodded. "Let me help you with those parcels."
He deftly extricated her from the footman, guided her past
the front desk towards an elevator, and relieved her of the
most troublesome parcel. "I almost didn't recognize you,"
he said quietly. "You've done a good job."

"It feels really strange, being a blonde. People look at
you differently. And it's so heavily lacquered it feels like
my head's embedded in a wicker basket. It'll probably
crack and fall off when I go to bed."

"Come on inside." He held the door for her, then dialed
the sixth floor. As the door closed, he added: "That's a nice
outfit. Almost too smart to be seen with the likes of me."

She pursed her lips. "Looking like a million dollars
tends to get you treated better by the kind of people those
million dollars hire." She'd ended up in something not
unlike a department store, buying a conservatively cut
black two-piece outfit. It was a lot less strange than some
of the stuff she'd seen in the shops: New London's fashion, at least for those who still had money to spend, was
more experimental than Boston's. The lift bell chimed.
"Where are we staying?"

"This way." He led her along a corridor like any other
hotel corridor back home (except for the flickering
tungsten bulbs), then used an old-fashioned key to un-
lock a bedroom door.

"There's, uh, only one bed, Erasmus."

"We're supposed to be married, Miriam. I'll take the chaise."

She blinked at the acrid bite of his words. "I didn't mean it like that."

"I'm sorry." He rubbed his forehead. "Blame Margaret's sense of humor." He looked at her again, appraisingly: "With hair that color, and curly, and—you've been using paints, haven't you? Yes, looking like that, I don't think anyone'll recognize you at first sight."

"I think it's ugly. But Mrs. Christobell—she ran the salon—seemed to think it was the height of fashion." She carefully hung her hat and jacket on the coat-rail then touched her hair gingerly. "That feels really odd. Better keep me away from candle flames for a while."

"I think I can manage that." He laid his hat and newspaper on the occasional table. "You did very well at making yourself look completely unlike yourself—it's going to take some getting used to."

"That goes for me, too. I'm not sure I like it." She headed for the table, but before she could reach it he ducked in and pulled a chair out for her. "Thanks, I think." She sat down, bent forward to get closer to her shoes, and sighed. "I need to get these off for a bit—my feet are killing me."

"Did you spend everything, or do you have some money left?"

"Not much." She focused on his expression. "Did you think I can keep up appearances by looting your shop?"

"No, but I—" He rubbed his forehead wearily. "Forget it."

"I had to do something about my appearance, make myself less recognizable. And I had to get hold of a respectable outfit, if I want to pass for your . . . spouse. And I had to buy shoes that fit, and a couple of changes of underwear, and some other stuff. It costs money, and takes time, but it's necessary. Are you still taking your medicine?"

He frowned at her effusion: "Yes, every day, as you said."

"Good." She managed to smile. "One less problem to solve." She crossed her legs. "Now, what have you been up to?"

"Getting the job done." He looked in her direction, not focusing, and she shivered. *Who is he seeing?* "I'm supposed to catch the train back to Boston tomorrow, but I wasn't planning on staying long—I'm needed in Fort Petrograd, out west." He blinked suddenly, and looked her in the eye. "You don't have to come with me—you can stay in my apartment if you prefer."

"And do what, precisely? Sit down, pacing like that is making me itch."

"I don't know." He pulled out the chair opposite and sat down. "I've got a job to do, and you turned up right in the middle of it."

"I could keep the shop open." She sounded doubtful, even to herself. *Do I want to be on my own in Boston? What if Angbard sends someone to look for me?* It would be the first place they checked. *Best not to wait until they start looking, then.*

"That's not practical." He frowned. "I trust you to do it—that's not in question—but there are too many problems. Business is very poor, and I'm already under observation. If I take a wife that's one thing, but employing a shop assistant while I take off to the wilds of California is something else: the local thief-takers aren't *completely* stupefied. I'm supposed to be a pawnbroker, not a well-off store-holder." He shook his head. "Unless you've got any better ideas?"

"I think . . . well, there's some stuff I need to pick up in Boston. And then I need to get back in touch with my relatives, but carefully. How about if I went with you? How long will you be gone?"

"At least a week; it's three days each way by train, and flying would attract the wrong kind of attention." He smiled lopsidedly. "Frankly, I'd be grateful if you'd accompany me. It'd strengthen my cover on the way out—we could be traveling on our honeymoon—and if we arrived back together I could introduce you to the neighbors as someone from out west. Wife, sister, brother's widow, whatever. And, to be truthful, the three days out—one gets tired of traveling alone."

"Oh yes," she said fervently. "Don't I know it." *It was traveling alone that got me into this mess, that courier run to Dunedin. That, and boredom, and wondering what Angbard was doing funding a fertility clinic*— "Before we skip town, though. There are some things I left in my office, at the works. I really need to get my hands on them. Do you think there's any way I could retrieve them?"

"You left your relatives running the business, didn't you? Do you know if it's still going? Or if you'd be welcome there if it is?"

"No." She realized she was shaking slightly. "No to both questions. I don't know anything. I might not be welcome. But it's important." She'd left a small notebook PC locked in a drawer in her office, and a portable printer, and a bunch of CD-ROMs with a complete archive of U.S. Patent Office filings going up to the 1960s. In this world, that was worth more than diamonds. But there was something on the computer that was even more valuable to her. In a moment of spare time, she'd scanned her locket using the computer's web cam, meaning to mess around with it later. If it was still there, if she could get her hands on it, and if it worked—*I'm free*. She could go anywhere and do anything, and she'd had a lot of time to think about Mike's offer of help, back in the basement of Hogarth Villas. It wasn't the only option, but just being able to get back to her own world would be a vast improvement on her current situation. "I need to get my stuff."

"Would it be—" He licked his lips nervously. "It's not safe, Miriam. If they're looking for you, they'll look there."

"I know, I just need—" she stopped, balling her hands into fists from frustration. "Sorry. It's not your fault. You're right, it's risky. But it's also important. If I can get

my things, I can also world-walk home. To the United
States, that is. I can—"

"Miriam." He waited almost a minute before continuing, his voice gentle. "Your relatives know where you'd
go. They might have established a trap there. Can you
think of another way to get what you need?"

"Huh?" She took a deep breath. "Yes. Roger!"

"Roger?"

She leaned across the table and took Burgeson's hand:
"I need to write him a letter. If the business is still running, he'll be working there. He's reliable—he's the one I
used to send you messages—I can ask him to take the
items whenever it's safe for him, and have a cousin deliver them to your shop when we get back." Erasmus
pulled back slightly: she realized she was gripping his
hand too hard. "Can I do that?"

He smiled ruefully as he shook some life back into his
fingers. "Are they small and concealable?"

"About so big—" she indicated "—and about ten
pounds in weight. They're delicate instruments, they need
to be kept dry and handled carefully."

"Then we'll get you some writing paper and a pen before we board the train." He nodded thoughtfully. "And
you'll tell him not to take the items for at least a week,
and to have his cousin deliver them to somewhere else, a
different address I can give you. A sympathizer. In the
very worst possible circumstances they will know that
you've visited Boston, my Boston, in the past week."

"Thank you." The knot of anxiety in her chest relaxed.

He stood up, pushing his chair back. "It's getting on.
Would you care to accompany me to dinner? No need to
change—the carvery downstairs has no code."

"Food would be good, once I get my shoes back on,"
she said ruefully. "If we've got that much travel ahead of
us I'm going to have to break them in—what are you going to Fort Petrograd for?"

"I have to see a man about a rare book," he said flippantly, offering Miriam her jacket. "And then I think

I should like to take a stroll along a beach and dip my toes in the Pacific Ocean . . ."

More wrecked buildings, another foggy morning.

Otto, Baron Neuhalle, had seen these sights twice already in the past week. His majesty had been most explicit: "We desire you to employ no more than a single battalion in any location. The witches have uncanny means of communication, as well as better guns than anything our artificers can make, and if the entire army is concentrated to take a single keep, it will be ambushed. To defeat this pestilence, it will first be necessary to force them to defend their lands. So you will avoid the castles and strong places, and instead fall upon their weaker houses and holdings. You will grant no quarter and take no prisoners of the witches, save that you put out their eyes as soon as you take them into captivity, that they may work no magic. Some of the witches make their peasants grow weeds and herbs in their fields, instead of food. You will fire these fields and slay the witches, but you will not kill their peasants—it is our wish that they be fed from the stores of their former lords and masters. The witches seem to value these crops, so they are as much a target as their owners."

His horse snorted, pawing the ground nervously at the smells and shouts from the house ahead. Neuhalle glanced at the two hand-men waiting behind him, their heavy horse-pistols resting across their saddles. "Follow," he ordered, then nudged his mount forward.

Before the first and fourth platoons had arrived, this had been a large village, dominated by the dome of a temple and the steeply pitched roof of a landholder's house—one of the Hjorth family, a poor rural hanger-on of the tinker clan. Upper Innmarch hadn't been much by the standards of the aristocracy, but it was still a substantial two-story building, wings extending behind it to form a horseshoe around a cobbled yard, with stables and outbuildings.

Now, half of the house lay in ruins and smoke and flames
belched from the roof of the other half. Bodies lay in the
dirt track that passed for a high street, soldiers moving
among them. Shouts and screams from up the lane, and a
rhythmic thudding noise: one of his lances was battering
on the door of a suspiciously well-maintained cottage,
while others moved in and out of the dark openings of
round-roofed hovels, like killer hornets buzzing around
the entrances of a defeated beehive. More moans and
screams split the air.

"Sir! Beg permission to report!"

Neuhalle reined his horse in as he approached the
sergeant—distinguished by the red scarf he wore—and
leaned towards the man. "Go ahead," he rasped.

"As ordered, I deployed around the house at dawn and
waited for Morgan's artillery. There was no sign of a
guard on duty. The occupants noticed around the time the
cannon arrived: we had hot grapeshot waiting, and Morgan put it through the windows yonder. The place caught
readily—too readily, like they was waiting for us. Fired a
few shots, then nothing. A group of six attempted to flee
from the stables on horseback as we approached, but
were brought down by Heidlor's team. The villagers either ran for the forest or barricaded themselves in, Joachim
is seeing to them now." He looked almost disappointed;
compared to the first tinker's nest they'd fired, this one
had been a pushover.

"I think you're right: the important cuckoos had already fled the nest." Neuhalle scratched at his scrubby
beard. "What's in the fields?"

"Rye and wheat, sir."

"Right." Neuhalle straightened his back: "Let the men
have their way with the villagers." These peasants had
been given no cause to resent the witches: so let them fear
the king instead. "Any prisoners from the house?"

"A couple of serving maids tried to run, sir. And an
older woman, possibly a tinker though she didn't have a
witch sign on her."

"Then give them the special treatment. No, wait. Maids? An older woman? Let the soldiers use them first, *then* the special treatment."

His sergeant looked doubtful. "Haven't found the smithy yet, sir. Might be a while before we have hot irons."

Neuhalle waved dismissively. "Then hang them instead. Just make sure they're dead before we move on, that will be sufficient. If you find any unburned bodies in the house, hang them up as well: we have a reputation to build."

"The peasants, sir?"

"I don't care, as long as there are survivors to bear witness."

"Very good, sir."

"That will be all, Sergeant Shutz."

Neuhalle nudged his horse forward, around the burning country house. He had a list of a dozen to visit, strung out through the countryside in a broad loop around Niejwein. The four companies under his command were operating semi-independently, his two captains each tackling different targets: it would probably take another week to complete the scourging of the near countryside, even though at the outset his majesty had barely three battalions ready for service. *It won't be a long war,* he hoped. *It mustn't be. Just a series of terror raids on the Clan's properties, to force them to focus on the royal army—and then what? Whatever Egon is planning,* Neuhalle supposed. Nobody could accuse the young monarch of being indecisive—he was as sharp as his father, untempered by self-doubt, and deeply committed to this purge. Neuhalle's hand-men rode past him, guns at the ready: *It had better work,* he hoped. *If Egon loses, Niejwein will belong to the witches forever.*

The courtyard at the back of the house stank of manure and blood, and burning timber. A carriage leaned drunkenly outside the empty stable doors, one wheel shattered.

"Sir, if it please you, we should—" The hand-man gestured.

"Go ahead." Neuhalle smiled faintly, and unholstered the oddly small black pistol he carried on his belt: a present from one of the witch lords, in better times. He racked the slide, chambering a cartridge. "I don't think they'll be interested in fighting. Promise them quarter, then hang them as usual once you've disarmed them." *Just as his majesty desires.* His eyes turned towards the wreckage. "Let's look this over."

"Aye, sir."

They'd cut the horses free and abandoned the carriage, but there was still a strong-box lashed to the roof, and an open door gaping wide. Otto dismounted carefully, keeping his horse between himself and the upper floor windows dribbling smoke—no point not being careful—and walked over to the vehicle. There was nobody inside, of course. Then the roof. The box wasn't large, but it looked heavy. Neuhalle's grin widened. "You, fetch four troopers and have them take this down. Place a guard on it."

"Aye sir!" His hand-man nodded enthusiastically: Neuhalle had promised his retainers a tithe of his spoils.

"There'll be more just like it tomorrow." There was a loud crack, and Neuhalle looked round just in time to see the roof line of the west wing collapse with a shower of sparks and a gout of flames. "And tomorrow . . ."

7

OIL TALK

❦

Just as the guard handed Eric back his mobile phone, it rang.

"Hey, good timing!" The cop chuckled.

Eric flipped it open, ignoring the man. It had already been a long day: back home it was about six in the evening, and he still had to fly back. "Smith here."

"Boss?" It was Deirdre, his secretary: "I'm aware this is an insecure line, but I thought you might want to know that Mike is back from his sales trip, and he says he's got a buyer."

"Jesus!" Eric stood bolt-upright. "Are you sure? That's amazing!" The sense of gloom that had been hanging over him for days lifted. He checked his watch: "Listen, I'll be back in town late tonight—can you get him into the office for an early morning debrief? Around six hundred hours?" *I'll have to tell Gillian something, he realized. Not just an apology. Take her somewhere nice?*

"I, I don't think that will be possible," Deirdre said, sounding distracted.

"Why not?" It came out too sharply: "Sorry, I didn't mean to snap at you. What's the problem?"

"He's, um, he had a traffic accident. He's taken a beating, but he'll be all right once he's out of hospital. Judith Herz is with him."

"Whoa!" Eric blinked furiously. He glanced round the guardroom, noticing the cop sitting patiently behind the counter, the polite SS agent with the car keys. "—Listen, I'll call you back from a secure terminal once I'm under way. Should be about an hour. I'll be expecting the best report you can pull together. If possible get Judith on the line for me, if she's spoken to him in person."

He could just about see Deirdre's eye-rolling nod: "That's about what I expected, boss. I'll be ready for you."

"Okay, bye."

He closed the phone with a snap and turned to Agent Simms: "Come on, we've got a plane to catch!"

There was a secure terminal aboard the Gulfstream, and Eric wasted no time in getting to it as soon as they were airborne. But what Judith Herz had for him wasn't encouraging.

"He got chewed up—one leg is badly broken with surface lacerations, he's got bruising and soft tissue injuries consistent with being in a fight, and he's got a nasty infected wound. I got him checked in to the nearest trauma unit and it looks like he'll pull through and keep the leg, but he's not going to be up and about any time soon. Someone stuck a syringe full of morphine in him and dumped him at a roadside in upstate New York. They called an ambulance using a stolen mobile phone, and no, we didn't get a trace on it—they turned it on just before they called and switched off immediately after. He was still wearing his cover gear, but they'd disarmed him."

"Shit. Excuse me." Eric took a few moments to gather his scattered thoughts. Too many things were going on at once. His head was still spinning from the stuff in the buried laboratory under Building Forty-seven. He'd just about gotten used to the idea that Mike had made it home alive—and that was *really* good news—but this latest tidbit was a little hard to take. "Okay. So someone sent him back to us? Any sign of Sergeant Hastert and his team?"

"Mike was awake when I saw him, sir." He stiffened at her tone of voice, anticipating the bad news to come: "He wasn't very lucid, but he said Hastert and O'Neil were killed. They walked in on some kind of war and they got caught in the crossfire. I'm sorry, sir: he wasn't very clear, but he wanted you to know they died trying to get him out."

"Shit." Eric rubbed his eyes tiredly. "Any good news? Or was *that* the good news?"

"He says he made contact with the target briefly, but there were problems. And something about her mother."

"What's her mother got to do with things?"

"We didn't get that far, sir. Like I said, he's been chewed up badly. I mean, it looks like someone took a whack at his left leg with a chain saw then left it to fester for a couple of days. That's on top of the bruising and a cracked rib. The medics shoved me out of the room just as he was getting to the good stuff—he's out of the operating theater now but he won't be talking for a while. But I'm pretty sure he was trying to say something about the target's mother saving him. I don't know what he meant by that, he was medicated and being prepped for surgery at the time, but I figure you'll want to follow it up."

"Dead right I will." Eric took a deep breath. "Alright. So he's out of the operating theater now. As soon as he's safe to move, I want him in a military hospital with an armed guard *in* the room with him at all times—for his own protection. If they can find an underground room to put him in, so much the better. If possible, move him tonight—I want him safe, right now his brains are our crown jewels. Tell Deirdre to get John from OPFAC Four to coordinate with Milton and Sarah on setting it up. Page them if they've gone home, this is important. Got that?"

"I'm on it. Anything else? Will you be coming in tonight?"

Eric shook his head tiredly. "I'm touching down around half past midnight. If you get any pushback between now and then, call me and I'll come in. If it goes smoothly, I might as well get some sleep before I debrief him." A thought struck him. "Another thing. I want a guard with him at all times, with a voice recorder in case he says anything. And I don't want random doctors or nurses eavesdropping."

"Already taken care of." Herz's laconic response made him want to kick himself. Of course it was taken care of: Herz was terrifyingly efficient when it came to police work like handling witnesses.

"Good. Good work, I mean, really good." *I'm babbling. Stop it.* "Well, I won't keep you any longer. If you need backup, call me. Bye."

The seatbelt light was off, the plane boring a hole in the sky towards the darkening eastern horizon. Eric unfastened his belt and stood up, then went forward to the desk where Dr. James was poring over a pile of printouts.

"What is it?" No polite small-talk from James: he was almost robotic in his focus.

"It's CLEANSWEEP. I just got confirmation that we've had a positive outcome."

It was Dr. James's turn to do a double take—or punch the air, if so inclined—and Eric was curious to see how he'd jump. Dr. James was not, it seemed, one for demonstrative gestures: he simply put his papers down, removed his spectacles, and said, mildly, "Explain."

"Agent Fleming is back. He's alive, but has injuries. His condition is stable and I've ordered him transferred to a secure facility pending debriefing. The preliminary report is that the specops team walked into a red-on-red crossfire of some sort, but Fleming was returned to us by someone who presumably wants to talk. There appears to be a factional split in fairyland. I'll know more tomorrow, when I've begun his debriefing: for now, I gather his injuries required operating theater time so we won't get much more out of him just yet."

James began to polish his bifocals with a scrap of tissue. "*Good.*" His fingertips moved in tiny circles, pinching the lens like a crab worrying at a fragment of decaying flesh. "You'll debrief him without witnesses. Record onto a sealed medium and type up the report yourself. Use a typewriter, not a word processor." He looked up at Eric with dead-fish eyes: "the fewer witnesses the better."

Eric cleared his throat. "You know that's in direct contravention of our operational doctrine?"

James nodded. "Sit down." Eric sat opposite him. James glanced round, to make sure there were no open ears nearby, then carefully balanced the bifocals on the bridge of his nose. "Off the record."

"Yes?" Eric did his best to conceal the sinking feeling those words gave him.

"You're a professional, and you're used to playing by the rules. That's all very well. The reason that rule book exists is to prevent loose cannons from rolling around the deck, knocking things over and making a mess. We designed the policy on debriefing to ensure that no asshole can piss in the coffeepot and embarrass the owners. However, right now, you're working directly for the owners. Standard policy wasn't designed for this type of war and therefore we have to make a new rule book up as we go along—where it's necessary. Your job is to build up a HUMINT resource, taking us back into a kind of operational model we haven't ever been really good at, and last tried in the sixties and seventies. But the flip side of HUMINT is COINTEL, and if we can spy on them, they can spy on us. So the zeroth rule of this operation is, minimize the eyeballs—minimize the risk of leaks. Clear?"

Eric nodded, involuntarily. Then a late-acting bureau-

cratic reflex prompted him to protest: "That's all very
well, and I agree with your reasoning, but it doesn't help
me out if they come after me with an audit."

James stared at him coldly. "Where's your loyalty,
boy?"

"You're asking me to commit a federal felony, on your
word. If you want to run HUMINT assets on the ground,
their rule number one is that they've got to be able to trust
their controllers. You're *my* controller." He crossed his
arms, hoping his anger wasn't immediately obvious to
the other man.

James stared at him a moment longer, then nodded
minutely. "So that's the way it is."

"It's the way it's got to be," Eric shot back. "It's not just
me who's got to trust you, it's the whole goddamn chain of
command, all the way down." *Which right now consists of
one guy in a hospital bed, but let's not remind him of that.*
"—History says that the smart money is on this coming out,
if not now, then in twenty years' time. This administration
will be fodder for the history books by then—hell, with his
heart condition, Daddy Warbucks will probably be sleeping with the fishes—but I'm a career officer, and so are the
folks in my outfit. If you don't give us a fig leaf, you're asking us to suck up time in Leavenworth. And we don't get to
go on to a juicy research contract with the Heritage Insti-
tute, or a part-time boardroom post with some defense con-
tractor when this is over."

"What do you want?" James's intonation was precise
and his voice even, but Eric didn't let it fool him.

"Something vague, but in writing. The vaguer the better.
Something like, 'In the interests of operational security
and in view of the threat of enemy intelligence-gathering
attempts aimed at compromising our integrity, all investi-
gations are to be restricted to those with a need to know,
and normal committee oversight will be suspended until
such time as the immediate threat recedes.' Just keep
it vague. Then if I have to take the stand, I've simply

misunderstood your intent. I'm obeying an order by a superior, you didn't intend your orders to breach the law. Nobody needs to get burned."

James snorted abruptly, startling Eric. "Is that all?"

Eric shrugged. "That's how it's done. That's what kept the shit in check during Iran-Contra. Or did you expect me to fall on my sword when all I need is a note signed by teacher to say I'm an overachiever?"

"Bah." James glanced away, but not before Eric noticed a twinkle of crocodilian amusement in his eye. "I thought you were an Air Force officer, not a politician."

"You don't get above captain if you're politically challenged, sir. With all due respect, it makes life easier for me if I can advise you—where appropriate—of steps I can take to do my job better. That's one of them. Off the record, of course."

"I'll get you your fig leaf, then. Signed on the Oval Office blotter, if that makes you feel better. Now, talk to me." James leaned back, making a steeple of his fingertips.

Eric relaxed infinitesimally. "Someone sent Mike back to us. He didn't come by himself; his leg's busted up. That tells us something about what sort of operation we're fighting."

"Go on . . ."

"I haven't debriefed him yet. But at a guess, what we've already done has hurt their operations on the east coast, and sending agents through after them is going to scare the shit out of them. They're going to have to negotiate or escalate. Leaving aside the business with GREENSLEEVES and the nuke, we're going to have to negotiate or escalate, too. Now, it's not for me to advise on policy, but I suspect we're going to find that Mike was sent back by someone who stands to gain from negotiating with us. Call them faction 'A'. The red-on-red action suggests there's a rival faction, call them 'B'. So we *really* need to keep a lid on this, because if the 'B' faction figures that the 'A' faction want to negotiate, they may try to torpedo things by escalating. And if GREENSLEEVES wasn't bluffing about the nuke, we could be in a world of hurt."

Dr. James nodded minutely. "Your advice?"

"We have to find that nuke, or rule it out. And we have to keep them talking while JAUNT BLUE get their shit together. Right now, we're fumbling around in the dark— but so are they. All they know is, we've whacked a bunch of their operations and figured out how to get an agent across. And if they're in trouble internally, presumably they'd love to get us off their backs while they clean up their own mess. They probably think we don't know about the nukes, and we can be pretty sure that they don't know about JAUNT BLUE. Everything we know about them suggests they just don't think in those terms, other- wise they'd be crawling all over us."

"So. You propose that we debrief Agent Fleming, then use him to establish a back channel to the leadership of Group 'A,' with the goal of stalling them with the promise of negotiations while we clean up the missing nuke and get some results from JAUNT BLUE. Is that a fair sum- mary?"

Eric blinked, then rubbed his forehead. "You put it bet- ter than I did," he said ruefully. "Long day."

"Going to be longer," James said laconically. He leaned back and stared at the ceiling air vents for a while, until Eric began to think he was planning on taking a nap: but just as he was about to stand up and leave, James sat up abruptly and looked at him. "Your analysis is valid, but incomplete because there are some facts you are un- aware of."

Uh? "Obviously," Eric said cautiously. "Should I be?"

"I think so." James stared at him, his expression decep- tively mild. "Same rules as the Fleming debriefing. This goes nowhere near a computer or a telephone. You fol- low?"

Eric nodded.

"Number one. Obviously, I do not want—nobody

wants—to see a terrorist nuke detonated in an American city. Even if it's in the People's Republic of Massachusetts, that would be very bad. But you need to understand this: if the worst happens, if that bomb goes off, a use will be found for it. The bloody shirt will be waved. Do you understand?"

Eric licked his suddenly dry lips. "Who's the fall guy?"

"The Boy Wonder's got a hard-on for Mr. Hussein, and PNAC will fall in line, but—" Dr. James shook his head. "I'm not sure who, Colonel. All I can tell you is, it will be someone who we can hammer for it. The hammer is ready, and if the United States doesn't wield it from time to time the other players may begin to wonder if we're still willing. So if JAUNT BLUE is ready, the target might be the Clan. And if JAUNT BLUE isn't ready, we'll hit someone else, someone we can reach and need to nail flat. North Korea, Iraq, Iran, whoever. But. Whatever else happens, if there's a hard outcome, it will be used to strengthen our hand. We'll have carte blanche." He stared at Eric. "The code name for this plan—and I stress, it's a contingency plan, a political spin to put on a disaster—is MARINUS BERLIN."

"Jesus." Eric looked away. "That's disgusting."

"Yes. I know. But what else can we do?"

"Find the bomb."

"Yes!" James's frustration boiled over in Eric's: "If you've got some kind of magic superpowers that let you stare through concrete walls and pinpoint missing nukes, then I'd like to hear about them, Colonel. Failing that, if you have any better ideas, I'm sure Daddy Warbucks would like to know what else to fricking do if terrorists nuke one of our cities?"

Shit. "I'm sorry. Like I said, we're looking. I'll see if I can scare up some backup when we get back, okay?"

"You'd better. Because falling on our swords is not on the agenda for this administration, son. We're not going to hand the country to the other team just because some assholes from another dimension fuck with us, any more

than we did when bin Laden got uppity and bit the feeding hand." James paused. "I shouldn't have blown up
then. Forget I said anything, it's not your fault. There's a
lot at stake here that you aren't in on: the big picture is
really scary. All the oil in fairyland, for starters."

"All the *what*?"

Dr. James looked as if he'd bitten a lemon while expecting an orange. "Oil, son. Makes the world go round. You
know what the business with al-Qaeda is about? Oil.
We're in Saudi Arabia because of the oil: bin Laden wants
us out of Saudi. We're going to go into Iraq because of the
oil. Oil is leverage. Oil lets us put the Chinks and Europe-
ans in their place. And we're running short of it, in case
you hadn't noticed, there's this thing called peak oil coming and we've got analysts scratching their heads to figure
out how we're going to field it. We're not going to run out,
but demand is going to exceed supply and the price is going to start climbing in a few years. Our planetary preem-
inence relies on us having cheap oil for our industries,
while everyone else pays through the nose for it. But we
can't guarantee to keep prices low if we're having to send
our boys out to sit in the desert and keep the wells pumping. So it was looking bad until six months ago, but now
there's a new factor in the equation . . ."

He took a deep breath. "The Clan. A bunch of medieval
jerks, squatting on our territory—or a good cognate of it.
What's going down in Texas, Colonel Smith? Their version of Texas, not our Texas: what are they *doing* there?
I'll tell you what they're doing: they're sitting on twice
as much oil as Saddam Hussein, and that's what's got
Daddy Warbucks's attention. Because, you see, if JAUNT
BLUE delivers, eventually all that good black stuff is going to be ours . . ."

"Are we nearly there yet?"

Huw glanced in the driver's mirror, taking his eyes off
the interstate for a couple of seconds. Elena sprawled

across one half of the back seat of the Hummer H2 truck, managing to look louche and bored simultaneously. Petulant, that was the word. A twenty-one-year-old Clan princess—no, merely a contessa in waiting, should she inherit—fresh from her Swiss finishing school and her first semester at college: out in the big bad world for the first time, with two brave knights to look after her. File off the serial numbers and you could mistake her for a spoiled preppy kitten. Of course, the jocks who'd be clustering around the latter type didn't usually carry swords. Nor did normal preppies know how to handle the FN P90 in the trunk. Still, Huw let his eyes linger on her tight jeans and embroidered babydoll tee for a second longer than was strictly necessary, before he glanced back at the road and the GPS navigation screen.

"About twenty miles to go. Eighteen minutes. We turn off in ten."

"Bo-ring." She faked a yawn at him, slim hand covering pink lip gloss.

"I'm bored too," snarked Hulius, from his nest in the front passenger seat. He took an orange from the glove box and began to peel it with his dagger. Citrus droplets swirled in the aircon breeze.

"We're all bored," Huw said affably. "Are you suggesting I should break the speed limit?"

Hulius paled. "No—"

"Good." Huw smiled. The white duke took a dim view of traffic infractions, and supplemented the official fines with additional punishments of his own choice: ten strokes of the lash for a first offense. *Don't ever, ever draw attention to yourselves* was the first rule they drilled into everyone before letting them out the door. Which was why couriers on Post duty dressed like lawyers, and why the three of them were driving down the interstate at a sober two miles under the speed limit, in a shiny new Hummer, with every *i* dotted and *t* crossed on the paperwork that proved them to be a trio of MIT graduate students with rich parents, off on a field trip.

The green dot on the map inched south along Route 95, slowly converging on Baltimore and the afternoon traffic. The aircon fans hissed steadily, but Huw could still feel the heat beating down on the back of his hand through the tinted glass. Concrete rumbled under the magically smooth suspension of the truck. The scrubby grass outside was parched, burned almost brown by the summer heat. He'd made a journey part of the distance down this way once before on horseback, in a place with no air-conditioning or cars: it had been a fair approximation of hell. Doing the journey in a luxury SUV was heaven—albeit a particularly boring corner of it. "Have you checked the charge on the goggles yet?"

"They're in the trunk. They'll be fine." Hulius pulled off a slice of orange and offered it to Huw. "you worry too much."

"It's your neck I'm worrying over. Would you rather I didn't worry, bro?"

"If you put it that way . . ."

The last half hour of any journey was always the longest, but Huw caught the sign in time, and took the exit for Bel Air and parts east: then a couple more turns onto dusty roads linking faceless tracts of suburb with open countryside. The dots converged. Finally he reached a stretch of trees and a driveway led up to an unprepossessing house. He brought the truck to a halt in front of the day room windows and killed the engine.

"You're sure this is the place?" Elena pushed herself upright then stretched, yawning.

"Got to be." Huw rooted around in the dash for the bunch of house keys and the letter from the realtor. Then he opened the door and jumped out, taking a deep breath as the oppressive summer humidity washed over him. "Number 344. Yup, that's right."

Sneakers crunched on gravel as he walked towards the front door. Behind him, a clattering: Elena unloading the flat Pelikan case from the trunk. Huw glanced up at the peeling white paint under the guttering, the patina of dust.

Then he rang the doorbell and waited for a long minute, until Elena, holding the case behind him as if it was a guitar, began tapping her toes and whistling a tuneless melody of impatience. "It pays to be cautious," he finally explained, before he stuck the key in the lock. "People hereabouts take a dim view of unexpected visitors."

The key turned. Inside, the hallway was hot and close, smelling of dust and old regrets. Huw breathed a sigh of relief. He'd set this up by remote control, one of ten test sites running down the coastline and across the continent all the way to the west coast, spaced five hundred kilometers apart. The Realtor had been only too glad to rent it to him for a year, money paid up front: it had been unsalable ever since its former owner, a retired widower, had died of a heart attack in the living room one bleak winter evening. You could remove the carpet and the furniture, and even do something about the smell, but you couldn't remove the reputation.

Huw hunted around for the fuse board for a while, then flipped the circuit breaker. A distant whir spoke of long-dormant air-conditioning. He checked that the hall lights worked, then nodded to himself. "Okay, let's get moved in."

It took the three of them half an hour to unload the Hummer. Besides backpacks full of clothing, they brought in a number of wheeled equipment cases, a laptop computer, and couple of expensive digital camcorders. Finally, the air mattresses. "Elena? You take the back bedroom. Yul, you and I are roughing it up front in the master room."

Huw dragged his mattress into the front room and plugged the electric pump in. Some of the houses were still furnished, but not this one. *Be prepared* wasn't just for scouts. Her Grace Helge had done pretty much this same job, on a smaller, much less organized scale—but Huw had been thinking about it for the week since the white duke had called him in, and he thought he had some new twists on it. He mopped at his forehead. "Listen, we're about done here and it's half past lunchtime, so why don't we head into town and grab a pizza while the air-conditioning makes this place habitable?"

"Works for me." Hulius grimaced. "Where's Lady Elena?"

"Here." Elena leaned against the banister rail outside the door. "Food would be good." She grinned impishly. "How about a couple of bottles of wine?" Like all Clan members, her attitude to wine was very un-American—tempered only by the duke's iron rule about attracting unwanted attention in public.

Huw nodded—thoughtfully, for he was still getting used to playing the role of responsible adult around the other two. "We'll pick something up if we pass a liquor store. But no drinking in public, okay?"

"Sure, dude."

"Let's go, then."

An hour later they were back in the under-furnished living room with pizza boxes, a stack of six-packs of Pepsi, and a discreet brown paper bag. "Okay," said Huw, licking his fingers. "Taken your pills yet?"

"Um, 'scuse me." Elena darted upstairs, returning with a toilet bag. "Hate these things," she mumbled resentfully. "Make me feel woozy." She threw back her head when she swallowed. *What fine bones she has,* thought Huw, watching her with unprofessional enthusiasm. That was one of the reasons she was along on this trip: because she was sixty kilograms, the stocky Hulius could carry her piggyback if necessary.

"Where were we?" asked Hulius, pausing with a slice of Hawaiian halfway to his mouth.

Huw checked his wristwatch. "About an hour and a half short of time zero. You guys eat, I'll repeat the plan, interrupt if you want me to explain anything."

"Okay," said Hulius. Elena nodded, rolling her eyes as she chewed.

"First, we assemble the stage one kit. Clothing, boots,

cameras, guns, telemetry belts. We triple-test the belt bat-
teries and set them running at five minutes to zero hour.
There's no post on this trip, even if we get some results.
Elena piggybacks on Yul, on the first attempt. If you fail,
we call it a wash today, switch off the telemetry, and
break open the wine. If you succeed, you evaluate your
surroundings and proceed to Plan Alpha or Plan Bravo,
depending. Now." He tore off a wedge of cooling pizza:
"It's your turn to tell me what you're supposed to do as
soon as you find yourself wherever the hell you're going.
Hoping to go. Plan Alpha first. Elena, describe your
job . . . ?"

The carvery in the hotel wasn't anything Miriam would
have described as a classy restaurant, but after being
locked in the basement of a brothel for most of a week it
felt like the Ritz. Miriam was ravenous from a day pounding the sidewalks: but Erasmus, she noticed over the soup,
ate slowly but methodically, clearing his plate with grim
determination. "Hungry?" she asked, lowering her spoon.

"I try never to leave my food." He nodded, then tore off
another piece of bread to mop his soup bowl clean. "Old
habit. Bad manners, I'm afraid: I apologize."

"No offense taken." Miriam nodded. "You need to put
on weight, anyway. I haven't heard you coughing today,
but you're so thin!"

"Really?" He made as if to raise his napkin to cover his
mouth, then grinned at her. "When you start you know
about it, but when something goes away . . . it's an unnoticed miracle." A waiter arrived, silently, and removed
their bowls. "I don't feel ancient and drained anymore.
But you're right, I need to eat. I wasn't always a sack of
bones." He shook his head, and the grin slipped into rue-
ful oblivion.

"It was your time in the north, wasn't it?" The statement slipped out before Miriam could stop it.

Erasmus stared at her. "Yes, it was," he said quietly.

She licked her lips. "Sorry. Didn't mean to say that."

"Yes you did." He glanced sidelong at the other occupants of the room: no one was paying them any obvious attention. "But it's all right, I don't mind."

"I don't mean to pry." The waiter was returning, bearing two plates. She leaned back while he deftly slid her entree in front of her. When he'd gone, she looked back at Burgeson. "But I'd be crazy not to be curious. Months ago, when I said I didn't care what your connections were . . . I didn't expect things to go this way."

He shrugged, then picked up his knife and fork. "Neither did I," he said shortly. "You are curious as to the nature of what you've gotten yourself into?"

She took a sip of wine, then began to methodically slice into the overcooked lamb chops on her plate. "This probably isn't the right place for this conversation."

"I'm glad you agree."

He wasn't making this easy. "So. Tomorrow . . . train back home? Then what?"

"It'll be a flying visit. Overnight, perhaps." He shoveled a potato onto his fork, holding it in place with a fatty piece of mutton: "I need to pick up my post, make arrangements for the shop, and notify the Polis." His cheek twitched. "I've reserved a suite on the night mail express, leaving tomorrow evening. It joins up with the Northern Continental at Dunedin, we won't have to change carriages."

"A suite?" She raised an eyebrow. "Isn't that expensive?"

Erasmus paused, another forkful of food halfway to his mouth: "Of course it is! But the extra expense, on top of a transcontinental ticket, is minor." He grimaced. "You expect travel to be cheaper than it is. It can be—if you don't mind sleeping on a blanket roll with the steerage for a week."

"Yes, but . . ." Miriam paused for long enough to eat some more food: "I'm sorry. So we're going straight through Dunedin and stopping in Fort Petrograd? How many days away?"

"We'll stop halfway for a few hours. The Northern Continental runs from Florida up to New London, cuts northwest to Dunedin, stops to take on extra carriages, nonstop to New Glasgow where it stops to split up, then down the coast to Fort Petrograd. We should arrive in just under four days. If we were really going the long way, we could change onto the Southern Continental at Western Station, keep going south to Mexico City, then cross the Isthmus of Panama and keep going all the way to Land's End on the Cape. But that's a horrendous journey, seven thousand miles or more, and the lines aren't fast—it takes nearly three weeks."

"Hang on. The Cape—you mean, you have trains that run all the way to the bottom of South America?"

"Of course. Don't your people, where you come from?"

They ate in silence for a few minutes. "I'd better write that letter to Roger right now and mail it this evening."

"That would be prudent." Burgeson lowered his knife and fork, having swept his plate clean. "You'll probably want to go through my bookcases before we embark, too—it's going to be a long ride."

After the final cup of coffee, Burgeson sighed. "Let us go upstairs," he suggested.

"Okay—yes." Miriam managed to stand up. She was, she realized, exhausted, even though the night was still young. "I'm tired."

"Really?" Erasmus led the way to the elevator. "Maybe you should avail yourself of the bathroom, then catch an early night. I have some business to attend to in town. I promise to let myself in quietly."

He slid the elevator gate open and as she stepped inside she noticed the heavily built doorman just inside the entrance. "If it's safe, that works for me."

"Why would it be unsafe? To a hotel like this, any whiff of insecurity for the guests is pure poison."

"Good."

Back in the room, Miriam jotted down a quick note to her sometime chief research assistant, using hotel stationery. "Can you get this posted tonight?" she asked Erasmus. "I'm going to have that bath now . . ."

The bathroom turned out to be down the corridor from the bedroom, the bath a contraption of cold porcelain fed by gleaming copper pipework. There was, however, hot water in unlimited quantities—something that Miriam had missed for so long that its availability came as an almost incomprehensible luxury.

The things we take for granted, she thought, relaxing into the tub: the comforts of a middle-class existence in New Britain seemed exotic and advanced after months of detention in a Clan holding in Niejwein. *I could fit in here.* She tried the thought on for size. *Okay, so domestic radios are the size of a photocopier, and there's no Internet, and they use trains where we'd use airliners. So what? They've got hot and cold running water, and gas and electricity. Indoor plumbing.* The chambers Baron Henryk had confined her to had a closet with a drafty hole in a wooden seat. *I could live here.* The thought was tempting for a moment— until she remembered the thin, pinched faces in the soup queue, the outstretched upturned hats. Erasmus's hacking cough, now banished by medicines that she'd brought over from Boston—her own Boston. No antibiotics: back before they'd been discovered, a quarter to a third of the population had died of bacterial diseases. She sighed, lying back carefully to avoid soaking her brittle-bleached hair. *It's better than the Clan, but still . . .*

She tried to gather her scattered thoughts. New Britain wasn't some kind of nostalgic throwback to a gaslight age: it was dirty, smelly, polluted, and intermittently dangerous. Clothing was expensive and conservative because foreign sweatshops weren't readily available: the cost of transporting their produce was too high even in peacetime—and with a wartime blockade in force, things were even worse. Politics was dangerous, in ways she'd barely begun to understand: there was participatory democracy for a price, for a very limited franchise of rich land-owning men who thought themselves the guardians of the people and the rulers of the populace, shepherding the masses they did not consider to be responsible enough for self-determination.

It wasn't only women's rights that were a problem here—and *that* was bad enough, as she'd discovered: women here had fewer civil rights than they had in Iran, in her own world; at least in Iran women could vote—but here, anyone who wasn't a member of the first thousand families was second-class, unable to move to a new city without a permit from the Polis, a subject rather than a citizen. "Fomenting democratic agitation" was an actual on-the-books felony that could get you sent to a labor camp in the far north. Outright chattel slavery might not be a problem—it seemed to have fizzled away in the late nineteenth century—but the level of casual racism she'd witnessed was jarring and unpleasant.

I just want to go home. If only I knew where home is!

The water was growing cold. Miriam finished her ablutions, then returned to the hotel room. It was close and humid in the summer heat, so she raised the sash window, dropping the gauze insect screen behind it. *Erasmus can let himself in,* she thought, crawling between the sheets. *How late will he*—she dozed off.

She awakened to daylight, and Erasmus's voice, sounding heartlessly cheerful as he opened the shutters: "Rise and shine! And good morning to you, Miriam! I hope you slept well. You'll be pleased to know that your letter made the final collection: it'll have been delivered already. I'll be about my business up the corridor while you make yourself decent. How about some breakfast before we travel?"

"Ow, you cruel, heartless man!" She struggled to sit up, covering her eyes. "What time is it?"

"It's half-past six, and we need to be on the train at ten to eight."

"Ouch. Okay, I'm awake already!" She squinted into the light. Burgeson was fully dressed, if a bit rumpled-looking. "The chaise was a bit cramped?"

"I've slept worse." He picked up a leather toilet bag. "If you'll excuse me? I'll knock before I come in."

He disappeared into the corridor, leaving Miriam feeling unaccountably disappointed. *Damn it, it's unnatural to be that cheerful in the morning!* Still, she was thoroughly awake. Kicking the covers back, she sat up and stretched. Her clothing lay where she'd left it the evening before. By the time Erasmus knocked again she was prodding her hair back into shape in front of the dressing-table mirror. "Come in," she called.

"Oh good." Erasmus nodded approvingly. "I've changed my mind about breakfast: I think we ought to catch the morning express. How does that sound to you? I'm sure we can eat perfectly well in the dining car."

She turned to stare at him. "I'd rather not hurry," she began, then thought better of it. "Is there a problem?" Her pulse accelerated.

"Possibly." He didn't look unduly worried, but Miriam was not reassured. "I'd rather not stay around to find out."

"In that case." Miriam picked up the valise and began stuffing sundries into it. "Let's get moving." The skin in the small of her back itched. "Are we being watched?"

"Possibly. And then again, it might just be routine. Let me help you." Erasmus passed her hat down from the coat rack, then gathered up her two shopping bags. "The sooner we're out of town the better. There's a train at ten to seven, and we can just catch it if we make haste."

Downstairs, the hotel was already moving. "Room ninety-two," Erasmus muttered to the clerk on the desk, sliding a banknote across: "I'm in a hurry."

The clerk peered at the note then nodded. "That will be fine, sir." Without waiting, Erasmus made for the front door, forcing Miriam to take quick steps to keep up with him. "Quickly," he muttered from the side of his mouth. "Keep your eyes open."

The sidewalk in front of the hotel was merely warm, this early in the morning. A newspaper boy loitered opposite, by the Post Office: early-morning commuters were about. Miriam glanced in the hotel windows as she followed Erasmus along the dusty pavement. A flicker of a newspaper caught her eye, and she looked ahead in time to see a man in a peak-brimmed hat crossing the road, looking back towards them. *Shit*. She'd seen this pattern before—a front and back tail, boxing in a surveillance subject. "Are we likely to be robbed in the street?" she asked Erasmus's retreating back.

He stopped dead, and she nearly ran into him: "No, of course not." He didn't meet her eyes, looking past her. "I see what you see," he added in a low, conversational tone. "So. Change of plan—again." He offered her his arm. "Let's take this nice and easy."

Miriam took his arm, holding him close to her side. "What are we going to do?" she muttered.

"We're going to deliberately get on the wrong train." He steered her around a pillar box, then into the entrance to the station concourse, and simultaneously passed her a stubby cardboard ticket. "We want to be on the ten to seven for Boston, on platform six. But we're going to get on the eight o'clock to Newport, on platform eight, opposite platform six, and we're going to get on right at the front."

Miriam nodded. "Then what?"

"It's sixteen minutes to seven." He smiled and waved his ticket at the uniformed fellow at the end of the platform: Miriam followed his example. "At twelve minutes to the hour, we cross over to the right train. If we're stopped or if you miss it, remember your cover, we just got on the wrong train by mistake. All right? Let's go . . ."

Miriam took a deep breath. *This doesn't sound good,* she realized, her pulse pounding in her ears as an irrational fear made her guts clench. She resisted the urge to look over her shoulder, instead keeping hold of Burgeson's arm until he steered her towards a railway carriage that seemed to consist of a row of small compartments, each with its own doors and a running-board to allow access to the platform. As she reached the train, she glanced sideways along the platform. The same two men she'd seen on the street were

walking towards her: as she watched, one of them peeled
off toward the carriage behind. *It's a box tail all right.* She
forced herself to unfreeze and climbed into the empty
eight-seat compartment, and Erasmus's arms.

"Hey!"

"This is the hard bit." He steered her behind him, then
pulled the door to and swiftly dropped the heavy leather
shutters across the windows of the small compartment.
Then he walked to the door on the other side of the carriage and opened it. "I'll lower you."

"I can climb down myself, thanks." Miriam looked over
the edge. It was a good five feet down to the track bed.
"Damn." She lowered herself over the dusty footplate.
"Got the bags?"

"Right behind you."

The track bed was covered in cinders and damp, unpleasant patches. She patted her clothes down and reached
up to take the luggage Erasmus passed her. A second later
he stood beside her, breathing hard. "Are you all right?"

"A touch of—of—you know." He wheezed twice, then
coughed, horribly. "All right now. *Move.*" He pointed her
across the empty tracks, towards a flight of crumbling
brick steps leading up the side of the platform. "Go on."

She hurried across the tracks then up the steps. She
glanced back at Erasmus: he seemed to be in no hurry, but
at least he was moving. *Shit, why now?* This was about
the worst possible moment for his chest to start causing
trouble. She looked round, taking stock of the situation.
The crowd on the platform was thinning, people bustling
towards open doors as if in a hurry to avoid a rain storm.
A plump man in a tricorn hat was marching up the platform, brandishing a red flag. Nobody was watching her
climb the steps from the empty track bed. *Come on, Erasmus!* She took a step towards the train, then another, and
picked up her pace. A few seconds later, an open door
loomed before her. She pulled herself up and over the
threshold. "Is this compartment reserved?" she asked,
flustered: "My husband—"

A whistle shrilled. She looked round, and down. Erasmus stood on the platform below her, panting, clearly out of breath. "No reservations," grumbled a fat man in a violently clashing check jacket. He shook his newspaper ostentatiously and made a great show of shifting over a couple of inches.

Miriam reached down and took Erasmus's hand. It felt like twigs bound in leather, light enough that her heave carried him halfway up the steps in one fluid movement. She stepped backwards and sat down, and he smiled at her briefly then tugged the door closed. The whistle shrilled again as the train lurched and began to pull away. "I didn't think we were going to make it," she said.

Burgeson took a deep breath and held it for a few seconds. "Neither did I," he admitted wheezily, glancing back along the platform towards the two running figures that had just lurched into view. "Neither did I . . ."

8

BREAKTHROUGHS

It's all very simple, Huw tried to reassure himself. *It'll take us somewhere new, or it won't.* True, the Wu family knotwork worked fine, as a key for travel between the worlds of the Gruinmarkt and New Britain. But the limited, haphazard attempts to use it in the United States had all failed so far. Huw had a theory to explain that: Miriam was in the wrong place when she'd tried to world-walk.

You couldn't world-walk if there was a solid object in your position in the destination world. That was why doppelgangering worked, why if you wanted protection against assassins for your castle in the Gruinmarkt you needed to secure the equivalent territory in the United States—or in any other world where the same geographical location was up for grabs. That explained why the Wu family had been able to successfully murder a handful of Clan heads over the years, triggering and fueling the vicious civil war that had decimated the Clan between the nineteen-forties and the late nineteen-seventies. And their lack of the pattern required to world-walk to the United States explained why, in the long run, the Wu family had fallen so far behind their Clan cousins.

"There are a bunch of ways the knotwork might work," he'd tried to explain to the duke. "The fact that two different knots let us travel between two different worlds is interesting. And they're similar, which implies they're variations on a common theme. But does the knotwork specify two endpoints, in which case all a given knot can do is let you shuttle between two worlds, A and B—or does it define a vector relationship in a higher space? One that's quantized, and commutative, so if you start in universe A you always shuttle from A to B and back again, but if you transport it to C you can then use it to go between C and a new world, call it D?"

The duke had just blinked at him thoughtfully. "I'm not sure I understand. How will I explain this to the committee?"

Huw had to give it some thought. "Imagine an infinite chessboard. Each square on the board is a world. Now pick a piece—a knight, for example. You can move to another square, or reverse your move and go back to where you started from. That's what I mean by a quantized commutative transformation—you can only move in multiples of a single knight's move, your knight can't simply slide one square to the left or right, it's constrained. Now imagine our clan knotwork is a knight—and the Wu family's design is, um, a special kind of rook that can move exactly three squares in a straight line. You use the knight, then the rook: to get back to where you started you have to reverse your rook's move, then reverse the knight's move. But because they're different types of move, they don't go to the same places—and if you combine them, you can discover new places to go. An infinite number of new places."

"That is a very interesting theory. Test it. Find out if it's true. Then report to me." He raised a warning finger: "Try not to get yourself killed in the process."

The pizza crusts were cold and half the soda was drunk. It was mid-afternoon, and the house was cooling down now that the air-conditioning had been on for a while. Huw sat in the front room, staring at the laptop screen. According to the geographical database, the ground underfoot was about as stable as it came. There were no nearby rivers, no obvious escarpments with debris to slide down and block the approaches. He closed his eyes, trying to visualize what the area around the house might look like in a land bare of human habitation. "You guys ready yet?" he called.

"Nearly there." There was a clicking, rattling noise from the kitchen. Elena was tweaking her vicious little toy again. ("You're exploring: your job is to take measurements, look around, avoid being seen, and come right back. But if the worst happens, you aren't going to let anyone stop you coming back. Or leave any witnesses.")

"Ready." Hulius came in the door, combat boots thudding.

Huw glanced up. In his field camouflage, body armor, and helmet Hulius loomed like a rich survivalist who'd been turned loose in an army surplus store. "where's your telemetry pack?"

"In the kitchen. Where's your medical kit?"

Huw gestured at the side of the room. "Back porch." He slid the laptop aside carefully and stood up. "How's your blood pressure?"

"No problems with it, I'm not dizzy or anything."

"Good. Okay, so let's go . . ."

Huw found Elena in the kitchen at the back of the rental house. She had her telemetry belt on, and the headset, and had rigged the P90 in a tactical sling across her chest. "Ready?" he asked.

"I can't wait!" She bounced excitedly on her toes.

"Let me check your equipment first." She surrendered with ill grace to Huw's examination. "Okay, I'm switching it on now." He poked at the ruggedized PDA, then waited until the screen showed an off-kilter view of the back of his head. "Good, camera's working." He turned to Hulius. Gruffly: "Your turn now."

"Sure, dude." Hulius stood patiently while Huw hung the telemetry pack off his belt, under the big fanny pack of ration packs, drink cans, and survival tools. Hulius's was heavier, and included a Toughbook PC and a short-wave radio—unlike Elena he might be sticking around for a while.

"Got signal."

"Cool. I'm ready whenever you are."

"Okay, I'll meet you out back."

Huw headed for the front room to collect the big aid kit and the artist's portfolio, his head spinning. *Demo time. Right?* Nobody had done this before; not this well-organized, anyway. He felt a momentary stab of anxiety. *If we'd done this right, we'd have two evenly matched world-walkers, able to lift each other, not a line backer and a princess.* The failure modes scared him shitless if he stopped to think about them. Still, Yul and 'Lena were eager volunteers. That counted for something, didn't it?

The back door, opening off the kitchen, stood open, letting in a wave of humidity. Hulius and Elena stood in the overgrown yard, Elena facing Yul's back as he crouched down. "Ready?" called Huw.

"Yo!"

Huw placed the first aid kit carefully on the deck beside him, then unzipped the art portfolio. "Elena, you ready?"

"Whenever big boy here gets down on his knees."

"I didn't know you cared, babe—"

Huw stifled a tense grin. "You heard her. Piggyback up, I'm going to uncover in ten. Good luck, guys."

Hulius crouched down and Elena wrapped her arms around his chest from behind. He held his hands out and she carefully placed her feet in them. With a grunt of strain, he rose to his feet as Huw dropped the front cover of the folio, revealing the print within—carefully keeping it facing away from himself. "Go!"

He tripped the stopwatch, then put the folio down,

closing it. Heart hammering, he watched the yard, stopwatch in hand. Five seconds. Elena would be down and
looking around, a long, slow, scan, her headset capturing
the view. Ten seconds. The weather station on her belt
should be stabilizing, reading out the ambient temperature, pressure, and humidity. Fifteen seconds. Her first
scan ought to be complete, and the smart radio scanner
ought to be logging megabits of data per second, searching for signs of technology. If there were no immediate
threats she should be taking stock of Yul, making sure his
blood pressure was stable from the 'walk. Thirty seconds.
Huw began to feel a chilly sweat in the small of his back.
By now, Hulius should have planted a marker and be on
his way to the nearest cover, or would be digging in to
wait out the one-hour minimum period before he could
return. He'd have a bad headache right now—if he used
the one-hour waypoint he'd be in bed for twenty hour
hours afterwards, if not puking his guts up. Otherwise
he'd stay a while longer . . .

Fifty-five. Fifty-eight. Fifty-nine. Sixty. *Oh shit.* Sixty-
one. Sixty-two.

The scenery changed. Huw's heart was in his mouth
for a moment: then he managed to focus on Elena. She
was holding her hands out, thumbs-up in jubilation.
"Case green! Case green!"

Huw sat down heavily. *I think I'm going to be sick.* It
had been the longest minute of his life. "What happened?" he asked, his voice thick with tension: "Which
schedule is Yul running to?"

She climbed the steps to the rear stoop. Her submachine gun was missing. "Let's go inside, I need to take
some of this stuff off before I melt."

Huw held the door open for her with barely controlled
impatience. "What happened?" He demanded.

"Relax, it's all right, really." She began to unfasten her
helmet and Huw moved in hastily to unplug the camera.
It was beaded with moisture and he swore quietly when
he saw that the lens was fogged over.

"You need to remove the telemetry pack first, I need to get this downloaded."

"Oh all right then! Here's your blasted toy." For a moment she worked on her equipment belt fastenings, then held it up at arm's length with an expression of distaste. Huw grabbed it before she let it drop. "It's perfectly safe over there. A lot cooler than it is here, and there are trees everywhere—"

"What kind of trees?"

She shrugged vaguely. "Trees. Like in the Alps. Dark green, spiny things. Christmas tree trees. You want to know about trees? Send a tree professor."

"Okay. So it's cold and there are coniferous trees. Anything else?"

Elena laid her helmet on the kitchen worktop and began to unfasten her body armor. "It was raining and the rain was cold. We couldn't see very far, but it was quiet—not like over here."

Huw shook his head: *City girl.*

"Anyway, I checked over Yul and he said he felt fine and there was no sign of anybody, so I gave him the P90 and tripped back over. Whee!"

Huw managed to confine his response to a nod. "When is he coming back?"

"Uh, we agreed on case green. That means four hours, right?"

"Four hours." Elena laid her armor out on the kitchen table then began to unlace her combat boots. "Then we can break out the wine, yay!"

"I'll be in the front room," Huw muttered, cradling the telemetry belt. "Would you mind staying here and watching the back window for a few minutes? If you see anything at all, call me."

In the front room, Huw poked at the ruggedized PDA, switching off the logging program. He plugged it into the laptop to recharge and hotsync, then sighed. The video take would be a while downloading, but the portable weather station had its own display. He unplugged it from the PDA, flicked it on, and looked at the last reading. Temperature: 16 Celsius. Pressure: 1026 millibars. Relative humidity: 65%. "What the fuck?" He muttered to himself. Sixteen Celsius—sixty Fahrenheit—in Maryland, in August? With high pressure? That was the bit that didn't make sense. It was over ninety outside, with 1020 millibars. "It's twenty Celsius degrees colder over there? And the trees are conifers?"

The penny dropped. "No wonder nobody could use the Wu family knotwork up in Massachusetts—it's probably under half a mile of ice!"

"Hey, you talking to me?" Elena called from the kitchen.

Huw glanced at the laptop. "Be right back, buddy," he told it, then carefully put it down on the battered cargo case, picked up the brown paper bag with the wine, and walked back towards Elena to wait for Hulius's return.

It was afternoon, according to the baleful red lights on the small TV opposite Mike's bed. He blinked at it sleepily, feeling no particular inclination to reach out for the remote control that sat on the trolley beside his bed. The curtains were drawn across what he took for a window niche, and he was alone in the small hospital room with nothing for company but the TV, the usual clutter of spotlights and strange valves and switches on the wall behind his bed, and the plastic cocoon they'd wrapped his leg in. The cocoon— *it's like something out of* Alien, he thought dreamily. Drainage tubes ran from it to the side of the bed, and there was a trolley with some kind of gadget next to him, and a hose leading to his left wrist. A drip. That was it. *I'm on a drip. Therefore, I must be home. I drip, therefore I am.* The thought was preposterously funny in a distant, swirly kind of way. Come to think of it, all his thoughts seemed to be leaving vapor trails, bouncing off the inside of his skull in slow motion. His leg ached, distantly, but it was nothing important. *I'm home. Phone home. Maybe I should phone Mom and Pop? Let them know I'm all right.* No, that wouldn't work—Mom and Pop died years ago, in the car crash with Sue. *Forget it.* He managed to roll his eyes towards the table the TV stood on. There was no telephone. *Some hospital bedroom this is . . .*

He was too hot. Much too hot. He was wearing pajamas: that was it. Fumbling for the buttons with his right hand, he realized he was fatigued. It felt as if his arm was weak, a long way away. He managed to get a couple of buttons undone, just as the door opened.

"As you can see he's, oh my—"

"Mike? Can he hear me?"

"I'm too hot." It came out funny.

"I'm real sorry, Mr. Smith, but he's running a fever. We've got him on IV penicillin for the infection, and morphine—"

"Penicillin? Isn't that old-fashioned; I mean, aren't most bacteria resistant to it these days?"

"That's not what the path lab report says about this one, thank Jesus; you're right, most infections are resistant, but he's had the good fortune to pick up an old-fashioned one. So, like I was saying, he's on morphine, his leg's an almighty mess, and they used a whole lot of Valium on him last night so he wouldn't pull out his tubes."

"Mike?"

The voice was familiar, conjuring up images of a whirring hand exerciser, a tense expression. "Boss?"

"Mike? Did you try to say something?"

Lips are dry. He tried to nod.

"Ah, h—heck. Is it the Valium? Or the morphine?"

"He ought to be better in a couple of hours, Mr. Smith."

"Okay. You hang in there, Mike. I'll be right back."

The door closed on discussion, and the sound of footsteps walking away. Mike closed his eyes and tried to gather his thoughts. *In the hospital. Doped up. Leg hurts a little. Morphine? Colonel Smith. Got to talk to the colonel . . .*

An indefinite time later, Mike was awakened by the rattle of the door opening.

"Huh—hi, boss." The cotton wool wrapping seemed to

have gone away: he was still tired and a little fuzzy, but thinking didn't feel like wading through warm mud anymore. He struggled, trying to sit up. "Huh. Water."

There was a jug of water sitting on the bedside trolley, and a couple of disposable cups. Eric sat down on the side of the bed and filled a cup, then passed it to him carefully. "Can you manage that? Good."

"'S better." *What's the colonel wanting? Must be really anxious for news to be here himself* . . . He cleared his throat experimentally. "How . . . how long?"

"It's Sunday afternoon. You were dumped on our doorstep on Friday evening, two and a half days past your due date. Do you feel like talking, or do you need a bit more time?"

"More water. I'll talk. Is . . . is official debrief?"

"Yes, Mike. Fill me in and I promise to leave you alone to recover." Eric smiled tightly. "If you need anything, I'll see what I can sort out. Guess you're not going to be in the office for a while." He passed the refilled cup over and Mike drained it, then struggled to sit up.

"Here, let me—gotcha." The motorized bed whined. Colonel Smith placed a small voice recorder on the bedside table, the tape spool visibly rotating inside it. "That comfortable?"

"Y-yeah. You want to know what happened? Everything was on track until I got into the palace grounds. Then everything went to hell . . ."

For the next hour Mike described the events of the past week in minute detail, racking his brains for anything remotely relevant. Eric stopped him periodically to flip tape cassettes, then began to supply questions as Mike ran down. Mike held nothing back, his own ambiguous responses to Miriam notwithstanding. Finally, Eric switched the recorder off. "Off the record. Why did you tell her we'd play hardball? Did you think we were going to burn her? How did you think it's going to sound if we have to go to bat with an oversight committee to keep your ass out of jail?"

Mike reached towards the water again. He swallowed, his throat sore. "You should know: if you want to run HUMINT assets, you can't treat them like machines. They have to trust you—they *absolutely* have to trust you. So I gave her the unvarnished truth. If I'd spun her a line of bullshit, do you really think she'd have believed me? She knows me well enough to know when I'm lying."

Smith nodded. "Go on."

"Her situation is shitty enough that—hell, her mom said she's on the run—she's short on options. If I'd told her we'd welcome her with open arms she'd have smelled a rat, but this way she's going to carry on thinking about it, and then eventually start sniffing the bait. At which point, we can afford to play her straight, and she's starting with low expectations. Offer her a deal—she cooperates with us fully, we look after her—and you'll get her on board willingly. You'll also get leverage over her mother, who is still in place and in a position to tell us what the leadership is up to. But I think the most important thing is, you'll have a willing world-walker who will do what we want, and—I figure this is important—try to be helpful. I can't quantify that, but I figure there's probably stuff we don't know that a willing collaborator can call out for us, stuff a coerced subject or a non–world-walker would be useless for. If Doc James gets some crazy idea about turning her into a ghost detainee, we're not going to be able to do that, so I figured I'd start by lowering her expectations, then raise the temperature at the next contact."

"Plausible." Eric nodded again. "It's a plausible excuse."

Mike put the cup down. His throat felt sore. "Is this going to go to oversight?"

Eric was watching him guardedly. "Not unless we fuck up."

"Thought so." *Get your cynical head on, Mike.* "How do you meant to handle her, then?"

"We go on as planned." Eric looked thoughtful. "For what it's worth I agree with you. I had a run-in with

James over how we deal with contacts, and while he's a whole lot more political than I thought, he's also a realist. Beckstein isn't a career criminal, you're right about that side of things. Not that it'd be a problem to nail her on conspiracy charges, or even treason—the DoJ has a hard-on for anyone it can label as a terrorist, especially if they're collaborating with enemy governments to make war on the United States—but there's no need to bring out the big stick if we don't need it. If you can coax her into coming in willingly, I'll do my best to persuade James to reactivate one of the old Cold War defector programs. You can tell her that, next time you see her."

"Cold War defector program?"

"How do you think we used to handle KGB agents who wanted to come over? They'd worked for an enemy power, maybe did us serious damage, but you don't see many of them doing time in Club Fed, do you? You don't burn willing defectors, not if you want there to be more defectors in future. There were a couple of Eisenhower-era presidential directives to handle this kind of shit, and I think they're still in force. It's just a matter of working on James and figuring out what the correct protocol is."

"Okay, I think I see what you're getting at." Mike eased back against the pillows. "It fits with the timetable. The only problem is, she hasn't gotten back in touch this week, has she? Are you tapping my home telephone?"

"You know I can't tell you that." Eric looked irritated. "I'm not aware of any contact attempts, but I'll make inquiries. I'd be surprised if nobody was watching your apartment—or mine, for that matter—but that's not my call to make."

"Okay. Then can you tell me where I am? Or when I'm going to be let out of this place, or what the hell is happening to my leg in there?" Mike gestured loosely at the bulky plastic brace and the cocoon of dressings. "It's kind of disturbing . . ."

"Shit." Eric glanced away. "I don't know," he admitted. "I'll ask one of the medics to tell you. They told me was your leg was broken, got chewed up pretty badly—who the hell expected them to be using mantraps in this day and age?"

"It's not this day and age over there," Mike offered dryly.

Eric laughed, a brief bark: "Okay, you got me! Listen, I figure the medics should give you the full rundown. What they told me is that you'll be off your legs for a few weeks and you won't be running any marathons for the rest of this year, but you should make a full recovery. They were more worried about the infection you brought home, except it responds well to penicillin, of all things. Something about there being no antibiotic resistance in the sample they cultured . . . anyway. You're in a private wing of Northern Westchester. We've closed it off to make it look like it's under maintenance, the folks who're seeing you are all cleared, there are guards on the front desk, and as soon as you're ready to move we're going to send you home. Officially you're on medical leave for the next month, renewed as long as the doctors think necessary. Unofficially, once I confirm this with Dr. James, you're going to be on station waiting for Iris Beckstein to get in touch. You can call in backup if you see fit—even a full surveillance team and SWAT backup—but from what you're telling me, she's got tradecraft, which would make that a high-risk strategy. Think you're up to it?"

"I'll have to be." Mike reached for the water again. "What a mess."

"That's what you get when you go back to running agents." Eric stood up. "Enough of that, I've got to go type all this up." He frowned. "Be seeing you . . ."

BEGIN TRANSCRIPT:

(Coldly.) "You realize that if anyone else had done this, I'd have had them shot."

"Yes, dear: I was counting on it. This way, hopefully the auld bitches won't be expecting it."

"Sky Father, give me patience! What did you think you were playing at? We've got a war on, in case you hadn't noticed—"

"Oh, really? And I suppose the sky is a funny non-red color, too? I'm not playing, I'm deadly serious: this is more important than your little war."

"Damn it, woman! Can't you leave your mother's embroidery circle alone just this once?"

(Exasperated sigh.) "Who exactly do you think it was that started the war, brother?"

"What—excuse me. You can't be serious. Do you really expect me to believe that she's in cahoots with Egon?"

"Absolutely not! It would be beneath her dignity to be in cahoots with anyone below the rank of the Romish Pope-Emperor. But you know, she's always been opposed to the idea of marrying into the royal family, hasn't she? 'Marrying beneath our station,' indeed. She set up this stupid business with Creon by way of Henryk, in order to provoke Egon. And really, do you believe for a moment that Egon was a real threat to us, absent her maneuvering? She set Helge up as a target while she had me under her proxy's thumb in Niejwein. If she hadn't overreached herself I'd still be stuck there."

"That's . . . curiously plausible. Hmm. You said she overreached herself. Do you mean Hildegarde didn't expect Egon to mount the putsch then and there?"

"I doubt it." (Pause.) "She wouldn't have shown her precious nose at the betrothal if she thought it was going to be cut off by the hussars, would she? But her intent was there. I know her schemes, the way her mind works. I think she meant to provoke Egon into doing something stupid, like the way he poisoned his younger brother all those years ago. She doesn't like Helge, as you might have noticed. After what she did to her sister, do you question her ruthlessness?"

"All right." (Pause.) "Your mother's embroidery circle dabbles in dangerous waters, and it is a bad idea to cross them. They've stirred up a third of the nobility against us and Egon's raiders are harrowing the countryside with fire and the sword—at least until we force him to group his army so that we can crush it beneath our boot-heel. As we shall, when the time comes, and make no mistake—they have carronades and musketry, but we have machine guns and radios. But, still. You have not yet explained why you did that thing. You'd best try to explain it to me, and get your story straight—the council will be a much less receptive audience, sister."

"Alright. You're not going to like it, though. Between your incredibly foolish machinations and mother-dearest's scheming, I've nearly lost my only child. That's not all I've lost, I'll concede, but unlike some of our relatives, I hold her dear. If I can get her back, I will move heavens and underworld to do so. That's the first thing I'd like to remind you of. The second point is—and this had better not be advanced before the council, or we are all lost beyond redemption—your niece knows about the insurance policy, but thanks to Henryk's stupidity and mother-dearest's venality, she's on the outside. If you'd told me what bait you'd used on her, I could have settled things, but oh no—"

"Henryk's men got to her first. He knows—knew—too, you understand that?"

"I've never understood why any of the old assholes should be allowed near the breeding program—"

"Stop and think about it. If we didn't at least let them observe, they'd have to assume it's a conspiracy against them. (As indeed it is, but not in such crude terms.) Henryk's participation was vital, to prevent a new civil war."

"Still. It's a delicate matter, you used it as a carrot for Helge to get her teeth into, then you complain when the other donkey in the stable bites her?"

"Enough. We can discuss might-have-beens some other time. But what of the American spy?"

"If you must. When I found out who he was—at first he was an 'injured clansman,' you should remember—my first thought was to hang him from the nearest available tree: but it turned out he'd already spoken to her. It was too late."

"Sky Father, you mean—"

"He was sent here to 'talk to Miriam.' He didn't know where she'd gone after the battle—my guess is, with a Wu family locket, she's somewhere in New Britain right now—but that's not the point. She spoke to him. Let me assure you that hanging her ex-boyfriend would be exactly the most effective way to make her turn traitor. She grew up in America, remember. In my opinion, the least damaging option was to spin him a line of disinformation, let his leg fester a bit, then send him back. If we're really lucky, we've got ourselves a back channel all the way to the White House. And if not—well, let's just say, whoever debriefs him is going to get a usefully skewed view of our politics."

(Pause.) "That will probably keep the council from demanding your head."

"I know." (Pause.) "Now let me draw you a diagram. The Americans have captured world-walkers and worked out how to make them serve. That means they know what they're dealing with. Helge—being Miriam—is on the run, she knows about the breeding program, and one of their agents has already tried to seduce her. Why haven't you tried to kill her?"

"She's my niece. You are not the only one who feels some residual loyalty, Patricia."

"Rubbish. There's another reason, isn't there? Is it something she knows? No? Oh. Something she did, no—the betrothal?"

"Henryk wanted to ensure a fruitful marriage. He was in a hurry. He sent Dr. ven Hjalmar to see to her."

"Tell me you didn't . . ."

"*I* didn't. *Henryk* did. With the queen mother's connivance, of course. That's the point, you see. It's going to be a world-walker."

"Oh no!"

"Oh yes. It was always going to be a very short betrothal, just long enough for the pregnancy test to be confirmed. And, do you know something? Once we've put down the pretender, all the surviving witnesses who were present at the palace will swear that it was, in fact, a lawful marriage ceremony, not just a betrothal."

"Holy mother of snakes! You're telling me that with Egon out of the picture, she's carrying the lawful heir to the throne?"

"Yes. You did ask why I hadn't issued a death warrant, didn't you?"

(Pause.) "Angbard, I've really got to hand it to you: that is the most crazy, fucked-up, Machiavellian conspiracy I've heard of since Watergate." (Pause.) "Does Hildegarde know?"

(Pause.) "You know, I really hadn't thought about that."

"Because as soon as she finds out, she's going to hit the roof." (Pause.) "Who did you send after Helge?"

"I sent Lady Brilliana after her. She's to stop Helge if she shows signs of turning traitor—beyond that, she's to try to bring her home. Ideally before the pregnancy goes too far."

"Brilliana? That's a good choice. Might even be enough, if we're lucky."

"Enough? I hardly think Helge will be able to prevent her—"

"I meant, enough to stop the auld bitches' assassins. If you'll excuse me, Angbard, I have urgent arrangements to make. Is the prescription I asked for ready yet?"

"It's in the outer office."

(Chuckle.) "So you weren't planning to kill me after all! Admit it!"

"Don't tempt me. You believe Hildegarde will try to kill Helge?"

"Who said anything about Hildegarde? She'll be pissed about me having a granddaughter to call my own, especially one who's an heir and a world-walker, but it's still her lineage. No, what you've really got to worry about are the other members of the old ladies' embroidery circle and poisoning society. Hmm. Then again, Helge thinking she's Miriam—thinking she's an American woman—could really spoil all your plans."

"I hardly think that changes anything—"

"Really? You're telling me you've never heard of *Roe v. Wade?*"

(Pause.) "Who?"

END TRANSCRIPT

Miriam found the journey uncomfortable. It wasn't the compartment, for the seats were padded and the facilities adequate, but the lack of privacy. Of the eight places—there were two bench seats that faced each other across the compartment—she and Erasmus occupied one side. The other was taken by the plump man in the loud coat, sitting beside the window, and a pinch-faced woman of uncertain years who clutched her valise to her lap, her long fingers as double-jointed as the legs of a crane fly. When she wasn't flickering suspicious glances at the fellow in the check jacket, she parked her watery gaze on a spot fifteen centimeters behind Miriam's head. Whenever the discomfort of being stared at got the better of her, Miriam tried to stare right back—but the sight of the woman's stringy, gray hair sticking out from under the rim of her bonnet made her feel queasy.

It was also hot. Air-conditioning was an exotic, ammonia-powered rarity, as likely to poison you as to quell the heat. A vent on the ceiling channeled fresh air down through the compartment while the train was moving, but it was a muggy, humid day and before long she felt sticky and uncomfortable. "We should have waited for the express," she murmured to Erasmus, provoking a glare from Crane Fly Woman.

"It arrives a few minutes later." He sighed. "Can't be late for work, can I?" He put a slight edge on his voice, a grating whine, and caught her eye with a sidelong glance. The fat man rattled his newspaper again. He seemed to be concentrating on a word puzzle distantly related to a crossword, making notes in the margin with a pencil.

"Never late for work, you." She tried to sound disapproving, to provide the shrewish counterpart to his henpecked act. *What's going on?* She sniffed, and glanced out of the window at the passing countryside. *Where did Erasmus go last night? Why were those guys tailing us? Was it him or me they were after?* The urge to ask him about the incident was a near-irresistible itch, but one glance at the fellow travelers told her that any words they exchanged would be eavesdropped on and analyzed with vindictive, exhaustive curiosity.

Luckily, things improved after an hour. The train stopped at Bridgeport for ten minutes—a necessity, for only the first-class carriages had toilets—and as she stretched her legs on the platform, Erasmus murmured: "The next compartment along is unoccupied. Shall we move?"

As the train moved off, Miriam kicked back at last, leaning against the wooden paneling beside the window. "What was that about? At the station." She prodded idly at an abandoned newspaper on the bench seat opposite.

Erasmus looked at her from across the compartment. "I had to see a man last night. It seems somebody wanted to know who he was talking to, badly enough to set up a watch on the hotel and tail all his contacts. They got slack: I spotted a watcher when I opened the curtains."

"Why didn't they just move in and arrest you?"

"You ask excellent questions." Erasmus looked worried. "It might be that if they were Polis, they didn't want to risk a poison pill. You can interrogate people, but they won't always tell you what you want to know, and if they do, it may come too late. If you take six hours out to break a man, by the time you get him to spill his guts his own people will have worked out that he's been taken, and they won't be home when you go looking for them."

"Oh." Her voice was very small. *Shouldn't you have*

been expecting this? She asked herself. Then she looked back at his eyes. "There's more, isn't there?"

He nodded, reluctantly. "They didn't smell like Polis." His expression was troubled. "There was something wrong about them. They looked like street thugs, backstairs men, the kind your, ah, business rivals employed." The Wu family's street fixers, in other words. "The Polis aren't afraid to raise a hue and cry when their quarry breaks cover. And the way they covered us was odd."

She glanced down at the floor. "It's possible it's not you they're looking for," she murmured. *I should have thought of this earlier: they know Erasmus is my friend, why wouldn't they be watching him? They're probably watching Paulette, too*—her business agent in Boston, back home in the world of airliners and antibiotics—*I'm a trouble magnet.* "Hair dye and a cover identity may not be enough."

"Explain." He leaned forward.

"Suppose someone in Boston spotted you leaving in a hurry, a day or two after I'd disappeared. They handed off to associates in New London. Either they followed you to your hotel, or they figured you'd pay for a room under your own name. They missed a trick; they probably thought you were visiting a brothel for the usual reason—" Were his ears turning red? "—but when you reappeared with a woman they knew they'd found the trail. We threw them with the streetcar, and then I turned up at the hotel separately and in disguise, but they picked us up again on the way into the station and if we hadn't done the track side scramble they'd be—" Her eyes widened.

"What is it?"

"We'll have to be really careful if we go back to Boston."

"You think they're looking for you, yes?"

"Well—" Miriam paused. "I'm not sure. It could be the Polis tailing you. But if they were doing that, why wouldn't they turn over Lady Bishop's operation? I think it's more likely someone who decided you might lead them to me. In which case it could be nearly anyone. The cousins in this world, maybe. Or it could be the Polis looking for *me*, although I figure that's unlikely. Or it could be the Clan, in which case the question is, which faction is it? It's not as if—"

"The Clan factions would be a problem?"

"Yes." She nodded. "I've been thinking about it. Even if, *if,* I wanted to go back, I'd have to approach it really carefully. A random pickup could be disastrous. I need to get in touch with them or they'll think I've gone over the wall, and that's—I don't want to spend the rest of my life hiding from assassins. But I've got to get in touch with the right people there, see if I can cut some kind of deal. I've got information they need, so I might be able to work something out—but I don't trust that slimy shit Morgan who they put in charge of the Boston office."

Erasmus shrugged. "But they've lost us, haven't they? They can't possibly overtake us before—"

"You're wrong. They've got two-way radios better than anything the Royal Post can build. If it *is* Clan security, they'll have us in the Gruinmarkt before we get off the platform."

Erasmus nodded thoughtfully. "Then we won't be on this train when it arrives, will we?" He reached into his valise and pulled out a dog-eared gazetteer. "Let's see. If we get off at Hartford, the next stopping train is forty-two minutes behind us. If we catch that one, we can get off at Framingham and take the milk train into Cambridge, then hail a cab. We'll be a couple of hours later getting home, but if we do our business fast we can make the express, and we won't be going through the city station. You know about the back route into the cellar. Do you think your stalkers know about it?"

Miriam blotted at her forehead. "Olga would. But she's not who I'm worried about. You're right, if we do it your way, we can probably get around them." She managed a strained smile. "I really don't need this. I don't like being chased."

"It won't be for long. Once we're on the transcontinental, there's no way they'll be able to trace us."

The shadows were lengthening and deepening, and the omnipresent creaking of cicadas provided an alien chorus as Huw sat in the folding chair on the back stoop, waiting for Hulius. Elena had installed her boom box in the kitchen, and it was pumping out plastic girl-band pop from the window ledge. But she'd gone upstairs to powder her nose, leaving Huw alone with the anxiety gnawing at his guts like a family of hungry rats. For the first hour or so he'd tried working on the laptop, chewing away at the report on research methodologies he was writing for his grace, but it was hard to concentrate while he couldn't stop imagining Yul out there in the chilly twilit pine forest, alone and in every imaginable permutation of jeopardy. *You put him there,* Huw's conscience kept reminding him: *You ought to be there instead.*

Well yes, he'd tell his conscience—which he liked to imagine was a loosely knit sock-puppet in grime-stained violet yarn, with webcams for eyes—*but you know what would happen. I don't have Yul's training. And Yul doesn't have the background to run this project if anything happened to me.* It sounded weak to his ears, even though it was true. He'd known Yul back when he'd been a towheaded blond streak of mischief, running wild through the forest back of Osthalle keep with a child's bow and a belt of rabbit scalps to show for it—and Huw had been a skinny, sickly, bookish boy, looked down on pityingly by his father and his hale, hunting-obsessed armsmen. The duke's visit changed all that, even though the intensive English tuition and the bewildering shift to a boarding school in the United States hadn't felt like much of an improvement at the time. It wasn't until years later, when he returned to his father's keep and went riding with Yul again, that he understood. Yul was a woodland creature, not in an elfin or fey sense, but like a wild boar: strong, dangerous, and shrewd within the limits of his vision. But not a dreamer or a thinker.

Yul had gone to school, too, and there'd even been talk of his enlisting in the U.S. Marine Corps for a while—the duke's security apparatus had more than a little use for graduates of that particular finishing school—but in the end it came to naught. While Huw had been sweating over books or a hot soldering iron, Hulius had enlisted in Clan security, with time off to serve his corvee duty with the postal service. And now, by a strange turnaround of fate that Huw still didn't quite understand, he was sitting with a first-aid kit on the back stoop of a rented house at twilight, worrying his guts out about his kid brother, the tow-headed streak who'd grown up to be a bear of a man.

Huw checked his wristwatch for about the ten-thousandth time. It was coming up on eight fifteen, and the sun was already below the horizon. Another half hour and it would be nighttime proper. *I could go over and look for him,* he told himself. *If he misses this return window, I could go over tomorrow.* Elena's video footage had been rubbish, the condensation on her helmet camera lens blurring everything into a madcap smear of dark green shade and glaring sunlight, but Hulius was wearing a radio beacon. If anything had happened—

Something moved. Huw's head jerked round, his heart in his mouth for an instant: then he recognized Yul's tired stance, and the tension erupted up from his guts and out of his mouth in a deafening whoop.

"Hey, bro!" Yul reached up and unfastened his helmet. "You look like you thought I wasn't coming back!" He grimaced and rubbed his forehead as he shambled heavily towards the steps. "Give me medicine. Strong medicine."

Huw grabbed him for a moment of back-slapping relief. "It's not easy, waiting for you. Are you alright? Did anything try to eat you? Let's get you inside and get the telemetry pack off you, then I'll crack open the wine."

"Okay." Hulius stood swaying on the stoop for a mo-

ment, then took a heavy step towards the doorway. Huw
picked up the first aid kit and laptop and hurried after him.

"Make your weapons safe, then hand me the telemetry
pack first—okay. Now your backpack. Stick it there, in
the corner." He squinted at his brother. Yul looked much
more wobbly than he ought to be. "Hmm." Huw cracked
the first-aid kit and pulled out the blood pressure cuff.
"Get your armor off and let's check you out. How's the
headache?"

"Splitting." Hulius pawed at the Velcro fastenings on
his armor vest, then dumped it on the kitchen floor. He
fumbled at the buttons on his jacket. "I can't seem to get
this open."

"Let me." Huw freed the buttons then helped Hulius get
one arm free of its sleeve. "Blood pressure, *right now.*"

"Aw, nuts. You don't think—"

"I don't know what to think. Chill out and try to relax
your arm." The control unit buzzed and chugged, pumping air into the pressure cuff around Yul's arm. Huw
stared at it as it vented, until the digits came up. "One
seventy four over one ten." *Shit.* "You remember to take
your second-stage shots on time, two hours ago?"

"Uh, I, uh, only remembered half an hour ago." Hulius
closed his eyes. "Dumb, huh?"

Huw relaxed a little. "Real dumb. You're not used to
doing back-to-back jumps, are you?" *Lightning Child, he
could have sprung a cerebral hemorrhage!* "The really
bad headache, that's a symptom. You need those pills.
They take about an hour to have any effect, though, and if
you walk too soon after you take them you can make
yourself very ill."

"It's just a headache—"

"Headache, balls." Huw began to pack up the blood
pressure monitor. "All you can feel is the headache, but if
your blood pressure goes too high the arteries and veins
inside your brain can burst from it. You don't want that to
happen, bro, not at your age!" Relief was making him angry. *Change the subject.* "So how was it?"

"Oh, it was quiet, bro. I didn't see any animals. Funny thing, I didn't hear any birds either; it was just me and the trees and stuff. Quite relaxing, after a while."

"Okay, so you had a nice relaxing stroll in the woods." *Why needle him? It's not his fault you were chewing your guts out.* "Sorry." He glanced away from Hulius just as the door opened and Elena bounced in.

"Hulius! You're back! *Squeee!*"

Huw winced as Elena pounced on his brother. Judging from the noises he made, the headache couldn't be too serious. Huw cleared his throat: "I'll be in the front room, downloading the take. You guys, you've got ten minutes to wash up. We're going out for dinner, and I'm buying." He picked up the telemetry pack and slunk towards the living room, trying to ignore the giggling and smooching behind him. *Young love*—he winced again. He might be out from under the matrons' collective thumb, but being expected to chaperon Hulius and Elena was one of the more unpleasant side effects of the manpower shortage. *If the worst happened . . . At least they're both inner family, and eligible.* A rapid wedding was a far more likely outcome than an honor killing if their affair came to light.

Back in the front room, he set the tablet PC down and plugged it in. Yul's camera had worked out okay, although there wasn't a hell of a lot to see. He'd come out in a forested area, with nothing but trees in all directions, and spent the next hours stooging around semi-aimlessly without ever coming across open ground. The weather station telemetry told its own story, though. Sixty degrees Fahrenheit had been the daytime peak temperature, and towards nightfall it dipped towards freezing. *I bet there's going to be a frost over there tonight.*

Huw poked at the other instrument readings. The scanner drew a blank; nobody was transmitting, at least on any wavelength known to the sophisticated software-directed radio he'd acquired from a friend who was still working at the Media Lab. The compact air sampler wouldn't tell him much until he could send it for analysis—much as he might want one, nobody was selling a backpack-sized mass spectroscope. He poked at the video, tripping it into fast-forward.

Trees. More trees. Elena hadn't been wrong about the tree surplus. *If we could figure out a way to get them back, we could corner the world market in cheap pine logs . . .* Yul had followed the plan at first, zipping around in a quick search then planting a spike and a radio beacon. Then he'd hunkered down for a while, probably listening. After about half an hour, he'd gotten up and begun walking around the forest, frequently pausing to scrape a marker on a trunk. *Good boy.* Then—

"Oh you have *got* to be kidding me."

Huw hit the pause button, backed up a few frames, and zoomed in. Yul had been looking at the ground, which lay on a gentle slope. There were trees everywhere, but for once there was a view of the ground the trees were growing in. For the most part it was a brownish carpet of dead pine needles and ferns, interspersed with the few hardy plants that could grow in the shadow of the coniferous forest— but the gray-black chunks of rocky material off to one side told a different story. Huw blinked in surprise, then glanced away, his mind churning with possibilities. Then he bounced forward through the next half hour of Hulius's perambulations, looking for other signs. Finally, he put the laptop down, stood up, and went back into the hall.

"Yul?" he called.

"Hello?" A door opened, somewhere upstairs.

"Why didn't you tell me about the ruins, Yul?"

Hulius appeared at the top of the staircase, wearing a towel around his waist, long blond hair hanging damply: "what ruins?"

"The black stones in the forest. Those ruins."

"What stones—" Yul looked blank for a moment, then his expression cleared. "Oh, *those*. Are they important?"

"Are they—" Huw tugged at his hair distractedly. "Lightning Child! Do I have to explain everything in words of one syllable? Where's Elena?"

"She's in the—hey, what's up?"

I'm hyperventilating again. Stop it, Huw told himself. Not that it seemed to help much. "There's no radio, it's really cold, and you stumbled across a fucking road! Or what's left of one. Not a dirt track or cobblestones, but asphalt! Do I have to do all the thinking around here?"

"What's so special about asphalt?" Hulius asked, hitching up his towel as he came downstairs.

"What's so special? Well, maybe it means there was a civilization there not so long ago!" Nervous energy had Huw bouncing up and down on the balls of his feet. "Think, bro. If there was a civilization there, what else does it mean?"

"There were people there?" Hulius perked up. "Hey, I think that rates at least a bottle of wine . . ."

"We're going back over, tomorrow," Huw said bluntly. "I'll e-mail a report to the duke tonight. Then we're going to double-check on that road and see where it leads."

9

PURSUIT

The small house hunkered a short way back from the sidewalk, one of a row of houses in an area that wasn't exactly cheap—nowhere in Boston was cheap—but that had once been affordable for ordinary working people. Brilliana knew it quite well. She'd been watching it discreetly for over an hour, and she was pretty sure that nobody was home and, more important, nobody else was watching it. Which suited her just fine, because if it was under surveillance what she was about to do would quite possibly get her killed.

Swallowing to clear her over-dry mouth, Brill opened the car door and stepped out into the hot summer sunlight. She slung the oversized leather handbag on her left shoulder, discreetly checking that she could get a hand into it in a hurry, then let the door of the rental car swing shut. The key was in the ignition: the risk of someone stealing the car was, in her view, minor compared to the risk of not being able to get away fast if things went wrong.

The road was clear. She glanced both ways before crossing it, a final check for concealed watchers. *I hope Paulie's all right,* she fretted. The ominous turn of recent events was bad enough for those who could look after themselves. Paulette wasn't a player, and didn't have the wherewithal to escape if things spun out of control. And Brill owed her. Not that she'd had much time to demonstrate it, lately—the past week had run her ragged, and this was the first free day she'd had to spend in the United States for weeks.

She paused for a moment at the front door, straining for any sign of wrongness, then shrugged. The key slid into the lock and turned smoothly: Brill let herself inside, then closed the door behind her. "Paulie?" She called softly.

No reply. The house felt empty. Brill began to relax. *She's shopping, or at work.* Whatever "work" meant these days—Brill couldn't be sure, but the huge mess that Miriam had landed in had probably cut Paulie loose from her sinecure. She glanced around the living room. The flat-screen TV was new, but the furniture was the same. *Yo, big spender!* Paulette wasn't stupid about money. She kept a low profile. Hopefully she'd avoided being caught up in the dragnet so far.

Brill put her bag down on the kitchen counter and pulled out a black box. Switching it on, she paced out the ground floor rooms, front to back, checking corners and walls and especially light fittings. The bug detector stayed stubbornly green-lit. "Good," she said aloud as she stashed it back in the bag. Next, she pulled out another box equipped with a telephone socket and extension cable, and plugged each of the phone handsets into it in order. A twitter of dialing tones, but the speaker on the box stayed silent: nobody had sneaked an infinity bug onto her landline. That left the Internet link, and Brill didn't know enough about that to be sure she could sweep Paulie's computer for spyware; but she was pretty sure that unplugged PCs didn't snoop on conversations.

"Okay . . ." Brill picked up her bag and scouted the top floor briefly, then returned to the kitchen. The carton of half-and-half in the fridge was fresh, and there was a neat pile of unopened mail on the tabletop, the most recent postmarked the day before. And there was no dust. She checked her watch: ten past four. *Might as well wait,* she thought, and began to set up the coffee machine.

An hour later, Brill heard footsteps on the front path, and a rattle of keys. She dropped her magazine and stood up silently, standing just inside the living room door as the front door opened. One person, alone. She tensed for a moment, then recognized Paulette. "Hey, Paulie," she called.

"What!" A clatter of dropped bags. Brill stepped into the passageway. "Brill! How did you—"

Brill raised a finger to her lips. Paulette glared at her, then bent down to pick up the spilled grocery bags. "Let me," Brill murmured. "Shut the door." She gathered the bags: Paulette didn't need prompting twice, and locked the front door before turning back to stare at her, hands on hips.

"What do you want?"

Brilliana shrugged apologetically. "To talk to you. Do you have a cellular telephone?"

"Yes." Paulie's hand tightened on her handbag.

"Please switch it off and remove the battery."

"But—" Paulie looked round once, then shook her head. "Like that, is it?" she asked, then reached into her bag and pulled out a phone. "What happens next?" Brilliana waited. After a moment Paulette slid the battery out of the phone. "Is that what you wanted?"

Brill nodded. "Thank you. I'd already swept your house for bugs. Would you like a coffee? I'm afraid I've been here a while, it's probably stale, but I could make some more—"

Paulette managed a brief chuckle of laughter. "You slay me, kid."

"No, never." Brill managed a wan smile. "I apologize

for breaking in. But I had to check that you weren't under observation."

"Observation—" Paulette frowned "—why do I get the feeling I'm not going to like this?"

"Because." Brill took a deep breath: "You're not going to like it. Before I say any more—when did you last see Miriam?"

"Shit, kid." For a moment Paulette's face twisted in pain. "She's in trouble, isn't she?"

"When did you last see her?" Brilliana repeated.

"Must be, let me see . . . about three months ago. We did lunch. Why?" Her expression was guarded.

Brill sighed. "You're right, she's in trouble. The good news is, I've been ordered to get her out of it. The duke thinks it can be papered over, if she cooperates. I can't promise you anything, but if you happen to see her, if you could make sure that's the first thing you tell her . . . ?"

Paulie frowned. "I'm telling you the truth."

"I know that," Brill said quietly. "Not everybody would choose to believe you, though. They'd want to believe you're protecting her. She's missing, Paulie. Nobody's seen her for a week, and we're pretty sure she's on the run. I'm talking to you because I figure if she makes it over here you're one of the first people she'll turn to for help—"

"What do you mean, if?"

"It is a long story." Brill pulled out one of the kitchen chairs and sat down. "I know part of it. I think you know another part of it?" She raised an eyebrow, but Paulette stared at her mulishly and refused to answer. "All right. Three months ago, Miriam did something really foolish. She stole some information about a project she was not supposed to know of, and then she tried to bluff her way into it. It's a Clan operation on this side, that's all I'm allowed to say, and she tampered with the Clan's postal service—that alone is a high crime. To make matters worse, she was caught by the wrong person, a conservative member of the council's security oversight board.

What Miriam did, that sort of thing—" she shrugged uncomfortably "—carries the death penalty. I'm not exaggerating. Sneaking into that particular operation—" She stopped. "You know the one I'm talking about?"

Paulie nodded once, sharply. "She told me what she was going to do. I tried to talk her out of it, but she wasn't listening."

Brilliana rolled her eyes. "I am going to pretend I didn't hear what you just said, because if I had heard you say it, certain superiors of mine would want to know why I didn't kill you on the spot."

"Ah—" Paulette's face paled. "Thanks, I think."

"No problem. Just remember, those are the stakes. Don't let anyone else know that you know." Brill gestured at the coffee machine. "Shall I refill it? This may take some time."

"Be my guest." There was no trace of irony in Paulette's voice. "You meant that. About the Clan's involvement in a fertility clinic being so secret people can be killed out of hand for knowing about it?"

Brill stood up and walked over to the coffee machine. "Yes, Paulie, I am absolutely serious. The project the center is working on is either going to change the structure of the Clan completely, and for the better—or it will trigger a civil war. What's more, the authorities here are now aware of the Clan's existence. There have been disturbing signs of covert operations . . . If they discover what has been happening at the clinic, we can't be certain how they will respond, but the worst case is that several thousand innocent teenagers and their parents will find themselves on a one-way trip down the rabbit hole." She finished with the coffeemaker and switched it on.

"I find that hard—"

"What do you think the clinic's doing?" Brill demanded.

"What?" Paulette shook her head. "It's a fertility clinic, isn't it? It helps people have babies. Artificial insemination, that kind of . . ." she trailed off.

"Yup," Brill said lightly. "And they've been helping

couples have children for nearly twenty years now. The fact that the children just happen to be de facto outer family members, carriers of the world-walking trait, is an extra. The clinic is still helping couples who're desperate to have children." She looked down at the table. "Half of the children are female. In due course, some of them will be getting letters from a surrogacy agency, offering them good money for the use of their wombs. And they'll be helping other couples have children, too. Children who will be world-walkers. And when they grow up, they'll get a very special job offer."

Paulette nodded slowly. "I'd gotten that much."

"About twenty years from now, the Clan's going to have to absorb a thousand Miriams, and their male counterparts. They'll all crop up at once, over about a decade. A torrent of world-walkers. At the peak of our power, before the civil war, there were less than ten thousand of us; now, I'm not sure, but I think only a couple of thousand, at most. Think what that change means. One of the reasons everyone has been bearing down on Miriam is that she's, she's a *prototype*, if you like. Raised outside the Clan. Not uncivilized, but she thinks like an American. They all want to see how—if—she can be integrated. If she's going to fit in. If Miriam can learn to be part of the Clan, then so can the children. But if not . . . in fifty years time they could be a majority of our members. And the established elders will not willingly give up their power, or that of their children, in favor of uncivilized upstarts. Think what Miriam is going to do to their lives, if she makes a mess of things now!" Brill stopped abruptly. Her shoulders were shaking.

"What's it to you?" Paulie demanded. She stared at Brilliana for a few seconds, then jammed her fist across her mouth. "Oh. Oh shit. I'm sorry. I didn't realize."

"Not your fault. My mother had . . . difficulties. Around the time the clinic was being set up. Angbard proposed to my father that he and my mother . . ."

"Oh. Oh dear."

"My father has *issues*," Brill said bitterly. "I believe that is the accepted euphemism. Over here, it's easy enough to say 'test tube baby.'" Over there . . ." She lapsed into silence as the coffee machine began to burble and spit. "In any case. To the matter in hand: Miriam stuck her nose into sensitive business—making life much harsher for people she has never met—and was imprisoned, under house arrest. Baron Henryk decided to see if he could domesticate her, using the stick alongside the carrot."

"What kind of carrot? And stick?"

"He promised not to execute her, if she married the King's younger son, the Idiot. She agreed—reluctantly. And to ensure the succession, he arranged for artificial insem—are you all right, my lady?"

Paulette finished coughing. "Bastards." She stared at Brill blearily. "The bastard. He did *that*?"

Brill shrugged. "Evidently. He didn't tell Angbard: this all came to light later, by which time it was too late. There was a betrothal ceremony, to be followed by a wedding at the palace. Egon—the Idiot's elder brother—got wind of it, and realized he would be a liability once the younger brother's wife bore a child, so he—"

"Hang on, this is the crown prince we're talking about? Why would his younger brother's offspring be a threat?"

"Creon might be damaged, but he's outer family. There's a test. The clinic only developed it in the past two years. Egon is not even outer family, he is merely royalty. Obviously, he was afraid that once a royal Clan member was to hand, he might suffer an unfortunate hunting accident. So he contrived an explosion in the great hall and proceeded to kill his father, usurp the throne, and start a civil war in the Gruinmarkt. In the middle of all this, Miriam disappeared. She is either here, or in New Britain. I have agents searching for her over there, and over here—"she shrugged again"—I thought she'd come to you if she was in trouble."

"Oh sweet Mary, mother of God . . ." The coffeemaker spluttered and hissed as Paulette stood up and shuffled over to it. She pulled two mugs down from the cupboard: "How do you take yours? White, no sugar, isn't it?"

"Yes, please." Brill waited while Paulette filled the mugs and carried them over to the table. Finally she said, in a small voice, "Her plight is perilous."

Paulette froze for a few seconds. "I seem to recall you said this was good news. Is there anything worse?"

"Oh, plenty." Brill picked up her mug. "Your government knows about us now. We have reason to believe they know Miriam is connected to us, too. They obviously don't know about you yet, because they haven't dragged you off to a secret underground detention facility. Hopefully they won't notice you—they are tracing the Clan courier routes, which you have never been connected with—but if she shows up on your doorstep, there is a chance they will follow her and find you." She reached into her handbag and pulled out a business card case. "Here's my mobile number. If Miriam shows up, ring me at once. If I'm not there, the phone will be answered by a trusted associate. Tell them the word *bolt-hole*. You will remember that?"

"Bolt-hole." Paulette licked her lips.

"They'll tell you where to go and what to do. From that moment on, we will ensure your security. Once we've got Miriam back, if you want to go home we'll make sure it's safe to do so." She paused. Paulette was staring at something on the table. Following her gaze, Brill noticed her handbag was gaping. "Oh. I am sorry." She reached across and flipped it shut.

"You're carrying. Concealed."

"Yes." Brill met her gaze evenly. "It's not meant for you."

"Why—" Paulette stopped for a moment. "Why don't you shoot me? If there's such a security risk? Surely I know too much?"

"I don't believe you know anything that could jeopardize our security. The breeding program is being moved:

the patient records are already in a safe location while a new clinic is set up. So, strictly speaking, you can't actually harm us. Besides." She pulled up a wan grin: "I try not to kill my friends."

Paulette chuckled weakly. After a moment, Brill joined in. *Especially when the friend in question is one of the two people who Miriam is most likely to go to for help,* she added silently, and resolved to check back on what progress her employees had made with the other one as soon as possible.

Things in New Britain had clearly gone to hell in a hand-basket while she'd been away, but Miriam's first intimation that they might have more personal consequences for her came from the set of Erasmus's shoulders as the streetcar rumbled and clanked past the end of the street.

"What is it?" she asked, as he raised his newspaper to shield his face from the window.

"We're getting off at the next stop," he said, standing up to ring the bell. The streetcar turned a corner, wheels screeching on their track, and began to slow. "Come on."

Miriam followed him out onto the high street's sidewalk. "Something's wrong, isn't it?"

"The shop's under surveillance." His expression was grim.

"I see." They walked past a post box.

"I'm going back there, by the back alley." He reached into an inner pocket and passed her a small envelope. "You might want to wait in the tearoom up New Bridge Way. If I don't reappear within half an hour—"

"I've got a better idea," she interrupted. "I'm going first. If there's someone inside—"

"It's too—"

"No, Erasmus, going in on your own is the dumbest thing you can do. Come on, let's go."

He paused by the entrance to an alleyway. "You don't want to make my life easy, woman."

"I don't want to see you get yourself arrested or mugged, no."

"Hah. Remember last time?"

"Come on." She entered the alley.

Piles of rubbish subsided against damp-rotted brickwork: galvanized steel trash cans composting week-dead bones and fireplace ashes. Miriam stifled a gag reflex as Burgeson fumbled with a rusting latchkey set in a wooden gate. The gate creaked open on an overgrown yard piled with coal and metalwork. Erasmus headed for a flight of cellar steps opening opposite. Miriam swallowed, and squeezed past him. "What exactly are we picking up?" she asked.

He glanced over his shoulder: "Clothing, cash, and an antiquarian book."

"Must be some book." He nodded jerkily. "Who was watching the shop?"

"Two coves. Ah, you mean why? I'm not sure. They didn't look like Polis to me, as I said. I think they may be your friends."

"In which case—" She briefly considered a direct approach, but rejected it as too risky: if they *weren't* Clan Security, or if ClanSec had gotten the wrong idea about her, she could be sticking her head in a noose. "—we can just nip in and out without them seeing us. But what if there's someone in your apartment, waiting?"

"There'd better not be." They were at the foot of the steps now.

"I'm getting sick of this." She pushed the door open. "Follow me."

She duckwalked into a cellar, past a damp-stained mattress, then through a tangle of old and decrepit wooden furniture that blocked off the back wall. Erasmus followed her. There was a hole in the brickwork, and he bent down to retrieve a small electric lantern from the floor just inside it. As he stood up, he began to cough.

"You can't go in like that, they'll hear you." Miriam

stared at him in the gloom. "Give me the lamp. I'll check out the shop."

"But if you—"

She rested a hand lightly on his shoulder. "I'll be right back. Remember, I'm not the one with the cough." *And besides, I'm sick of just waiting for shit to happen to me.* At least this made it feel as if she was back in control of her destiny.

Erasmus nodded. He handed over the lantern without a word. She took it carefully and shone it along the tunnel. She'd been this way before, six months ago. *Is this entirely sensible?* She asked herself, and nearly burst into hysterical laughter: nothing in her life had been *entirely sensible* for about a year, now, since her mother had suggested she retrieve a shoe box full of memories from the attic of the old family house.

The smuggler's corridor zigzagged underground, new brick and plasterwork on one side showing where neighboring tenement cellars had been encroached on to create the rat run. A sweet-sick stink of black water told its own story of burst sewerage pipes. Miriam paused at a T-junction, then tiptoed to her left, where the corridor narrowed before coming to an end behind a ceiling-high rack of pigeonholes full of dusty bundles of rags. She reached out and grabbed one side of the rack. It slid sideways silently, on well-greased metal runners. The cellar of Erasmus's store was dusty and hot, the air undisturbed for days. Flicking the lamp off, Miriam tiptoed towards the central passage that led to the stairs up to the shop. Something rustled in the darkness and she froze, heart in mouth: but it was only a rat, and after a minute's breathless wait she pressed on.

At the top of the stairs, she paused and listened. *It's empty,* she told herself. *Isn't it? It's empty and all I have to do is take two more steps and I can prove it.* Visions paraded through her mind's eye, the last time she'd ventured into a seemingly unoccupied residence, a horror-filled flashback that nailed her to the spot. She swallowed convulsively, her hand tightening on the rough handrail nailed to the wall. She'd gone into Fort Lofstrom, ahead of the others, and Roland had died—*This is crazy. Nothing's going to happen, is it?*

She took a step forward, across inches that felt like miles: then another step, easier this time. The short passage at the top of the stairs ended in the back room. She crept round the door: everything was as empty as it should be. The archway leading to the main room—there was an observation mirror, tarnished and flyspecked. Relaxing, she stepped up to the archway and peered sidelong into the shop itself.

It was a bright day, and sunbeams slanted diagonally across the dusty window display shelves and the wooden floor boards. The shop was empty, but for a few letters and circulars piling up under the mail slot in the door. If it had been dark, she wouldn't have noticed anything out of the ordinary, and if she'd been coming in through the front door she wouldn't have seen it until it was too late. But coming out of the dimness of the shop . . . her breath caught as she saw the coppery gleam of the wire fastened to the door handle. The sense of déjà vu was a choking imposition on her fragile self-confidence. She'd seen too many trip wires in the past year: Matt had made a bad habit of them, damn him, wherever he was. She turned and retraced her steps, gripping the banister rail tightly to keep her hands from shaking.

"The shop is empty, but someone's been inside it. There's a wire on the door handle." She shuddered, but Erasmus just smiled.

"This I must see for myself."

"It's too dangerous!"

"Obviously not," he replied mildly. "You're still alive, aren't you?"

"But I—" she stopped, unable to explain the dread that gripped her.

"You saw it in time. It won't be a petard, Miriam, not if

it's the Polis, probably not if it's your relatives. Your bête noir, the mad bomber, is unlikely, isn't he? We'll take care not to trip over any other wires. I'll wager you it turns out to be a bell, wired to wake up a watcher next door. Someone wants to know when I return, that's all."

"That's *all*?" She wanted to stamp her feet in frustration. "They broke into your shop and installed a trip wire and you say that's all? Come on, let's go—you can buy new clothes—"

"I need the book." He was adamant.

She took a deep breath. "I don't like it."

"Neither do I, but . . ." He shrugged.

Paradoxically, Miriam felt herself begin to relax once they returned to the back room. Trip wires and claymore mines were Matthias's stock in trade, a nasty trick from the days of the Clan-on-Clan civil war. But Matthias wasn't a world-walker, and he couldn't be over here, could he? He'd gone missing in the United States six months earlier, a week before the first series of targeted raids had shut down the Clan's postal service. While she waited patiently, Erasmus sniffed around his shelves, the writing desk and dusty ledgers, the battered sink with the tin teapot and oil burner beside it, the cracked frosted-glass window pane with the bars on the outside. "Nobody's touched these," he said after a few minutes. "I'm going to look in the shop."

"But it's under observation! And there's the wire—"

"I don't think anyone outside will be able to see in, not while the sun's out. And I want to fetch some stuff. Come help me?"

Miriam tensed, then nodded.

Erasmus slowly walked into the front of the shop, staying well back from the windows. He paused between two rails of secondhand clothing. "That's interesting," he said quietly.

"What is it?"

He pointed at the door handle. "Look." The copper wire ran to the door frame, then round a nail and down to the floor where it disappeared into a small gray box, unobtrusively fastened to the skirting board. "What's that?"

Miriam peered at the box. It was in shadow, and it took her a few seconds to make sense of what she was seeing. "That's not a claymore—" She swallowed again.

"What is it?" he asked.

It was gray, with rounded edges—as alien to this world as a wooden automobile would be in her own. And the stubby antenna poking out of its top told another story. "I think it's a rad—a, uh, an electrograph." And it sure as hell wasn't manufactured over here. "It might be something else."

"How very interesting," Erasmus murmured, stooping further to retrieve the letters. "You were right, earlier," he added, glancing her way: "if this was planted by the men who followed us in New London, they're not looking for me. They're looking for you."

And they're not the same as the men staking out the front door, damn it. She nodded. "Let's get your stuff and hit the road. I don't like this one little bit."

They hanged the servants beneath the warmth of the early afternoon sun, as Neuhalle's minstrel played a sprightly air on the hurdy-gurdy. It was hard work, and the men were drinking heavily during their frequent breaks. "It takes half the fun out of it, having to do all the heavy lifting yourself," Heidlor grumbled quietly as he filled his looted silver tankard from the cask of ale sitting on the cart.

Neuhalle nodded absently as another half-naked maid swung among the branches, bug-eyed and kicking. The bough groaned and swayed beneath its unprecedented crop, much of which was still twitching. "You don't have to," he pointed out. "Your men seem to be enjoying themselves."

"Maybe, but it's best to set a good example. Besides, they'll change their minds when they run out of beer."

The tree emitted another ominous creak, like the half-strangled belch of a one-eyed god. "Start another tree," Neuhalle ordered. "This one is satisfied. That one over there looks like he's willing to serve."

"Aye, sir."

"Sky Father will be grateful for your work today," Neuhalle added, and his sergeant's face split in a broad grin.

"Oh, aye, sir!"

It paid to put a pious face on such affairs, Otto reflected, to remind the men that the sobbing women and shivering, whey-faced lads they were dispatching were a necessary sacrifice to the health of the realm, a palliative for the ailment that had afflicted the royal dynasty for the past three generations. The servants of the tinker families—*no, the clan of witches,* Neuhalle reminded himself—weren't the problem: the real problem was the weakness of the dynasty and the debauched compliance of the nobility. Egon might be unable to sacrifice himself or another of the royal bloodline for the strength of the kingdom, but at least he could satisfy Sky Father by proxy. The old ways were bloody, true, but sometimes they provided a salutary lesson, strengthening the will of the state. And so these unfortunates' souls would be dedicated to Sky Father, the strength of their lives would escheat to the Crown, and their gold would pay for the royal army's progress.

Neuhalle was sitting on his camp chair with an empty cup, watching his soldiers man-handle a hog-tied and squalling matron towards the waiting tree, when a horseman rode up to the ale cart and dismounted. He cast about for a moment, then looped his reins around the wagon's shaft and walked towards Otto. Otto glanced at the fellow, and his eyes narrowed. He stood up: as he did so, his hand-men appeared, clearly taking an interest in the stranger with his royalist sash and polished breastplate.

"Sir, do I have the honor of addressing Otto, Baron Neuhalle?"

Second impressions were an improvement: the fellow was young, perhaps only twenty, and easily impressed—or maybe just stupid. "That would be me." Otto inclined his head. "And who are you?" He kept his right hand away from his sword. A glance behind the fellow took in Jorg, ready to draw at a moment's notice, and he nodded slightly.

"I have the honor to be Eorl Geraunt voh Marlburg, second son of Baron voh Marlburg, my lord. I am here at the word of my liege his majesty—" He broke off, nonplussed, at a particularly loud outbreak of wailing and prayers from the corral. "—I'm sorry, my lord, I bear dispatches."

Otto relaxed slightly. "I would be happy to receive them." He snapped his fingers. "Jorg, fetch a tankard of ale for Eorl Geraunt, if you please." Jorg nodded and headed for the ale cart, his hand leaving his sword hilt as he turned, and the other hand-man, Hein, took a step back. "Have you had a difficult time finding us?"

"Not too difficult, sir." Geraunt bobbed his head: "I had but to follow the trail of wise trees." Behind Otto, the crying and praying was choked off abruptly as his men raised further tribute to Sky Father. "His majesty is less than a day's hard ride away."

Otto glanced at Geraunt's horse. He could take a hint. "Henryk, if you could find someone to see to the eorl's horse . . ." He turned back to Geraunt as his other hand-man strode off. "How fares his majesty?"

Sir Geraunt grinned excitedly. "He does great deeds!" A nod at the tree: "Not to belittle your own, my lord, but he sweeps through the countryside like the scythe of his grandsire, reaping the fields of disorder and uprooting weeds!" He reached into the leather purse dangling from his belt and pulled out a parchment envelope, sealed with wax along its edges. "His word, as I stand before you, my lord."

"Thank you." Otto accepted the letter, glanced at the seal, then slit it open with his small knife. Within, he found the crabbed handwriting of one of Egon's scribes. "Hmm."

The message was short and to the point. He glanced round, as Jorg returned with Geraunt's beer and Heidlor walked over.

"Sergeant. How long until you are finished with the prisoners?"

Heidlor shrugged. "Before sundown, I would say, sir. Perhaps in as little as one bell."

Otto frowned. This was taking too long. "We have orders to march. Much as it pains me to deprive Sky Father of his own, I think we'd better speed things up. So once the men have finished decorating that branch—"he pointed: there was barely room for another three bodies "—hmm, how many are we left with? Two score?" This particular house had been full of refugees, and the village with collaborators. "Strip them naked, whip them into the woods, and fire the buildings with their clothes and chattels inside. We'll have to rely on winter to do the rest of our work here."

Sir Geraunt blanched. "Isn't that a bit harsh?" he asked.

"His majesty was most specific." Otto tapped his finger on the letter. "I don't have time to gently send them to their one-eyed father—you say his Majesty is a day's ride away? We have to meet with him by this time tomorrow. With my men."

"Oh, I see. If I may be permitted to ask, did he issue orders for my disposition, my lord? I am anxious to return—"

"You may ride with us." He turned and walked away, towards his tent. "I'm sure there'll be enough wise trees for everyone if he's right about this," he muttered to himself, for the summons was unequivocal: *It is time to seek a concentration of fluxes,* his majesty had ordained. To draw the tinker-witches into a real battle, by threatening a target they couldn't afford to lose with force they couldn't ignore. It would mean attacking a real target, not just another of these tedious manor estates. It would probably be either Fort Lofstrom or Castle Hjorth, and Otto would be willing to bet good money on the latter.

BEGIN TRANSCRIPT:

"Good evening, your grace!"

"Indeed it is, indeed it is, Eorl Riordan. A lovely evening. And how are you?"

"I am well, sir. As well as can be expected."

"For a fellow who is well, your face is uncommonly glum. Here, sit down. A glass of the Cabernet, perhaps?"

"Thank you, sir. What can I do for you?"

"Hmm, direct and to the point. Let me ask you a leading question, then. You may answer as indiscreetly as you care—it will go no farther than this room. How do you rate our performance?"

"Tactical or strategic? Or logistic and economic?"

"Whichever you deem most important. I want to know, in confidence, what you think we're doing wrong and what you think we're doing right."

"Doing *right*?" (Brief laughter.) "Nothing."

"That's—" (Pause.) "—a provocative statement. Would you elaborate?"

"Yes, your grace. May I start with a summary?"

"Be my guest."

"We are engaged in a war on two fronts. I shall ignore the first hostility for now, and concentrate on the second, because that's the one you assigned me to deal with. Hostilities started when the former crown prince usurped the throne. It is evident from the speed and nature of his actions that he had been planning to do so for some time, and that he had already assured himself of the support of a sufficiently broad base of the nobility, before he moved, to have some hope of success. However, his move may well have been reactive—a response to the imminent marriage of his younger brother. So to start with, we are fighting an opponent who has studied his enemies and who has prepared extensively for this conflict, but whose execution was rushed."

"Hmm. How do you evaluate his preparations?"

"They were confoundedly good, your grace. His

control over the royal Life Guards, for one thing—that was a nasty surprise. His ability to install explosives in the palace—his possession of them—speaks of a level of planning that has given me sleepless nights. The Pervert may be many things but he isn't stupid. Despite his well-known antipathy for our number, he has studied us closely. It is impossible to now ask his grand-dame how much lore she may have passed on to him, but we should take it as read that when he refers to us as 'witches' he knows exactly what we are capable of. For example, rather than holding Niejwein and the castles surrounding it, he immediately departed for the field, where I am told he sleeps among his troops, never in the same tent twice. Sir, he clearly knows how the civil war was fought: he knows exactly what tactics we would first think to use against an enemy noble, and his defenses are as good as anything we could muster for one of our own."

"You've considered the usual routes, I take it? An assassination team from the other side?"

"Yes, your grace. It would be suicidal. For one thing, as I said, he sleeps among his men, in the field, always moving—for another, he has body doubles. We have identified at least two of them on different occasions, and they're good actors: there is a good chance we would be striking at a puppet rather than their master. Finally, he has bodyguards. And I fear we have been too liberal with our gifts over the past decades: either that, or they've captured some hedge-lord's private cabinet of arms, because I have confirmation that his Majesty's hand-men carry MP-5s."

(Pause.) "All right, so the Pervert's a hard target. Now. The strategic picture?"

"Certainly, your grace. The enemy has divided his forces into battalion strength raiding units. They're in the field and they're hurting us. It's a—this is embarrassing— a classic insurgency. The royal battalions fall on our outlying villages, hit them hard, massacre and destroy everything they can get their hands on, then disappear into the forest again. It's absolutely not how you'd expect an eastern monarch to fight, it's downright dishonorable—but it's how the Pervert is fighting. He's serious, sir, he's trying to force us to divide our strength. And he's succeeded. We've had to move as many dependents as possible over to the other side, and keep couriers on standby everywhere. And even that's not enough. We've used helicopters to rush armed detachments into position on the other side a couple of times, and it worked on that bastard Lemke—he won't be burning any more villages—but the more we do it, the greater the risk that the Americans will notice. He's got us on the defensive, and each time he hits us we either lose a village or we lose men we can't afford to—and he gains honor. This week I've lost eleven dead and fourteen injured badly enough they won't be fighting again for months. That's not including the outer family members, dependents, servants, peasants and the like. I think we've accounted for a good couple of hundred of the foe, but they're not stupid: usually the first warning of an attack we have is when a cannon ball comes through a manor house door. There's a limit to what a lance with M-16s and a SAW can do against a battalion of dragoons and a cavalry squadron—some of whom have Glocks."

"Ah, yes. I thought you'd bring that up. Be glad you don't have to explain it to the council, Eorl Riordan. They know it's wrong, but they still can't help but petition for protection, which is why three quarters of our number are guarding strategic hamlets or sitting in helicopter hangars on the other side. It's what we exist for, and we're being nibbled to death by mice. What would you do, were you in charge?"

"I'd set out a mouse trap, your grace. We can't afford to suffer the death of a thousand cuts—Clan Security has, what? Two hundred inner family? Nearly a thousand armed and trained retainers? And up to six hundred world-walkers to call in for the corvee, if we need logistic support. The usurper outnumbers us five to one, but we've got SAWs and two-way radio while they're limited to roundshot, grapeshot, and horseback couriers. We should be able to massacre those raiding parties, if we can just once anticipate not only their next target, but their path of advance."

"Hmm. Suppose I were to tell you exactly where the enemy is planning to mass for a major strike, next Tuesday. Not just one of their battalions, but three of them, a goodly chunk of the royal army. Would that enable you to prepare a suitable reception for him?"

"Would—your grace! Please say it's true!"

(Pause.) "The source is . . . troubling. I would not completely discount all risk of it being a deliberate leak, intended to lure us into a trap. Still. Be that as it may, I am informed—by one who stands to profit from that information—that there is a high probability of an attack on Castle Hjorth within the next two weeks. Which strikes me as suicidal, given the location and defenses of the castle, so I advise you to bear in mind the possibility that even if my source is telling the truth, they are not telling us everything. But, having said that, I want you to work out what we're going to do about it. Because if it is true, my informer tells me that the Pervert himself will lead the attack. And this might be our best opportunity to kill him and end the war."

END TRANSCRIPT

10

INTERACTION

༄

A s it happened, Mike didn't get to go home that day—or the next. "You live on your own in a second-floor apartment, and you've got a lovely spiral fracture plus soft tissue injuries and a damaged Achilles tendon, Mr. Fleming. Listen, I'll happily sign you out—if you fill in a criminal negligence waiver for me, first. But I really think it's a bad idea right now. Maybe tomorrow, when we've got you a nice fiberglass box and a set of crutches, after we set you up with an appointment with physio. But if you check out today, you'll wish you hadn't."

The time passed slowly, with the inane babble of daytime TV as a laugh track, interrupted occasionally by nursing orderlies and interns checking up on him. Smith hadn't left him any reading matter, classified or otherwise, and he was close to climbing the walls by the morning of the second day after Smith's visit, when he had a surprise visitor: Judith Herz, the FBI agent who'd been sucked into Family Trade at the same time at Mike.

"Smith sent me. You're checking out," she said crisply, and dropped an overnight bag on the chair. "Here's your stuff, I'll be back in ten."

She shut the door briskly, leaving Mike shaking his head. *What got her so pissed?* He opened the bag and pulled out the clothing. It was the stuff he'd been wearing over a week ago, before the CLEANSWEEP mission ran off the rails. He shook it out and managed to get the trouser leg over his cast without too much trouble. By the time Herz opened the door again, he was buttoning his jacket. "Yes?" he asked.

"I'm your lift." She waved a key fob at him. "You going to be okay walking, or do you need a wheelchair?"

Mike frowned. "I'll walk. Give me time, I'm not used to these things." He eased his weight onto the crutches and took an experimental step forward. "Let's go."

She said nothing more all the way to the parking lot. As they neared a black sedan Mike's impatience got the better of him. "You're not in the taxi business. What's the big problem?"

"I wanted to talk to you without eavesdroppers." She squeezed the key fob: lights flashed and doors unlocked.

"Okay, talk." Mike's stomach twisted. *Last time someone said that to me, he ended up dead.*

She opened the passenger door. "Here, give me those, I'll put them in the trunk." A minute later she slid behind the wheel and moved off. "Your house is under surveillance."

"Yeah, I know."

She gave him a look. "Like that, is it? Care to explain why?"

"Because—" he stopped in mid-sentence "—what business of yours is it?"

She braked to a stop, near the end of the exit ramp, looking for a gap in the traffic. "It'd be kind of nice to know that I've been taken off hunting for a ticking bomb and told to stake out a colleague's house for a good reason." Her voice crackled with quiet anger.

Mike swallowed. *Good cop,* he realized. *What to say . . . ?* "It's not me you're staking out. I'm expecting a visitor."

"Okay." She hit the gas hard, pushing out into a too-small gap in the traffic: a horn blared behind them for a moment, then they were clear. "But they'd better be worth it."

Mike swallowed again. "Listen. You know the spooks are calling the shots. I got dragged off into fairyland, but you don't have to follow me down the rabbit hole."

"Too late. I'm in charge of the team that's watching you. I just found out about it yesterday. If it's not you, who am I meant to be keeping an eye open for?"

"Someone who may be able to tell us whether he was bluffing or if there really *is* a bomb—and if so, where he might have planted it."

Herz swung left into the passing lane. "Good answer." Her fingers tightened on the wheel. "That's what I wanted to hear. Is it true?"

Mike took a deep breath. "The NIRT guys are still working their butts off, right?"

"Yes . . ."

"Then in the absence of a forensics lead or an informant you're not delivering much value-added, are you? They're the guys with the neutron scattering spectrometers and the Geiger counters. You're the detective. What did the colonel tell you to do?"

Herz took an on-ramp, then accelerated onto the interstate: "Stake you out like a goat. Watch and wait, twenty-four by seven. You're supposed to tell me what to do, when to wrap up the case."

"Hmm." *What have I gotten myself into here?* "I really ought to get the colonel to tell me whether I can fill you in on a couple of codewords."

Herz set the cruise control and glanced at him, sidelong. "He told me you'd been on something called CLEANSWEEP, and this is the follow-up."

Mike felt the tension ease out of his shoulders. "I hate

the fucking spook bullshit," he complained. "Okay, let me fill you in on CLEANSWEEP and how I got my leg busted up. Then maybe I can help you figure out a surveillance plan . . ."

Miriam watched from the back room while Erasmus systematically looted his own shop. "Go through the clothing and take anything you think you'll need," he told her. "There's a traveling case downstairs that you can use. We're going to be away for two weeks, and we'll not be able to purchase any necessities until we reach Fort Kinnaird."

"But I can't just—" Miriam shook her head. "Are you sure?"

"Whose shop is it?" He flashed her a cadaverous grin. "I'll be upstairs. Got to fetch a book."

The traveling case in the cellar turned out to be a battered leather suitcase. Miriam hauled it up into the back room and opened it, wrinkling her nose. It looked clean enough, although the stained silk lining, bunched at one side, made her wonder at its previous owner's habits. She stuffed the contents of her valise into it, then scoured the rails in the back for anything else appropriate. There wasn't much there: Erasmus had run down the stock of clothes since she'd last seen the inside of his shop. A search of the pigeonholes behind the counter yielded a fine leather manicure case and a good pen. She was tucking them into the case when Erasmus reappeared, carrying a couple of books and a leather jewelry case.

"What's that?" she asked.

"Stock I'm not leaving in an empty shop for two weeks." He pulled another suitcase out from a cubby behind his desk and opened it: "I'm also taking the books to prove I'm their rightful owner, just in case." It all went in. Then he opened the partition at the back of the counter and rummaged around inside. "You might want to take this . . ." He held a small leather box out to Miriam.

"What—" She flicked the catch open. The pistol was tiny, machined with the precision of a watch or a camera or a very expensive piece of jewelry. "Hey, I can't take—"

"You must," Burgeson said calmly. "Whether you ever need to use it is another matter, but I believe I can trust you not to shoot me by mistake, yes?"

She nodded, jerkily.

"Then put it away. I suggest in a pocket. The case and spare rounds can go—here." He picked out the pistol then slipped the case through a slit in the lining of the suitcase that Miriam hadn't even noticed. "It's loaded with three rounds in the cylinder, the hammer is on the empty fourth chamber. It's a self-arming rotary, when you pull the trigger it will cock the hammer—double action—do you see?" He offered it to her.

"I don't—" She nodded, then took the pistol. "You really think I'll need it?"

"I hope you won't." He glanced away, avoiding her gaze. "But these are dangerous times."

He bustled off again, into the front of the shop, leaving Miriam to contemplate the pistol. *He's right*, she realized with a sinking heart. She double-checked that the hammer was, indeed, on the empty chamber, then slipped it into her coat pocket just as Erasmus returned, clutching a wad of envelopes.

"You have mail." He passed her a flimsy brown wrapper.

"I have—" She did a double take. "Right." There was no postage stamp; it had been hand-delivered. She opened it hastily. The neat copperplate handwriting she recognized as Roger's. The message was much less welcome:

Polis raided yr house, watching yr factory. Am being watched, can't help. Think yr stuff is still where it was, locked in the office.

"Shit!"

She sat down hard on the wooden stool Erasmus kept in the back office.

"What troubles you?"

She waved the note at him. "I need to collect this stuff," she said.

"Yes, but—" he read the note rapidly, his face expressionless. "I see." He paused. "How badly do you need it?"

The moment she'd been half-dreading had arrived. How would Burgeson respond if she told him the unvarnished truth?

"Very." She meshed her fingers together to avoid fidgeting. "The machine I need to collect has . . . well, it's more than just useful to me. It stores pictures, and among them there's a copy of the original knotwork design I need if I'm going to get back to my own world by myself. If I've got it, I'm not stuck with a choice between permanent exile here and a, a feudal backwater. Or going back to the Clan. If I *do* decide to make contact with them and ask to be taken in, it's a bargaining lever that demonstrates my bona fides because I had a choice. And if I don't, it gives me access to my own, my original, world. Where it's possible to get hold of things like the medicine I got you."

He waited for several seconds after she finished speaking. "That's not all, is it?" he said gently.

She swallowed. "Are you planning on keeping me a prisoner here?" She asked. "Because that's what denying me the ability to go back to the United States amounts to."

"I'm not!" He began explosively, then stopped to draw a deep breath: "I apologize. I did not mean to imply that I thought you were going to cut and run." He grimaced. "But there's more to this device of yours than a mere pictographic representation, isn't there?"

"Well, yes," she admitted. "For one thing, it contains a copy of every patent filed in my home country over more than a century." Erasmus gaped at her. "Why do you think I started out by setting up a research company?"

"But that must be—that's preposterous!" He struggled visibly to grapple with the idea. "Such a library would occupy many shelf-feet, surely?"

"It used to." Miriam felt a flash of hope. "But you saw the DVD player. Every second, that machine has to project thirty images on screen, to maintain the illusion of motion. How much storage do you think they take up? In my world, we have ways of storing huge amounts of data in very small spaces."

"And such a library would be expensive," he added speculatively.

"Not if it was old. And the cost of the storage medium was equivalent to, say, a reporter's notebook." Her patent database might not include anything filed in the past fifty years, but a full third of its contents were still novelties in New Britain.

"We must seem very primitive to you." He was scrutinizing her, Miriam realized, with a guarded expression that was new and unwelcome.

"In some ways, yes." She relaxed her hands. "In other ways—no, I don't think so. And anyway, there are probably any number of other worlds out there that are as far beyond this one, or the one I came from, as this is beyond the Gruinmarkt. Where the Clan come from," she clarified. "Bunch of medieval throwbacks." *Throwbacks who are your family,* she reminded herself. "Look, from my point of view, I need to make sure I've got something, anything, that'll stop them coming after me if they realize I survived the massacre." *Assuming they survived.* "If I've got the laptop I can threaten to throw myself on the mercy of the security agencies in the U.S., whoever Mike is working for. Or I can claim loyalty and demonstrate that I didn't do that, even though I could have. And if I don't have anything to do with them I can use it to set up in business again, over here."

"Do you plan to throw yourself on the mercy of your friend's agency?" Erasmus asked, raising an eyebrow.

Miriam shuddered. "It's a last resort," she said slowly. "If the Clan come after me and try to kill me, they might be able to keep me alive." *But then again*—Mike's words came back to haunt her: *They're using world-walkers as mules, there's a turf war inside the bureaucracy.* Things might go really well. And then again, she might end up vanishing into some underground equivalent of Camp X-ray, into a nightmarish gulag that would make house arrest in Niejwein seem like paradise. "But I don't want to risk it unless I have to."

"So what are you going to do?" he asked gently. She blinked, and realized he was watching her hands. A double take: *He gave me a pistol,* she realized.

"I'm going to take back what's mine," she said calmly, "and I'm going to get clean away with it. Then we're going to go on a long rail trip while the fuss dies down." She stood up. "Do you mind if I go through your stock again? There's some stuff I need to borrow . . ."

Two hours later, a mousy-looking woman in black trudged slowly past a row of warehouses and business premises, pushing a handcart. Her back hunched beneath an invisible load of despair, she looked neither left nor right as she trailed past an ominously quiet light metal works and a boarded-up fabric warehouse. The handcart, loaded with a battered suitcase and a bulging sack, told its own story: another of the victims of the blockade and the fiscal crisis, out on her uppers and looking for work, or shelter, or a crust before nightfall.

The streets weren't deserted, but there was a lack of purposeful activity; no wagons loading and unloading bales of cloth or billets of mild steel, and a surfeit of skinny, down-at-heels men slouching, hands in pockets, from one works to another—or optimistically holding up crude signboards saying WILL WORK FOR FOOD. Some messages were universal, it seemed.

The woman with the handcart paused in the shadow of the textile mill, as if out of breath or out of energy on whatever meager rations she'd managed that morning. Her dull gaze drifted past a couple of idlers near the gates to a closed and barricaded glass factory: idlers a trifle better fed than the run of the mill, idlers wearing boots that—if she'd stopped to look—she might have noticed were suspiciously well-repaired.

A little further up the road, a shabby vendor with a baked potato stand was watching another boarded-up building. The woman's gaze slid past him, too. After a minute or so she began to put one weary foot in front of another, and pushed her cart along the sidewalk towards the boarded-up works.

As she hunched over the handles of her cart, Miriam rubbed her wrist and squinted at the small pocket watch she'd wound around it. *Any minute now*, she told herself, half-sick with worry. The last time she'd tried something like this she'd ended up in Baron Henryk's custody, guarded by cold-faced killers and under sentence of death. If she was wrong about the watchers, if there were more of them, this could end up just as badly.

From the alleyway running alongside the boarded-up workshop there was a crash and a tinkle of broken glass. Miriam shuffled slowly along, overtly oblivious as the potato-vendor left his stand and strolled towards the side of the building. Behind him the two idlers she'd tagged began to walk briskly in the opposite direction, setting up a pincer on the other end of the alley. She felt a flash of triumph. Now all it would take was for the street kids Erasmus had paid to do their job . . .

The watchers were out of sight. Miriam dropped the handles of her cart, grabbed her suitcase, and darted towards the workshop's office doorway. A heavy seal and a length of rope held the splintered main door closed with the full majesty of the law, and not a lot besides: she grimaced and tugged hard at the seal, ducking inside as the door groaned and threatened to collapse on her. *One minute only,* she told herself. It might take them longer to work out that the urchins were a distraction, but she wasn't betting on it.

Inside the entrance the building was dark and still, and cold—at least, as cold as anything got at this time of year. Moving fast, with an assurance born of having worked here for months, Miriam darted round the side of the walled-off office and felt for the door handle. It had always been loose, and her personal bet—that the Polis wouldn't lock up inside a building they were keeping under surveillance—paid off. The door handle flexed as she stepped inside her former office, raising her suitcase as a barrier.

She needn't have bothered. There was nobody waiting for her: nothing but the dusty damp smell of an unoccupied building. The high wooden stools lay adrift on the floor under a humus of scattered papers and overturned drawers. A flash of anger: *The bastards didn't need to do this, did they?* But in a way it made things easier for her. Dealing with a stakeout by the secret police hereabouts was trivially easy compared to sneaking her laptop out past Morgan and making a clean getaway.

Thirty seconds. The nape of her neck was itching. Miriam stumbled across the overturned furniture, then bent down, fumbling in the leg well below one scribe's position. The hidden compartment under the desk was still there: her hands closed on the wooden handle and pulled down and forward to open it. It slid out reluctantly, scraping loudly. She tugged hard, almost stumbling as it came out and the full weight of its contents landed on her arms.

The suitcase was on the floor. *Forty-five seconds.* She fumbled with the buckles for a heart-stopping moment, but finally the lid opened. Scooping the contents out of the hidden drawer—the feel of cold plastic slick against her fingertips—she swept them into the pile of bundled clothing within, then grabbed the bag by its handles. There was no time to buckle it closed: she picked it up in one hand and scurried back into the body of the empty works.

One minute. Was that a shout from outside? Miriam glanced briefly at the front door. *Doesn't matter,* she thought: *they'll work it out soon enough.* Moving by dead reckoning, her free hand stretched out to touch the wall beside her, she headed deeper into the building, following the deepening shadows. Another turn and the shadows began to lighten. At the end of the corridor she turned left and the grimy daylight lifted, showing her the dust and damage that had been brought to bear on her business, in the name of the law and by the neglect of her peers. It was heartbreaking, and she stopped, briefly unable to go on. *I'll rebuild it,* she told herself. *Somehow.* The most important tools were in her suitcase, after all.

Then she heard them. A bang from the front door, low-pitched male voices, hunters casting around for the scent. Burgeson's distraction had worked its purpose, but if she didn't hurry, it would be all for nothing. Grimly determined, Miriam stepped into the abandoned workshop and gripped her suitcase. Standing beneath the skylight, she pulled the locket out of her pocket and narrowed her eyes, focusing on it and clearing her mind of everything else as the police agents stumbled towards her through the darkness.

This is it, she told herself. *No more nice-guy Miriam. Next time someone tries to do this to me, I'm not going to let them live long enough to regret it.*

And then the world changed.

Huw slept badly after he finished drafting the e-mail report to the duke. It wasn't simply the noises Yul and Elena were making, although that was bad enough—young love, he reflected, was at its worst when there wasn't enough to go round—but the prospects of what he was going to have to face on the morrow kept him awake long after the other had fallen asleep.

A new world. There couldn't be any other explanation for the meteorological readings. Temperatures that low, that kind of subarctic coniferous forest, hadn't been found in this part of the world since the last of the ice ages. The implications were enormous. For starters, this was the second new world that the Wu family's knotwork could take a world-walker to. *What happens if I use the original knot, from somewhere in this fourth world? Probably it takes me to yet another* . . . even without discovering new topologies, ownership of both knotwork designs implied access to a lot more than three, or even four, worlds. *The knots define a positional transformation in a higher order space. Like the moves of different pieces on a chessboard—able to go forward or backward, but if you used your bishop to make a move in one direction, then swapped your bishop for a rook, you could go somewhere else.* It meant everything was up for grabs.

For over a century the Clan's grandees had doppelgangered their houses—building defenses in the other world they knew of, to protect their residences from stealthy attack—without realizing that the Wu family could attack them from a third world. Now there was a fourth, and probably a fifth, a sixth . . . where would it end? *Our core defensive strategy has just been made obsolete, overnight.* And that wasn't the worst of it. The Wu family knot was a simple mistake, the lower central whorl superimposed over the front of the ascending spiral, rather than hidden behind it. There would be other topologies, encoding different positional transformations. That much seemed clear to Huw, although he'd had to limit his forays into Mathematica to half an hour per day—trying to work out the knot structure was a guaranteed fast-track route to a migraine. *There will be other worlds.*

He lay awake long after Yul and Elena had dozed off, staring at the ceiling, daydreaming about exploration and all the disasters that could befall an unwary world-walker. *We'll need oxygen masks.* (What if some of the worlds had never evolved photosynthesis, so that life was a thin scum of sulfur-reducing bacteria clustered around volcanic vents, at the bottom of a thick blanket of nitrogen and ammonia?) *Trickster-wife, we may need space suits.* (What if the planet itself had never formed?) *Need to map the coastlines and relief, see if plate tectonics evolves deterministically in all worlds* . . .

He blinked at the sunlight streaming in through the

front window. How had it gotten to be morning? His mouth tasted of cobwebs and dust, but his head was clear. "Gaah." There was no point pretending to sleep.

Someone was singing as he wandered through into the kitchen, rubbing his eyes. It was Elena: she'd found the stash of kitchenware and was filling the coffee maker, warbling one of the more salacious passages of a famous saga to herself with—to Huw—a deeply annoying air of smug satisfaction.

"Humph." He rummaged in the cupboard for a glass but came up with a chipped coffee mug instead. Rinsing it under the cold water tap, he asked, "Ready to face the day?"

"Oh yes!" She trilled, closing up the machine. She turned and grinned at him impishly. "It's a wonderful day to explore a new world, don't you think?"

"Just as long as we don't leave our bones there." Huw took a gulp of the slightly brackish tap water. "Yuck." *Ease up, she's just being exuberant,* he told himself. "Where's Yul?"

"He's still getting dressed—" She remembered herself and flushed. "He'll be down in a minute."

"Good." Huw pressed his lips together to keep from laughing. *Memo to self: do not taunt little brother's girlfriend, little brother will be tetchy.* "Coffee would be good, too, thanks," he added.

"What are we going to do today?" she asked, eyes widening slightly.

"Hmm. Depends."

"I was thinking about doing breakfast," rumbled Hulius, from the doorway.

"That—" Huw brightened "—sounds like a great idea. Got to wait for the duke's say-so before we continue, anyway," he added. "Breakfast first, then we can get ready for a camping trip."

Huw drove into town carefully, hunting for the diner he'd spotted the day before. He steered the youngsters to a booth at the back before ordering a huge breakfast—fried eggs, bacon, half a ton of hash browns, fried tomatoes, and a large mug of coffee. "Go on, pig out," he told Elena and Hulius, "you're going to be sorry you didn't later."

"Why should I?" asked Elena, as the waitress ambled off towards the kitchen. "I'll be sorry if I'm fat and ugly before my wedding night!"

Huw glanced at his brother: Yul was studiously silent, but Huw could just about read his mind. *Not the sharpest knife in the box . . .* "We're going back to the forest," Huw explained laboriously, "and we're staying there for at least one night, maybe two, in a tent. It's going to be very cold. Your body burns more calories when you're cold."

"Oh!" She glared at him. "Men!" Yul winked at him, then froze as the waitress reappeared with a jug of coffee. "No sense of humor," she humphed.

"Okay, so we're humor-impaired" Huw started on his hash browns. "Listen, we—" he paused until the waitress was out of earshot "—it depends what orders we receive, alright? It's possible his grace will tell me to sit tight until he can send a support team . . . but I don't think it's likely. From what I can gather, we're shorthanded everywhere and anyone who isn't essential is being pulled in for the corvee, supporting security operations, or running interference. So my best bet is, he'll read my report and say 'carry on.' But until I get confirmation of that, we're not going across."

Elena stabbed viciously at her solitary fried egg. "To what end are we going?"

"To see if that stuff Yul found really is the remains of a roadbed. To look around and get some idea of the vegetation, so I can brief a real tree doctor when we've got time to talk to one. To plant a weather station and seismograph. To very quietly see if there's any sign of inhabitation. To boldly go where no Clan explorer has gone before. Is that enough to start with?"

"Eh." Yul paused with his coffee mug raised. "That's a lot to bite off."

"That's why all three of us are going, this time." Huw

took another mouthful. "And we're all taking full packs instead of piggybacking. That ties us down for an hour, minimum, if we run into trouble, but going by your first trip, there didn't seem to be anybody home. We might have wildlife trouble, bears or wolves, but that shouldn't be enough to require an immediate withdrawal. So unless the duke says 'no,' we're going camping."

They managed to finish their breakfast without discussing any other matters of import. Unfortunately for Huw, this created a zone of silence that Elena felt compelled to fill with enthusiastic chirping about Christina Aguilera and friends, which Hulius punctuated with nods and grunts of such transparently self-serving attentiveness that Huw began to darkly consider purchasing a dog collar and leash to present to his brother's new keeper.

Back at the rented house, Huw got down to the serious job of redistributing their packs and making sure everything they'd need found a niche in one rucksack or another. It didn't take long to put everything together: what took time was double-checking, asking *what have I forgotten about that could kill me?* When finally they were all ready it was nearly noon.

"Okay, wait in the yard," said Huw. He walked back inside and re-set the burglar alarm. "Got your lockets?" This time there was no need for the flash card, no need to keep all their hands free for emergencies. "On my mark: three, two, one . . ."

The world shifted color, from harsh sunlight on brown-parched grass to overcast pine-needle green. Huw glanced round. A moment earlier he'd been sweating into his open three-layer North Face jacket: the chill hit him like a punch in the ribs and a slap in the face. There were trees everywhere. Elena stepped out from behind a waist-high tangle of brush and dead branches and looked at him. A moment later Hulius popped into place, his heavy pack looming over his head like an astronaut's oxygen supply. "All clear?" Huw asked, ignoring the pounding in his temples.

"Yup." Yul hefted the meter-long spike with the black box of the radio beacon on top, and rammed it into the ground.

"It looks like it's going to rain," Elena complained, looking up at the overcast just visible between the tree-tops. "And it's cold."

Huw zipped his jacket up, then slid his pack onto the ground carefully. "Yul, you have the watch. Elena, if you could start unpacking the tent?" He unhooked the scanner from his telemetry belt and set it running, hunting through megahertz for the proverbial needle in a thunderstorm, then began to unpack the weather station.

"I have the watch, bro." Yul's backpack thudded heavily as it landed in a mat of ferns, followed by the metallic clack as he chambered a round in his hunting rifle. "No bear's going to sneak up on you without my permission."

"I'm so glad." Huw squinted at the scanner, then nodded. "Okay, nothing on the air. Radio check. Elena?"

"Oh, what? You want—the radio?"

"Go ahead."

Elena reached into her jacket pocket and produced a walkie-talkie. "Can you hear me?"

Huw winced and turned down the volume. "I hear you. Your turn, Yul—" Another minute of cross-checks and he was happy. "Okay. Got radio, got weather station, acquired the beacon. Let's get the tent up."

The tent was a tunnel model, with two domed compartments separated by a central awning, for which Huw had a feeling he was going to be grateful. Elena had already unrolled it: between them they managed to nail the spikes in and pull it erect without too much swearing, although the tunnel ended up bulging in at one side where it wrapped around an inconveniently placed trunk.

Huw crossed the clearing then, stretching as high as he could, slashed a strip of bark away from the trunk of the tree nearest the spike. Then he turned to Yul. "Where was that chunk of asphalt?"

"That way, dude." Hulius gestured down the gentle

slope. The trees blocked the line of sight within a hundred meters. "Want to go check it out?"

"You know it." Huw's stomach rumbled. *Going to have to find a stream soon,* he realized, *or send Elena back over to fill up the water bag.* "Lead off. Stay close and stop at twenty so I can mark the route."

It was quiet in the forest, much too quiet. After a minute, Huw realized what he was missing: the omnipresent creaking of the insect chorus, cicadas and hopping things of one kind or another. Occasionally a bird would cry out, a harsh cawing of crows or the *tu-whit tu-whit* of something he couldn't identify marking out its territory. From time to time the branches would rustle and whisper in the grip of a breeze impossible to detect at ground level. But there was no enthusiastic orchestra of insects, no rumble of traffic, nor the drone of engines crawling across the upturned bowl of the empty sky. *We're alone,* he realized. And: *it feels like it's going to snow.*

Yul stopped and turned round. He grinned broadly and pointed at the nearest tree. "See? I've been here before."

Huw nodded. "Good going." His headache eased slightly. "How much farther is it?"

"About six markers, maybe a couple of hundred meters."

"Right." Huw glanced round at Elena. "You hear that?"

"Sure." She chewed rhythmically as she reached up with her left hand to flick a stray hair away from her eyes. She didn't move her right hand away from the grip on the P90, but kept scanning from side to side with an ease that came from long practice—she'd done her share of summer training camps for the duke.

"Lead on, Yul." Huw suppressed a shiver. Elena—was she really as brainless as she'd seemed over breakfast? Or was she another of those differently socialized Clan girls, who escaped from their claustrophobic family connections by moonlighting as manhunters for ClanSec? He hadn't asked enough questions when the duke's clerk had gone down his list of names and suggested he talk to her.

But the way she moved silently in his footsteps, scanning for threats, suggested that maybe he ought to have paid more attention.

Ten, fifteen minutes passed. Yul stopped. "Here it is," he said quietly.

"I have the watch." Elena turned in a circle, looking for threats.

"Let me see." Huw knelt down near the tree Hulius had pointed to. The undergrowth was thin here, barely more than a mat of pine needles and dead branches, and the slope almost undetectable. Odd lumpy protuberances humped out of the ground near the roots of the tree, and when he glanced sideways Huw realized he could see a lot farther in one direction before his vision was blocked by more trees. He unhooked the folding trench shovel from his small pack and chopped away at the muck and weedy vegetation covering one of the lumps. "Whoa!"

Huw knew his limits: what he knew about archeology could be written on the sleeve notes of an Indiana Jones DVD. But he also knew asphalt when he saw it, a solid black tarry aggregate with particles of even size—and he knew it was old asphalt too, weathered and overgrown with lichen and moss.

"Looks like a road to me," Yul offered.

"I think you're right." Huw cast around for more chunks of half-buried roadstone. Now that he knew what he was looking for it wasn't difficult to find. "It ran that way, north-northeast, I think." Turning to look in the opposite direction he saw a shadowy tunnel, just about as wide as a two-lane road. Some trees had erupted through the surface over the years, but for the most part it had held the forest at bay. "Okay, this way is downhill. Let's plant a waypoint and—"he looked up at the heavy overcast"—follow it for an hour, or until it starts to rain, before we head back." He checked his watch. It was just past two in the afternoon. "I don't want to get too far from base camp today."

Hulius rammed another transponder spike into the earth by the road and Huw scraped an arrow on the nearest tree,

pointing back along their path. The LED on top of the
transponder blinked infrequently, reassuring them that
the radio beacon was ready and waiting to guide them
home. For the next half hour they plodded along the shallow downhill path, Hulius leading the way with his hunting rifle, Elena bringing up the rear. Once they were on
the roadbed, it was easy to follow, although patches of asphalt had been heaved up into odd mounds and shoved
aside by trees over the years—or centuries—for which it
had been abandoned. Something about the way the road
snaked along the contours of the shallow hillside tickled
Huw's imagination. "It was built to take cars," he finally
said aloud.

"Huh? How can you tell?" asked Yul.

"The radius of curvature. Look at it, if you're on foot
it's as straight as an arrow. But imagine you're driving
along it at forty, fifty miles per hour. See how it's slightly
banked around that ridge ahead?" He pointed towards a
rise in the ground, just visible through the trees.

They continued in silence for a couple of minutes.
"You're assuming—" Yul began to say, then stopped,
freezing in his tracks right in front of a tree that had thrust
through the asphalt. "*Shit.*"

"What?" Huw almost walked into his back.

"Cover," Yul whispered, gesturing towards the side of
the track. "It's probably empty, but . . ."

"What?" Huw ducked to the side of the road—followed
by Elena—then crept forward to peer past Yul's shoulder.

"There," said Hulius, raising one hand to point. It took
a moment for Huw to recognize the curving flank of a
mushroom-pale dome, lightly streaked with green debris.
"You were looking for company, weren't you? I've got a
bad feeling about this . . ."

It wasn't the first time Miriam had hidden in the woods,
nursing a splitting headache and a festering sense of injus-

tice, but familiarity didn't make it easier: and this time she'd had an added source of anxiety as she crossed over, hoping like hell that the Clan hadn't seen fit to doppelganger her business by building a defensive site in the same location in their own world. But she needn't have worried. The trees grew thick and undisturbed, and she'd made sure that the site was well inland from the line the coast had followed before landfill in both her Boston and the strangely different New British version had extended it.

She'd taken a risk, of course. Boston and Cambridge occupied much the same sites in New Britain as in her own Massachusetts, but in the Gruinmarkt that area was largely untamed, covered by deciduous forest and the isolated tracts and clearings of scattered village estates. She'd never thought to check the lay of the land colocated with her workshop, despite having staked out her house: for all she knew, she might world-walk right into the great hall of some hedge lord. But it seemed unlikely— Angbard hadn't chosen the site of his fortified retreat for accessibility—so the worst risk she expected was a twisted ankle or a drop into a gully.

Instead Miriam stumbled and nearly walked face-first into a beech tree, then stopped and looked around. "Ow." She massaged her forehead. This was bad: she suddenly felt hot and queasy, and her vision threatened to play tricks on her. *Damn, I don't need a migraine right now.* She sat down against the tree trunk, her heart hammering with the release of tension. A flash of triumph: *I got away with it!* Well, not quite. She'd still have to cross back over and meet up with Erasmus. But there were hours to go, yet . . .

The nausea got worse abruptly, peaking in a rush that cramped her stomach. She doubled over to her right and vomited, whimpering with pain. The spasms seemed to go on for hours, leaving her gasping for breath as she retched herself dry. Eventually, by the time she was too exhausted to stand up, the cramps began to ease. She sat up and leaned back against the tree, pulled her suitcase close, and shivered uncontrollably. "I wonder what brought that on?" She mumbled under her breath. Then in an effort to distract herself, she opened the case.

The contents of the hidden drawer were mostly plastic and base metal, but they gleamed at her eyes with more promise than a chest full of rubies and diamonds. A small Sony notebook PC and its accessories, a power supply and CD drive. With shaking hands she opened the computer's lid and pushed the power button. The screen flickered, and LEDs flashed, then it shut down again. "Oh, of course." The battery had run down in the months of enforced inactivity. Well, no need to worry: New Britain had alternating current electricity, and the little transformer was designed for international use, rugged enough to eat their bizarre mixture of frequency and voltage without melting. (Even though she'd had a devil of a time at first, establishing how the local units of measurement translated into terms she was vaguely familiar with.)

Closing the suitcase, she felt the tension drain from her shoulders. *I can go home*, she told herself. *Any time I want to.* All she had to do was walk twenty-five paces north, cross over again at the prearranged time, and then find an electric light socket to plug the computer into. "Huh." She glanced at her watch, surprised to discover that fifty minutes had already passed. She'd arranged to reappear in three hours, the fastest crossing she felt confident she could manage without medication. But that was before the cramps and the migraine had hit her. She stood up clumsily, brushed down her clothes, and oriented herself using the small compass she'd found among Burgeson's stock. "Okay, here goes nothing."

Another tree, another two hours: this time in the right place for the return trip to the side alley behind the workshop. Miriam settled down to wait. *What do I really want to do?* she asked herself. It was a hard question to answer. Before the massacre at the betrothal ceremony—already nearly a week ago—she'd had the grim luxury of certainty. But now . . . *I could buy my way back into the game,* she realized. *The Idiot's dead so the betrothal makes no sense anymore. Henryk's probably dead, too. And I've got valuable information, if I can get Angbard's ear.* Mike's presence changed everything. Hitherto, all the Clan's strategic planning and internecine plotting had made the key assumption that they were inviolable in their own estates, masters of their own world. But if the U.S. government could send spies, then the implications were likely to shake the Clan to its foundations. *They've been looking for the Clan for years,* she realized. But now they'd found the narcoterrorists—*one world's feudal baron is another world's drug lord*—the whole elaborate game of charades that Clan security played was over. The other player could kick over the card table any time they wanted. *You can doppelganger a castle against world-walkers, but you can't stop them crossing over outside your walls and planting a backpack nuke.* In an endgame between the Clan and the CIA or its world-walking equivalent, there could be only one winner.

"So they can't win a confrontation. But if they lose . . ." She blinked. They had Iris, Patricia, her mask-wearing mother. *Could I let her go?* The thought was painful. And then there were others, the ones she could count as friends. Olga, Brill, poor innocent kids like Kara. Even James Lee. She could cut and run, but she'd be leaving them to—*no, that's not right.* She shook her head. Where did this unwelcome sense of responsibility come from? *Damn it, I haven't gone native!* But it was too late to protest: they'd tied her into their lives, and if she just walked out on them, much less walked willingly into the arms of enemies who'd happily see them all dead or buried so deep in jail they'd never see daylight, she'd be personally responsible for the betrayal.

"They'll have to go." Somewhere beyond the reach of a government agency that relied on coerced and impris-oned world-walkers. "But where?" New Britain was a possibility. Her experiment in technology transfer had worked, after all. *What if we went overt?* She wondered.

If we told them who we were and what we could do. Could we cut a deal? Build a military-industrial complex to defend against a military-industrial complex. *The Empire's under siege. The French have the resources to . . .* she blanked. *I don't know enough.* A tantalizing vision clung to the edges of her imagination, a new business idea so monumentally vast and arrogant she could barely contemplate it. Thousands of world-walkers, working with the support and resources of a continental superpower, smuggling information and ideas and sharing lessons leeched from a more advanced world. *I was thinking small. How fast could we drag New Britain into the twenty-first century?* Even without the cohorts of new world-walkers in the making that she'd stumbled across, the product of Angbard's secretive manipulation of a fertility lab's output, it seemed feasible. More than that: it seemed desirable. *Mike's organization will assume that any world-walker is a drug mule until proven otherwise. It won't be healthy to be a world-walker in the USA after the shit hits the fan. We'll need New Britain.*

Miriam shook herself and checked her watch. The hours had drifted by: the shadows were lengthening and her headache was down to a dull throb. She stood up and dusted herself down again, picked up her suitcase, and focused queasily on the locket. "Once more, with spirit . . ."

Bang.

Red-hot needles thrust into her eyes as her stomach heaved again: a giant gripped her head between his hands and squeezed. Cobblestones beneath her boots, and a stink of fresh horseshit. Miriam bent forward, gagging, realizing *I'm standing in the road*—and a narrow road it was, walled on both sides with weathered, greasy brickwork—as the waves of nausea hit.

Bang.

Someone shouted something, at her it seemed. The racket was familiar, and here was a car (or what passed for one in New Britain) with engine running. Hands grabbed at her suitcase: she tightened her grip instinctively.

"Into the car! *Now!*" *Erasmus,* she realized fuzzily.

"'M going to be *sick*—"

"Well you can be sick in the car!" He clutched her arm and tugged.

Bang.

Gunshots?

She tottered forward, stomach lurching, and half-fell, half-slid through the open passenger compartment leg well, collapsing on the wooden floor. The car shuddered and began to roll smoothly on a flare of steam.

BANG. Someone else, not Erasmus, leaned over her and pulled the trigger of a revolver, driving sharp spikes into her outraged eardrums. With a screech of protesting rubber the car picked up speed. *BANG.* Erasmus collapsed on top of her, holding her down. "Stay on the floor," he shouted.

The steam car hit a pothole and bounced, violently. It was too much: Miriam began to retch again, bringing up clear bile.

"Shit." It was the shooter on the back seat, wrinkling his face in disgust. "I think that's—"he paused"—no, they're trying to follow us on foot." The driver piled on the steam, then flung their carriage into a wide turn onto a public boulevard. The shooter sat down hard, holding his pistol below seat level, pointing at the floor. "Can you sit up?" he asked Miriam and Erasmus. "Look respectable fast, we're hitting Ketch Street in a minute."

Erasmus picked himself up. "I'm sorry," he said, his voice shaky. Miriam waited for a moment as her stomach tried to lurch again. "Are you all right?"

"Head hurts," she managed. Arms around her shoulders lifted her to her knees. "My suitcase . . ."

"On the parcel shelf."

More hands from the other side. Together they lifted her into position on the bench seat. The car was rattling and rocking from side to side, making a heady pace— almost forty miles per hour, if she was any judge of speed, but it felt more like ninety in this ragtop steamer.

She gasped for air, chest heaving, trying to get back the wind she'd lost while she was throwing up. "Are you alright?" Burgeson asked again. He'd found a perch on the jump seat opposite, and was clutching a grab-strap behind the chauffeur's station on the right of the cockpit.

"I, it never hit me like that before," she admitted. Amidst the cacophony in her skull she found a moment to be coldly terrified: world-walking usually caused a blood pressure spike and migraine-like symptoms, but nothing like this hellish nausea and pile-driver headache. "Something's up with me."

"Did you get what you wanted?" he pressed her. "Was it worth it?"

"Yeah, yes." She glanced sideways, tiredly. "We haven't been introduced."

"Indeed." Erasmus sent her a narrow-eyed look. "This is Albert. Albert, meet Anne."

Gotcha. "Nice to meet you," she said politely.

"Albert" nodded affably, and palmed his revolver, sliding it into a pocket of his cutaway jacket. "Always nice to meet a fellow traveler," he said.

"Indeed." *Fellow traveler, is it?* She fell silent. Burgeson's political connections came with dangerous strings attached. "What's with the car? And the rush?"

"You didn't hear them shooting at us?" Erasmus looked concerned, as if questioning her sanity.

"I was busy throwing up. What happened?"

"Stakeout," he said. "About ten minutes after your break-in they surrounded the place. If you'd come out the front door—" The brisk two-fingered gesture across his throat made the message all too clear. "I don't know what you've stirred up, but the Polis are *very* upset about something. So I decided to call in some favors and arrange a rescue chariot."

"Albert" nodded. "A good thing too," he said darkly. "You'll excuse me, ma'am." He doffed his cap and began to knead it with his fingers, turning it inside out to reveal a differently patterned lining. "I'll be off at the next crossroads." Erasmus turned and knocked sharply on the wooden partition behind the chauffeur: the car began to slow from its headlong rush.

"Where are we—"Miriam swallowed, then paused to avoid gagging on the taste of bile"—where are we going?"

The car slowed to a near halt, just short of a streetcar stop. "Wait," said Erasmus. To "Albert" he added: "The movement thanks you for your assistance today. Good luck." "Albert" nodded, then stepped onto the sidewalk and marched briskly away without a backward glance. The car picked up speed again, then wheeled in a fast turn onto a twisting side street. "We're going to make the train, I hope," Erasmus said quietly. "The driver doesn't know which one. Or even which station. I hope you can walk."

"My head's sore. But my feet . . ." She tried to shrug, then winced. Only minutes had passed, but she was having difficulty coming to terms with the ambush. "They were trying to kill me. No warnings."

"Yes." He raised one eyebrow. "Maybe your friend was under closer surveillance than he realized."

Miriam shuddered. "Let's get out of here," she suggested.

It took them a while to make their connection. The car dropped them off near a suburban railway platform, from which they made their way to a streetcar stop and then via a circuitous route Erasmus had evidently planned to throw off any curious followers. But an hour later they were waiting on a railway platform in downtown Boston, not too far from the site of Back Bay Station in Miriam's home world. *Geography dictates railroads,* she told herself as another smoky locomotive wheezed and puffed through the station, belching steam towards the arched cast-iron ceiling trusses. *I wonder what else it dictates?* The answer wasn't hard to guess: she'd seen the beggars waiting outside the ticket hall, hoping for a ride out west. Erasmus nodded to himself beside her, then tensed. "Look," he said, "I do believe that's ours."

Miriam glanced towards the end of the long, curving

platform, through the thin haze of steam. "Really?" The long ant column of carriages approaching the platform seemed to vanish into the infinite distance. It was certainly long enough to be a transcontinental express train.

"Carriage eleven, upper deck." He squinted towards it. "We've got a bit of a walk . . ."

The Northern Continental was a city on wheels—wheels six French feet apart, the track gauge nearly half as wide again as the ordinary trains. The huge double-deck carriages loomed overhead, brass handrails gleaming around the doors at either end. Burgeson's expensive passes did more than open doors: uniformed porters took their suitcases and carried them upstairs, holding the second and third class passengers at bay while they boarded. Miriam looked around in astonishment. "This is ridiculous!"

Erasmus smiled lopsidedly. "You don't like it?"

"It's not that—" Miriam walked across to the sofa facing the wall of windows and sat down, bemused. The walls of the compartment were paneled in polished oak as good as anything Duke Angbard had in his aerie at Fort Lofstrom, and if the floor wasn't carpeted in hand-woven Persian rugs, she was no judge of carpet. It reminded her of the expensive hotels she'd stayed at in Boston, when she'd been trying to set up a successful technology transfer business and impress the local captains of industry. "Does this convert into a bed, or . . . ?"

"The bedrooms are through there." Erasmus pointed at the other end of the lounge. "The bathroom is just past the servants' quarters—"

"Servants' quarters?"

Erasmus looked at her oddly. "Yes, I keep forgetting. Labor is expensive where you come from, isn't it?"

Miriam looked around again. "Wow. We're here for the next three or four days?"

A distant whistle cut through the window glass, and with a nearly undetectable jerk the carriage began to move.

"Yes." He nodded. "Plenty of time to take your shoes off."

"Okay." She bent down automatically, then blinked stupidly. "This doesn't come cheap, does it?"

"No." She heard a scrape of chair legs across carpet and looked up, catching Erasmus in the process of sitting down in a spindly Queen Anne reproduction. He watched her with his wide, dark, eyes, his bearing curiously bird-like. Behind him, Empire Station slid past in ranks of cast-iron pillars. "But one tends to be interfered with less if one is seen to be able to support expensive tastes."

"Right . . . so you're doing this, spending however much, just to go and see a man about a book?"

A brief pause. "Yes." Erasmus smiled faintly.

Miriam stared at him. *And you gave me a gun to carry? Either you're mad, or you trust me, or . . .* she couldn't complete the sentence: it was too preposterous. "That must be some book."

"Yes, it is." He nodded. "It has already shaken empires and slain princes." His cheek twitched at some unspoken unpleasantness. "I have a copy of it in my luggage, if you'd like to read it."

"Huh?" She blinked, stupidly. "I thought you said you were going to see a man about a book? As in, you were going to buy or sell one?"

"Not exactly: perhaps I should have said, I'm going to see a man about *his* book. And if all goes well, he's going to come back east with us." He glanced down at his feet. "Does Sir Adam Burroughs mean anything to you?"

Miriam shook her head.

"Probably just as well," Erasmus muttered to himself. "I think you ought to at least look at the book, after dinner. Just so you understand what you're getting into."

"Alright." She stood up. "Is there an electrical light in the bedroom? I need to plug my machine in to charge . . ."

The fridge was half empty, the half-and-half was half past yogurt, and Oscar thought he was a burglar. That was the downside of coming home. On the upside: Mike could finally look forward to sleeping in his own bed without fear of disturbances, he had a crate of antibiotics to munch on, and Oscar hadn't thrown up on the carpet again. *Home. Funny place, where are the coworkers and security guards? Out on the street, obviously.* Mike watched Herz drive off from the porch, then closed the door and went inside.

The crutches got in the way, and the light bulb in the hallway had blown, but at least Oscar wasn't trying to wrap his furry body around the fiberglass cast in a friendly feline attempt to trip up the food ape. *Yet.* Mike shuffled through into the living room and lowered himself into the sofa, struggled inconclusively with the one shoe he was wearing, and flicked on the TV. The comforting babble of CNN washed over him. *I need some time out,* he decided. *This being hospitalized shit is hard work.* Spending half an hour as a couch potato was a seductive prospect: a few minutes later, his eyelids were drooping shut.

Perhaps it was the lack of hospital-supplied Valium, but Mike—who didn't normally remember his dreams— found himself in a memorable but chaotic confabulatory realm. One moment he was running a three-legged race through a minefield, the sense of dread almost choking him as Sergeant Hastert's corpse flopped drunkenly against him, one limp arm around his shoulders; the next, he was lying on a leather bench seat, unable to move, opposite Dr. James, the spook from head office. "It's important that you find the bomb," James was saying, but the cranky old lady on the limousine's parcel shelf was pointing a pistol at the back of his head. "Matthias is a traitor; I want to know who he was working for."

He tried to open his mouth to warn the colonel about the old madwoman with the gun, but it was Miriam crouching on the shelf now, holding a dictaphone and making notes. "It's all about manipulating the currency exchange rates," she explained: then she launched into an enthusiastic description of an esoteric trading scam she was investigating, one that involved taking greenbacks into a parallel universe, swapping them for pieces of eight, and melting them down into Swiss watches. Mike tried to sit up and pull Pete out of the line of fire, but someone was holding him down. Then he woke up, and Oscar, who'd been sitting on his chest, head-butted him on the underside of his chin.

"Thanks, buddy." Oscar head-butted him again, then made a noise like a dying electric shaver. Mike figured his bowl was empty. He took stock: his head ached, he had pins and needles in one arm, the exposed toes of his left foot were cold to the point of numbness, and the daylight outside his window was in short supply. "Come here, you." He reached up to stroke the tomcat, who was clearly intent on exercising his feline right to bear a grudge against his human whenever it suited him, and not a moment longer. For a moment he felt a bleak wave of depression. The TV was still on, quietly babbling inanities from the corner of the room. *How long is this going to take?* Mrs. Beckstein had said it could be weeks, and with Colonel Smith tasking him with being her contact, that could leave him stuck indoors here for the duration.

He pushed himself upright and hobbled dizzily over to the kitchen phone—the cordless handset had succumbed to a flat battery—and dialed the local pizza delivery shop from memory. Working out what the hell to do with this surfeit of time (which he couldn't even use for a fishing trip or a visit to his cousins) could wait 'til tomorrow.

The next morning, the long habit of keeping office hours—despite a week of disrupted sleep patterns—dragged Mike into unwilling consciousness. He took his antibiotics, then spent a fruitless half-hour trying to figure out how to shower without getting water in his cast, which made his leg itch abominably. *This is hopeless,* he told himself, when the effort of trying to lift an old wooden stool into the shower left him so tired he had to sit down: *I really am ill.* The infection—thankfully under control—had taken out of him what little energy the torn-up and broken leg had left behind. The difficulty of accomplishing even minor tasks was galling, and sitting at home on full pay, knowing that serious, diligent people like Agent Herz were out there busting their guts to get the job done made it even worse. But there was just about nothing he could do that would contribute to the mission, beyond what he was already doing: sitting at ground zero of a stakeout.

Mike had never been a loafer, and while he was used to taking vacations, enforced home rest was an unaccustomed and unwelcome imposition. For a while he thought about getting out and picking up some groceries, but the prospect of getting into the wagon and driving with his left leg embedded in a mass of blue fiberglass was just too daunting. *Better wait for Helen,* he decided. His regular cleaner would be in like clockwork tomorrow—he could work on a shopping list in the meantime. *There's got to be a better way.* Then he shook his head. *You're sick, son. Take five.*

Just after lunchtime (a cardboard-tasting microwave lasagna that had spent too long at the bottom of the chest freezer), the front doorbell rang. Cursing, Mike stumbled into the hall, pushing off the walls in a hurry, hoping whoever it was wouldn't get impatient and leave before he made it. He paused just inside the vestibule and checked the spy hole, then opened the door. "Come in!" He tried to take a step back and ended up leaning against the wall.

"No need to put on a song and dance, Mike, I know you feel like shit." Smith nodded stiffly. "Go on, take your time. I'll shut the door. We need to talk about stuff." He was carrying a pair of brown paper grocery bags.

"Uh, okay." Mike pushed himself off from the wall and half-hopped back towards the living room. The crutch would have come in handy, but he knew his way around well enough to use the furniture and door frames for support. "What brings you here?" He called over his shoulder. "I thought I was meant to be taking it easy."

"You . . . are." Smith glanced around as he came into the main room. *Not used to visiting employees at home*, Mike realized. "But there's some stuff we need to talk about."

I do not need this, Mike lowered himself onto the sofa. "You couldn't tell me in the hospital?" he asked.

"You were still kind of crinkle-cut, son. And there were medics about."

"Gotcha." Mike waved at the door to the kitchen. "I'd offer you a coffee or something but I'm having a hard time getting about . . ."

"That's alright." Smith put one of the grocery bags down on the side table, then walked over to the kitchen door and put the other on the worktop inside. Then he made a circuit of the living room. He held his hands tightly behind his back, as if forcibly restraining himself from checking for dust on top of the picture rail. "I won't be long."

"Are we being monitored?"

Smith glanced at him. "I sure hope so." He gestured at the walls. "Not on audio, but there's a real expensive infrared camera out there, son, and a couple of guys in a van just to keep an eye on you."

"There are?" Mike knew better than to get angry. "What are they expecting to see?"

"Visitors who don't arrive through the front door." Smith slung one leg over the arm of the recliner and leaned on it, inspecting Mike pensively.

"Oh, right." For a second, Mike felt the urge to kick his earlier self for passing on absolutely everything he'd learned. The impulse passed: he'd been fever-ridden, and anyway it was what he was supposed to do. But still, if he hadn't done so, he wouldn't be stuck out here under virtual house arrest. He might be back in hospital, with no worries about groceries. And besides, Smith had a point. "You might want to warn them I'm expecting a housekeeper to show tomorrow—she drops by a couple of times a week."

"I'll tell them." Smith paused. "As it happens, I know you're not being listened in on, unless you lift the receiver on that phone—I signed the wiretap request myself. There's stuff we need to talk about, and this place is more private than my office, if you follow my drift."

"I'm not being listened in on right now? Suits me." Mike leaned back in the sofa. "Talk away. Sorry if I don't, uh, if I'm not too focused: I feel like shit."

"Yes, well." Smith glanced at him. "That's why you're on sick leave. You may be interested to know that your story checks out: that is, Beckstein's mother disappeared six months ago. Her house is still there, the bills are being paid on time, but there's nobody home. We haven't gotten a trace on her income stream so far; her credit cards and bank account are ordinary enough, but the deposits are coming in from an offshore bank account in Liechtenstein and that's turning out to be hard to trace. Anyway, I think we can confirm that she's one of them." He stood up again and paced over to the kitchen door then back, as if his legs were incapable of standing still. "This is a, a tactical mess. We'd hoped to get at least a few successful contacts in place before our ability to operate in fairyland was blown. What this means is that they, uh, Beckstein senior's faction, are going to be alert for informants from now on. On the other hand, if they're willing to talk we've got an—admittedly biased—HUMINT source to develop. Contacts, in other words."

Mike stared at him. Smith was just about sweating bullets. "Who do we talk to in the Middle East?" he asked. "I mean, when we want to know what al-Qaeda is planning?"

"That's a lot more accessible. This, these guys, it's like China in the fifties or sixties." Smith looked as if he was sucking on a lemon. "Look." He picked up the second grocery bag and handed it to Mike. "This stuff is strictly off the books because, unfortunately, we're off the map here, right outside the reservation."

"What—" Mike upended the bag and boxes fell out. A mobile phone, ammunition, a pistol. "The fuck?"

"Glock 18, like their own people use. The phone was bought anonymously for cash. Listen." Smith hunkered down in front of him, still radiating extreme discomfort. "The phone's preprogrammed with Dr. James's private number. This is running right from the top. If you have to negotiate with them, James can escalate you all the way to Daddy Warbucks."

Mike was impressed, despite himself. *They're briefing the vice president?* "What's the gun for?"

"In case the other faction come calling for you."

Shit. "Hadn't thought of that," he admitted. "What do you want me to do?"

Smith took a deep breath. "Find out if GREENSLEEVES was blowing smoke. If all he had was a couple of slugs of hot metal, that's still bad—but right now it would be really good if we could call off the NIRT investigation. On the other hand, you might want to point out to the Beckstein faction what would happen if one of our cities goes up."

"Huh. What would happen? What could we do, realistically?" Mike stared at him.

Smith paused for a few seconds. "I'm just guessing here, you understand. I'm not privy to that information. But my guess is that we would be very, very angry—for all of about thirty minutes." He swallowed. "And then we'd retaliate in kind, Mike. The SSADM backpack nukes have been out of inventory since the early seventies and the W54 cores were retired by eighty-nine, but they don't have to stay that way. The schematics are still on file and if I were a betting man I'd place a C-note on Pantex being able to run one up in a few weeks, if they haven't done so already. Daddy Warbucks and the Wolfman are both gung-ho about developing a new generation of nukes. It could get really ugly really fast, Mike. A smuggler's war, tit for tat. But we'd win, because they've got better logistics but we've got a choke hold on the weapons supply. And if it comes to it, I don't think we'd hold back from making it a war of extermination. It's not hard to stick a cobalt jacket on a bomb when there's zero risk of the fall-out coming home."

"Wow, that's ugly all right." 9/11 had been bad enough: the nightmare Smith was dangling before him was infinitely worse. "Anything else?"

"Yep." The colonel stood up. "From now on, until you're through with this thing or we call it off, you're in a box. We don't want you in day-to-day contact with the organization. The less you know, the less you can give away."

"But I—oh. You're thinking, if they kidnap me—"

"Yes, that's what we're afraid of."

"Right." Mike swallowed. "So. I'm to tell Mrs. Beckstein about Matt's bomb threat, and we either want it handed over right now, or convincing evidence that he was bluffing. Otherwise, they're looking at retaliation in kind. What else?"

"You give her the mobile phone and tell her who it connects to. There's a deal on the table that she might find interesting." Smith nodded to himself. "And there's one other thing you can pass on at the same time."

"Yes?"

"Tell her we're working on the world-walking mechanism. Her window of opportunity for negotiation is open right now—but if she waits too long, it's going to slam shut." He stood up. "Once we aren't forced to rely on captured couriers, as soon as we can send the 82nd Airborne across, we aren't going to need the Clan anymore. And we want her to know that."

In Otto's opinion one camp was much like another: the only difference was how far the stink stretched. His majesty's camp was better organized than most, but with three times as many men it paid to pay attention to details like the latrines. King Egon might not like the tinkers, but he was certainly willing to copy their obsession with hygiene if it kept his men from the pest. And so Otto rode with his retinue, tired and dusty from the road, past sur-

prisingly tidy rows of tents and the larger pavilions of
their eorls and lords, towards the big pavilion at the heart
of the camp—in order to ask the true whereabouts of his
majesty.

The big pavilion wasn't hard to find—the royal banner
flying from the tall mast anchored outside it would have
been a giveaway, if nothing else—but Otto's eyes narrowed at the size of the guard detachment waiting there.
*Either he mistrusts one of his own, or the bluff is dou-
bled,* he thought. Handing his horse's reins to one of his
hand-men he swung himself down from the saddle, wincing slightly as he turned towards the three guards in household surcoats approaching from the side of the pavilion.
"Who's in charge here?" he demanded.

"I am." The tallest of them tilted his helmet back.

Otto stiffened in shock, then immediately knelt, heart
in mouth with fear: "My liege, I did not recognize you—"

"You weren't meant to." Egon smiled thinly. "No shame
attaches. Rise, Otto, and walk with me. You brought your
company?"

"Yes—all who are fit to ride. And your messenger, Sir
Geraunt."

"Good." The king carefully shifted the strap on his exotic and lethal weapon, pointing the muzzle at the ground
as he walked around the side of the tent. Otto noticed the
two other household guards following, barely out of
earshot. They, too, carried black, strangely proportioned
witch weapons. "I've got something to show you."

"Sire?" Behind him, Heidlor was keeping his immediate bodyguard together. *Good man.* The king's behavior
was disturbingly unconventional—

"The witches can walk through another world," remarked Egon. "They can ambush you if you keep still
and they know where you are. Armies are large, they attract spies. Constant movement is the best defense. That,
and not making a target of one's royal self by wearing
gilded armor and sleeping in the largest tent."

Ah. Otto nodded. So there was a reason for all this strangeness, after all. "What would you have me do, sire?"

Behind the royal pavilion there was a hummock of mounded-up earth. Someone—many someones—had labored to build it up from the ground nearby, and then cut a narrow trench into it. "Pay attention." His majesty marched along the trench, which curved as it cut into the mound. Otto followed him, curious as to what his majesty might find so interesting in a heap of soil. "Ah, here we are." The trench descended until the edges were almost out of reach above him, then came to an abrupt end in an open, circular space almost as large as the royal pavilion. The muddy floor was lined with rough-cut planks: four crates were spaced around the walls, as far apart as possible. The king placed a proprietorial hand on one of the crates. "What do you make of it?"

Otto blanked for a moment. He'd been expecting something, but this . . . "Spoils?" he asked, slowly.

"Very good!" Egon grinned boyishly. "Yes, I took these from the witches. Hopefully they don't realize they're missing, yet. Tonight, another one should arrive."

"But they're—" Otto stared. "Treasure?" His eyes narrowed. "Their demon blasting powder?"

"Something even better." A low metal box, drab green in color, lay on the planking next to the crate. Egon bent down and flicked open the latches that held the lid down. "Behold." He flipped the lid over, to reveal the contents— a gun.

"One of the tinkers'," Otto noted, forgetting to hold his tongue. "An arms dump?"

"Yes." Egon straightened up. "My sources told me about them, so I had my—helpers—go looking." He looked at Otto, his face unreadable. "Twenty years ago, thirty years ago, the witch families handed their collective security to the white duke. He standardized them. Their guns, your pistol—" he gestured at Otto's holster—"when you run out of their cartridges, what will you do?"

Otto shrugged. "It's a problem, sire. We can't make anything like these."

Egon nodded. "They have tried hard to conceal a dirty little secret: the truth is, neither can they. So they stockpile cartridges of a common size and type, purchased from the demons in the shadow world. Your pistol uses the same kind as my carbine. But they kept something better for themselves. This is a, an M60, a *machine gun.*" He pronounced the unfamiliar, alien syllables carefully. "It fires bigger bullets, faster and farther. It outranges my six pounder carronades, in fact. But it is useless without cartridges, big ones that come on a metal belt. And they are profligate with ammunition. So the duke stockpiled cartridges for the M60s, all over the place."

Otto looked at the gun. It was bigger than the king's MP5, almost as long as a musket. Then he looked at the crate. "How much do you have, sire?"

"Not enough." Egon frowned. "Four crates, almost eighty thousand rounds, six guns. And some very fine blasting powder."

"Only six—" Otto stopped. "They haven't noticed?"

The king lowered the lid back on top of the gun. "Ten years ago, the witches began to re-equip with a better weapon." He patted the MP5: "These are deadly, are they not? But it is a side-arm. They held the M60s to defend their castles and keeps. But they're heavy and take a lot of ammunition. They have a new gun now, the SAW. And it takes different ammunition, lighter, with a shorter range— still far greater than anything we have, though, near as far as a twelve pounder can throw shot, and why not? A soldier with one of the new demon-guns can carry twice as much ammunition, and war among the witches is always about mobility. So they gradually forgot about the M60s, leaving the crates of ammunition in the cellars of their houses, and they forgot about the guns, too." The royal smile reappeared. "But their servants remembered."

"Sire. How would you have me use these guns?"

The royal smile broadened.

"The foe has been informed, by hitherto unimpeach-able sources, that I will be attacking Castle Hjorth in the next week. They will concentrate in defense of the castle, which as the gateway to the Eagle hills would indeed be a prize worth capturing. Baron Drakel, who is already on his way there at the head of a battalion of pike and mus-ketry, has the honor of ensuring that the witches have tar-gets to aim their fire at. Meanwhile, the majority of the forces camped here will leave on the morrow for the real target. Your task is to spend a day with your best hand-men, and with my armorers, who will remain behind, in-structing you in the use of the machine guns, and the explosives. Then you will follow the main force, who will not be aware of your task."

"Sire! This is a great honor, I am sure, but am I to un-derstand that you do not want to bring these guns to bear in the initial battle?"

"Yes." Egon stared at the baron, his eyes disturbingly clear. "There are traitors in the midst of my army, Otto. I know for a fact that you are not one of them—"Otto shud-dered as if a spider had crawled across his grave"—but this imposes certain difficulties upon my planning."

Otto glanced round. The two royal bodyguards stood with their backs to him. "Sire?"

"The witches cannot be defeated by conventional means, Otto. If we besiege them, they can simply vanish into their shadow world. There they can move faster than we can, ob-tain weapons of dire power from their demonic masters, and continue their war against us. So to rid my kingdom of their immediate influence, I must render their castles and palaces useless as strong points."

Egon paced around the nearest ammunition crate. "At the outset, I determined to pin them down, forcing them to defend their holdings, to prove to my more reluctant sworn men that the witches are vulnerable. Your raids were a great success. For every village you put to the sword, another ten landholders swore to my flag, and for that you will be rewarded most handsomely, Otto." His eyes gleamed. "But to allow you to live to a ripe old age in your duchy—"he continued, ignoring Otto's sharp intake of breath"—we must force the witches to concentrate on ground of our choice, and then massacre them, while denying them the ability to regroup in a strong place. To that end, it occurs to me that a castle can be as difficult to break *out* of as it is to break *in* to—especially if it is surrounded by machine guns. This is a difficult trick, Otto, and it would be impossible without the treachery of their servitors and hangers-on, but I am going to take the Hjalmar Palace—and use it as an anvil, and you the hammer, to smash the witches."

Traveling across New Britain by train in a first-class suite was a whole lot less painful than anything Amtrak or the airlines had to offer, and Miriam almost found herself enjoying it—except for the constant nagging fear of discovery. Discovery of what, and by whom, wasn't a question she could answer—it wasn't an entirely rational fear. *I still feel like an impostor everywhere I go,* she realized. Erasmus's attempts to engage in friendly conversation over dinner didn't help, either: she'd been unable to make small talk comfortably and had lapsed into a strained, embarrassed silence. The tables in the wide-gauge dining car were sufficiently far apart, and the noise of the wheels loud enough, that she wasn't worried about being overheard: but just being on display in public made her itch as if there was a target pinned to her back. The thing she most wanted to ask Erasmus about was off-limits, anyway—the nature of the errand that was taking a lowly shopkeeper haring out to the west coast in the lap of luxury. *I'm going to see a man about his book?* That must be some book—this journey was costing the local equivalent of a couple of around-the-world airline tickets in first class, at a time when there were soup kitchens on the street corners and muggers in the New London alleyways who were so malnourished they couldn't tackle a stressed-out woman.

That was more than enough reason to itch. Things had gone bad in New Britain even faster than they had in her own personal life, on a scale that was frightening to think about. But the real cause of her restlessness was closer to home. *Sooner or later I'm going to have to stop drifting and do something,* she told herself. Relying on the comfort of near-strangers—or friends with secret agendas of their own—rankled. *If only I had that laptop working! Or I could go home and call Mike. Set things moving. And then*—her imagination ran into a brick wall.

After dinner they returned to the private lounge, and Miriam managed to unwind slightly once they were on their own. There was a wet bar beside the window, and Erasmus opened it: "Would you care for a brandy before bed?"

"That would be good." She sat down on the chaise. "They really overdid the dessert."

"You think so?" He shook his head. "We're traveling in style. The chef would be offended if we didn't eat."

"Really?" She accepted the glass he offered. "Hmm." She sniffed. "Interesting." A sip of brandy and her stomach had something else to worry about: "I'd get fat fast if we ate like that regularly."

"Fat?" He looked at her oddly. "You've got a long way to go before you're fat."

Oops. It was another of those momentary dislocations that reminded Miriam she wasn't at home here. New British culture held to a different standard of beauty from Hollywood and the New York catwalks: in a world where agriculture was barely mechanized and shipping was slow, plumpness implied wealth, or at least immunity from starvation. "You think so?" She found herself unable to suppress a lopsided smile of embarrassment, and dealt with it by hiding her face behind the brandy glass.

"I think you're just right. You've got a lovely face, Miriam, when you're not hiding it. Your new hairstyle complements it beautifully."

He looked at her so seriously that she felt her ears flush. "Hey! Not fair." A sudden sinking feeling, *Is that what this is about? He gets me alone and then—*

"I'm—" He did a double-take. "Oh dear! You— Did I say something wrong?"

Miriam shook her head. He seemed sincere: *Am I misunderstanding?* "I think we just ran into an etiquette black hole." He nodded, politely uncomprehending. "Sorry. Where I come from what you said would be something between flattery and an expression of interest, and I'm just not up to handling subtlety right now."

"Expression of . . . ?" It was his turn to look embarrassed. "My mistake."

She put the glass down. "Have a seat." She patted the chaise. Erasmus looked at it, looked back at her, then perched bird-like on the far end. *Better change the subject*, she told herself. "You were married, weren't you?" she asked.

He stared at her as if she'd slapped him. "Yes. What of it?"

Whoops. "I, uh, was wondering. That is. What happened?"

"She died," he said tersely. He glanced at the floor, then raised his brandy glass.

Miriam's vision blurred. "I'm sorry."

"Why? It's not your fault." After a long moment, he shrugged. "You had your fellow Roland. It's not so different."

"What—"she swallowed"—happened to her?" *How long ago was it?* she wondered. Sometimes she thought she'd come to terms with Roland's death, but at other times it still felt like yesterday.

"Twenty years ago. Back then I had prospects." He raised an eyebrow as if considering his next words. "Some would say, I threw them away. The movement—well."

"The movement?"

"I was sent to college, by my uncle—my father was dead, you know how it goes—to study for the bar. They'd relaxed the requirements, so dissenters, freethinkers, even atheists, all were allowed to affirm and practice. His majesty's father was rather less narrow than John Frederick, I don't know whether that means anything to you. But anyway . . . I had some free time, as young students with a modest stipend do, and I had some free thoughts, and I became involved with the league. We had handbills to write and print and distribute, and a clear grievance to bring before their lordships in hope of redress, and we were optimistic, I think. We thought we might have a future."

"The league? You had some kind of political demands?" Miriam racked her brains. She'd run across mention of the league—*league of what* had never been clear—in the samizdat history books he'd loaned her, but only briefly, right at the end, as some sort of hopeful coda to the authorial present.

"Yes." He looked distant. "Little things like a universal franchise, regardless of property qualifications and religion and marital status. Some of the committee wanted women to vote, too—but that was thought too extreme for a first step. And we wanted a free press, public decency and the laws of libel permitting."

"Uh." She closed her mouth. "But you were . . ."

The frown turned into a wry smile. "I was a young hothead. Or easily led. I met Annie first at a public meeting, and then renewed her acquaintance at the *People's Voice* where she was laying type. She was the printer's daughter, and neither he nor my uncle approved of our liaison. But once I received my letters and acquired a clerk's post, I could afford to support her, which made her father come round, and my uncle just muttered darkly about writing me out of his will for a while, and stopped doing even that after the wedding. So we had a good four years together, and she insisted on laying type even when the two boys came along, and I wrote for the sheets—anonymously, I must add—and we were very happy. Until it all ended."

Miriam raised her glass for another sip. Somehow the contents had evaporated. "Here, let me refill that," she said, taking Erasmus's glass. She stood up and walked past him to get to the bar, wobbling slightly as the carriage jolted across a set of points. "What went wrong?"

"In nineteen eighty-six, on November the fourteenth, six fine fellows from the northeast provinces traveled to the royal palace in Savannah. There had been a huge march the week before in New London, and it had gone off smoothly, the petition of a million names being presented to the black rod—but the king himself was not in residence, being emphysemic. That winter came harsh and early, so he'd decamped south to Georgia. It was his habit to go for long drives in the country, to take the air. Well, the level of expectation surrounding the petition was high, and rumors were swirling like smoke: that the king had read the petition and would agree to the introduction of a bill, that the king had read the petition and threatened to bring home the army, that the king had this and the king had that. All nonsense, of course. The king was on vacation and he refused to deal with matters of state that were anything less than an emergency. Or so I learned later. Back then, I was looking for a progressive practice that was willing to take on a junior partner, and Annie was expecting again."

Miriam finished pouring and put the stopper back in the decanter. She passed a glass back to him: "So what happened?"

"Those six fine gentlemen were a little impatient. They'd formed a ring, and they'd convinced themselves that the king was a vicious tyrant who would like nothing more than to dream up new ways to torment the workers. You know, I think—judging by your own history books—how it goes. The mainstream movement spawns tributaries, some of which harbor currents that flow fast and deep.

The Black Fist Freedom Guard, as they called themselves, followed the king in a pair of fast motor carriages
until they learned his habitual routes. Then they assassinated him, along with the queen, and one of his two
daughters, by means of a petard."

"They what?" Miriam sat down hard. "That's crazy!"

"Yes, it was." Erasmus nodded, calmly enough. "George
Frederick himself pulled his dying father from the wreckage. He was already something of a reactionary, but not,
I think, an irrational one—until the Black Fist murdered
his parents."

"But weren't there guards, or something?" Miriam shook
her head. *What about the secret service?* she wondered. If
someone tried a stunt like that on a U.S. president it just
wouldn't work. It wouldn't be allowed to work. Numer-
ous whack-jobs had tried to kill Clinton when he was in
office: a number had threatened or actually tried to off the
current president. Nobody had gotten close to a president
of the United States since nineteen eighty-six. "Didn't he
have any security?"

"Oh yes, he had security. He was secure in the knowl-
edge that he was the king-emperor, much beloved by the
majority of his subjects. Does that surprise you? John
Frederick goes nowhere without half a company of guards
and a swarm of Polis agents, but his father relied on two
loyal constables with pistols. They were injured in the attack, incidentally: one of them died later."

He took a deep, shuddering breath, then another sip
of the brandy. "The day after the assassination, a state
of emergency was declared. Demonstrations ensued. On
Black Monday, the seventeenth, a column of demonstra-
tors marching towards the royal complex on Manhattan
Island were met by dragoons armed with heavy steam re-
peaters. More than three hundred were killed, mostly in
the stampede. We were . . . there, but on the outskirts, Annie and I. We had the boys to think of. We obviously
didn't think hard enough. The next day, they arrested me.
My trial before the tribunal lasted eighteen minutes, by

the clock on the courtroom wall. The man before me they sentenced to hang for being caught distributing our news sheet, but I was lucky. All they knew was that I'd been away from my workplace during the massacre, and I'd been limping when I got back. The evidence was merely circumstantial, and so was the sentence they gave me: twelve years in the camps."

He took a gulp of the brandy and swallowed, spluttering for a moment. "Annie wasn't so lucky," he added.

"What? They hanged her?" Miriam leaned toward him, aghast.

"No." He smiled sadly. "They only gave her two years in a women's camp. I don't know if you know what that was like . . . no? Alright. It was hard enough for the men. Annie died—"he stared into his glass—"in childbed."

"I don't understand—"

"Use your imagination," Erasmus snapped. "What do you think the guards were like?"

"Oh god." Miriam swallowed. "I'm so sorry."

"The boys went to a state orphanage," Erasmus added. "In Australia."

"Enough." She held up a hand: "I'm sorry I asked!"

The fragile silence stretched out. "I'm not," Erasmus said quietly. "It was just a little bit odd to talk about it. After so long."

"You got out . . . four years ago?"

"Nine." He drained his glass and replaced it on the occasional table. "The camps were overfull. They got sloppy. I was moved to internal exile, and there was a—what your history book called an underground railway. 'Erasmus Burgeson' isn't the name I was known by back then."

"Wow." Miriam stared at him. "You've been living under an assumed identity all this time?"

He nodded, watching her expression. "The movement provides. They needed a dodgy pawnbroker in Boston, you see, and I fitted the bill. A dodgy pawnbroker with a history of a couple of years in the camps, nothing serious, nothing *excessively* political. The real me they'd hang for sure if they caught him, these days. I hope you don't mind notorious company?"

"I'm—" She shook her head. "It's crazy." *You were writing for a newspaper, for crying out loud! Asking for voting rights and freedom of the press! And those are hanging offenses?* "And if what you were campaigning for back then 'is crazy, so am I." Her eyes narrowed. "What's the movement's platform now? Is it still just about the franchise, and freedom of speech? Or have things changed?"

"Oh yes." He was still studying her, she realized. "Eighty-six was a wake-up cry. The very next central council meeting that was held—two years later, in exile— announced that the existence of a hereditary crown was a flaw in the body politic. The council decreed that nothing less than the overthrow of the king-emperor and the replacement of their Lordships and Commons by a republic of free men and women, equal before the law, would suffice. The next day, the Commons passed a bill of attainder against everyone in the movement. A month after *that* the pope excommunicated us—he declared democracy to be a mortal sin. But by that time we already knew we were damned."

11

ђot pursuit

Another day, another Boston. Brill walked up the staircase to the front office and glanced around. "Where's Morgan?" she demanded.

"He's in the back room." The courier folded his news sheet and laid it carefully on the desk.

"Don't call ahead." She frowned, then headed straight back to the other office, overlooking the back yard colocated with Miriam's house's garden in the other Boston, in New Britain.

The house—Miriam's house, according to the deeds of ownership, not that it mattered much once she'd allowed her commercial submarine to surface in the harbor of the Clan's Council deliberations—was a stately lump of shingle-fronted stonework with a view out over the harbor. But over here the building was distinctly utilitarian, overshadowed by a row of office towers. The architecture in New Britain was stunted by relatively high material and transport costs: planting fifty-thousand-ton lumps of concrete and steel on top of landfill was a relatively recent innovation in New Britain, and hadn't corrupted their skyline yet. But this one was different.

Oskar was waiting outside the door to the rear office. He looked bored. The cut of his jacket failed to conceal his shoulder holster. "How long are you here for?"

"I came to see Morgan." She stared him in the eye. "Then I need to cross over, get changed into native garb, and draw funds. I may be some time. It depends."

"Cross over. Right." Oskar twitched. "You know there's a problem."

"Problem?"

"You'd better ask the boss." Oskar backed up, rapped on the door twice, then opened it for her.

"Who—" Morgan looked up. He had his feet up on the mahogany desk, a half-eaten burger at his right hand, and judging by his expression her appearance was deeply unwelcome.

"Hello there. Don't let me keep you from your food."

"Lady Brilliana!" He swung his feet down hastily, almost knocking his chair over in his hurry to stand up.

"Sit down." She walked around the desk and pulled out the chair on his right, then sat beside him. "Oskar tells me there's a *problem*. On the other side."

Morgan twitched even more violently than Oskar had. "You're telling me. Have you come to fix it?"

"Tell me about it first."

"You haven't—" He swallowed his words, but the look of dismay was genuine enough in her estimate.

"I need to cross over and run a search in New Britain," she said evenly. "If there's a problem with our main safe house in Boston, I need to know it."

"The Polis—the security cops? They raided the house. We barely pulled everybody out in time."

Brilliana swallowed a curse. "When was this?"

"Three days ago. I thought everyone knew—"

"Was it coordinated action?" she demanded.

Morgan shook himself, visibly trying to pull himself

together. "I don't think so," he admitted. "The situation over there's been going to the midden, frankly, and the Polis are running around looking for saboteurs and spies under every table. Six weeks ago they turned over the workshop and shut it down: some of the staff were arrested for sedition. We were already lying low—"

"What about Burgeson?" Brill demanded.

"Oh," he said. "That."

"Yes, *that*." She nodded. "I came as soon as I heard. How long has the watch been running?"

"All week, since before the raid. I can't be sure, my lady, but I think our activities might be what attracted the interest of the Polis. We were using the house as a staging post, and when he went down to New York . . ." His shrug was eloquent.

"I see." Brilliana paused for a moment. *It would fit the picture,* she considered. If the Polis were already watching the house, and spotted strangers based there keeping watch on a suspect, that would get their attention. *And if Burgeson headed for London and the strangers followed him . . .* that would be when they'd bring down the hammer, right enough. "But you lost the trail in Man—New London."

"He started evading," Morgan protested. "Like a seasoned agent!"

"He was last seen with a female companion," Brilliana pointed out coldly. "Which was the whole point of the watch on him."

"It's not her," Morgan dismissed her concern. "Some bint he picked up from a brothel in New London—"

"You sound awfully sure of that. Would you like to place a little wager on it? Either way? The last joint on your left little finger, against mine?"

She grinned as she said it: he turned white. "No, no," he mumbled. "It'd be just my luck if—look, he was deliberately trying to throw his tail, that's what Joseph said! And the business with them changing trains? I had Oskar and Georg waiting at the station but Burgeson and his companion weren't on it when it pulled in."

"Morgan. *Morgan.*" Brill smiled again. The way it made Morgan wince was truly wonderful. On the other hand, he probably thought she was reporting direct to the thin white duke. "I already know that you're undermanned and don't have enough pairs of boots on the ground. And you've lost your forward base, due to enemy action, not negligence." At least, not *active* negligence. Nobody could accuse Morgan of spontaneous activity—he might be stupid, but at least he possessed the mitigating quality of bone-deep laziness. His sins were seldom those of commission. "So why are you trying so hard to convince me it's not your fault? Anyone would think you were trying to hide something! Whereas if it's just Burgeson giving you the slip . . ." She shrugged.

"It's embarrassing, that's what it is." He squinted at her suspiciously. "And I know what you think of me."

You do? Really? The temptation to tell him the truth was hard to resist, but she managed to restrain herself. *Later.* "The shop. You've checked the door alarm, haven't you?"

"I've had it staked out since the train departed." Morgan looked pleased with himself.

"Right. Team in the street? A wire and transmitter on the door?" He nodded. "You know there's a secret back way in? And you know about Helge's experience with trip wires?" His smile slipped. "Here's what's going to happen. Oskar and I are going to disguise ourselves then cross over via the backup transfer site. While we are checking the shop out—and I expect our birds have flown the coop, long since—you'll finish your lunch then send a messenger across to cable the railway ticket office asking if they have any reservations in the name of, let's see, a Mr. and Mrs. Burgeson would spring to mind? That *is* the alias they were using at the hotel? And if so, I want to know where they're going, and where the train stops en route, so I can meet them before they get to the final destination." Brill had allowed her voice to grow quieter, so that Morgan was unconsciously leaning towards her as she finished the sentence.

"But if they're on a train—they could be on their way to Buenos Aires, or anywhere!"

"So what? The organization bizjet is on standby for me at Logan." She stood up. "I'll be back in two hours, and I expect a detailed report on the surveillance operation and Burgeson's current location, so I can set up the intercept and work out who to draft in." She took a deep breath. "We'd better be in time. And you'd better find out where they're going, because if we lose her again, the duke will be *really* pissed."

The council of war took place in a conference room in the Boston Sheraton, just off the Hyatt Center, with air-conditioning and full audio-visual support. All but two of the eighteen attendees were male, and all wore dark, conservatively cut business suits: they were polite but distant in their dealings with the hotel staff. The facilities manager who oversaw their refreshments and lunch buffet got the distinct impression that they were foreign bankers, perhaps a delegation from a very starchy Swiss institution. Or maybe they were a committee of cemetery managers. It hardly mattered, though. They were clearly the best kind of customer—quiet, undemanding, dignified, and utterly unlikely to make a mess or start any fights.

"Helmut. An update on the opposition's current disposition, if you please," said the graying, distinguished-looking fellow seated at the head of the table. "Are there any indications of a change in their operational deployments?"

"Yes, your grace." Helmut—a stocky fellow in his mid-thirties with an odd pudding-bowl haircut, stood up and opened his laptop. His suit jacket flexed around muscled shoulders: he obviously worked out between meetings. "I have prepared a brief presentation to show the geographical distribution of targets . . ."

The video projector flickered on, showing a map of the eastern seaboard as far inland as the Appalachians, gridded out in uneven regions that bore little resemblance to state boundaries. Odd names dotted the map, vaguely Germanic, as one might expect from a Swiss lending institution. Helmut recited a list of targets and names, clicking the laptop's track pad periodically to advance through a time series of transactions. It was curiously bloodless, especially once he began discussing the losses.

"At Erkelsfjord, resistance was offered: the enemy burned the house, hanged all those of the outer family and retainers who surrendered—twenty-eight in all—then stripped the peasants and drove them into the woods, firing the village. We lost but one dead and two injured of the inner families. At Isjlmeer, quarter was offered and accepted. The lentgrave accepted and, with his family, left the keep, whereupon he and all but two sons and one daughter were struck down by crossbow fire. The servants were flogged, stripped, and taken into slavery, but the villagers were left unharmed. The next day, a different company of light cavalry struck Nordtsman's Keep. The baron was present and had raised his levies and, forewarned, had established a defensible perimeter: he took the enemy with enfilading fire from their left flank, forcing a retreat. Total enemy casualties numbered sixty-seven bodies, plus an unknown number who escaped.

"At Giraunt Dire, the eorl emplaced his two light machine guns to either side of the bridge across the river Klee, beating off an attack by two companies of horse led by Baron Escrivain . . ."

The map flickered with red dots, like smallpox burning up the side of a victim's face. As the conflict progressed, dotted red arrows appeared, tracking the course of the pestilence. The litany of sharp engagements began to change, as more of the defenders—forewarned and prepared—put up an effective defense. Helmut's presentation kept a running tally in the bottom right corner of the screen, a profit and loss balance sheet denominated in gallons of blood. Finally he came to an end.

"That's the total so far. Thirty-one attacks, twenty-two

successful and nine beaten off with casualties. In general, we have lost an average of two inner members per successful attack and one per successful defense; our losses of retainers and outer family members are substantially higher. The enemy has lost at least three hundred dead and probably twice that number wounded, although we cannot confirm the latter figure. The four columns appear to be converging near Neuhalle, and it is noteworthy that this one has at no time ventured further than a fifteen-mile march from one of the pretender's sworn vassals' keeps."

The projector switched off: Helmut directed a brief half-bow towards the other end of the table, then sat down.

The silence lay heavy for nearly a minute after he finished speaking, the only sounds in the room the white noise of the air-conditioning and the faint scribble of pens on the notepads of a couple of the attendees. Finally, the chairman directed his gaze towards a bluff, ruddy-faced fellow in early middle age, whose luxuriant handlebar mustache was twitching so violently that it threatened to take wing. "Carl. You appear to have something on your mind. Would you care to share it with us?"

Carl glanced around the table. "It's a calculated outrage," he rumbled. "We've got to nail it fast, too, before the decree of outlawry convinces everyone that we're easy game. While we're pinned down in our houses and keeps, the pretender can run around at will, taking whichever target is cheapest. It sends entirely the wrong message. Why hasn't he been assassinated yet?"

"We've tried." The chairman stared at him coldly. "It's difficult to assassinate a target when the target is taking pains to avoid mapped killing grounds and is sleeping and working surrounded by troops. Do you have any constructive suggestions, or shall we move on?"

There was a crunching sound. Eyes swiveled towards Carl's hand, and the wreckage of what had been a Pelikan Epoch mechanical pencil. Carl grunted. "A conventional infiltrator could get close to him . . ."

The chairman nodded, very slightly, and a certain tension left the room. "That might work, but as you already observed, if it takes too long it doesn't buy us anything. He's already in the field, and levies are being recruited to his vassals' forces. I've had no reports of the pretender adding to his own body of men. To all intents and purposes he is surrounded by a thousand bodyguards at all times. Moreover, if we just kill him, it'll trigger a race for the succession among his vassals—and the only outcome that is guaranteed is that every last one of them will consider us a mortal threat. To resolve this problem, we're going to have to defeat his forces in detail as well as producing an heir to the throne."

"But he's refusing to concentrate where we can hit him!" Carl opened his meaty hand above his blotter: two hundred dollars' worth of pencil scattered across the pad in fragments. "We must do something to bring him to battle! Otherwise he will continue to make us look like fools!"

"You're quite right."

Carl looked up at the chairman. "Your grace?"

"I'd like to call Eorl Riordan next, Carl. Eorl Riordan, would you care to explain next week's operation to the baron?"

"Certainly, your grace." The new speaker, square-jawed and short-haired, had something of a wardroom air about himself. "On the basis of intelligence indicating that the pretender is preparing a major offensive against one of our most prominent fortifications, his grace asked me to prepare a plan for the defense of Castle Hjorth—which we have reason to believe is the most likely target—with fallback plans to ensure that our other high-value fortifications remain defensible. The resulting plan requires us to stockpile supplies at the likely targets in preparation for the arrival of a mobile reinforcement group. The reinforcement group will be based in this world, while courier elements in our Gruinmarkt assets will rotate regularly and report on their status. As soon as one of our sites goes dark, or as soon as we receive confirmation of contact from one of our scouts in the field, the reinforcement group will redeploy to the target area. The primary target, Castle Hjorth, is already locked down and defended by a platoon of outer family guards, backed up by a team of eighteen couriers on logistic support. When the enemy attacks, here's how we intend to defend ourselves . . ."

The dome was big.

Huw hadn't been able to grasp the scale of it at first: it was buried in the forest, and apart from the segment looming over the clear roadway, the trees had obscured its curvature. But as he studied it, moving quietly from tree trunk to deadfall as Elena and Hulius stood watch, he came to realize that it was huge. It was also very old, and looked— although he wasn't about to jump to any conclusions— abandoned.

There was a convenient fallen tree trunk about twenty meters out from the rough white dome. Huw settled down behind it, waved to the kids, and pulled out his compact binoculars and the walkie-talkie. "Yul, do you read?"

"Yes, bro." Yul sounded almost bored. "Got you covered."

"Copy," Elena added tersely.

"No features visible on the outside." Huw scanned laterally with the binoculars, looking for anything that would give him traction on the thing. "Going by the trees . . . I make it fifty to eighty meters in radius. Very approximate. There's green stuff on the surface. Looks rough, like concrete. I'm going to approach it when I finish talking. If anything happens I'll head towards the road. Over."

Nothing was moving. Huw took a deep breath. He was nervously aware of his heartbeat, thudding away like a bass drum: *What is this doing here?* All too acutely, he felt a gut-deep conviction that historic consequences might hinge on his next actions. *Helge didn't feel anything like this when she stumbled on the Wu family's world, did she?* Well, probably not—but that world was inhabited, and by people who spoke a recognizable language, too. No evidence of weird climatological conditions, no strange concrete domes in ancient subarctic forests. He checked his web cam briefly, then stood up in full view of the dome.

Anticlimax: nothing happened. *Well, that's a relief.* The small of his back itched. He walked around the deadfall, pacing towards the dome. Close up, he realized it was bigger than he'd thought: the curve of its flank was nearly vertical at ground level, stretching away above and to either side of him like a wall. *Hmm, let's see.* He looked down at the base, which erupted smoothly from a tumble of ferns and decaying branches. Then he looked up. From this close, he could see the treetops diverge from the curve of the convex hull. "Scratch the size estimate, it's at least a hundred meters in radius."

A gust of wind rattled the branches above him. The top of the dome was hard to make out against the background of gray clouds. Huw shivered, then reached out and touched the dome. It was cold, with the grittiness of concrete or sandstone. He leaned close and peered at it. The surface was very smooth, but occasional pockmarks showed where it had been scarred by the surface cracking away under the chisel-like blows of ice forming in tiny fissures on its surface. Finally, he leaned against it and listened.

"I don't hear anything, and it's cold—probably at ambient temperature. I think it's empty, possibly abandoned. I'm going to proceed around it, clockwise."

The direction he'd chosen took him downslope, away from the road. He walked very slowly, pausing frequently, taking care not to look back. If someone was observing him, he didn't want to tip them off to Yul and Elena's presence. The dome extended, intact, curving gradually away from the road. In places, trees had grown up against it, roots scrabbling for purchase in the poor soil. It took Huw a quarter of an hour to realize that none of them had actually levered their way into the concrete or stone or whatever the dome was made of. "It's not quite a flawless finish," he reported, "but I've got a hunch it's been here a very long time." He rubbed his gloved hands together to warm them: there was a distinct bite in the air, and the gusts were growing more frequent.

In the end, the hole in the dome came as a surprise to Huw. He'd been expecting some sort of opening, low down on the slope: or perhaps a gatehouse of some sort. But one moment he was walking around the huge, curving flank of the thing, and the next moment the curved edge of the dome disappeared, as if a giant the size of the Goodyear blimp had taken a huge bite out of it. Huw stopped for a minute, inspecting the edge of the hole with his binoculars. "The opening starts at ground level and extends two thirds of the way to the top of the dome. Must be at least fifty meters wide. I'm going closer . . . the edge looks almost melted." He looked down. The trees were thinner on the ground, shorter, and the ground itself fell away in front of the opening, forming a shallow bowl. *Like a crater*, he realized. *Hey*—a trickle of water emerged from the shadowy interior of the dome, feeding down a muddy, overgrown channel into a pond in the depression. The pond was almost circular. *Something cracked the dome open. Something from*—he walked away from the opening, trying to get a perspective on it—*something firing downwards, from above.*

He shook his head, and suddenly the whole scene dropped into perspective. The dark shadows inside the dome, looming: *piles of debris*. The melted edges: *either the dome is self-healing, or it's made of something a whole lot more resilient than concrete*. It hadn't shattered like masonry—it had melted like wax. He keyed his walkie-talkie again: "The dome's split open here. Something energetic, punching down out of the sky. A long time ago." *The way the crater had filled with water, the*

way the trees were so much shorter than their neighbors,
almost as if—

Huw fumbled with his telemetry belt, then slipped one
hand free of its glove in order to pull out the Geiger tube.
"Got you," he muttered, holding it out in front of him.
"Let's see." He flicked the switch on the counter pack, then
advanced on the depression. The counter clicked a few
times, then gave a warning crackle, like a loose connection. Huw paused, swinging around. It popped and crackled, then as he took a step forward it buzzed angrily.
"Hmm." He turned around and walked back towards the
dome. The buzzing subsided, back down to a low crackle.
He moved towards the edge of the dome. As he approached
the melted-looking edges the counter began to buzz—then
rose to an angry whine as he brought the tube to within a
couple of centimeters of the edge. "Shit!" He jumped back.
"Yul, Elena, listen up—the edge of the hole is radioactive.
Lots of beta and maybe alpha activity, not much gamma.
I don't think—"he swallowed"—I don't think we're going
to find anyone alive in here. And I don't want you touching
the edge of the dome, or walking through the stream running out of it."

He swallowed again. *What am I going to tell the duke*
this time? He wondered.

A hypothesis took root and refused to shake free:
Imagine a nuclear installation or a missile command site
or a magic wand factory. Or something. There'd been a
war. It all happened a long time ago of course—hundreds
of years ago. Everyone was dead, nobody lived here anymore. During the war, someone took a shot at the dome
with a high energy weapon. Not an ordinary H-bomb, but
something exotic—a shaped nuclear charge, perhaps, designed to punch almost all of its energy out into a beam of
radiation going straight down. Or a gamma-ray laser
powered by a couple of grams of isomeric hafnium.
Maybe they used an intercontinental ballistic magic
wand. Whatever it was, not much blast energy reached

the ground—but the dome had been zapped by a stabbing knife of plasma like Lightning Child's fiercest punch, followed by a storm of secondary radiation.

Huw looked up at the underside of the dome. A gust of wind set up a sonorous droning whistle, ululating like the ghost of a dead whale. The dome was thick. He froze for a moment, staring, then raised his binoculars again. He raised his dictaphone, and began speaking. "The installation is covered by a dome, and back in the day it was probably guarded by active defenses. You'd need a nuke to crack it open because the stuff it's made of is harder and more resilient than reinforced concrete, and it's at least three, maybe four meters thick. Coming down from the zenith, perhaps eighty meters off-center, the shotgun-blast of lightning-hot plasma has sheared through almost fifteen meters of this—call it supercrete? Carbon-fiber reinforced concrete?—and dug an elliptical trench in the shallow hillside. It must have vaporized the segment of the dome it struck. How in Hell the rest of the dome held—must have a tensile strength like buckminsterfullerene nanotubes. That's probably what killed the occupants, the shockwave would rattle around inside the dome . . ."

The tree branches rustled overhead as the drone of the dead whale rose. Huw glanced up at the clouds, scudding past fast in the gray light. He sniffed. *Smells like snow.* Then he glanced over his shoulder, and turned, very deliberately, to raise a hand and wave.

Elena was the first to catch up with him. "Crone's teeth, Huw, what have you found?"

"Stand away from there!" He snapped as she glanced curiously at the edge of the gaping hole in the dome. "It's radioactive," he added, as she looked round and frowned at him. "I think whatever happened a long time ago was . . . well, I don't think the owners are home."

"Right." She shook her head, looking up at the huge arch that opened the dome above them. "Wow. What are we going to do?"

"Yo." Yul trotted up, rifle cradled carefully in his arms. "What now—"

Huw checked his watch. "We've got half an hour left until it's time to head back to base camp. I don't know about you guys, but I want to do some sightseeing before I go home. But first, I think we'd better make sure it doesn't kill us in the process." He held up his Geiger counter: "Get your tubes out." A minute later he'd reset both their counters to click, rather than silently logging the radiation flux. "If this begins to crackle, stop moving. If it buzzes, back away from wherever the buzzing is highest-pitched. If it howls at you, run for your life. The higher the pitch, the more dangerous it is. And don't touch *anything* without checking it out first. Never touch your counter to a surface, but hold it as close as you can—some types of radiation are stopped by an inch of air, but can kill you if you get close enough to actually touch the source. Got that? If in doubt, don't touch."

"What are we looking for again, exactly?" Yul raised an eyebrow.

"Magic wands. C'mon, let's see what we've got."

The trouble with trains, in Miriam's opinion, was that they weren't airliners: you actually went *through* the landscape, instead of soaring over it, and you tended to get bogged down in those vast spaces. About the best thing that could be said about it was that in first class you could get a decent cooked meal in the dining car then retire to your bedroom for a night's sleep, and wake up seven or eight hundred miles from where you went to bed. On the other hand, the gentle swaying, occasional front-to-back lurching of the coaches, and the perpetual clatter of wheels across track welds combined to give her a queasy feeling the like of which she hadn't felt since many years ago she'd let her then-husband argue her into a boating holiday.

I seem to be spending all my time throwing up these days. Miriam sat on the edge of her bed, the chamber pot clutched between her hands and knees in the pre-dawn light. *What's wrong with me?* A sense of despondency washed over her. *All I need right now is a stomach bug* . . . she yawned experimentally, held her breath, and let her back relax infinitesimally as she realized that her stomach was played out. *Damn.* She put the pot back in its under-bunk drawer and swung her legs back under the sheets. She yawned again, exhausted, then glanced at the window in mild disgust. *Might as well get started now*, she told herself. There was no way she'd manage another hour's sleep before it was time to get up anyway: the train was due to pause in Dunedin around ten o'clock, and she needed to get her letter written first. The only question was what to put in it . . .

She glanced at the door to the lounge room. Erasmus insisted on sleeping in there—not that it was any great hardship, for the padded bench concealed a pullout bed—which would make it just about impossible for her to get the letter out without him noticing. *Well, there's no alternative,* she decided. She was fresh out of cover stories: who else could she be writing to, when she was on the run? *Sooner or later you've got to choose your allies and stick by them.* So far, Erasmus had shown no sign of trying to bar her from pursuing her own objectives. *I'll just have to risk it.*

Sighing, she rummaged in the bedside cabinet for the writing-box. People here were big on writing letters—no computers or e-mail, and typewriters the size of a big old laser printer meant that everyone got lots of practice at their cursive handwriting. There was an inkwell, of course, and even a cheap pen—not a fountain pen, but a dipping pen with a nib—and a blotter, and fine paper with the railway corporation crest of arms, and envelopes. *Envelopes.* What she was about to attempt was the oldest trick in the book—but this was a world that had not been blessed by the presence of an Edgar Allan Poe.

Biting her lip, Miriam hunched over the paper. Best to keep it brief: she scribbled six sentences in haste, then pulled out a clean sheet of paper and condensed them into four, as neatly as she could manage aboard a moving train.

Dear Brill, I survived the massacre at the palace by fleeing into New Britain. I have vital information about a threat to us all. Can you arrange an interview with my uncle? If so, I will make contact on my return to Boston (not less than seven days from now).

Folding it neatly, she slid the note into an envelope and addressed it, painstakingly carefully, in a language she was far from easy with.

Next, she took another sheet of paper and jotted down instructions upon it. This she placed, along with a folded six-shilling note, inside another envelope with a different name and address upon it.

Finally, she took the locket from under her pillow, and copied the design onto the envelope, making a neat sketch of it in place of a postage stamp—taking pains to cover each side of the knotwork as she drew the other half, so that she couldn't accidentally visualize the whole.

And then she waited.

Dunedin was the best part of a thousand miles from New London, a good nine hundred from Boston—the nearest city in her own world to it was Joliet. In this world, with no Chicago, Dunedin had grown into a huge metropolis, the continental hub where railroad and canal freight met on the southern coast of the great lakes. There was a Clan post office in Joliet, and a small fort in the unmapped forests of the world the Clan came from— a no-man's-land six hundred miles west of the territory claimed by the eastern marcher kingdoms—and now a post office in Dunedin too, a small house in the suburbs where respectable-looking men came and went erratically. Miriam had been there before, had even committed the address to memory for her courier runs: an anonymous villa in a leafy suburb. But the train would only pause for half an hour to change locomotives; she wouldn't have time to deliver it herself.

Eventually she heard shuffling and muttering from the other side of the door—and then a tentative knock. "Who is it?" she called.

"Breakfast time." It was Erasmus. "Are you decent?"

"Sure." She pulled on her shoes and stood up, opening the through door. The folding bunk was stowed: Erasmus looked to have been up for some time. He smiled, tentatively. "The steward will bring us our breakfast here, if you like. Did you sleep well?"

Miriam yawned. "About as well as can be expected." She steeled herself: "I need to post a letter when we get to Dunedin."

"You do?"

She nodded. The chair opposite the bench seat was empty, so she sat in it. "It's to, to one of my relatives who I have reason to trust, asking if it's safe for me to make contact."

"Ah." Erasmus nodded slowly. "You didn't mention where you are or where you're going?"

"Do I look stupid?" She shrugged. "I told Brill to be somewhere in a week's time, and I'd make contact. She wasn't at the royal reception so she's probably still alive, and if she gets the letter at all she's in a position to act on it. In any event, I don't expect the letter to reach her immediately, it'll take at least a couple of days."

"That would be—ah." He nodded. "Yes, I remember her. A very formidable young woman."

"Right." Miriam managed a smile. "If she shows up in Boston in a week's time, you'll know what it means. If she tells me it's safe to come in from the cold, then and *only* then I'll be able to talk to my relatives. So. What do you think?"

"I think you ought to send that letter." Erasmus nodded again. "What will you do if a different relative shows up looking for you?"

"That's when I have to go to ground." She twitched:

"I've got to try. Otherwise I'll end up spending the rest of my life looking over my shoulder, always keeping an eye open for assassins."

"Who doesn't?" he said ironically, then reached up and pulled the bell rope. "The steward will post the letter for you. Now let's get some breakfast . . ."

12

SURPRISE PARTY

Despite the summer heat, the grand dining hall in the castle harbored something of a damp chill. Perhaps it was the memory of all the spilled blood that had run like water down the years: despite the eighty-degree afternoon outside, the atmosphere in the hall made Eorl Riordan shiver.

"Erik, Carl, Rudi. Your thoughts?"

Carl cleared his throat. Unlike the other two, he was attired in local style, although his chain shirt would have won few plaudits at a Renaissance Faire on the other side. Machine-woven titanium links backing a Kevlar breastplate and U.S. Army–pattern helmet—the whole ensemble painted in something not unlike urban camo pattern—would send entirely the wrong, functional message. Even without the P90 submachine gun strapped to his chest, and the sword at his hip.

"I think he'd be stupid to invest us. The fort's built well, nobody's ever taken it in the past three hundred years, and it has a commanding view of the river and land approaches. Even with cannon, it'll take him a while to breach the outer curtains. I've inspected the outer works and Villem was right—we've got a clear field of beaten fire over the six hundred yards around the apron. If he had American artillery, maybe, or if we give him time to emplace bombards behind the ridge line—but a frontal investment would be a fruitless waste of lives. And the pretender may be many things, but I will not insult his victims by calling him stupid."

"What about treachery?" asked Erik. A younger ClanSec courtier of the goatee-and-dreadlocks variety, his dress was GAP-casual except for the Glock, the saber, and the bulky walkie-talkie hanging from his belt.

Eorl Riordan looked disapproving. "That's only one of the possibilities." He held up a hand and began counting off fingers. "One, the pretender really is stupid, or has taken leave of his senses. Two, it's a tactical diversion, planned to tie us up defending a strategic necessity while he does something else. Three, treachery. Four, weapons or tactics we haven't anticipated. Five . . . two or more of the above. My assessment of the Pretender is the same as yours, Sieur Carl: He's crazy like a rat. I forgot to bring a sixth finger, so kindly use your imaginations—but I think he is playing a game with the duke's intelligence, and he wants us here for some reason that will not rebound to our benefit. So. Let's set up a surprise, shall we? Rudi, how are the scouts doing?"

"Nothing to report." Rudi was another of the younger generation, wiry and gangling in hoodie and cutoffs. "They're checking in regularly but we've only got twelve of them between here and Isjlemeer: he could march an army between them and we might never know. I can't give you what you want unless you let me use Butterfly, whatever the duke thinks of it." He grinned, knowingly.

Riordan snorted. "You and your kite. You know about the duke's . . . feelings?"

"Yep." Rudi just stood there, hands in pockets. Riordan, about to take him to task, noticed the oversized watch on Rudi's skinny left arm and paused. "It's too late to get started today but, weather permitting, I could give you what you want tomorrow."

It was a tempting offer. Riordan considered it. Normally he'd have been down on the ass of a junior officer who suggested such a thing like a mountain lion, but he'd been given a very specific job to get done, and Rudi wasn't wrong. He made a quick executive decision. "You can do your thing tomorrow on *my* authority, if we haven't made contact first. The duke will forget to be angry if you get results. But." He shook a finger at Rudi: "There *will* be consequences if you make an exhibition of your craft. Do you understand?"

"Uh, yes, sir. There won't be any problems. Apart from the weather, and, worst case, we've still got the scouts."

"Go get it ready," Riordan said tersely. Rudi nodded, almost bowing, and scurried out of the room in the direction of the stables. Riordan didn't need telepathy to know what was going through his mind: the duke had almost hit the roof back when Rudi had first admitted to smuggling his obsession across, one component at a time, and it had been all Riordan and Roland had been able to do to talk Angbard out of burning the machine and giving the lad a severe flogging. It wasn't Rudi's fault that forty years ago a premature attempt to introduce aviation to the Gruinmarkt had triggered a witchcraft panic—superstitious peasants and "dragons" were a volatile combination—but his pigheaded persistence in trying to get his ultralight off the ground flew in the face of established security doctrine. Riordan glanced at Carl. "Yes, I know. But I don't think it can make the situation any worse at this point, and it might do some good. Now, the defensive works. We've got a couple of hours to go until sunset. Think your men will be expecting a surprise inspection . . . ?"

* * *

Brill realized she was being watched as soon as she turned to lock the front door of the shop behind her.

She'd spent a frustrating hour in Burgeson's establishment. The monitor on the door was working exactly as intended—she couldn't fault Morgan for that—but the fact remained, it hadn't been triggered. And it didn't take her long to figure out that somebody had been in the shop recently. The drawers in the desk in the back office were open, someone had been rummaging through the stock, and the dust at the top of the cellar stairs was disturbed. She'd looked down the steps into the darkness and cursed, realizing exactly what had happened. Morgan had secured the front door, and even the back door onto the yard behind the shop, but it hadn't occurred to him that a slippery customer like Burgeson might have a rat run out through the cellar. *Better check it out,* she thought grimly, extracting a pocket flashlight from her handbag.

The cellar showed more signs of recent visitors: disturbed dust, a suspicious freshness to the air. She glanced around tensely, aiming the flashlight left-handed at the nooks and crannies of the cellar. *The floor . . .* she focused the beam, following a scuffed trail in the dust. *Right.* The trail led through a side door into another cellar room full of furniture, and dead-ended against a wooden cabinet full of labeled cloth bundles. Brill walked towards it, staring. The back of the cabinet was dark, too dark. "Clever," she muttered, peering past a bundle: there was a gap between the cabinet and the side wall, and behind it, she saw another wall—two feet farther in. The smell of dust, and damp, and something else—something oily and aromatic, naggingly familiar—tugged at her nostrils. She took a sharp breath, then slipped behind the cabinet and edged along it, through the hole in the bricks at the other end of the cellar, into the tunnel. There was a side door into another, hidden back room: the smell was stronger here. Tarpaulins covered wooden barrels, a thin layer of dust caking them. She raised a cover, glanced inside, and nodded to herself. If someone—Burgeson?

Miriam?—hadn't left the back door open, the smell
wouldn't have given it away, but down here the stink of
oiled metal was almost overpowering. She let the tarp
fall, then slid back out of the concealed storeroom. *So
Miriam keeps dangerous company,* she reminded herself,
her lips quirking in a faint smile. *Maybe that's no bad
thing right now.*

But it certainly wasn't a *good* thing, and as she turned
to lock the front door she paid careful attention to the re-
flections in the window panes in front of her. Maybe it was
pure coincidence that a fellow in a threadbare suit was
lounging at the corner of the alley, and maybe it wasn't,
but with at least twenty rifles stashed in that one barrel
alone, Brill wasn't about to place any bets. She walked
away briskly, whistling quietly to herself—let any watchers hurry to keep up—and turned left into the high street.
There were more people here, mostly threadbare men
hanging around the street corners in dispirited knots,
some of them holding out hats or crudely lettered signs.
She paused a couple of doors down the street to glance in
a shop window, checking for movement behind her. Alley
Rat was trying to look inconspicuous about fifty feet behind her, standing face-to-cheek with one of the beggars
who wore a shapeless cloth hat and frayed fingerless
gloves as gray as his face.

Tail. Brill tensed, glancing up the street. "How annoying," she murmured aloud. There were no streetcars in
sight, but plenty of alleyways. *Worse than annoying,* she
added to herself as she thrust her right hand into her bag.
Try to shed him, first . . .

She started moving again, hurrying, letting her stride
lengthen. She glanced over her shoulder—no advantage to
be gained in hiding her awareness now, if she needed cover
from civilians she could just say she was being chased—
and spotted Mr. Threadbare and Mr. Hat blundering
towards her, splitting in a classic pincer. Most of the bystanders had evaporated or were feigning inattention—
nobody wanted to be an audience for this kind of street

theater. Brill took a deep breath, stepped backwards until she came up against the brick wall of a shop, then held her handbag out towards Mr. Hat, who was now less than twenty feet away. "Stop right there," she said pleasantly, and when he didn't, she shot him twice. The hand bag jerked, but the suppressor and the padding kept the noise down to the level of an enthusiastic hand clap. She winced slightly and shook her wrist to dislodge a hot cartridge as Mr. Hat went to one knee, a look of utter surprise on his face, and she spun sideways to bear on Mr. Threadbare. "Stop, I said."

Mr. Threadbare stopped. He began to draw breath. She focused on him, noting absently that Mr. Hat was whimpering quietly and slumping sideways against a shop front, moving one hand to his right thigh. "Who do you think—"

Brill jerked her hand sideways and shot Mr. Hat again. He jerked and dropped the stubby pistol he'd been drawing, and she had her bag back on Mr. Threadbare before he could reach inside his jacket. "If you want to live, you will walk ten feet ahead of me," she said, fighting for calm, nerves screaming: *Where's their backup? Clear the zone!* "Move."

Mr. Threadbare twitched at Mr. Hat: "But he's—"

An amateur. Brill tensed up even more: amateurs were unpredictable. "Move!"

Mr. Threadbare moved jerkily, like a puppet in the hands of a trainee. He couldn't take his eyes off Mr. Hat, who was bleeding quite copiously. Brill circled round the target and toed the gun away from him, in the direction of the gutter. Then she gestured Mr. Threadbare ahead of her, along the sidewalk. For a miracle, nobody seemed to have noticed the noise. Mr. Threadbare shuffled slowly: Brill glanced round quickly, then nodded to herself. "Left into the next alleyway."

"But you—"

She closed the gap between them and pushed the gun up against the small of his back. "Don't turn. Keep walking." He was shaking, she noticed, and his voice was weak. "Left here. Stop. Face the wall. Closer. That's right. Raise your right hand above your head. Now raise your left." Nobody in the alley, no immediate witnesses if she had to world-walk. "Who do you work for?"

"But I—" He flinched as brick dust showered his face.

"That's your last warning. Tell me who you work for."

"Red Hand thief-taker's company. You're in big trouble, miss, Andrew was a good man and if you've killed—"

"Be quiet." He shut up. "You tailed me. Why?"

"You burgled the pawnbroker's—"

"You were watching it. Why?"

"We got orders. The Polis—"

Thief-takers—civilian crime prevention, mostly private enterprise—working for the polis—government security? "What were you watching for?" She asked.

"Cove called Burgeson, and some dolly he's traveling with. He's Wanted, under the Sedition Act. Fifty pounds on his head and the old firm's taking an interest, isn't it?"

"Is it now?" Brill found herself grinning, teeth bared. In the distance, a streetcar bell clanged. "Kneel."

"But I told you—"

"I said, kneel. Keep your hands above your head. Look away, dammit, that way, yes, over there. I want you to close your eyes and count to a hundred, slowly. One, two, like that, I'll be counting too. If you leave this alley before I reach a hundred, I may shoot you. If you open your eyes before I reach a hundred, I may shoot you. Do you understand?"

"Yes, but—"

"Start counting. Aloud."

On the count of ten, Brill backed away towards the high street. Seeing Mr. Threadbare still counting as fervently as a priest telling his rosary, she turned, lowered her handbag, and darted out into the open. The streetcar was approaching: Mr. Hat lolled against a wall like an early drunk. She held her arm out for the car, forcing her cheeks into an aching smile. *Miriam, what have you gotten yourself into this time?*

* * *

The Hjalmar Palace fell, as was so often the case, to a combination of obsolescent design, treachery, and the incompetence of its defenders. And, Otto ven Neuhalle congratulated himself, only a *little* bit of torture.

About three hundred years ago, the first lord of Olthalle had built a stone round tower on this site, a bluff overlooking the meeting of two rivers—known in another world as the Assabet and Sudbury—that combined to feed the Wergat, gateway to the western mountains. Over the course of the subsequent decades he and his sons had fought a bitter grudge war, eventually driving the Musketaquid wanderers west, deeper into the hills and forests of the new lands where they'd not trouble the ostvolk. But then there'd been a falling out in the east, among the coastal settlements. An army had marched up the river and burned out the keep and its defenders, leaving smoking ruins and a new lentgrave to raise the walls afresh. He learned from his predecessor's mistake, and built his walls thick and high.

More years passed. The Olthalle tower sprouted a curtain wall with five fine round bastion towers and a gatehouse larger than the original keep. Within the grounds, airy palace wings afforded the baron's family a measure more comfort than the heavily fortified castle. The barons of Olthalle fell on hard times, and seventy years earlier the Hjalmars had married into the castle, turning it into a gathering place for the clan of recently ennobled tinker families. They'd bridged the Wergat, levying tolls, then they'd driven a road into the hills to the west and wrestled another fortune from the forests. The town of Wergatfurt had grown up a couple of miles downstream, a thriving regional market center known for its timber yards and smithies. His majesty had been unable to leave such a vital asset in the hands of the witches—the Hjalmar estates were a dagger aimed at the heart of the kingdom. And so, it had come to this . . .

The festivities had started at dawn, when Sir Markus, beater for the royal hunt, had led his levies up to the gates of Wergatfurt and laid his demand before the burghers of the town. Open the gates to the royal army, accept the Thorold Palace edicts, surrender any witches and their get, and be at peace—or defy the king, and suffer the consequences. He had put on a brave show, but (at Otto's urging) had carefully not placed troops on the town's south-western, upstream, side. And he'd given them until noon to answer his demands.

Of course, Otto's men were already in position in the woods, half a kilometer short of the palace itself. And when they brought the first of the captives to him in early afternoon, bound so tight that the fellow could barely move, he had found Otto in an uncharacteristically good humor. "You're Griben's other boy, aren't you? What a surprising coincidence."

"You—" The lad swallowed his words. Barely old enough to be sprouting his first whiskers, barely old enough to know enough to be afraid: "What do you want?"

Otto smiled. "An excuse not to hang you."

"I don't know—" The boy's brow furrowed, then the meaning of Otto's words sank in. "Lightning's blood, you're just going to burn me anyway, aren't you?" He glared at Otto with all the hollow bravado he could muster. "I'm no traitor!"

"Perhaps." Otto glanced towards the stand of trees that concealed his position from the castle's outermost watch-towers. "But you're not one of them, either. You don't have their blood-spell, you'd never have inherited their wealth, all you are to them is a servant. A dead, loyal servant—the moment my men find another straggler who's willing to listen to reason." He turned back to the prisoner. "It's quite simple. Show me the way in and I'll have Magar here turn you loose in the woods, a mile downstream of here. We never met, and nobody saw you. Or." He shrugged: "We hold you for the king. I hear he's a traditionalist; takes a personal interest in the old folkways.

And he doesn't approve of people who put his arms-men to the trouble of laying siege to a castle. If you're lucky he'll hang you." Otto paused for effect. "I hear he holds with the Blood Eagle for traitors." His nose wrinkled: the kid had pissed himself. And fainted.

"You mean to scare him to death, sir?" asked Magar, toeing the prone prisoner with professional disdain: "Because if so, I can go fetch a burial detail . . ."

"I don't think that'll be necessary." Otto peered at the unconscious boy. The Pervert's carefully cultivated reputation for perpetrating unspeakable horrors on people who crossed him had certainly come in useful on this campaign, he reflected: *All I have to do is hint about his majesty and they just fall apart on me.* It was an interesting lesson. "You understand that when I said you'd turn him loose in the woods, I didn't promise that *you* wouldn't kill him."

"Aye, I got that much, sir." The boy was twitching. Magar kicked him lightly in the ribs. "You, wake up."

Otto bent over the prisoner, so that when the lad opened his eyes there'd be no escape. "What's it to be?" Otto asked, not unkindly. "Do you want to—" He straightened up and looked over the boy's head. "—time's up, looks like we've got another prisoner coming in—"

"I'll show you! I'll show you!" The boy was almost hysterical, tears of terror flowing down his cheeks.

"Really?" Otto smiled at him. "Thank you. That wasn't so hard now, was it?"

The problem with castles was not that they were hard to get into, but that they tended to be equally hard to get out of. And people take shortcuts.

To enter the Hjalmar Palace by road, a polite visitor would ride across the well-manicured apron in front of the walls, itself a killing zone two hundred meters across, then up the path to the gatehouse. There was a moat, of course, a ten-meter-wide ditch full of water diverted from

the river (and, during particularly hot moments of a
siege, layered in burning oil). A stone bridge spanned half
the width of the moat. The gatehouse was a small castle
in its own right, four round towers connected by stone
walls a meter thick, and its wooden drawbridge was a
welcome mat that could be withdrawn back to the castle
side of the moat if the occupants weren't keen on entertaining visitors. In case that wasn't a sufficiently pointed
deterrent to intruders, the bridge towers were topped by
steel shields and the ominous muzzles of belt-fed machine guns, and the drawbridge itself opened into a zigzagging stony tunnel blocked at several choke points by
metal grilles, and covered from above by a killing platform from which the defenders could rain molten lead.

And that was before the visitors reached the outer
walls, which in addition to the usual glacis and arrow
slits, had acquired (under the custody of the Hjalmar
branch of the Clan) such luxuries as imported razor wire,
claymore mines, and defenders with automatic weapons.

But such defenses are inconvenient. To leave the central keep by the front door required a descent down a
steep flight of steps, a march around half the circumfer-
ence of the tower, then the traversal of a murder tunnel
through the foundations of one of the inner bastions, then
a ride halfway along the circular road that lined the inner
wall, then another murder tunnel, then the gatehouse,
four portcullises, and the drawbridge—it could take half
an hour on foot. And so, successive generations of defenders had come up with shortcuts. They'd installed
sally ports in the bases of bastions to allow raiding parties
to enter and leave. Toilet outfalls venting over the moat
could, at a pinch (and with nose held tight) serve for a
hasty exit. A peacetime road battered through the wall,
straight into the stable yard, ready to be blocked by a
deadfall of boulders at the first alarm. And then there
were the usual over-the-wall quick routes out for soldiers
and servants in search of an evening's drinking and fucking in the beer cellars of Wergatfurt.

In the case of the Hjalmar Palace, the weak point in its defenses was the water supply. The water supply had to feed the moat, if attackers tried to dam it off from the river: it also had to keep the defenders in drinking water. Some tactical genius a century or two earlier had dug a trench nearly two hundred meters long, under the curtain wall to the river. He'd lined it with stone, floored it with fired clay pipe, then roofed it over and buried it. It wasn't just a backup water supply: it was a tactical back door for raiding parties and scouts, a fire escape for the terminally paranoid. The stone blockhouse on the upstream slope of the hill was overgrown with bushes and trees, nearly invisible unless you knew what you were looking for, and when properly maintained—as it was, now—it was guarded by sentries and booby traps. An intruder who didn't know the word of the day, or the positioning of the trip wires for the mines embedded in the walls of the tunnel, or the different code word for the guards in the water-house attached to the walls of the inner keep, would almost certainly die.

Unfortunately for the roughly one hundred guards, stable hands, cooks, smiths, carpenters, dog handlers, lamplighters, servants, and outer family members sheltering behind those walls, Baron Otto ven Neuhalle knew all of these things, and more.

Even more unfortunately for the defenders, one of the unpalatable facts of life is that in close quarters—at ranges of less than three meters—firearms were generally less useful than swords, of which Neuhalle's troop had many. Nor were they expecting an attacking force armed with machine guns of their own to appear on the walls of the keep itself.

By the time night fell, his troops were still winkling the last few stubborn holdouts out of their stony shells, but the Hjalmar Palace was in his hands.

And now to start building the trap, Otto told himself, as he summoned his hand-men to him and told them exactly what was needed.

* * *

The first day at home was the worst. Mike was still getting used to the plastic cocoon on his leg, not to mention
being short on clean clothes, tired, and gobbling antibiotics and painkillers by the double handful. But a second
night in his own bed put a different complexion on things.
He awakened luxuriously late, to find Oscar curled up on
the pillow beside him, purring.

The fridge was no more full than it had been the day
before, but the grocery bag Smith had dumped in the
kitchen turned out to be full of honest-to-god groceries, a
considerate touch that startled Mike when he discovered
it. *He might be a hyperactive hard-ass, but at least he
cares about his people,* Mike decided. He fixed himself a
breakfast of bagels and cream cheese and black coffee,
then tried to catch up on the lighter housework, running
some clothes through the washing machine and doing
battle with the shower again—this time more successfully. *I must be getting better,* he told himself optimistically.

Around noon, he got out of the house for a couple of
hours, driven stir-crazy by the daytime TV. It took him
nearly ten minutes to get the car seat adjusted, and an
hour of hobbling around Barnes and Noble and a couple
of grocery stores left him feeling like he'd run a
marathon, but he made it home uneventfully. Then he discovered that he hadn't figured on carrying the grocery
sacks and bag of books and magazines up the front steps.
He ended up so exhausted that by the time he got the last
bag in and closed the door he was about ready to drop. He
hobbled into the lounge clutching the bookbag, and lowered the bag onto the coffee table before he realized the
lounger was already occupied.

"So, Mr. Fleming! We meet again." She giggled, ruin-
ing the effect. It was unnecessary, in any case: the pistol
in her lap more than made up for her lack of menace.

"Jesus!" He staggered, nearly losing his balance.

"Relax. I do not intend to shoot you. Are you well?"

"I'm—" He bit back his first angry response. *What are you doing in my house?* That question was the elephant in the living room: but it wasn't one he felt like asking the Russian princess directly, not while she was holding a gun on him. "No, not very." He shuffled towards the sofa and lowered himself down into it. "I'm tired. Been shopping," he added, redundantly. *And how did you get past Judith's watch team?* "What brings you here?"

"Patricia sent me to see how you were," she explained, as if it was the most natural thing in the world for killer grannies from another dimension to send their ice-blonde hit-woman bodyguards to check up on him. "She was concerned that you might be unwell—your leg was hard to keep clean in the carriage."

"Yeah, right." Mike snorted. "She's got nothing but my best interests at heart."

Olga leaned forward, her eyes wide: "It is the truth, you know! You will be of little use to us if you die of battle fever. Are you well?"

"I'm as well as—"he bit back the words, *any man facing an armed home intruder*—"can be expected. Spent a couple of days in hospital. Off work for the next several weeks." He paused. "Getting about. A bit."

"Good." Olga sat back, then made the pistol disappear: "Excuse me." She looked apologetic. "Until I was sure it was you . . ."

"That's alright," Mike assured her gravely. "I quite understand. We're all paranoids together here." A thought struck him. "How did you get in?"

She smiled. "Your housekeeper is taking the day off."

"Ah." *Shit.* Mike had a sharp urge to bang his head on the wall. *Who's staking who out?* Of course, she'd had time to set everything up while he was in hospital; possibly even before they'd dropped him back in the right universe. The Russian princess and her world-walking friends could have been watching his apartment for days before Herz and her team moved in to set up their own surveillance op. *They don't work like the Mafia, they work like a government,* he recalled. *A feudal government.* "So Pat—what did you call her? Sent you to check up on me. I thought she was going to mail me instead?"

"Your mail is being intercepted," Olga pointed out. "Consequently, we felt it best to talk to you in person. There is mail, too, and you can respond to it if you wish. Have you reported to your liege yet?"

"Have I?" The sense of grinding gears was back: Mike forced himself to translate. "Uh, yes." He nodded, stupidly. "I have a cellular phone for you. It's off the official record. There's a preprogrammed number in it that goes direct to my boss's boss. He's authorized to negotiate, and if necessary he can talk to the top. Office of the Vice President. But it's all deniable, as I understand things." He pointed at the paper bag on the side table. "It's in there."

Olga didn't move. "What guarantee have we that as soon as we dial the number, you assassins won't locate the caller? Or that there isn't a bomb in the earpiece?"

"That's—" Mike swallowed. "Don't be silly."

"I'm not being silly. Just prudent." She reached out and took the bag, removed the phone, and started to fiddle with the case. "We'll be in touch. Probably not with this telephone, however."

"There are certain requirements," Mike added.

"What?" She froze, holding the battery cover in one hand.

"The sample that Matthias provided." He watched her minutely. "I'm told they're willing to negotiate with you. But there's an absolute precondition. Matt told us he'd planted a bomb, on a timer. We want it disarmed, and we want the pit. If it goes off, there's no deal—not now, not ever."

Olga's expression shifted slightly. *She's not a poker player,* Mike realized. "A time bomb? I understand that is not good, but what do your lords think we can do about such a thing? Surely it's no more than a minor . . ." She trailed off. "What kind of bomb?"

Mike said nothing, but raised an eyebrow.

"Why would he plant a bomb?" she persisted. "I don't see what he could possibly hope to achieve."

Too much subtlety, maybe. "He brought a sample of plutonium with him when he wanted to get our attention. It worked."

"A sample of ploo-what?" Her expression of polite incomprehension would have been hilarious in any other context.

"Oh, come on! What world did you—" Mike stopped dead. *Whoops.* "You're serious, aren't you?"

"I don't understand what you're talking about," she said coolly.

He boggled for a moment, as understanding sank in. *She's not from around these parts, is she?* "Do you know what an atom bomb is?"

"An atom bomb?" She looked interested. "I've seen them in films. An ingenious fiction, I thought." Pause. "Are you telling me they're real?"

"Uh." *You're* really *not from around here, are you?* On the other hand, if you stopped a random person in a random third-world country and asked them about atom bombs and how they worked, what kind of answer would you get? He licked his lips. "They're real, all right. Matthias had a sample of plutonium." No sign of recognition. "That's the, the explosive they run on. It's very tightly controlled. Even though the amount he had is nothing like enough to make a bomb, it caused a major panic. Then he claimed to actually have a bomb. We want it. Or we want the rest of your plutonium, and we want to know exactly how and where you got it so that we can verify there's no more missing. That's a nonnegotiable precondition for any further talks."

"Huh." She frowned. "You are serious about this. How bad could such a bomb really be? I saw *The Sum of All Fears* but that bomb was so magically powerful—"

"The real thing is worse than that." Mike swallowed. He'd spent the past couple of weeks deliberately not thinking about Matt's threat, trying to convince himself it was a bluff: but Judith had told him about the broken nightmare they'd found in the abandoned warehouse, and it wasn't helping him get to sleep.

"Assuming Matthias wasn't bluffing, and planted a real atom bomb near Faneuil Hall. Make it a small one. Imagine it goes off right now." He gestured at the window. "It's miles away, but it'd still blow the glass in, and if you were looking at it directly, it would burn your eyes out. You'd feel the heat on your skin, like sticking your head into an open oven door. And that's all the way out here." If it was the size of the one Judith found, Boston and Cambridge would be a smoking hole in the coastline—but multi-megaton H-bombs weren't likely to go world-walking and were in any case unlikely to explode if they weren't maintained properly. "We don't want to lose Boston. More importantly, *you* don't want us to lose Boston. Because if we *do*—"he noticed that she was looking pale "—you saw the reaction to 9/11, didn't you? I guarantee you that if someone nukes one of our cities, the response will be a thousand times worse."

"I—I don't know." The Russian princess was clearly rattled: "I was not aware of this. This bomb that Matthias claimed to—I don't know about it." She shook her head. "I will have to tell Patricia. We'll have to investigate."

"You will? No shit." Mike didn't even try to keep the sarcasm out of his voice. "This other faction in your clan—if it's theirs, they're playing with fire. Maybe they don't understand that."

She finished extracting the battery from the mobile phone. "You said that this, it goes to the vice president?"

"To one of his staff," Mike corrected her.

"We'll be in touch." She slid it into a pocket gingerly, as if it might explode. "I will see you later." She stood up briskly and walked into the front hall, and between one footstep and the next she vanished.

Mike stared at the empty passage for a moment, then shook his head. The shakes would cut in soon, but for now all he could feel was a monstrous sense of irony. "What a mess," he muttered. Then he reached for the phone and dialed Colonel Smith's number.

The dome was huge, arching overhead like the wall of a sports stadium or the hull of a grounded Zeppelin. Small, stunted trees grew in the gap in its wall, their trunks narrow and tilted towards the thin light. Mud and rubble had drifted into the opening over the years, and the dripping trickle of water suggested more damage deep inside. Huw shuffled forward with arthritic caution, poking his Geiger counter at the ground, the rocks, the etiolated trees—treating everything as if it might be explosive, or poisonous, or both. The results were reassuring, a menacing crackle that rarely reached the level of a sixty-cycle hum, much less the whining squeal of real danger.

As he neared the dribble of water, Huw knelt and held the counter just above its surface. The snap and pop of stray radiation events stayed low. "The pool outside the dome is hot, and the edges of the dome are nasty, but the stream inside isn't too bad," he explained to his microphone. "If the dome's leaky, the stream probably washed most of the hot stuff out of it ages ago." He looked up. "This place feels *old*."

Old, but still radioactive? He felt like scratching his head. Really dangerous fallout was mostly dangerous precisely because it decayed very rapidly. If what had happened here was as old as it felt, then most of the stuff should have decayed long ago. The activity in the dome's edge was perplexing.

"You want a light, bro?"

Huw glanced over his shoulder. Yul was holding out the end of a huge, club-like Maglite. "Thanks," he said, shuffling the Geiger counter around so that he could heft the flashlight in his right hand. He pressed the button just as a cold flake of snow drifted onto his left cheek. "We don't have long."

"It's creepy in here," Elena commented as he swung the light around. For once, Huw found nothing to disagree with in her opinion. The structures the dome had protected were in ruins. A flat apron of magic concrete peeped through the dirt in places, but the buildings—rectangular or cylindrical structures, rarely more than two or three stories high—were mostly shattered, roofs torn off, walls punched down. Their builders hadn't been big on windows (although several of them sported gaping doorways). The skeletal wreckage of metal gantries and complex machinery lay around the buildings. Some of them had been connected by overhead pipes, and long runs of rust-colored ductwork wrapped around some of the buildings like giant snakes. "It looks like a chemical works that's been bombed."

Huw blinked. "You know, you might be right," he admitted. He walked towards the nearest semi-intact building, a three-story high cylindrical structure that was sheltered from the crack in the dome by a mass of twisted rubble and a collapsed walkway. "Let's see, shall we?"

The Geiger counter calmed down the farther from the entrance they progressed, to Huw's profound relief. He picked his way carefully over a low berm of crumbled concrete-like stuff, then reached the nearest gantry. It looked familiar enough—a metal grid for flooring, the wreckage of handrails sprouting from it on a triangular truss of tubes—but something about its proportions was subtly wrong. The counter was content to make the odd click. Huw whacked the handrail with his torch: it rang like metal. Then he took hold of it and tried to move it, lifting and shoving. "That's odd." He squinted in the twilight. A thin crust of flaky ash covered the metal core. Paint, or something like it. That was comfortingly familiar—but the metal was too light. Yet it hadn't melted. "Got your hammer?" He asked Yul, who was looking around, gaping like a tourist.

"Here."

He took the hammer and whacked the rail, hard. "It's

not soft like aluminum. Doesn't melt easily." He tugged it, and it creaked slightly as it shifted. "You have *got* to be kidding me."

"What's wrong?" Hulius asked quickly.

"This railing. It's too light to be steel, it's not aluminum, but who the fuck would make a handrail out of titanium?"

"I don't know. Someone with a lot of titanium? Are you sure it's titanium? Whatever that is."

"Fairly sure," Huw said absently. "I don't have any way to test it, but it's light enough, and hard, and whatever flash-fried the shit in here didn't touch it. But titanium's expensive! You'd have to know how to make lots of it really cheap before you got anywhere near to making walkways with it . . ." He trailed off, glancing up at the twilight recesses of the dome overhead. "Let's get on with this."

The black rectangle, set in the cylindrical structure at ground level, looked like a doorway to Huw. It was high enough, for sure, but there were no windows and no sign of an actual door. He waited for Yul and Elena to close up behind him, then walked towards it. The counter was quiet. There was a pile of debris just inside the opening, and he approached it cautiously, sniffing at the air: there was no telling what might have made its lair in here. Thinking about the chill outside reminded him of wolves, of saber-toothed tigers and worse things. He shivered, and pointed the torch into the gloom.

"Over there." Elena scuttled sideways, her gun at her shoulder, pointing inside.

"Where—" Huw blinked as she flicked on the torch bolted beneath her barrel. "Oh." The thing she was pointing at might have been a door once, but now it lay tumbled on the floor across a heap of junk: crumbled boxes, bits of plastic, pieces of scaffolding. And some more identifiable human remains, although wild animals had scattered the bones around. "Good, that's helpful." He stepped across the threshold, noting in the process that the wall was about ten centimeters thick—too thin for brick or concrete—and the inner wall was flat, with another sealed door set in it.

A skull leered at him from the far corner of the room, and as the shadows flickered across the pile of crap inside the doorway he saw what looked like a stained, collapsed one-piece overall. The overall glowed orange in the light, slightly iridescent, then darkened to black where ancient blood had saturated the abdominal area. Huw held his breath, twisting the flashlight to focus on the shoulder, where some kind of patch was embossed on the fabric. He squinted. "Yul, can you get a photograph of that?" he said, pointing.

"What's it say—" Yul closed in. "That's not Anglischesprach. Or . . . Huh, I don't recognize it, whatever it is."

"Dead right." Huw held the light on the remains while Yul pulled out his camera and flashgunned it into solid state memory. "What do you think it means?"

"Why would you expect Anglische here?" Elena asked archly.

"No reason, I guess," Huw said, trying to conceal how shaken he was. He pointed the torch back at the skull sitting on the floor. "Hang on." He peered closer. "The teeth. Shit, *the teeth!*"

"What?" Elena's flashlight swung around wildly for a moment.

"Point that away from me if you're going to be twitchy—"

"It's okay, little brother. I've got it." Yul hooked a finger into each eye socket and spun the skull upside down for Huw to examine. It had been picked clean long ago and had aged to a sallow dark yellow-brown, but the teeth were all there.

"Look." Huw pointed at the upper jaw. "Bony here has *all his dentition.* And." He peered at them. "There are no fillings. It's like a plastic model of what a jawbone ought to be. Except for this chipped one here, this incisor."

"Whoa!" Hulius lowered the skull reverently. "That's some orthodontist."

"Don't you get it?" Huw asked impatiently.

"Get what?" Yull asked flippantly.

"That's not dentistry," Huw said, gritting his teeth. "You know what it's like back home! The Americans, they're good at faking it, but they're not *this* good." He glanced at the door on the inner wall. *No obvious hinges,* he realized. *Fits beautifully.* "Domes the size of a sports stadium that try to heal themselves even when you crack them open with a nuke. Metal walkways made out of titanium. Perfect dentistry." He snapped his fingers. "You got the ax?"

"Sure." Yul nodded. "What do you want me to hit?"

"Let's see what's inside that door," Huw decided. "But then we leave. Magic wands? Dentistry."

"They're more advanced than the Americans," Elena commented. "Is that what you're saying?"

"Yes," Huw said tensely. "I'm not quite sure what it means, though . . ."

"What about their burglar alarms?"

"After all this time?" Huw snorted. "Let's see what else is in here. Yul?"

"I'm with you, bro." He winked at Elena. "This is a real gas!"

And with that, he swung the fire ax at the edge of the door.

The Boeing Business Jet had reached cruising altitude and was somewhere over the Midwest, and Brill had just about managed to doze off, when her satellite phone rang.

"Who's speaking?" She cleared her throat, trying to shake cobwebs free. The delay and the echo on the line made it sound like she was yelling down a drainpipe.

"It's me, Brill. Update time."

"*Scheiss*—one minute. I'll take it in the office." She hit the button to raise her chair then stood up and walked back towards the door at the rear of the first-class cabin. Rather than a cramped galley or a toilet, it opened onto a compact boardroom. As the only passenger on the luxury jet she had it all to herself except for the cabin attendants, but she still preferred to have a locked door between herself and any flapping ears. "Okay, Olga. What ails you?"

"Are you secure?"

Brill yawned, then sat down. Beyond the windows, twilight had settled over the plains. It was stubbornly refusing to lift, despite the jet's westward dash. "I'm on the BBJ, arriving at SFO in about three hours. I was trying to get some sleep. Yes, I'm secure."

"I've got to report to Angbard, so I'd better keep this brief. I went to see Fleming today. You know what that little shit Matthias did? He convinced the DEA, this new FTO outfit, everybody who matters, that he'd planted a gadget in downtown Boston. Then he managed to get himself killed before he could tell them where it was. So now they're blaming us, and they want it handed over."

"He *what?*" Brill blinked and tried to rub her eyes, one-handed.

"I'm not kidding. Fleming wasn't kidding either—at least, he believed what he'd been told. I played dumb with him, pretending not to know what he was talking about, but afterwards I went and told Manfred and he ran an audit. The little shit was telling the truth. One of our nukes is missing."

"*God on a stick!* If the Council finds out—"

"It gets worse. Turns out it's one of our FADMs. Long-term storable, in other words, and there's a long-life detonation controller that's *also* turned up missing. The implosion charges were remanufactured eighteen months ago, so it's probably nearing a service interval, but those charges were modified to survive storage under adverse conditions for up to a decade. If we don't find it, we're in a world of hurt—what do you think they'll do if Boston or Cambridge goes up?—and if we *do* find it and hand it over as a sign of our commitment to negotiate, it'll take them all of about ten seconds to figure out where it came from."

Brilliana closed her eyes and swore, silently for a few seconds. She'd known about the Clan's nuclear capability; she and Olga were among the handful of agents whose job would be to emplace the weapons, if and when the shit ever truly hit the fan. But the nukes weren't supposed to go walkies. They were supposed to sit on their shelves in the anonymous warehouse, maintained regularly by the engineers from Pantex while U.S. Marine Corps guards patrolled the site overhead.

Based on a modified W54 warhead pattern, the FADMs were a highly classified derivative of the MADM atomic demolition device. They'd been built during the mid-1970s as backup for the CIA's Operation Gladio, to equip NATO's "stay behind" forces in Europe—after a Soviet invasion—with a storable, compact, tactical nuclear weapon. Most nukes required regular servicing to replace their neutron-emitting initiators and the plastic explosive implosion charges. The FADM had been tweaked to have a reasonable chance of detonation even after several years of unmaintained storage; the designers had replaced the usual polonium initiator with an electrically powered neutron source, and adding shields to protect the explosive lenses from radiation-induced degradation. The wisdom of supplying underground cells with what was basically a U.S. inventory–derived terrorist nuke had been revisited during the Reagan administration, and the weapons returned to the continental USA for storage—but they'd been retained long after the other man-portable demolition nukes had been destroyed, because the advantages they offered had been too good for certain spook agencies to ignore. More recently, the current administration—pathologically secretive and dealing with the aftermath of 9/11—had wanted every available arrow in their quiver, even if they were broken by design.

And they *were*. Because the Clan, with their ability to get into places that were flat-out impossible for home-grown intruders, had been treating them as their own personal nuclear stockpile for the past two decades.

"Listen, why are you telling me this? Why haven't you briefed Uncle A? It's his headache—"

"Uncle A is fielding another problem right now: the pretender's just rolled over the Hjalmar Palace and there's a three-ring, full-dress panic going down in Concord. He's pulling me in—I'm supposed to be looking for a thrice-damned mole, who everybody tells me is probably a disgruntled outer family climber, and in case you'd missed it, we've got a civil war on. The bomb's been missing for months, it'll wait a couple of hours more. But I think when you get back from the west coast you're going to find that finding it is suddenly everyone's highest priority. And I've got a feeling that the spy who's feeding Egon and the nuclear blackmail thing are connected. Matt wasn't working alone, and I smell a world-walker in the picture. So I figure you and I, we should do some snooping together." She paused. "Just what are you doing out in California, anyway? Is it something to do with the Wu clan?"

Brill sighed. "No, it's Helge. We've located her. While I was flailing around in Boston doing the breaking and entering bit, she mailed me a letter via the New Britain office at Dunedin. The duty clerk caught it in time, opened it, and faxed the contents on: meanwhile we identified her aboard a westbound train that's en route for Northern California. I need to find her before the New Britain secret police arrest her. So I'm taking a shortcut."

"Huh. Much as I like her, isn't finding Matt's plaything a slightly higher priority?"

"Not when she's carrying the heir to the throne, Olga." She waited for the explosion of spluttering to die down. "Yes, I agree completely. You and I can have a little talk about professional ethics with Dr. ven Hjalmar later, perhaps? Assuming he survives the current unpleasantness, I'd like to make sure that he needs a new pair of kneecaps. But you've got to admit that we'll need a king—or queen—after we nail Egon, won't we? And if he really *did* artificially impregnate her with Creon's seed, and if we have witnesses to the handfasting, then it seems to me that . . . well, which would you rather deal with? Egon trying to have us all hanged as witches, or Miriam as queen regent with Uncle A pulling the strings?"

"I'm not sure," Olga said grimly. "She'll be furious." She paused. "Gods, that's why he sent you, isn't it? She trusts you. If anyone can get her calmed down and convince her to play along, it'd be you. But if not . . ."

"Uncle A wants her back in play," Brill said, mustering up what calm she could. "But if she's left loose, she's as dangerous as that time bomb you're hunting. Isn't she?"

"Yes," Olga said, sounding doubtful.

"She was getting too close to James Lee, the hostage," Brill added.

Olga's voice went flat. "She was?"

"We don't need another faction on the board," Brill said.

"No. I can see that." Olga paused. "You'll just have to charm her, won't you?"

"Yes," Brill agreed. "Now, if you don't mind, I'm going back to sleep. Give my regards to Uncle."

"I'll tell him. Bye . . ."

Quietly closing the boardroom door behind her, Brill padded back to her first-class chair. She paused at the storage locker next to it, and opened it briefly: the specialized equipment was undisturbed, and she nodded, satisfied. It was the biggest single advantage of flying on the Clan Committee executive jet, in her opinion—in the course of her business she often required access to certain specialized items, and commercial airlines tended to take a dim view of her carrying her sniper kit as hand luggage. She sat down and strapped herself in, then tilted her chair back and dimmed the overhead lights. Tomorrow was going to be a long day, starting with arranging a reception for a train at a station she didn't even know the precise location of, and trying to make contact with Miriam one jump ahead of the Homeland Security Directorate goon squad who'd surely be waiting for her when the train arrived.

13

BOMBARDIERS

It was a good morning for flying, thought Rudi, as he checked the weather station on the north tower wall. *No, make that a great morning.* After all, he'd never flown over his homeland before. It would be a personal first, not to mention one in the eye for the stick-in-the-muds. Visibility was clear, with a breeze from the southwest and low pressure, rising slowly. He bent over the anemometer, jotting down readings in the logbook by the dawn light. "Hans? I'll be needing the contents of both crates. Get them moved into the outer courtyard. I'll need two pairs of hands to help with the trike—make sure they're not clumsy. I'll be down in ten minutes."

"Aye, sir." His footman, Hans, gave him an odd look, but hurried down off the battlements all the same. He clearly thought his master was somewhat cracked. *Well, he'll change his mind before the day is out,* Rudi told himself. *Along with everyone else. Just as long as nothing goes wrong.* He was acutely aware that he hadn't kept his flying hours up since the emergency began, and there were no luxuries (or necessities) like air traffic control or meteorology services over here.

In fact, he didn't even have as much fuel as he'd have liked: he'd managed to squirrel away nearly twenty gallons of gas before some killjoy or other—he harbored dark suspicions about Erik—had ratted out his scheme to Riordan, who'd had no option but to shout a lot and notify the duke. Who in turn had threatened to have him flogged, and lectured him coldly for almost half an hour about the idiocy of not complying with long-standing orders . . .

Rudi had bitten his tongue while the duke threatened to burn the trike, but in the end the old man had relented just a little. "You will maintain it in working order, and continue to practice your skills in America, but you will not fly that thing over our lands without my explicit orders, delivered in person." Eorl Riordan wasn't the duke, but on the other hand, he was in the chain of command: and that was enough for Rudi. *Flying today.*

It took him closer to half an hour to make his way down to the courtyard, by way of his room—his flying jacket and helmet were buried deeper than he'd remembered, and he took his time assembling a small survival kit. Then he had to divert via the guardhouse to check out a two-way radio and a spare battery. "Where do you think you're going, cuz?" asked Vincenze, looking up from the girlie magazine he was reading: "A fancy dress party?"

Rudi grinned at him. "Got a date with an angel," he said. "See you later."

"Heh. I'll believe it when I see it—" But he was talking to Rudi's back.

Down in the courtyard next to the stables, he found that Hans had enlisted a couple of guards to move the crates, but hadn't thought to bring the long tubular sack or the trike itself. "Come on, do I have to do everything myself?" he demanded.

"I didn't know what you wanted, sir," Hans said apologetically. "You said it was delicate . . ."

"Huh. Okay. Come here. Take this end of the bag. I'll take the other. It's heavy. Now! The courtyard!"

Half an hour later, performing in front of an audience of mostly useless gawpers (occasionally he'd need one of them to hold a spar in position while he tightened a guy wire), Rudi had the wing unpacked and tensioned. At eight meters long and weighing fifty kilos the Sabre 16 had been murder to world-walk across—it was too long to fit in the Post Office room—but it was about the smallest high performance trike wing he'd been able to find. At least he'd been able to unbolt the engine from the trike body. "Go get the trike," he told Hans and the guards. "Push it gently, it'll roll easily enough once you get it off the straw."

Another half hour passed by in what felt like seconds. By then he'd gotten the wing mounted on top of the trike's mast and bolted together. The odd machine—a tricycle with a pair of bucket seats and a petrol engine with a propeller mounted on the back—was beginning to resemble a real, flyable ultralight. He was double-checking his work, making sure there was no sign of wear on any of the cables and that everything was secure, when someone cleared his throat behind him. He glanced round: it was Eorl Riordan, along with a couple of sergeants he didn't recognize. "How's it going?" asked Riordan, his tone deceptively casual.

"It's going all right, for now." Rudi glanced up at the sky. *Partial cloud cover, at least five thousand feet up*—no problem for the time being. "Thing is, I'm about to trust my neck to this machine. There's no backup and no air traffic control and no help if something goes wrong. So I want to make sure everything is perfect before I take her up."

"Good." Riordan paused. "You've got a radio."

"Yeah. And binoculars." He gestured to the small pile sitting beside the fuel drum. "If you need it, I can take a camera. But right now, this is going to be pretty crude, visual flying only in good weather, staying below two thousand feet, and if I see anything I'll probably only be able to pinpoint it to within a mile or so. I max out at about fifty-five miles per hour, so that's not going to take me far from here, and I've got enough fuel for a couple of three-hour-long flights, but I'd prefer not to go up twice in one day. It's pretty physical."

"Three hours and a hundred and fifty miles ought to be enough." Riordan nodded to himself. "What I wanted to say—I'd like you to do a circuit of the immediate area. If there's any sign of troops on the ground within thirty miles, I'd like to know about it. We're expecting a move from the southeast, and I know it's well forested down there so I don't expect miracles, but if you do see anything, it's probably important. Also, I'd like you to take a look at Wergatfurt. We got an odd call half an hour ago, there's something going on down there. Can you do that?"

"Probably, yes." Rudi patted his pocket. "I'm using relief maps from the other side for navigation, it's close enough to mostly work, and the Wergat's pretty hard to miss. The only thing I will say is, if the weather starts closing in I need to get down on the ground fast. The Hjalmar palace is about an hour, hour and ten minutes away from here, as the trike flies—it'll cut into my ability to do a sweep around to the north. Are you sure you want that?"

Riordan rubbed the side of his nose thoughtfully. "I think . . . if you don't see signs of soldiers southeast of here within thirty miles, then I definitely want to know what's going on down along the Wergat. If you see those soldiers, call me up and we'll discuss it." He nodded to himself. Then he pointed at Rudi's survival kit. "Why the gun? Can you shoot from a moving aircraft?"

"It's not for when the trike's flying: but if anything goes wrong while I'm forty miles out, over open forest . . ."

Riordan nodded. "Good luck."

"Thank you, sir. I'll try not to need it."

* * *

In the end, what saved them was Huw's nose hair.

It was, Huw sometimes reflected, one of those fine ironies of life that despite being unable to grow a proper beard, he suffered inordinately from the fine hairs that clogged his nostrils. Nostril hair was neither sexy nor obviously problematic to people who didn't have to put up with it: it was just . . . *icky*. That was the word Elena had used when she caught him in the bathroom with an open jar of Vaseline and one finger up a nostril. Yet it played seven shades of hell with his sense of smell, and had driven his teenage self into an orgy of nose-picking that resulted in a series of nosebleeds before he'd figured out what to do about it. And now . . .

In the flashlight-lit wreckage of a building inside a shattered dome, standing before a wall with a tightly sealed doorway in it, his kid brother raised a fire ax and swung it down hard towards the left side of the door.

As the ax struck the door, Huw, who was standing a good two meters behind and to the left of him, sneezed. The sneeze had been building up for some time, aggravated by the cold, damp air in this new world and the low priority Huw had attached to his manicure in the face of the mission of exploration. Nevertheless, the eruption took Huw by surprise, forcing him to screw his eyes shut and hunch his shoulders, turning his face towards the floor. The noise startled Yul, who began to turn to his right, towards Huw. The movement took him out of the direct line of the door. And it also surprised Elena, who was standing off to the right near the entrance to the building with her vicious little machine pistol at the ready. She ducked, and this took her out of the direct line of sight on the portal.

Which was why they survived.

As the ax blade bit into the edge of the door, there was a brilliant flash of violet-tinted light. Huw registered it as as flicker of red behind his closed eyelids and might have ignored it—but the rising noise that followed it was impossible to write off.

"Ouch! What's that—" Yul began.

Huw, opening his eyes and straightening up, grabbed his brother's arm, and yanked. "Run!"

The hissing sound from the edge of the door grew louder; the center of the door bowed inward slightly, as if under the pressure of a giant fist from their side. Yul barely spared it a glance before he dropped the axe and took to his heels. Huw was a stride behind him. Two seconds brought them to the twilit entrance to the room. "Hit the ground!" yelled Huw, catching one glimpse of Elena's uncomprehending face as he threw himself forward and rolled sideways, away from the open doorway.

Behind them, the creaking door—far thinner than Huw had realized—creaked once more, and gave way. All hell broke loose.

The hissing and whistling gave way to a deep roaring, and the breeze in Huw's face began to strengthen. Huw glanced over his shoulder once, straining to look over the length of his body towards the inner chamber. A strange mist curdled out of the air, obscuring whatever process was at work there. The wind was still strengthening. "Take cover!" he called out. "There's hard vacuum on the other side of that—thing—watch out for flying debris!" *It'll blow itself out soon,* he told himself. *Won't it?* A sudden frisson of fear raised the hair on the back of his neck: *That skeleton was* old, *the door can't have held in a vacuum that long. So something's pumping the air on the other side out, something that's still working . . .*

But that didn't make sense. *Come on, Huw,* think! The wind wasn't slackening. Dust and leaves blew past, vanishing towards the gulping maw behind the doorway. Huw pushed himself up on hands and knees and began to crawl sideways, away from the damaged front of the building. He waved to Yul and Elena, beckoning them after. The seconds stretched out endlessly. The wind was refusing to die. "Meet me behind the building!" He

yelled, jabbing his hands to indicate the direction. Yul
raised a thumb and began to crawl away, tracking round
the building.

Once Huw was away from the frontage, he risked
standing up. Out of the direct line of the door, the wind
was a barely noticeable breeze. "Huh." He slapped the
knees of his fatigues, then hurried round to meet Yul and
Elena. *It's still running,* he realized. *Can't be a pump; it'd
take a jet engine to shift that much mass flow.* He glanced
around. A nasty idea was inching its way into his mind:
Utterly preposterous, but . . .

"Well, bro, what do you reckon?"

Yul was characteristically unfazed by his near-miss.
Elena, however, was anything but pleased: "What were
you playing at? Hitting that thing with an ax, we could all
have been killed!"

"It looked like a door to me," Yul shrugged.

"Did you see the flash—"

"Flash?" Huw glanced at her. "There was a flash?"

"Yes, a bright flash of light as the big oaf here hit it!"
Elena swatted Yul on the arm. "You could have been
killed!" She chided him. Then she glared at Huw. "What
were you playing at?"

"I'm not sure yet." Huw licked his left index finger and
held it up to feel the breeze. "Yes, it's still going. Hmm."

"What *is* it?"

"I'm not sure," Huw said slowly, "but I'll tell you what
I think. It was behind the door, sealed in until Yul broke
something. It's got hard vacuum on the other side. like a,
a hole in space. Not a black hole, there's no gravitational
weirdness, but like—imagine a wormhole leading into
yet another world? Like the thing we do when we world-
walk, only static rather than dynamic? And the universe it
leads to is one where there's no planet Earth. You'd come
out in interplanetary space."

"But why—"

Huw rolled his eyes. "Why would anyone want such a
thing? How would I know? Maybe they used to keep a

space station there, as some kind of giant pantry? You put one of those doors in your closet, build airtight rooms on the other side of it, and you'll never have to worry about where to keep your clothes again—it gives a whole new meaning to wardrobe space. But you keep an airtight door in front of the—call it a portal—just in case."

He gestured around the dome. "Something bad happened here, a long time ago. Centuries, probably. The guy with the perfect teeth was trying to hide in the closet, but didn't make it. Over time, something went wrong on the other side—the space station or whatever you call it drifted off site—leaving the portal pointing into interplanetary space. And then we came along and fucked with the protective door."

Elena's eyes widened. "But won't it suck all the air out?"

Huw shrugged. "Not our problem. Anyway, it'll take thousands of years, at a minimum. There's plenty of time for us to come back and drop a concrete hatch over it." He brightened: "Or an airlock! Get some pressure suits and we can go take a look at it! A portal like that, if we can figure out how it works—" he stopped, almost incoherent with the sudden shock of enlightenment. "Holy Sky Father, Lightning Child, and Crone," he whispered.

"What is it, bro?" Yul looked concerned. "Are you feeling alright?"

"I've got to get back to base and report to the duke *right now*." Huw took a deep breath. "This changes everything."

After two days aboard the Northern Continental, Miriam was forced to reevaluate her opinion of railroad travel—even in luxury class. Back when she was newly married she and Ben had taken a week to go on a road trip, driving down into North Carolina and then turning west and north. They'd spent endless hours crawling across Illinois, the landscape barely changing, marking the distance they'd covered by the way they had to tune the radio to another station every couple of hours, the only marker of time the shifting patterns of the clouds overhead.

This was, in a way, worse: and in another way, much better. Travel via the Northern Continental was like being sentenced to an enforced vacation in a skinny luxury hotel room on wheels. Unfortunately, New British hotels didn't sport many of the necessities a motel back home would provide, such as air-conditioning and TV, much less luxuries like a health suite and privacy. Everything was kept running by a small army of liveried stewards, bustling in and out—and Miriam hated it. "I feel like I can't relax," she complained to Burgeson at one point: "I've got no space to myself!" And no space to plug her notebook computer in, for that matter.

He shrugged. "Hot and cold running service is half of what first-class travel is all about," he pointed out. "If the rich didn't surround themselves with armies of impoverished unfortunates, how would they know they were well off?"

"Yes, but that's not the point . . ." Back in Baron Henryk's medieval birdcage she'd at least been able to shunt the servants out of her rooms. Over here, such behavior would draw entirely the wrong kind of attention. She waved a hand in wide circles, spinning an imaginary hamster wheel. "I feel like I'm acting in a play with no script, on a stage in front of an audience I can't see. And if I step out of character—the character they want me to play—the reviewers will start snarking behind my back."

"Welcome to my world." He smiled lopsidedly. "It doesn't get any better after a decade, let me assure you."

"Yes, but—" Miriam stopped dead, a sarcastic response on the tip of her tongue, as the door at the carriage end opened and a bellboy came in, pushing a cart laden with clean towels for the airliner-toilet-sized bathroom. "You see what I mean?" she asked plaintively when he'd gone.

The train inched across the interior at a laborious sixty miles per hour, occasionally slowing as it rattled across cast-iron bridges, hauling its way up the long slope of the mountains. Three or four times a day it wheezed to a temporary halt while oil and water hoses dropped their loads into the locomotive's bunkers, and passengers stretched their legs on the promenade platform. Once or twice a day it paused in a major station for half an hour. Often Miriam recognized the names, but as provincial capitals or historic towns, not as the grand cities they had become in this strange new world. But sometimes they were just new to her.

On the first full day of the voyage (it was hard to think of anything so protracted as a train journey) she left the train for long enough to buy a stack of newspapers and a couple of travel books from the stand at the end of the platform at Fort Kinnaird. The news was next to impenetrable without enlisting Erasmus as an interpreter, and some of the stuff she came across in the travel books made her skin crawl. Slavery was, it seemed, illegal throughout the empire largely because hereditary indentured servitude was so much more convenient; one particular account of the suppression of an uprising in South America by the Royal Nipponese Ronin Brigade left her staring out of the window in a bleak, reflective trance for almost an hour. She was not surprised by the brutality of the transplanted Japanese soldiers, raised in the samurai tradition and farmed out as mercenaries to the imperial dynasty by their daimyo; but the complacent attitude to their practices exhibited by the travel writer, a middle-aged Anglican parson's wife from Hanoveria, shocked her rigid. Crucifying serfs every twenty feet along the railway line from Manaus to São Paulo was simply a necessary reestablishment of the natural order, the correction of an intolerable upset by the ferocious but civilized and kindly police troops of the Brazilian Directorate. (All of whose souls were in any case bound for hell: the serfs because they were misguided papists and the samurai because they were animists and Buddhists, the author felt obliged to note.)

And then there was the *other* book, and the description of the French occupation of Mesopotamia, which made the New British Empire look like a bastion of liberal enlightenment . . .

What am I doing here? she asked herself. *I can't live in this world! And is there any point even trying to make it a better place? I could be over in New York getting myself into the Witness Protection Program . . .*

On the second day, she gave in to the inevitable. "What's this book you keep trying to get me to read?" she asked, after breakfast.

Erasmus gave her a long look. "Are you sure?" he asked. "If you're concerned about your privacy—"

"Give." She held out a hand. "You want me to read it, right?"

He looked at her for a while, then nodded and passed her a book that had been sitting on the writing desk in full view, all along. "I think you'll find it stimulating."

"Let's see." She turned to the flyleaf. "Animal husbandry?" She closed it and glared at him. "You're having me on!"

"Why don't you turn to page forty-six?" he asked mildly.

"Huh?" She swallowed acid: breakfast seemed to have disagreed with her. "But that's—"she opened it at the right page"—oh, I see." She shook her head. "What do I do if someone steals it?"

"Don't use a bookmark." He was serious. "And if someone *does* steal it, pray to the devil that they're a fellow traveler."

"Oh." She stared at the real title page, her brow furrowed: *The Ethical Foundations of Equality,* by Sir Adam Burroughs. "It's a philosophy textbook?"

"A bit more than that." Burgeson's cheek twitched. "More like four to ten years' hard labor for possession."

"Really . . ." She licked her lips. It was a hot day, the

track was uneven, and between her clammy skin and her delicate stomach she was feeling mildly ill. "Can you give me a synopsis?"

"No." He grinned at her. "But I should like it very much if you would give *me* one."

"Whoa." She felt her ears flush. "And I thought you were being a perfect gentleman!"

He looked at her anxiously. "Did I say something offensive?"

"No," she said, as her guts twisted, "I'm just in a funny mood." Her hand went to her mouth. "And if you'll excuse me now, I'm feeling sick—"

Days turned into hours, and the minor nuisances of keeping a round-the-clock watch on a suburban house sank into the background. So when the call she'd been half-dreading finally came through, Judith Herz was sitting in the back of her team's control van, catching up on her nonclassified e-mail on a company-issue BlackBerry and trying not to think about lunch.

"Ma'am?" Agent Metcalf leaned over the back of the seat in front, offering her a handset tethered to the van's secure voice terminal: "It's for you."

She managed to muster a smile as she put down the BlackBerry and accepted the other phone: "Who is it?"

Metcalf didn't say anything, but his expression told her what she needed to know. "Okay. Give me some privacy." Metcalf ducked back into the front. A moment later, the door opened and he climbed out. She waited for it to close before she answered. "Herz here."

"Smith speaking. Authenticate." They exchanged passwords, then: "I've got an errand for you, Judith. Can you leave the watch team with Sam and Ian for a couple of hours?"

"A couple of—" She bit back her first response. "This had better be worth it, Eric. You're aware my watch team's shorthanded right now?"

"I think it's worth it," he said, and although the fuzz the secure channel imposed on the already-poor phone line made it hard to be sure, she got the impression that he meant it. "How far from the nearest MBTA station are you?"

Herz blinked, surprised. "About a twenty-minute walk, I figure," she said. "I could get one of the guys to drop me off, if you're willing to cut the front cover team to one man for a few minutes. Why, what's come up?"

"We've got a lead on your last job, and I thought you'd want to be in on the close-out. I'm out of town right now and I need a pair of eyes and ears I can trust on the ground. What do you say?"

"The last—" That was the search for the elusive nuke source GREENSLEEVES had claimed he'd planted. She swallowed, her throat suddenly dry. "You found it?"

"It's not definite yet but it looks like it's at least a level two." They'd defined a ladder of threat levels at the beginning of the search, putting them into a proper framework suitable for reporting on performance indicators and success metrics. A level five was a rogue smoke detector or some other radiation source that tripped the NIRT crews' detectors—all the way up to a level one, a terrorist nuke in situ. The nightmare in the lockup in Cambridge was still unclassified—Judith had pegged it for a level one, and still didn't quite believe in it—but a level two was serious; gamma radiation at the right wavelength to suggest weapons-grade material, location confirmed.

"Okay. Where do you want me to go?"

"Blue Line, Government Center. It's the station itself. Go there and head for the Scollay Square exit. Rich will meet you there. He and Rand are organizing the site search. The cover story we're going with is that it's an exercise, training our guys for how to deal with a terrorist dirty bomb—so you can anticipate some press presence. You'll be wearing your old organization hat and you can tell them the truth, you're an agent liaising with the anti-terror guys."

Herz felt like wincing. Wheels within wheels—how better to disguise a bunch of guys in orange isolation suits trampling around a metro station in search of a terrorist nuke than by announcing to the public that a bunch of guys in isolation suits would be tramping around the station in search of a pretend-nuke? "What if they don't find Matt's gadget?" She asked.

"That's okay, they've got a mock-up in the van. You'll just have to run in with it and tell any reporters who get in your way that we forgot to install it earlier."

A dummy nuke, in case we don't find a real one? Herz shook her head. "When does it kick off?"

"Rich is shooting for fourteen hundred hours."

"Okay, I'm on my way." She hung up the phone and cracked the window. Metcalf was smoking a cigarette. "Hey, Ian."

He turned, looking surprised. "Yes, ma'am?"

"We've got a call. Time to roll."

Metcalf carefully stubbed the cigarette out on the underside of his shoe then climbed back into the driver's seat. "What's come up?"

"I need a lift to Alewife. Got a T to catch."

He shook his head. "You're being pulled off the site?"

"It's urgent." She put an edge in her voice.

"I'm on it." He slid the van into gear and pulled away. "How long are you going to be?"

"A couple of hours." She picked up her briefcase and zipped it shut to stop her hands trembling with nervous anticipation. "I'll make my own way back."

The train ride to Downtown Crossing went fast, as did her connection to Government Center. Early afternoon meant that there was plenty of space in the subway trains, but the offices in the center of town would be packed. Herz tried not to think about it. She'd had months to come to terms with the idea that there might be a ticking bomb in the heart of her city—or not, that it might simply be a vicious hoax perpetrated by a desperate criminal—and now was not the time to have second thoughts about it. Still. "Our man has a thing about trip wires and clay-more mines," Mike Fleming had told her. *Right. Booby traps.* She resolved to keep it in mind. Not that it wasn't in the orchestral score everyone was fiddling along to, but if it slipped some other player's mind at the wrong moment . . .

On her way out of the station Herz had time to reflect on the location. The JFK Federal Building loomed on one side, a hulking great lump of concrete: around the corner in the opposite direction was the tourist district, Faneuil Hall and Quincy Market and a bunch of other attractions. The whole area was densely populated—not quite as bad as downtown Manhattan, but getting there. A small back-pack nuke would cause far more devastation and more loss of life than a ten-megaton H-bomb out in the sub-urbs. But the search teams had already combed this district—it was one of the first places they'd looked. *So what's come up now?*

Rich was waiting just inside the station exit, tapping his toes impatiently. "Glad you could make it," he said, leading her out onto the plaza. "We're ready to go."

Judith froze for a moment. There was an entire flying circus drawn up on the concrete: police cars with lights flashing, two huge trucks with an inflatable tent between them, Lucius Rand and his team wandering around in bright orange suits, hoods thrown back, chatting to each other, the police. There was even a mobile burger van—someone's idea of lunch, it seemed. "What's this?" She asked quietly.

"*This* is Operation Defend Our Rails," Rich announced portentiously. "In which we simulate a terrorist attack on a T station with weapons of mass destruction, and how we'd respond to it. Except," his voice dropped a dozen decibels, "it's not a simulation. But don't tell *them*." He nodded in the direction of a couple of bored-looking reporters with a TV camera who were filming the orange-suited team.

"What do the cops know?"

"They know nothing." Rich suddenly looked serious.

"Okay." Judith steered him towards what looked to be the control vehicle. "Tell me why we're here, then."

"Team Green rescanned the area with the new gamma spectroscope they just got hold of from Lockheed. The idea was to calibrate it against our old readings, but what they found—they thought it was an instrument error at first. Turns out that MBTA's civil engineers recently removed the false walls at the ends of the Blue Line platforms so they could run longer trains. That's when we began getting the emission spectra. More sensitive detectors, less concrete and junk in the way—that's how it works. There's an older platform behind the false walls, and it looks like there's something down there."

Down? "How far down?" she asked.

"Below the surface? Not far. This lot is all built up on reclaimed land—if that's what you're thinking."

She nodded. "Suppose it's not deep at all, in fairyland. Suppose it's on the surface. They could just waltz in and plant a bomb. Nobody would notice?"

"It's not that simple," said Dr. Rand, taking her by surprise. "Let's get you a hard hat and jacket and head down to the site."

"You've already opened it up?" she demanded.

"Not yet, we were waiting for you." He grinned unnervingly. "Step this way."

All railway stations—like all public buildings—have two faces. One face, the one Herz was familiar with, was the one that welcomed commuters every day: down the stairs into the MBTA station, through the ticket hall and the steps or ramps down to the platforms where the Blue Line trains and Green Line streetcars thundered and squealed. The other face was the one familiar to the MBTA workers who kept the system running. Narrow corridors and cramped offices up top, anonymous doors leading into dusty, ill-lit engineering spaces down below, and then the trackside access, past warning signs and notices informing the public that they endangered both their lives and their wallets if they ventured past them. "Follow me, sir, ma'am," said the MBTA transit cop Rand was using as an escort. "It's this way."

From one end of a deserted Blue Line platform—its entrance sealed off by police tape, the passengers diverted to a different part of the station—he led them down a short ramp onto the trackside. Herz glanced up. The roof of the tunnel was concrete, but it was also flat, a giveaway sign of cut and cover construction: there couldn't be much soil up there. Then she focused on following the officer as he led them alongside the tracks and then through an archway to the side.

"Wow." Judith glanced around in the gloom. "This is it?" Someone had strung a bunch of outdoor inspection lamps along the sixty-foot stretch of platform that started at shoulder height beside her. It was almost ankle-deep in dirt, the walls filthy.

"No, it's down here," said Lucius, pointing.

She followed his finger down, and realized with a start that the platform wasn't solid—it was built up on piles. The darkness below seemed almost palpable. She bent down, pulling her own flashlight out. "Where am I supposed to be looking?" she asked. "And has anyone been under here yet?"

"One moment," said Rand. "Officer, would you mind going back up for the rest of my team? Tell Mary Wang that I want her to bring the spectroscope with her."

Herz half-expected the cop to object to leaving two civilians down here on their own, but evidently someone had got to him: he mumbled an acknowledgment and set off immediately, leaving them alone.

"No, nobody's been under there yet," said Rand. "That's why you're here. You mentioned that the person behind this incident had some disturbing habits involving trip wires, didn't you? We're going to take this very slowly."

"Good," said Herz, suppressing an involuntary shudder.

The next half hour passed slowly, as half a dozen members of Rand's team made their way down to the platform with boxes of equipment in hand. Wang arrived first, wheeling a metal flight case trailing a length of electrical cable behind. She was petite, so short that the case nearly reached her shoulders. "Let's see where it is," she said encouragingly, then proceeded to shepherd the case along the platform at a snail's pace, pausing every meter or so to take readings, which she marked on the platform using a spray can.

"Where do you make it?" Rand asked her.

"I think it's under there." She pointed to a spot about two thirds of the way down the platform, near the rear wall. "I just want to double-check the emission strength and recalibrate against the reference sample."

Rand glanced at Herz and pulled a face. "Granite," he said. "Plays hell with our instruments because it's naturally radioactive."

"But Boston isn't built on—"

"No, but where did the gravel in the aggregate under the platform come from? Or the dye on those tiles?" His gesture took in the soot-smudged rear wall. "Or the stones in the track ballast?"

"But granite—"

"It's not the only problem we've got," Rand continued, in tones of relish that suggested he was missing the classroom: "Would you believe, bananas? Lots of potassium in bananas. You put a bunch of bananas next to a gamma source and a scattering spectrometer on the other side and they can fool you into thinking you're staring at a shipping container full of yellowcake. So we've got to go carefully." Wang and a couple of assistants were hauling her balky boxful of sensors over the platform again, peering at the instrument panel on top with the aid of a head-mounted flashlight.

"It's here!" she called, pointing straight down. "Whatever it is," she added conversationally, "but it sure looks like a pit to me. Lots of HEU in there. Could have come right out of one of our own storage facilities, it's so sharp."

"Nice work." Rand eased himself down at the side of the platform and lowered himself to the track bed. He looked up at Herz. "Want to come and see for yourself? Hey, Jack, get yourself over here!"

Judith jumped down to the track bed beside him. Her hands felt clammy. *Is this it?* she asked herself. The sense of momentous events, of living through history, ran damp fingertips up and down her spine. "Watch out," she warned.

"No problem, ma'am." Rand's associate, Jack, had an indefinite air about him that made her think, Marine Corps: but not the dumb stereotype kind. "Let's start by looking for lights."

Another half hour crept by as Jack—and another three specialists, experts in bomb disposal and booby traps—checked from a distance to ensure there were no surprises. "There are no wires, sir," Jack finally reported to Dr. Rand. "No IR beams either, far as I can tell. Just a large trunk over against the wall, right where Mary said."

The hair on Judith's neck rose. *It's real,* she admitted to herself. "Okay, let's take a closer look," said Rand. And without further ado, he dropped down onto hands and knees and shuffled under the platform. Herz blinked for a moment, then followed his example. *At least I won't have to worry about the dry-cleaning bill if Jack's wrong,* part of her mind whispered.

Jack had set up a couple of lanterns around the trunk. Close up, down between the pillars supporting the platform, it didn't look like much. But Rand seemed entranced. "That's our puppy all right!" He sounded as enthusiastic as a plane spotter who'd managed to photograph the latest black silhouette out at Groom Lake.

"What exactly is it?" Herz asked warily.

"Looks like an FADM to me. An enhanced storage version of the old SSADM, based on the W54 pit. Don't know what it's doing here, but someone is going to catch it in the neck over this. See that combination lock there?" He pointed. "It's closed. And, wait . . ." He fell silent for a few seconds. "Got it. Did you see that red flash? That's the arming indicator. It blinks once a minute while the device is live. This one's live. There's a trembler mechanism and a tamper alarm inside the casing. Try to move it or crack it open and the detonation master controller will dump the core safety ballast and go to detonate immediately." He fell silent again.

"Does 'detonate immediately' mean what I think it means?" asked Herz. *It's been here for months, it's not going to go off right away,* she told herself, trying to keep a lid on her fear.

"Yes, it probably does." Dr. Rand sounded distracted. "Hmm, this is an interesting one. I need to think about it for a while."

You need to— Herz wrenched herself back on track. "What happens now?" she asked.

"Let's go up top," suggested Rand.

"Okay." They scrambled backwards until they reached the track bed, and could stand up. "Well?" she asked.

"I got its serial number," Rand said happily. "Now we can cross-check against the inventory and see where it came from. If it's on the books, and if we can trust the books, then we can just requisition the PAL combination and open it up, at which point there's a big red OFF switch, sort of." A shadow crossed his face: "Of course, if it's a ghost device, like the big lump of instant sunshine you stumbled across in Cambridge, we might be in trouble."

"What kind of trouble? Tell me everything. I've got to tell the colonel."

"Well . . ." Rand glanced from side to side, ensuring nobody else was within earshot. "If it's just a pony nuke that's been stolen from our own inventory, then we can switch it off, no problem. *Then* we get medieval on whoever let it go walkabout. But you remember the big one? That wasn't in our inventory, although it came off the same production line. If this is the same, well, I *hope* it isn't, because that would mean hostiles have penetrated our current warhead production line, and that's not supposed to be possible. And we won't have the permissive action lock keys to deactivate it. So the best we can hope for is a controlled explosion."

"A controlled—"Herz couldn't help herself: her voice rose to an outraged squeal—"*explosion*?"

"Please, calm down! It's not as bad as it sounds. We know the geometry of the device, where the components sit in the casing. These small nukes are actually very delicate—if the explosive lens array around the pit goes off even a microsecond or two out of sequence, it won't implode properly. No implosion, no nuclear reaction. So what happens is, we position an array of high-speed shaped charges around it and blow holes in the implosion assembly. Worst case, we get a fizzle—it squirts out white-hot molten uranium shrapnel from each end, and a burst of neutrons. But no supercriticality, no mushroom cloud in downtown Boston. We've got time to plan how to deal with it, so before we do *that* we pour about a hundred tons of barium-enriched concrete around it and hollow out a blast pit under the gadget to contain the fragments." He grinned. "But these gadgets don't grow on trees. I'm betting that your mysterious extradimensional freaks stole it from our inventory. In which case, all I need to do is make a phone call to the right people, and they give me a number, and—"he snapped his fingers"—it's a wrap."

"But you forgot one thing," Judith said slowly.

"Oh, yes?" Rand looked interested.

"Before you do anything, I want you to dust for finger-prints around the lock," she said, barely believing her own words. "And you'd better hope we find prints from source GREENSLEEVES. Because if not . . ."

"I don't under—"

She raised a hand. "If these people have stolen one nuke, who's to say they haven't stolen others?" She looked him in the eye and saw the fear beginning to take hold. "We might have found Matt's blackmail weapon. But this isn't over until we know that there aren't any others missing."

Rudi hung above the forest with the wind in his teeth, a shit-eating grin plastered across his face (what little of it wasn't numb with cold) and the engine of the ultralight sawing along behind his left ear like the world's largest hornet. The airframe buzzed and shuddered, wires humming, but the vibration was acceptable and everything was holding together about as well as he'd hoped for. Unlike a larger or more sophisticated airplane, the trike was simple and light enough for one world-walker to shift in a week of spare time: and now Rudi was reaping his reward for all the headaches, upsets, reprimands, and other cold-sweat moments he'd put into it. "On top of the world!" He yelled at the treetops a thousand feet below him. "Yes!"

The sky was as empty as a dead man's skull; the sun burned down, casting sharp shadows over his right shoulder. Hanging below the triangular wing, with nothing below his feet but a thin fiberglass shell, Rudi could almost imagine that he was flying in his own body, not dangling from a contraption of aluminum and nylon powered by a jumped-up lawn mower engine. Of course, letting his imagination get away from him was not a survival-enhancing move up here, a thousand feet above the forests that skirted the foothills of the Appalachians in this world—but he could indulge his senses for a few seconds between instrument checks and map readings, saving the precious memories for later.

"Is that the Wergat or the Ostwer?" he asked himself, seeing the glint of open water off to the northwest. He checked his compass, then glanced at the folded map. One advantage of using an ultralight: with an airspeed of fifty-five, tops, you didn't wander off the page too fast. A few minutes later he got it pinned down. "It's the Ostwer all right," he told himself, penciling a loose ellipse on the map—his best estimate of his position, accurate to within a couple of miles. "Hmm." He pushed gently on the control bar, keeping one eye on the air speed indicator as he began to climb.

The hills and rivers of the western reaches of the Gruinmarkt spread out below Rudi like a map. Over the next half hour he crawled towards the winding tributary river—it felt like a crawl, even though he was traveling twice as fast as any race-bred steed could gallop—periodically scanning the landscape with his binoculars. Roads hereabout were little more than dirt tracks, seldom visible from above the trees, but a large body of men left signs of their own.

That's odd. He was nearly two thousand feet up, and a couple of miles short of the Ostwer—glancing over his left shoulder at a thin haze of high cloud that looked to be moving in—when a bright flash on the ground caught his eye. He stared for a moment, then picked up his binoculars.

Out towards the bend in the river—after the merger that produced the Wergat, where the trees thinned out and the buildings and walls and fields of Wergatfurt sprouted—something flashed. And there was smoke over the town, a thin smudge of dirty brown that darkened the sky, like a latrine dug too close to a river. "Hmm." Rudi leaned sideways, banking gently to bring the trike round onto a course towards the smoke, still climbing (there was no sense in overflying trouble at low altitude on one engine), and took a closer look with his binoculars.

He was still several miles out, but he was close enough to recognize trouble when he saw it. The city gates were open, and one guard house was on fire—the source of the smoke.

"Rudi here, Pappa One, do you read?"

The reply took a few seconds to crackle in his earpiece: "Pappa One, we read."

"Overflying Wergatfurt, got smoke on the ground, repeat, smoke. Guard house is on fire. Over."

"Pappa One to Rudi, please repeat, over."

"Stand by . . ."

Minutes passed, as Rudi checked his position against the river, and buzzed ever closer to the town and the palace three miles beyond it. The smoke was still rising as Rudi closed on the town, now at three thousand feet, safely out of range of arrows. He looked down, peering through binoculars, at a scene of chaos.

"Rudi here, Pappa One. Confirm trouble in Wergatfurt, cavalry force, battalion level or stronger. Cannon emplaced in town square, northeast guard tower on fire, tents outside city walls. Now heading towards Hjalmar Palace, over."

"Pappa One, Rudi, please confirm number of troops, over."

Rudi looked down. A flash caught his eye, then another one.

"Rudi here, am under fire from Wergatfurt, departing in haste, over." His hands were clammy. Even though none of the musketry could possibly reach him, it was unnerving to be so exposed. He pulled back on the bar to nose gently down, gathering speed: the sooner he checked out the palace and got the hell away from this area, the happier he'd be.

Tracking up the shining length of the river, Rudi headed towards the concentric walls of the castle overlooking the Wergat. The Hjalmar Palace was an enormous complex, sprawling across a hillside, surrounded on three sides by water. It stood in plain sight, proud of the trees that clothed the land around it. Rudi raised his glasses and stared at the walls. From a mile out, it looked perfectly normal. Certainly the cannon stationed in Wergatsfurt hadn't bitten any chunks out of those walls yet.

"Pappa One, Rudi, update please, over."

"Rudi here. Approaching Hjalmar Palace at two five hundred feet. Looks quiet. Over."

"Pappa One, Rudi, be advised palace has missed two watch rotations, over. Be alert for—"

Rudi missed the rest. Down below, sparks were flashing from the gatehouse. Startled, he let go of the binoculars and threw himself to the left, side-slipping away from the tower. A faint crackling sound reached his ears, audible over the buzz of the engine. "Rudi, Pappa One, am under fire from the palace, over." He leaned back to the right, feeling a bullet pluck at the fabric of his wing. *This shouldn't be happening,* he told himself, disbelieving: the altimeter was still showing two thousand feet. *How are they reaching me?* A horrible suspicion took hold. "Pappa One, Rudi, they've got—shit!"

For a moment he glanced down at the shattered casing of the radio, blinking stupidly. Then he leaned forward, trying to squeeze every shuddering mile per hour that was available out of the airframe, fuming and swearing at himself for not bringing a spare transceiver.

His unwelcome news—that whoever had taken the Hjalmar Palace had also taken its heavy machine guns, and knew how to use them—would now be delayed until he returned to Castle Hjorth.

It took them two hours to stagger back up the track to the waypoints blazed on the trees, and another half hour to reach the marked transit point. Walking in near-darkness with early flakes of snow whirling around them wasn't Huw's idea of a happy fun vacation: but his sense of urgency pushed him on, even though he was halfway to exhaustion. *We've got to tell someone about this,* he kept reminding himself. *Important* didn't begin to describe the significance of the door into nowhere. *We might not be the only people who can world-walk—or even the most effective at it.*

Eventually he staggered into the clearing where they'd pitched the tent—now a dark hump against a darker backdrop of trees, lonely and small in the nighttime forest. "You ready?" he asked Yul.

"I think you should go first, bro," his brother rumbled. "You're the one who understands that stuff."

"Yes but—" He made a snap decision: "—Follow me at once, both of you. We can recover the camp later if we need to. I may need witnesses to back me up."

"I'd kill for a bath!" Elena ended on a squeak. "Let's go!"

"Count of three," said Huw. He bared his wrist to the chilly air and squinted. "One, two—"

He lurched as the accustomed headache kicked in, then gasped as the humid evening air of home hit him in the face like a wet flannel. The noise of insects was almost deafening after the melancholy silence of the forest. To his left, Elena blinked into view and winced theatrically. "I'm going to the bathroom," she announced, unslinging her P90. "I may be some time."

"Whatever." Huw waited a few seconds before he turned to his brother, who was grinning like an idiot. "Is she always like this?"

"What? Oh, you should see her in polite society, bro." He stared after her longingly.

Huw punched him on the arm. "Come on inside, I've got to report this immediately."

He headed for the front room, shedding his pack and boots and finally his jacket and outer waterproof trousers as he went. The mobile phone was where he'd left it, plugged in and fully charged. He picked it up and unlocked it, then dialed by hand a number he'd committed to memory. It took almost thirty seconds to connect, but rang only once before it was answered. "This is Huw. The word today is 'interstitial.' Yes, I'm well, thank you, and yourself, sir. I want to speak to the duke immediately, if you can arrange it."

Hulius watched him from the doorway, a faintly amused expression on his face. From upstairs, the sound of running water was barely audible.

Huw frowned. "Please hold," Carlos had said. He was

the duke's man; he would have been told that Huw was working on a project for him, surely?

"Trouble?" asked Yul.

"Too early to say." Huw sat down on the bedroll, cradling the phone. "I'm on hold—oh. Yes, sir, I am. We're all there. I have an urgent report—what? Yes. Um. Um. Can you repeat that, please? Yes. Okay, I guess. Transfer me."

He clamped his free hand over the mouthpiece and grimaced horribly at Yul. "Shit. We've been nobbled."

"What—" Yul began, but Huw's face turned to an attentive mask before he could continue.

"Yes? My lady? Yes, I remember. What's going on? It's about—*oh,* yes, indeed. You want—you want us to meet you *where*?—When?—Tomorrow? But that's more than a thousand miles! We could fly—oh. Are you sure?" He rolled his eyes. "Yes, my lady. Um. We'll have to get moving right away. Okay. You have my number? We'll be there."

He hung up then put the phone down deceptively gently, as if he'd rather have thrown it out the window.

"What was *that* about?"

Huw looked up at his brother. "We'd better roust Elena out of her bath. Shit." He shook his head.

"Bro?"

"That was my lady d'Ost—one of his grace's agents. I got through to the duke's office but he's busy right now. Carlos passed on orders to submit a written report: meanwhile we're to get moving *at once*. We've got to drive all the way to the west coast and back on some fucking stupid errand. We're to take our guns, and we've got to be in Las Vegas by noon tomorrow, so we're going to be moving out *right now*. There's a private plane waiting for us near Richmond but we've got to get there first and it's going to take eight hours to get where we're going once we're airborne. Some kind of shit has hit the fan and they've got *my* name down as one of the trustees to deal with it!" He trailed off plaintively. "What's going on?"

Hulius grunted. "Two and a half thousand miles, bro. They must really want you there badly."

"Yeah. That's what I'm afraid of. Hmm, Lady d'Ost. I wonder what she does for the duke?"

Otto stared at the buzzing gnat in the distance, and swore.

"Gregor, my compliments to Sir Geraunt and I request the pleasure of his company in the grand hall as a matter of urgency."

The hand-man dashed off without saluting, catching the edge in his voice. The faint hum of the dot in the sky, receding like a bad dream of witchcraft, put Otto in mind of an angry yellowjacket. He could barely hear it over the ringing in his ears; the morning smelled of brimstone and gunsmoke. *Too early*, he thought. He'd barely taken the inner keep an hour ago: he'd counted on having at least a day to arrange things to his advantage. "Heidlor," he called.

"Sir?" Heidlor had been saying something to one of the gunners, who was now hastily swabbing out the barrel of his weapon.

"Get the fishermen into the grand hall and have them set their nets up between ankle and knee level, leaving areas free as I discussed. Once they've done the hall they're to do the barracks room, the duke's chambers, the kitchen, and the residences, in that order. The carpenters are to start on the runways in the grand hall as soon as the fishermen are finished, and to move on in the same order. This is of the utmost urgency, we can expect visitors at any time. Should any of the craftsmen perform poorly, make an example of them—nail their tools to their hands or something."

"Yes, sir." Heidlor paused. "Anything else?"

Otto swallowed his first impulse to snap at the man for hanging around: he had a point. "Find Anders and Zornhau. Their lances are to go on duty as soon as they are able. Station the men with the fishers and carpenters, one guard for each craftsman, with drawn steel. In the grand hall, place one man every ten feet, and a pistoleer in each corner. For the cleared spaces, position two guards atop a chair or table or something. Warn them to expect witches to manifest out of thin air at any moment. Rotate every hour." He paused for a moment. "That's all."

"Sir!" This time Heidlor didn't dally.

Otto turned on his heel and marched back towards the steps leading down from the battlements. He didn't need to look to know that his bodyguard—Frantz and four hand-picked pistoleers, equally good with witch gun or wheel lock, and armed with cavalry swords besides—were falling into line behind him. The way the witches fought, by stealth and treachery, his own life was as much under threat as that of any of his soldiers, if not more so.

The corkscrewing steps (spiraling widdershins, to give the advantage to a swordsman defending the upper floor) ended on the upper gallery of the great hall. Otto looked down on the fishermen and their guards, as they hastily strung their close-woven net across the floor at ankle height. Spikes, hammered heedlessly into the wooden paneling, provided support for the mesh of ropes. The carpenters were busy assembling crude runways on trestles above the netting, so that the guards could move between rooms without touching the floor. At the far end, near the western door that opened onto the grand staircase, there was a carefully planned open area: a killing ground for the witches who would be unable to enter from any other direction.

Sir Geraunt, the royal courier, was standing directly below him, looking around in obvious puzzlement. "Sir Geraunt!" Otto boomed over the balcony: "Will you join me up here directly?"

A pale face turned up towards him in surprise. "Sir, I would be delighted to do so, but this cat's cradle your artisans are weaving is in my way. If you would permit me to cut the knot—"

"No sir, you may not. But if you proceed through the door to your left, you will find the stairway accessible—for now."

A minute later Sir Geraunt emerged onto the balcony, shaking his head. A couple of weavers also emerged, lugging a roll of netting between them, but Otto sent them a wave of dismissal. "We are in less danger from the witches the higher we go, but the balcony must be netted in due course," he explained, for the younger man was still staring at the work in the room below with an expression of profound bafflement.

"My lord, I fail to understand what you are doing here. Is it some ritual?"

"In a way," Otto said easily. He walked to the edge of the balcony, and pointed down. "What do you see there?"

"A mess—" Sir Geraunt visibly forced himself to focus. "Nets strung across the floor, and walkways for your men. The witches appear from the land of shadows, do they not? Is this some kind of snare?"

"Yes." Otto nodded. It wouldn't do to let the witches retake the castle too easily—his majesty's little plan wasn't the kind of trick you could play twice. "Observe the open area, and the position of the guards—who are free to move where they will. I am informed by an unimpeachable source that the witches cannot arrive inside another object: that is, they may be able to appear within the building, but if the exact spot they desire to occupy is filled by a piece of furniture or a tree or another body, they are blocked. The netting is close enough to prevent them arriving anywhere on the covered floor. Thus, if they wish to pay us a visit, they must do so on the ground I leave to them. Where, you will note, my soldiers are awaiting them."

Sir Geraunt's eyes widened. "Truly, his majesty chose wisely in placing his faith in you!"

"Perhaps. We'll see when the foe arrive. That was why I called for you, as a matter of fact: the witches have unforeseen resources. A most peculiar carriage just over-

flew us, carrying a man who is now, without a doubt, has-
tening to their headquarters with word of our presence. I
had counted on having an entire day to prepare the defenses
here, and the surprise outside. To make matters worse,
my guards fired on the intruder—and missed. His majesty
is still a day away. I therefore expect the witches to attack
within a matter of hours."

The knight's reaction was predictable: "I stand before
you. What can I do on your behalf?"

Otto managed to produce a thin smile. "I expect to kill
a fair number of witches, but they have better guns than
my men, and probably other surprises beside. So I am
moving things forward. A reinforced company will stay
here to take the first attack. The survivors will fall back
through the tunnel to the river. Hopefully the resistance
will force them to concentrate in the castle, but our
witch-guns on the curtain walls, pointing inwards, will
bottle them up for long enough to execute his majesty's
plan . . ."

It was shaping up to be a good day, thought Eric, as he
twisting his left wrist with increasing effort to get the gyroball up to speed. A good day in a good week. Judith's
report from the scene under Scollay Square was the second bit of really good news after Mike Fleming's remark-
able reappearance. *Heads we win: Lucius punches in the
PAL code and switches off the bomb. Tails we don't lose:
we get to deal with a fizzle, but we keep Boston.* There
were cover stories available to deal with a fizzle, to sweep
it under the rug—it would be messy, but a whole different
matter from losing the core of a city. "I'm waiting on a
definite match when they finish fuming for prints," Judith
had told him from the scene, "but we got some good UV-
fluorescence images of patent prints in the dirt around the
lock, and it sure looks like GREENSLEEVES's prints."
Eric gave the ball another flick of the wrist. *Which means
we can take the kid gloves off now,* he thought, with a

warm glow of satisfaction. *Just as soon as we've con-firmed no other stock is missing.* And he went back to staring at his desk.

Back when telephone switchboards were simple looms of wires and plug boards, different networks needed different wires. You could judge how important an official was by how many phone handsets he had on his desk. Life had been a lot simpler in those days. Today, Eric had just the one handset—and it plugged into his computer instead of a hole in the wall. He glanced at the clock in his taskbar to confirm the call was late, just as the computer rang.

"Smith here." He leaned back.

"Eric? Mandy in two-zero-two."

"Hi Mandy, Jim here. Y'all had a good day so far?"

"I'll take roll call." Eric grinned humorously. The list of names on the conference call was marching down the side of his screen. "Looks like we're missing Alain and Sonya. I'd give them another five minutes, but I've got places to be and meetings to go to, so if we can get started?"

The field ops conference call was under way. Like any policing or intelligence-gathering operation, the hunt for the extradimensional narcoterrorists called for coordination and intelligence sharing: and with agents scattered across four time zones it couldn't be carried out by calling everyone into a briefing room. But unlike a policing job, some aspects of the task were extraordinarily sensitive and could not be discussed, and unlike a normal intelligence operation, things were too fluid and unstable to leave to the usual bureaucratic channels of written reports and weekly bulletins. So the daily ops call had become a fixture within FTO, or at least within that part of FTO that was focused on hunting the bad guys within the Continental United States. Each field office delegated a staff intelligence officer who could be trusted to filter the information stream for useful material and refrain from mentioning in public those projects that not everyone was

cleared for. Or so the post-hoc justification went. In practice, they gave Eric a chance to keep a finger on the pulse
of his department at ground level without spending all his
time bouncing around the airline map.

In practice, normally all it was usually good for was an
hour's intensive wrist exercise with the gyroball and a
frustrating ten minutes writing up a summary for Dr.
James. But today, Eric could smell something different in
the air.

". . . Following up the mobile phone thing via Wal-Mart,
we've made some progress over here."

Eric snapped to full alert, glancing at the screen. It
was Mandy, from the team in Stony Brook. "How many
phones?" He cut in.

"I was just getting to that." She sounded offended.
"The suspects bought two hundred and forty-six over the
past six months, all the same model, batches of ten at a
time, right up until yesterday. Wal-Mart has been very co-
operative, and we've been going over their videotapes—
they think it's some kind of fraud ring—and it looks like
a Clan operation for sure. It's the same two men each
week: if they follow the usual pattern—"the Clan had a
rigid approach to buying supplies, always paying cash for
small quantities at regular intervals"—we could lift them
next week. We've also got a list of phone IMEIs and SIM
numbers they bought and we're about to go to Cingular to
see if—"

"Don't do that," Eric interrupted again. He glanced
around frantically, looking for a pen and a Post-it: he
hadn't expected this much information, so soon. "We
have other resources to call on who are better at dealing
with this angle." To be precise, Bob and Alice at No Such
Agency, who—given a mobile phone's identifying
fingerprints—could tell you *everything* about them. This
was the trouble with ex-FBI staff: they did great investigative work, but they didn't know what external strings
they could pull with Defense. "E-mail me the list immediately," he ordered. "I'll take it from there."

"Certainly, I'll send them right after—"

"No, I meant *now*." The gyroball, unnoticed, wound down. "If any of those phones are switched on, we can get more than a trace." He took a deep breath. "I'm going offline now, waiting on that e-mail, Mandy." He hit the hangup button and shook his head, then speed-dialed a different number.

The phone picked up immediately. "James here."

"It's me. I assume you're in the loop over Lucius's little project? Well, Stony Brook has just hit the mother-lode, too. Mobiles, numbers. I'm forwarding everything to EARDROP. If any of them turn out to be live I intend to put some assets on the ground and tag them—then it's time to turn up the heat. If Herz confirms that the gadget under Government Center was planted by GREENSLEEVES, and Dr. Rand's friends confirm that no other weapons of the same class are missing, I propose to activate COLD-PLAY."

"Excellent," said James. "Get started, then get back to me. It's time to hurt these bastards."

Three coaches full of medieval weekend warriors drove in convoy through the Massachusetts countryside, heading towards Concord.

The coaches were on lease from a small private hire firm, and someone had inexpertly covered their sides with decals reading HISTORY FAIRE TOURING COMPANY. The passengers, mostly male but with some women among them, wore surcoats over chain mail, and the luggage racks overhead were all but rattling with swords and scabbards: the air conditioners wheezed as they fought a losing battle with the summer heat. They looked like nothing so much as the away team for the Knights of the Round Table, on their way to a joust.

The atmosphere in the coach was tense, and some of the passengers were dealing with it by focusing on irrelevancies. "Why do we have to wear all this crap?" complained Martyn, running his thumb round the neckline of his surcoat. "It's about as authentic as a jet fighter at the battle of Gettysburg."

"You'll grin and bear it," grunted Helmut. "It's cover, is what it is. You can swap it for camo when we link up with the wardrobe department. And it'll do in a hurry, if it comes to it . . ."

"Consider yourself lucky," Irma muttered darkly. "Ever tried to fight in a bodice?"

Martyn blew a raspberry. "Are we there yet?"

Helmut checked the display on his GPS unit. "Fifteen miles. Hurry up and wait." Someone down the aisle groaned theatrically. Helmut turned, his expression savage: "Shut the fuck up, Sven! When I want your opinion I'll ask for it."

The medieval knight at the wheel drove on, his shoulders slightly hunched, his face red and sweating. The lance members wore full plate over their machine-woven chain vests and Camelbak hydration systems—it was much lighter than it looked, but it was hellishly hot in the sunlight streaming through the coach windows. Heat prostration, Helmut reminded himself, was the reason heavy armor had gone out of fashion in this world—that, and its declining utility against massed gunfire. "Hydration time, guys, everyone check your buddies. Top off now. Victor, make with the water cart."

A police cruiser pulled out to overtake the coach and Helmut tensed, in spite of himself. Thirty assorted knights and maids on their way to a joust and a medieval faire shouldn't set the traffic cop's alarm bells ringing the way that thirty soldiers in American-style body armor would, but there was a limit to how much inspection their cover could handle. If the police officer pulled them over to search the baggage compartment he'd be signing his own death warrant: Helmut and his platoon of Clan Security soldiers were sitting on top of enough firepower to reenact a much more modern conflict.

"Keep going." The police car swept past and Helmut

sent Martyn a fishy stare. "Mine's a Diet Pepsi," Martyn said, oblivious. Helmut shook his head and settled back to wait.

Some time later, the driver braked and swung the coach into a wide turn. "Coming up on the destination," he remarked loudly.

Helmut sat up and leaned forward. "The others?"

"Braun is right behind me. Can't see Stefan but I'd be surprised if—"

Helmut's phone rang. Gritting his teeth, Helmut answered it. "Yes?"

"We see you. Just to say, the park's clear and we're keeping the bystanders out of things."

"Bystanders?"

The voice at the other end of the connection was laconic: "You throw a Renaissance Faire, you get spectators. Ysolde's telling them it's a closed rehearsal and they should come back tomorrow."

Helmut buried his fingertips in his beard and scratched his chin. "Good call. What about the—"he checked his little black book"—ticket seats?"

"They're going up. A couple of problems with the GPS but we should be ready for the curtain-raiser in about an hour."

Helmut glanced at his book again to confirm that *curtain-raiser* was today's code word for *assault team insertion*. One of the constraints they'd been working under ever since the big DEA bust six months ago was the assumption that at any time their cellular phones (carefully sanitized, stolen, or anonymously purchased for cash) might be monitored or tracked by hostile agencies. Clan Security—in addition to fighting a civil war in the Gruinmarkt—had been forced to rediscover a whole bunch of 1940s-era communication security procedures.

"Call me if there's a change in status before we arrive," Helmut ordered, then ended the call. "Showtime," he added, for the benefit of the audience seated behind him.

"It's not over until the fat lady sings," Martyn snarked in Irma's direction: she glared at him, then drew her dagger and began to ostentatiously clean her already-spotless nails.

The coach turned through a wide gateway flanked by signs advertising the faire, bumped across loose gravel and ruts in the ground, then came to a halt in a packed-earth car park at one end of a small open field. A couple of big top circus tents dominated it, and a group of men with a truck and a stack of scaffolding were busy erecting a raised seating area. To an untrained eye it might easily be mistaken for a public open-air event, close by Concord: that was the whole idea. Real SCA members or habitual RenFaire goers weren't that common, and those that might notice this event would probably write it off as some kind of commercial rip-off, aimed at the paying public. Meanwhile, the general reaction of that public to a bunch of people in inaccurate historical costume was more likely to be one of amusement than fear. Which was exactly what Riordan had proposed and Angbard had accepted.

In fact, the strip mall on the far side of the open space was owned by a shell company that answered to a Clan council director—because it was doppelgangered, located on the identical spot occupied by a Clan property in the other world. And the supposed historical faire was one of several ClanSec contingency plans designed to cover the rapid deployment of military units up to battalion size into the Gruinmarkt.

"Let's move those kit bags out," Helmut barked over his shoulder as the driver scrambled to open the baggage doors on the side of the coach. "I'll have the guts of any man who opens his kit before he gets it inside the assembly tent." His troopers scrambled to drag their heavy sports bags towards the nearer big top: he'd checked that they'd been properly packed, and while any hypothetical witnesses would see plenty of swords and "historical shit" as Erik called it, they wouldn't get even a hint of the SAWs

and M16s that were the real point of this masquerade—
much less the M47 Dragon that Stefan's fire support platoon were bringing to the party.

The setup in the tent would have surprised anyone expecting a show. Half a dozen men and women—officers in
Clan security, comptrollers of the postal service, and a
willowy blonde in a business suit who Helmut was certain
was one of the duke's harem of assassin-princesses—
were gathered around a table covered with detailed floor
plans: three more, armed with theodolites, laser range
finders, and an elaborate GPS unit were carefully planting
markers around the bare earth floor. At the far side, a work
crew was unloading aluminum scaffolding and planks
from the back of a truck, while another gang was frantically bolting them together at locations indicated by the
survey team. Helmut left his soldiers scrambling to pull
camouflage surcoats and helmets on over their armor, and
headed straight for the group at the table, halting two meters short of it.

The duke glanced up from the map. As usual, he was
impeccably tailored, dressed for the boardroom: a sixty-
something executive, perhaps, or a mid-level politician.
But there was a feral anger burning in his eyes that was
normally kept carefully banked: Helmut suppressed a
shudder. "Third platoon is dismounting and will be ready
to go in the next ten minutes," he said as calmly as he
could.

The duke stared at him for a moment. "Good enough,"
he rasped, then glanced sideways at his neighbor, whom
Helmut recognized—with a surprised double-take—as
Earl Oliver Hjorth, an unregenerate supporter of the
backwoods conservative cabal and the last man he'd have
expected to see in the duke's confidences. "I told you so."

The earl nodded, looking thoughtful.

"Is there any word from Earl Riordan?" The duke
turned his attention towards a plump fellow at the far side
of the table.

"Last contact was fifty-two minutes ago, sir," he said,

without even bothering to check the laptop in front of him. "Coming up in eight. I can expedite that if you want . . ."

"Not necessary." The duke shook his head, then looked back at Helmut. "Tell me what you know."

Helmut shrugged. Despite the full suit of armor, the gesture was virtually silent—there was neoprene in all the right places, another of the little improvements ClanSec had made to their equipment over the years. World-walkers were valuable enough to be worth the cost of custom-fitted armor, and they hadn't been idle in applying new ideas and materials to the classic patterns. "Stands to reason, he's hit the Hjalmar Palace, or you wouldn't have called us out. Is there any word from Wergatsfurt or Ostgat?"

The duke inclined his head. "Wergatsfurt is taken. Ostgat hasn't heard a whisper, as of—" He snapped his fingers.

"Thirty-seven minutes ago," said the ice blonde. She sounded almost bored.

"So we were strung out with a feint at Castle Hjorth and the Rurval estates, but instead he's concentrated eighty miles away and hit the Hjalmar Palace," summarized Helmut. He glanced around at the scaffolding that was going up. "It's fallen?"

"Within minutes," Angbard confirmed. He was visibly fuming, but keeping a tight rein on his anger.

"Treachery?"

"That's my concern," said the duke, with such icy restraint that Helmut backed off immediately. The blonde, however, showed no sign of surprise: she studied Helmut with such bland disinterest that he had to suppress a shudder.

So we've got a leak, he realized with a sinking feeling. *It didn't stop with Matthias, did it?* "Should I assume that the intruders know about doppelganger defenses?" He glanced round. "Should I assume they have world-walkers of their own?"

"Not the latter, Gray Witch be thanked." Angbard

hesitated. "But it would be unwise to assume that they don't know how to defend against us, so every minute delayed increases the hazard." He reached a decision. "We can't afford to leave it in their hands, any more than we can afford to demolish it completely. Our options are therefore to go in immediately with everything we've got to hand, or to wait until we have more forces available and the enemy has had more time to prepare for us. My inclination is towards the immediate attack, but as you will be leading it, I will heed your advice."

Helmut grimaced. "Give me enough rope, eh? As it happens, I agree with you. Especially if they have an informant, we need to get in there as fast as possible. Do we know if they are aware of the treason room?"

"No, we don't." Angbard's expression was thunderous. "If you wish to use it, you will have to scout it out."

"Aye, well, there are worse prospects." Helmut turned on his heel and raised his voice. "Martyn! Ryk! To me. I've got a job for you!" Turning back to the duke, he added: "If the treason room is clear, we'll go in that way, with diversions in the north guard room and the grand hall. Otherwise, my thinking is to assault directly through the grand hall, in force. The higher we go in—"he glanced up at the scaffolding, then over to the hydraulic lift that two guards were bringing in through the front of the tent"—the better I'll like it."

Motion sickness was a new and unpleasant experience to Miriam, but she figured it was a side effect of spending days on end aboard a swaying express train. Certainly it was the most plausible explanation for her delicate stomach. She couldn't wait to get solid ground under her feet again. She'd plowed through about half the book by Burroughs, but it was heavy going; where some of the other Leveler tracts she'd read had been emotionally driven punch-in-the-gut diatribes against the hereditary dictators, Burroughs took a far drier, theoretical approach.

He'd taken up an ideological stance with roots Miriam half-recognized—full of respectful references to Voltaire, for example, and an early post-settlement legislator called Franklin, who had turned to the vexatious question of the rights of man in his later years—and had teased out a consistent strand of political thought that held the dictatorship of the hereditary aristocracy to be the true enemy of the people. Certainly she could see why Burroughs might have been exiled, and his books banned, by the Hanoverian government. But the idea that he might be relevant to the underground still struck her as peculiar. *Do I really want to get involved in this?* she asked herself. It was all very well tagging along with Erasmus until she could get her hands on her laptop again and zip back to the United States, but the idea of getting involved in *politics* made her itch. Especially the kind of politics they had here.

"He's a theoretician, isn't he?" she asked Erasmus, as their carriage slid through the wooded hills. "What's Lady Bishop's interest?"

He stared out of the window silently, until she thought he wasn't going to reply. Then he cleared his throat. "Sir Adam has credibility. Old King George sought his counsel. Before Black Monday, he was a Member of Parliament, the first elected representative to openly declare for the radicals. And to be fair, the book—it's his diagnosis of the ailment afflicting the body politic, not his prescription. He's the chair of the central committee, Miriam. We need him in the capital—"

There was a sudden jerk, and Miriam was pushed forward in her seat. The train began to slow. "What's going on?"

"Odd." He frowned. "We're still in open country." The train continued to slow, brakes squealing below them. The window put the lie to Erasmus's comment almost immediately, as a low row of wooden shacks slid past. Brakes still squealing, the long train drifted to a halt. Erasmus glanced at her, worried. "This can't be good."

"Maybe it's just engine trouble? Or the track ahead?" *That's right, clutch at straws,* she told herself. Her hand went to her throat, where she had taken to wearing James Lee's locket on a ribbon: at a pinch she could lift Erasmus and land them both in the same world as the Gruinmarkt, but . . . "I can get us out of here, but I know nothing about where we'd end up."

"We've got papers." Now *he* sounded as if he was grasping at straws, and knew it.

"Don't anticipate trouble." She swallowed.

"Get your bag. If they want a bribe—"

"Who?"

"How should I know?" He pointed at the window: "Whoever's stopped the train."

The door at the end of the compartment opened abruptly, and a steward stepped inside. He puffed out his brass-buttoned chest like a randy pigeon: "Sorry to announce, but there's been a delay. We should be moving soon, but—" A bell sounded, ringing like a telephone outside the compartment. " 'Scuse me." He ducked back out.

"What kind of delay?" Miriam asked.

"I don't know." Erasmus stood up. "Got everything in your bag?" He raised an eyebrow.

Miriam, thinking of the small pistol, swallowed, then nodded. "Yeah." It was stuffy in the un–air-conditioned carriage, but she stood up and headed over to the coat rail by the door, to pick up her jacket and the bulging hand-bag she'd transferred the notebook computer into. "Thinking of getting off early?"

"If we have to." He frowned. "If this is—"

Footsteps. Miriam paused, her coat over her left arm. "Yes?" she asked coolly as the door opened.

It was a middle-aged man, wearing the uniform of a railroad ticket inspector. He looked upset. "Sir? Ma'am? I'm sorry to disturb you, but would you mind stepping this way? I'm sure we can sort this out and be on our way soon."

Erasmus glanced sideways at her. Miriam dry-swallowed,

wishing her throat wasn't dry. *Bluff it out, or . . . ?* "Certainly," he said smoothly: "Perhaps you can tell us what it's about?"

"In the station, sir," said the inspector, opening the door of the carriage. The steps were already lowered, meeting the packed earth of a rural platform with a weathered clapboard hut—more like a signal box than a station house—hunched beside it. Only the orange groves to either side suggested a reason for there to be a station here. The inspector hurried anxiously over towards the building, not looking back until he neared the door. Miriam caught Burgeson's eye: he nodded, slowly. *The Polis would just have come aboard and arrested us, wouldn't they?* she told herself. *Probably . . .*

As her companion approached the door, Miriam curled her fingers around the butt of her pistol. The inspector held the door open for them, his expression anxious. "The electrograph from your cousin requested a private meeting," he said apologetically. "This was the best I could arrange—"

"My *cousin*?" Miriam asked, her voice rising as the door opened: "I don't have a cousin—"

A whoosh of escaping steam dragged her attention up the line. Slowly and majestically, the huge locomotive was straining into motion, the train of passenger cars squealing and bumping behind it. Miriam spun round, far too late to make a run back for it. "Shit," she muttered under her breath. A steam car was bumping along the rutted track that passed for a service road to the station. "Double shit." Erasmus was frozen in the doorway, one hand seeming to rest lightly on the inspector's shoulder. Another car came into view along the road, trailing the first one's rooster-tail of dust.

"Please don't!" The inspector was nearly hysterical.

"Who set this up?" Erasmus asked, his tone deceptively calm.

"I don't know! I was only following orders!" Miriam ducked round the side of the station house again, glancing in through the windows. She saw an empty waiting room furnished only with a counter, beyond the transom of which was an evidently empty ticket office. *It's not the station,* she realized, near-hysteria bubbling under.

"Into the waiting room," she snapped, bringing the revolver out of her pocket. *"Move!"*

The inspector stared at her dumbly, as if she'd grown a second head, but Erasmus nodded: "Do as she says," he told the man. The inspector shuffled into the waiting room. Erasmus followed, his movements almost bored, but his right hand never left the man's shoulder.

"How long 'til they get here?" Miriam demanded.

"I don't know!" He was nearly in tears. "They just said to make you wait!"

"They," said Erasmus. "Who would *they* be?"

"Please don't kill me!"

The door to the ticket office was ajar. Miriam kicked it open and went through it with her pistol out in front. The office was indeed empty. On the ticket clerk's desk a message flimsy was waiting. Miriam peered at it in the gloom. DEAR CUZ SIT TIGHT STOP UNCLE A SENDS REGARDS STOP WILL MEET YOU SOONEST SIGNED BRILL.

Well, that *settles it.* Miriam lowered her gun to point at the floor and headed back to the waiting room.

"—The Polis!" moaned the inspector. "I've got three wee ones to feed! Please don't—"

Shit, meet fan. Even so, it struck her as too big a coincidence to swallow. *Maybe the Polis are tapping the wires? That would do it.* Brilliana had figured out where she was, which train she was on, and signaled her to wait, not realizing someone else might rise to the bait.

Burgeson's expression was grim. "Miriam, the door, please."

"Let's not do anything too hasty," she said. "There's an easy way out of this."

"Oh please—"

"Shut up, you. What do you have in mind?"

Miriam waved at the ticket office. "He's not lying about my cousin: she's on her way. Trouble is, if we bug out before she gets here she's going to walk into *them*. So I think we ought to sit tight." She closed the door anyway, and glanced round, looking for something to bar it with. "I can get us both out of here in an emergency," she said, a moment of doubt cutting in when she recalled the extreme nausea of her most recent attempts to world-walk.

The first car—*more like a steam-powered minivan,* Miriam noted—rounded the back of the station and disappeared from sight. Almost two minutes had passed since they reached the station. Miriam slid aside from the windows, while Burgeson did likewise. Boots thudded on the ground outside: the only sounds within the building were the pounding of blood in her ears and the quiet sobbing of the ticket inspector.

"Mr. Burgeson!" The voice behind the bullhorn sounded almost jovial: "And the mysterious Mrs. Fletcher! Or should I say, *Beckstein*?" He made it sound like an accusation. "Welcome to California! My colleague Inspector Smith has told me all about you both and I thought, why, we really ought to have a little chat. And I thought, why not have it somewhere quiet-like, and intimate, instead of in town where there are lots of flapping ears to take note of what we say?"

Across the room, Burgeson was mouthing something at her. His face was in shadow, making it hard to interpret. The inspector knelt in the middle of the floor, in a square of sunlight, sobbing softly as he rocked from side to side wringing his hands. The appearance of the Polis had quite unmanned him.

"Like this: parlez vous Francoise, Madame Beckstein?"

Miriam felt faint. *They think I'm a French spy?* Either the heat or the tension or some other strain was plucking her nerves like guitar strings. Somehow Erasmus had fetched up almost as far away as it was possible to get, twelve feet away across open ground overlooked by a window. To get him out of here one or the other of them would need to cross that expanse of empty floor, in front of—

The ticket inspector snapped, flickering from broken passivity to panic in a fraction of a second. He lurched to his feet and ran at the window, screaming, "*Don't hurt me!*"

Erasmus brought his right hand up, and Miriam saw the pistol in it. He hesitated for a long moment as the inspector fumbled with the window, throwing it wide and leaning out. "*Let me*—" he shouted: then a spatter of shots cracked through the glass, and any sense of what he had been trying to say.

The bullhorn blared, unattended, as the inspector's body slumped through the half-open window and Miriam, seeing her chance, ducked and darted across the room, avoiding the lit spaces on the floor, to fetch up beside Burgeson.

"I think they want you alive," he said, a death's-head grin spreading across his gaunt cheekbones. "Can you get yourself out of here?"

"I can get us both out—" She fumbled with the top button of her blouse, hunting for the locket chain.

"After how you were last time?"

Miriam was still looking for a cutting reply when the bullhorn started up again. "If you come out with your hands up we won't use you for target practice! That's official, boys, don't shoot them if they've got their hands up! We want to ask you some questions, and then it's off to the Great Lakes with you if you cooperate. That's also a promise. What it's to be is up to you. Full cooperation and your lives! Hurry, folks, this is a bargain, never to be repeated. Because you're on my manor, and Gentleman Jim Reese prides himself on his hospitality, I'll give you a minute to think about it before we shoot you. Use it carefully."

"Were you serious about waiting around for your friends?" Burgeson asked ironically. "Is a minute long enough?"

"But—" Miriam took a deep breath. "Brace yourself."

She put her arms around Erasmus, hugging him closely. His breath on her cheek smelled faintly stale. "Hang on." She dug her heels into the floor and lifted, staring over his shoulder into the enigmatic depths of the open locket she had wrapped around her left wrist. The knot writhed like chain lightning, sucking her vision into its contortions—then it spat her out. She gasped involuntarily, her head pulsing with a terrible, sudden tension. She focused again, and her stomach clenched. Then she was dizzy, unsure where she was. *I'm standing up*, she realized. *That's funny.* Her feet weren't taking her weight. There was something propping her up. A shoulder. *Erasmus's shoulder.* "Hey, it didn't—"

She let go of him and slumped, doubling over at his feet as her stomach clenched painfully. "I know," he said sadly, above her. "You're having difficulty, aren't you?"

The bullhorn: "Thirty seconds! Make 'em count!"

"Do you think you can escape on your own?" Burgeson asked.

"Don't—know." The nausea and the migraine were blocking out her vision, making thought impossible. "N-not."

"Then I see no alternative to—"Erasmus laid one hand on the doorknob"—this."

Miriam tried to roll over as he yanked, hard, raising the pistol in his right hand and ducking low. He squeezed off a shot just as Gentleman Jim, or one of his brute squad, opened fire: clearly the Polis did things differently here. Then there was a staccato burst of fire and Erasmus flopped over, like a discarded hand puppet.

Miriam screamed. A ghastly sense of déjà vu tugged at her: *Erasmus, what have you* done? She rose to her knees and began to raise her gun, black despairing fury tugging her forward.

There was another burp of fire, ominously rapid and regular, like a modern automatic weapon. *That's funny*, she thought vacantly, tensing in anticipation. She managed to unkink her left hand, but even a brief glance at the locket told her that it was hopeless. The design swum in her vision like a poisonous toadstool, impossible to stomach.

Erasmus rolled over and squeezed off two more shots methodically. Miriam shook her head incredulously: *You can't do that, you're dead!* Someone screamed hoarsely, continuously, out behind the station. Shouts and curses battered at her ears. The hammering of the machine gun started up again. Someone else screamed, and the sound was cut short. *What's going on?* she wondered, almost dazed.

The shots petered out with a final rattle from the machine gun. The silence rang in her ears like a tapped crystal wineglass. Her head ached and her stomach was a hot fist clenched below her ribs. "Erasmus," she called hoarsely.

"Miriam. My lady, are you hurt?"

The familiar, crystal-clear voice shattered the bell of glass that surrounded her. "Brill!" she cried.

"My lady, *are you alone in there*?"

Urgency. Miriam tried to take stock. "I think so," she managed. "I'm with Erasmus."

"She's not hurt, but she's sick," Burgeson called out. He shuffled backwards, into the shadowy interior of the waiting room, still clutching his pistol in his hand. He focused on Miriam. "It's your girl, Brill, isn't it?" he hissed.

"Yes," she choked out, almost overwhelmed with emotion. *He's not dead!* More than half a year had passed since that terrible moment in Fort Lofstrom, waiting beside Roland's loose-limbed body, hoping against hope. *And Brill—*

"Then I suggest we move out of here at once!" Brilliana called. "I'm going to stand up. Hold your fire."

"I'm holding," Erasmus called hoarsely.

"Good. I'm coming in now."

Another wild goose chase, Judith told herself gloomily. No sooner had she gotten back to the serious job of shad-

owing Mike Fleming like he was the president or something, no sooner had she managed to breathe a series of
extended gasps of relief at the news—that Source
GREENSLEEVES fingerprints had been all over the casing and it *was* missing from inventory and Dr. Rand had
punched in the PAL code and switched it off without any
drama, and all the other weapons in its class were present
and accounted for—than the colonel came down with his
tail on fire and a *drop everything* order of the day: absolutely typical. "Leave a skeleton team on site and get
everyone else up here *now*," he said, all trace of his usually friendly exterior gone. Crow's-feet at the corners of
his eyes that hadn't been there the week before. *Something's eating him*, she'd realized, and left it to Rich Wall
to ask what the rush job was and get his head bitten off.

Which was why, four hours later, she was sitting in the
back seat of an unmarked police car behind officers
O'Grady and Pike, keeping an eye on a strip mall and a
field with a big top in it and a sign saying HISTORY
FAIRE outside.

"What is it we're supposed to be *looking* for, ma'am?"
Pike asked, mildly enough.

"I'll tell you when I see it." The waiting was getting to
her. She glanced once more at the laptop with the cellular
modem and the GPS receiver sitting next to her. Seven red
dots pocked the map of Concord like a disease. Updated
in real time by the colonel's spooky friends Bob and Alice, no less, the laptop could locate a phone to within a
given GSM cell . . . but that took in the mall, the field, and
a couple of streets on either side. "There are tricks we can
play with differential signal strength analysis to pin down
exactly where a phone is," Smith had told her, "but it takes
time. So go and sit there and keep your eyes peeled while
we try to locate it."

The mall was about as busy—or as quiet—as you'd expect on any weekday around noon. Cars came, cars went.
A couple of trucks rumbled past, close enough to the
parked police car to rock it gently on its suspension.

O'Grady had parallel-parked in front of a hardware store just beside the highway, ready to move.

"We could be here a while," she said quietly. "Just as long as it isn't a wild goose chase."

"I didn't think you people went on wild goose chases," said Pike. Then she caught his eye in the rearview mirror. He reddened.

"We try not to," she said dryly, keeping her face still. Her FBI credentials were still valid, and if anyone checked them out they'd get something approximating the truth: on long-term assignment to Homeland Security, do not mess with this woman. "We're expecting company."

"Like that?" O'Grady gestured through the window. Herz tracked his finger, and stifled a curse. On the screen beside her, an eighth red dot had lit up in her cell.

"It's possible." She squinted at the coach. Men were coming out of the big top to open the gate, admitting it.

The laptop beeped. A ninth red dot on the map—and another coach of HISTORY FAIRE folks was slowing down to turn into the field.

"Just what do they do at a history faire anyway?" asked Pike. "Hey, will you look at that armor!"

"Count them, please," Judith muttered, pulling out her own phone. She speed-dialed a number. "Larry? I've got two coachloads that showed up around the same time as two more positives. Can you give me a background search on—"she squinted through her compact binoculars, reading off the number plates"—and forward it to Eric? He's going to want to know how many to bring to the party."

"What's that they're carrying?" Pike grunted.

Judith blinked, then focused on a group of men in armor, lugging heavy kit bags in through the door of the marquee. "This doesn't add up—" she began. Then one of the armored figures lifted the awning higher, to help his mates: and she got a glimpse at what was going on inside.

"Officers, we're not dressed for this party and I think we should get out of here *right now*."

"But they—" began Pike.

"*Listen* to the agent." O'Grady grimaced and started the engine. "Okay, where do you want me to go, ma'am?"

"Let's just get out of the line of sight. Keep moving, within a couple of blocks. I'm going to phone for backup."

"Is it a terror cell? Here?"

She met his worried eyes in the mirror. "Not as such," she said grimly, "but it's nothing your department can handle. Once you drop me off you're going to be throwing up a cordon around the area: my people will take it from here." She hit a different speed-dial button. "Colonel? Herz. You were right about what's going on here. I'm pulling out now, and you're good to go in thirty . . ."

Rudi squinted into the sunlight and swore as he tried to gauge the wind speed. The walls of Castle Hjorth loomed before him like granite thunderclouds—*except they're far too close to the ground, aren't they?* He shook his head, fatigue adding its leaden burden to his neck muscles, and glanced at the air speed indicator once more. *Thirty-two miles per hour, just above stall speed, too high . . .* the nasty buzzing, flapping noise from the left wing was quieter, though, the ripstop nylon holding. He leaned into the control bar, banking to lose height. Small figures scurried around the courtyard below him as he spotted the crude wind sock he'd improvised over by the pump house. *Okay, let's get this over with.*

The ultralight bounced hard on the cobblestones, rattling him painfully from spine to teeth, and he killed the engine. For a frightening few seconds he wondered if he'd misjudged the rollout, taking it too near the carriages drawn up outside the stables—but the crude brakes bit home in time, stopping him with several meters to spare. "Phew," he croaked. His lips weren't working properly and his shoulders felt as stiff as planks: he cleared his throat and spat experimentally, aiming for a pile of droppings.

Rudi had originally intended to go and find Riordan and make his report as soon as he landed, but as he took his hands off the control bar he felt a wave of fatigue settle over his shoulders like a leaden blanket. Flying the ultralight was a very physical experience—no autopilots here!—and he'd been up for just over three hours, holding the thing on course in the sky with his upper arms. His hands ached, his face felt as if it was frozen solid, and his shoulders were stiff—though not as stiff as they'd have been without his exercise routine. He unstrapped himself slowly, like an eighty-year-old getting out of a car, took off his helmet, and was just starting on his post-flight checklist when he heard a shout from behind. "Rudi!"

He looked round. It was, of course, Eorl Riordan, in company with a couple of guards. He didn't look happy. "Sir." He stood up as straight as he could.

"Why didn't you report in?" demanded the eorl.

Rudi pointed mutely at the remains of the radio taped to the side of the trike. "I came as fast as I could. Let me make this safe, and I'll report."

"Talk while you work," said Riordan, a trifle less aggressively. "What happened?"

Rudi unplugged the magneto—*no point risking some poor fool chopping their arm off by playing with the prop*—and began to check the engine for signs of damage. "They shot at me from the battlements and the gatehouse," he said, kneeling down to inspect the mounting brackets. "Took out the radio, put some holes in the wing. I was two thousand feet up—they've got their hands on modern weapons from somewhere." He shook his head. *Shit*. "If anyone's going in—"

"Too late."

Rudi looked up. Riordan's face was white. "Joachim, signal to the duke: defenders at the Hjalmar Palace have guns. No, wait." Riordan stared at Rudi. "Could you identify them?"

"I'm not sure." Rudi stood up laboriously. "Wait up." He walked round the wing—tipped forward so that the central spar lay on the ground—and found the holes he was looking for. "Shit. Looks like something relatively large. They were automatic, sir, machine guns most likely. Didn't we get rid of the last of the M60s a long time ago?"

Riordan leaned over him to inspect the bullet holes. "Yes." He turned to the messenger: "Joachim, signal the duke, defenders at the Hjalmar Palace have at least one—"

"Two, sir."

"Two heavy machine guns. Go now!"

Joachim trotted away at the double, heading for the keep. A couple more guards were approaching, accompanying one of Riordan's officers. For his part, the eorl was inspecting the damage to the ultralight. "You did well," he said quietly. "Next time, though, don't get so close."

Rudi swallowed. He counted four holes in the port wing, and the wrecked radio. He walked round the aircraft and began to go over the trike's body. There was a hole in the fiberglass shroud, only inches away from where his left leg had been. "That's good advice, sir. If I'd known what they had I'd have given them a wider berth." It was hard to focus on anything other than the damage to his aircraft. "What's happening?"

"Helmut and his men went in half an hour ago." Riordan took a deep breath. "When will you be ready to fly again?"

Whoa! Rudi straightened up again and stretched, experimentally. Something in his neck popped. "I need to check my bird thoroughly, and I need to patch the holes, but that'll take a day to do properly. If it's an emergency and if there's no other damage I can fly again within the hour, but—"he glanced at the sky"—there're only about three more flying hours in the day, sir. And I've only got enough fuel here for one more flight, anyway. It's not hard to get on the other side, but I wasn't exactly building a large stockpile. To be honest, it would help if we had another pilot and airframe available." He shrugged.

Riordan leaned close. "If we survive the next week, I

think that'll be high on his grace's plans for us," he admitted. "But right now, the problem we face is knowing what's going on. You didn't see any sign of the pretender's army, but that doesn't mean it isn't out there. Get your work done, get some food, then stand by to go out again before evening—even if it's only for an hour, we need to know whether there's an army marching down our throat here or whether the Hjalmar Palace is the focus of his attack."

Brill was one of the last people Miriam had expected to meet in California—and she seemed to have brought a bunch of others with her. "You're unhurt?" Brill asked again, anxiously.

The trio of Clan agents she'd turned up with—two men and a woman, sweating and outlandish in North Face outdoor gear—as if they'd just parachuted in from a camping expedition somewhere in the Rockies, in winter—had taken up positions outside the station. One of them Miriam half-recognized: *Isn't he the MIT postgrad?* Perhaps, but it was hard for her to keep track of all the convoluted relationships in the Clan, and right now—covering the approach track with a light machine gun from behind a bullet-riddled steam car—he didn't exactly look scholarly. Brilliana was at least dressed appropriately for New British customs.

"I'm unhurt, Brill." Miriam tried to hold her voice steady, tried not to notice Erasmus staring, his head swiveling like a bird, as he took in the scattered bodies and the odd-looking machine pistols Brill and the other woman carried. The Polis inspector and his men had tried to put up a fight, but revolvers and rifles against attackers with automatic weapons appearing out of thin air behind them "—Just got a bit of a headache." She sat down heavily on the waiting room bench.

"Wonderful! I feared you might attempt to world-walk." Brill looked concerned. "I must say, I was not expecting you to get this far. You led us a merry chase! But your letter reached me in time, and a very good thing too. His grace has been most concerned for your well-being. We shall have to get you out of here at once—"

Miriam noticed Brill's sidelong glance at Burgeson. "I owe him," she warned.

Erasmus chuckled dryly. "Leave me alive and I'll consider the debt settled in my favor."

"I think we can do better than that!" Brill drew breath. "I remember you." She glanced at Miriam. "How much does he know?"

"How much do you think?" Miriam stared back at her. This was a side to Brill that she didn't know well, and didn't like: a coldly calculating woman who came from a place where life was very cheap indeed. "They were lying in wait for us because they intercepted your telegram. The least we can do is get him to his destination. Leave him in this, and . . ." She shrugged.

Brill nodded. "I'll get him out of here safely. Now, will you come home willingly?" she asked.

The silence stretched out. "What will I find if I do?" Miriam finally replied.

"You need not worry about Baron Henryk anymore." Brill frowned. "He's dead; but were he not, the way he dealt with you would certainly earn him the disfavor of the council. He overplayed his hand monstrously with the aid of Dr. ven Hjalmar. The duke is minded to sweep certain, ah, events into the midden should you willingly agree to a plan he has in mind for you." Her distant expression cracked: "Have you been sick lately? Been unable to world-walk? Is your period late?"

Miriam blinked. "Yes, I—" she raised a hand to her mouth in dawning horror. "Fuck."

Brill knelt down beside her. "You have borne a child before, did you not?"

"But I haven't slept with—" Miriam stopped. "That fucking quack. *What did he do to me?*"

"Miriam." She looked down. Brill was holding her hands. "Ven Hjalmar's dead. Henryk is dead. *Creon* is dead. But we've got living witnesses who will swear blind that you were married to the crown prince at that ceremony, and this was the real reason why Prince Egon rebelled. Ven Hjalmar, with the queen mother's connivance . . . it's unconscionable! But we're at war, Miriam. We're at war with half the nobility of the Gruinmarkt, and you're carrying the heir to the throne. You're not a pawn on Angbard's chessboard anymore, Miriam, you're his queen. Whatever you want, whatever it takes, he'll give you—"

Miriam shook her head. "There's only one thing I truly want," she said tiredly, "and he can't give it to me." The claustrophobic sense of losing control that she'd fled from weeks ago was back, crushingly heavy. She lowered one hand to her belly, self-consciously: *Why didn't I think of this earlier?* she wondered. *All those examinations . . . Shit.* Then another thought struck her, and she chuckled.

"What ails you?" Brilliana asked anxiously.

"Oh, nothing." Miriam tried to regain control. "It's just that being figurehead queen mother or whatever scheme Angbard's penciled in for me isn't exactly a job with a secure future ahead of it. Even if you get this rebellion under control."

"My lady?"

"I was planning on bargaining," Miriam tried to explain. "But I don't need to, so I guess you want to know this anyway: it's too late. I ran into an old acquaintance on my way out of the burning palace. His people had been watching it when the shit hit the fan. It's the U.S. government. They've got agents into the Gruinmarkt, and it's only a matter of time before—"

"Oh, *that*," Brill snorted dismissively and stood up. "That's under control for now; your mother's running the negotiations."

Miriam held a hand before her eyes. *Make it stop*, she thought faintly. *Too much!*

"In any event, we have worse things to worry about now," she added. "Sir Huw was sent to do a little job for the duke that I think you suggested—he'll brief you about what he found on the flight home. The CIA or the DEA and their friends are the least of our worries now." Brill laid a hand on her shoulder. Quietly, she added: "We need you, Miriam. Helge. Or whoever you want to be. It's not going to be the same this time round. The old guard have taken a beating: and some of us understand what you're trying to do, and we're with you all the way. Come home with me, Miriam, and we'll take good care of you. We need you to lead us . . ."

The treason room was a simple innovation that Angbard's last-but-two predecessor had installed in each of the major Clan holdings: a secret back door against the day when (may it never arrive) Clan Security found itself locked out of the front. Like almost all Clan holdings of any significance, the Hjalmar Palace was doppelgangered—that is, the Clan owned, and in most cases had built on, the land in the other world that any world-walker would need to cross over from in order to penetrate its security.

For an empty field, the location where they'd set up the HISTORY FAIRE had a remarkably sophisticated security system, and the apparently decrepit barns at the far end of the field, collocated with the palatial eastern wing, were anything but easy to break into.

The treason room in the Hjalmar Palace had once been part of a guard room on the second floor of the north wing. That is, it had been part of the guard room until Clan Security had moved everybody out one summer, installed certain innovative features, then built a false wall to conceal it. The cover story was that they'd been installing plumbing for the nobs upstairs. In fact, the treason room, its precise location surveyed to within inches, was an empty space hidden behind a false wall, located twenty feet above the ground. The precise coordinates of the treason rooms were divided between the head of Clan

Security, and the office of the secretary of the Clan's commerce committee, and their very existence was a dark secret from most people.

Now, Helmut watched tensely as two of his men ascended towards the middle of the tent on a hydraulic lift.

"Ready!" That was Martyn. Big and beefy, he waved at Helmut.

"Me too," called Jorg. He pulled the oxygen mask over his head and made a show of adjusting the flow from his tank, then gave a thumbs-up while Martyn was still fiddling with his chin straps.

"Move out when you're both ready," Helmut called.

Martyn turned, lumbering, and switched on the tactical light clamped under the barrel of the MP5 he wore in a chest sling. Then he knelt down. Jorg climbed onto his back. The platform creaked and its motor revved slightly as he stood up, raising his left wrist to eye level before him. Silently and without any fuss, they disappeared from sight: a perfect circus trick.

Helmut nodded to the platform's operator. "Take it down three inches." The platform whirred quietly as it lowered. It wouldn't do for the returning world-walker to be blocked by the lift. He checked his watch. *Thirty seconds.* The drill was simple. Jorg would drop off Martyn's back, Martyn would swing round, and if there was any company he'd take them out while Jorg came right back over. If not, they'd inspect the room, plant the charges in the pre-drilled holes, set the timer to blow in half an hour, and then Jorg would carry Martyn back. After which, the next group through wouldn't need the masks—they wouldn't be entering a room that had been filled with carbon dioxide and sealed off behind a gas-tight membrane for fifty years.

Elapsed time, two minutes. Helmut shook his head, dizzy with tension. *If they've found the treason room and booby-trapped it* . . . He'd known Jorg as a kid. This wasn't something he wanted to have to explain to his mother.

"It's going to work," a voice at his shoulder said quietly.

Helmut managed not to jump. "I hope so, sir."

"It had better, because this is the real treason room, not the decoy." Angbard cast him a brief feral grin. "Unless my adversary is a mind reader . . ."

The thud of boots landing on metal dragged Helmut's head round. "Yo!" Jorg waved from the platform, which swayed alarmingly. He pulled his oxygen mask up: "It's clean!" Behind him, Martyn staggered slightly, fumbling with the lift controls. The platform began to descend, and Helmut drew in a breath of relief.

"Stand down," he told the guards who still stood with M16s aimed at the platform.

"Aw, can't I shoot him?" asked Irma. "Just a little?"

"You're going in next," Helmut said, deadpan. Now he was tense for an entirely different reason: anticipation, not fear. On the other side of the tent, Poul's couriers were already wheeling the siege tower forward. The aluminum scaffold on wheels didn't look very traditional, but with its broad staircase and the electric winch for hauling up supply packs it served the same purpose—a quick way into an enemy-held fortress. He looked up at Martyn. "Time check!"

"Catch."

Martyn tossed underarm and Helmut grabbed the grip-coated stopwatch out of the air. He stared at the countdown. "Listen up! Eighteen minutes and thirty seconds on my mark . . . Mark! First lance, Erik, lead off at plus ten seconds. I want an eyeball report no later than T plus thirty. Second lance, Frankl, you're in after the eyeball clears the deck. Third lance, you idle layabouts, we're going in thirty seconds after that. Line up, line up! Take your tickets for the fairground ride!" He headed off around the tent, checking that everyone knew their assigned role and nothing was out of place.

Minutes passed. The siege tower was finally set up on the carefully surveyed spot below the treason room. The couriers were still hammering stabilizer stakes into the ground around it as Erik led his lance up the ramp to the jump platform. The medical team was moving into position, maneuvering stretchers into position next to the winch: an ambulance sat next to one of the side doors to the tent, ready to go. Helmut checked the stopwatch.

"Sir Lieutenant." He glanced round, as Angbard nodded at him. The old man had a disturbing way of moving silently and unobtrusively. He straightened as the duke continued: "I don't intend to jog your elbow. You have complete discretion here. However, if there is an opportunity to take the commanding officer of the attacking force, or one of his lieutenants, alive, without additional risk to yourself or your men, then I would be *most* interested in asking him certain questions."

"Really?" He felt himself grinning in spite of himself. It wasn't an expression of amusement. "I can imagine, your grace." He glanced at the scaffolding. In a few minutes, it was quite possible that some or most of his platoon would be dead or injured. And right that moment, the idea of dragging the man who'd inflicted this shocking insult upon the Clan's honor up before his liege was a great temptation to Helmut. "I shall do everything in my power to oblige you, my lord. I can't promise it—not without knowing what is happening within the castle— but I'd like to make the bastards pay for everything they've done to us."

"Good." Angbard took a step back, and then, to Helmut's surprise, raised his fist in salute: "Lead your men to victory, knight-lieutenant! Gods speed your sword!"

Helmut returned the salute, then checked the time. *Minus one minute.* He raised a hand and waved at Erik, pointing to the stopwatch. "One minute!"

On the other side of the wall between the worlds, the timer would be counting down towards zero. Martyn and Jorg had packed the pre-drilled holes with blocks of C4 strung together on detcord, plugged in the timer, and synchronized it with the stopwatch in Helmut's hand. In a few seconds time, the thin false wall would be blasted into splinters of stone, throwing a deadly rain of shrapnel across the guardroom. It was intended to kill anyone inside, clearing a path for the assault lance waiting on the siege tower above. *Any second*—

Helmut raised his hand. "Time!"

Twelve pairs of boots shuffled forward above his head. The rattle of M16s and M249s being cocked, like a junkyard spirit clearing his throat: Erik's lance flipping out the knotwork panels beside their sights, squinting along their barrels and shuffling forward.

"Plus five!" called Helmut. "Six! Seven! Eight! Nine! Ten!"

The platform juddered on its base as the soldiers flickered out of sight. Helmut took a deep breath and turned towards the map table where the duke was conferring with his officers. Raised voices, alarm. Helmut glanced at the sergeant standing with his men beside the ramp. "Frankl, you know the plan. When the eyeball reports, go if it's clear. I'm—"the duke's raised voice made up his mind"—checking something."

"Is this confirmed?" Angbard demanded: the signals officer hunched defensively before him. "Is it?"

"Sir, all I have is Eorl-Major Riordan's confirmed report on Lieutenant Menger's overflight. If you want I can put you through to Castle Hjorth, but he's already redeploying—"

"Never mind." Angbard cut him dead as he turned to face Helmut. "They've got M60s," he said conversationally, although his cheeks showed two spots of color. "Your men need to know."

"M60s?" Helmut blanked for a moment. "Shit! The gatehouse!"

"More than that," the duke added. "It sounds like they captured a stockpile from one of the strategic villages. Eorl Riordan is redeploying his company. They should be arriving here within the next three hours."

"Right, right." Helmut nodded. "Well, that puts a different picture on things." He glanced at Angbard, anticipating the duke's dismissal. "If you'll excuse me, sir, my men need me?"

He turned and trotted back towards the siege tower. Overhead, on the platform, the first lance's messenger was shouting excitedly, something about the room being clear. "Listen up!" he called. "Change of plan. We're going in *now*. Housecleaning only, new plan is to secure the upper floors, strictly indoors. Anyone who goes outdoors gets their ass shot off: the bad guys have got their hands on a couple of M60s, and until we pinpoint them we're not going to be able to break out. Lance three, follow me in. Lance two, follow after."

He strode up the ramp as fast as he could, bringing his M16 down from his shoulder. The messenger was almost jumping from foot to foot. "It's clear, sir! It went really well. Erik said to tell you he's moving out into the upper gallery and will secure the roof line. Is that right?"

"It was." *Five minutes ago, before we knew they had machine guns on the bastions.* Helmut shook his head, an angry sense of injustice eating at his guts. Erik was probably already dead. "Okay, let's go to work." He glanced over his shoulder, at Irma and Martyn and the others in the lance he, personally, led: they were watching him, trusting him to lead them into the unknown. "For the glory of the Clan! Follow me . . ."

14

DOPPELGANGERED

Otto nearly didn't make it out of the castle. He was in the courtyard with Sir Geraunt and his personal guards, supervising the withdrawal of the body of his forces to the gatehouse and the prepared positions outside the castle walls, when there was a deafeningly loud thud from inside the central keep. "What's that?" Geraunt asked, stupidly.

"Nothing I planned." Otto turned to Heidlor, who was waiting for further instructions: "Stations! As I ordered!" The hand-man hurried off, and Otto met Sir Geraunt's curious gaze. "It'll be the enemy. Too damned early, blast them. Quickly, this way."

"But the fighting—"

Otto bit back his first response. "A commander who gets himself killed in the first engagement isn't terribly effective later in the battle," he muttered. "Come *on*." He hurried towards the gate tower's postern door. "You there! Stand by!"

A crackle of witch-gun fire echoed out of the central keep. On the top of the gate tower, and the tops of the four towers around the curtain wall, he saw the shields of the captured M60s swinging to bear on the keep.

More gunfire, and screams—this time, the flat boom of his own men's musketry, but far too little of it, too late. *Gods, they're good.* He could see it in his mind's eye: the witches appearing in the middle of a room, unable to enter in strength, surrounded by the cat's cradle of ropes while his men hacked at them desperately with blade and club, trying to keep them from advancing into the keep before the welcome mat was ready—

He paused at an arrow slit. A light blinked in one window high up in the keep, flashing a prearranged signal. He blinked, then swore. "What is it?" asked Sir Geraunt.

"They had a back door," Otto said tersely. Just as he feared: and they'd come through it hard and fast, hours sooner than his plan called for. "Every man of ours in the keep is as good as dead." He turned from the window and stopped: Sir Geraunt was between him and the staircase leading up to the top of the gatehouse.

"We must do something! Give me a score of men and I'll force an entrance—"

"No you won't." Otto breathed deeply. "Come on, follow me. It's premature, but." A grinding roar split the air overhead and he winced: it stopped for a moment, then started again, bursts of noise hammering at his ears like fists as the machine gun battery opened fire on the roofline of the keep, scything through the figures who had just appeared there. "Quickly!"

Up on top of the gatehouse the stench of burned powder and the hammering racket of the guns were well-nigh unbearable. Otto headed for the hetman he'd left in charge. "Anders. Report."

"They're pinned down!" Anders yelled over the guns. "They keep trying to take the roof and we keep sweeping them off it." The machine gun paused as two of his men

fumbled with gloves at the barrel, swearing as they inexpertly worked it free and tried to slot the replacement into
position.

"They seem to have learned to keep their heads down,"
Otto said dryly. A spatter of gunfire from a window in the
keep targeted the doorway to the northern tower: the
heavy guns on the south and west replied, chipping lumps
of stone out of the sides of the arrow slit. "Keep them bottled up. Conserve your fire if you can." He glared disap-
provingly at the two other towers, whose gunners were
pounding away at the enemy as if there was no shortage
of ammunition. "Carry on."

He ducked back down the stairs towards the guardroom
overlooking the gate tunnels. "March," he said, spotting a
sergeant: "What state did you leave the charges in?"

"The barrels are in position, my lord." March looked
pleased with himself. "The cords were ready when I left."

"Good!" Otto nodded. He looked around: there was an
entire lance of soldiers in the room. "Then let's set the
timers and fall back to our prepared positions." He made
the sign of the crone behind his back, where the men
couldn't see it: *If this fails* . . . It wasn't just the king's
men who knew how to fill a wise tree.

The duke was as tense as she had ever seen him: that worried Olga. Not that most of the junior nobility and officers
scurrying between communications and intelligence tables would recognize the signs—Angbard was not one to
fret obviously in public—but she had known him for
years, almost as a favorite uncle, and had observed him in
a variety of situations, and she'd seldom seen him as
edgy as this. From the set of his shoulders to the way he
held his hands behind his back as he listened to messen-
gers and barked orders, the duke was clearly trying to
conceal the extent of his ill-ease. *Is it really that bad?* she
wondered.

It had started with the messenger who arrived just minutes after the vanguard of the raiding group crossed over into the treason room: she'd been close enough to hear the news of the machine guns, and he could hardly fault the duke for being disturbed by *that*. But as time went by, and the minutes counted on from the incursion, the duke had become even more unhappy. The brief message from Brilliana—she'd been standing right behind him when he received it—had brightened his mood momentarily, but the lack of courier reports was obviously preying on his mind. Clan security didn't have enough bodies to keep him supplied with a blow-by-blow account of the action, and he knew better than to micromanage a skilled subordinate, but his patience had limits. And so, she waited by the duke's command table, keeping one eye on Eorl Hjorth—who she trusted as far as she could throw him. Hjorth's testimony to the council might well decide whether the duke remained in charge of Clan Security. *So we'll have to make sure that his testimony is favorable, won't we?*

"Sir, I have the hourly report from Eorl Riordan." The messenger offered Angard a print-out to scrutinize. The duke glanced up. "Where's Braun?" he demanded tensely.

"Sir." Braun—a wiry fellow, one of the distaff side of the Hjorth-Wu side—saluted.

"Messenger for Helmut, or whoever's in charge, immediate: sweep the cellars for explosive charges." The duke paused for a moment. "He's not to attempt to sally from the keep until Stefan's unit is in place to take out the machine guns." Olga glanced over her shoulder: the second platoon, with their heavy equipment, were already climbing the siege tower. "Instead, he's to ensure there are no surprises in the cellars under the keep. I think the pretender's trying to be *clever*." He delivered the final word with contemptuous satisfaction. "What—"

There was some kind of disturbance going on at the perimeter. Even as Braun charged off to brief a courier, and the heavy weapons platoon climbed the tower and vanished from its top deck three at a time, a distant noise reached Olga's ears, like the throbbing growl of distant traffic. She glanced up. *Lightning Child! Not here, not now!* A pair of guards detached themselves from the group near the awning and trotted towards the table. Reflexively, she moved her right hand close to her jacket pocket, interposing herself.

The first of the guards stopped three meters short and saluted. Olga relaxed slightly, for a moment. "Sir! We have hostiles in view. Sergeant Bjorg is calling a Threat Red."

"How many hostiles?" asked the duke, as if it was a minor point of interest.

Olga cleared her throat. "Sir, I think we should evacuate *now.*"

"Two choppers overhead at last sighting, sir, but it's not looking good on the ground, either: there've been no cars or trucks for a couple of minutes now." The throbbing was getting louder. *Almost as if—*

The duke shook himself. "Get everyone across immediately!" he barked. He pointedly refrained from looking up. "Third platoon, provide covering fire if necessary. Olga!"

"Your grace?" She stared at him.

"You're going across right now, with the headquarters staff. Keep an eye on Hjorth—he's mostly got our interests at heart, if he's smart enough to understand where they lie." The duke gestured at the siege tower. "Get moving!"

"But they're—" The bass roar of rotor blades was unmistakable now: not just one set, but the throb of multiple helicopters. Olga set her jaw. "After you, my lord!"

"You—" For a moment, the duke looked furious: then he nodded tightly, and stalked towards the tower. A squad from the third platoon raced to take up positions around the entrance and behind the low awning, as the duke's staff hurriedly grabbed their papers and equipment and trotted towards the platform from which they could cross into the treason room.

Olga ducked over to the side of the map table and

retrieved her rifle and kit—a very non-standard item, more suitable for a sniper than a soldier—then followed the exodus towards the tower. The roof of the tent billowed beneath the thunder, and for a terrifying moment she wondered if she was about to see a SWAT team dropping right through the fabric roof on ropes—but no, *the cops won't do that: they'll go for a siege. Unless—*

The voice of an angry god battered through the walls. *"Come out with your hands up! You have ten seconds to comply!"*

Olga grimaced. *Bastards,* she thought absently. For a routine weekly briefing this was certainly turning out to be an interesting one. *I wonder how they tracked us?* It couldn't be the phone Mike had given her—that wasn't even in the same county.

The queue at the tower had backed up, bottlenecked at the foot of the stairs, but it was moving fast, the worldwalkers jumping as soon as they reached the top step with reckless disregard for whatever might be waiting for them on the other side. Olga could see the duke up ahead, near the top step. He glanced over his shoulder as if looking for her, then reached the platform and disappeared. She took a deep breath, relieved. The throbbing roar of rotor blades and the flapping of the canvas roof were making it hard to think: *But we were negotiating: why attack now?* she thought. *Why?* It made little sense. *Unless they think—*

A punishingly loud blast of gunfire ripped through the side of the tent, slapping the fire team behind the main entrance into the ground. *"We can see you. Drop your weapons and come out immediately!"*

Olga stared at the mangled bodies for a fraction of a second, then forced herself to palm her locket open and focus. Some of the surviving guards were shooting blind, suppressive fire through the walls of the tent, while ahead of her half the bodies in the queue were doing just as he was—trying to cross over blind, heedless of hazard. Some of them would make it, some wouldn't, but at least the crush would clear. The design on the inside of her amulet spiraled and twisted, dragging her eyes down towards a vanishing point. Somewhere behind her, a concussive blast: and then she stumbled forward into a smoke-filled space, the air thick with suspended dust, her head pounding and her stomach coiling. *I made it,* she thought. Then: *We're mousetrapped.*

"Milady!" Her eyes widened as she turned towards the Clan soldier, lowering the pistol that had appeared in her hand before she consciously noticed his presence.

"Where's the duke?" she snapped.

"This way." He turned and she followed him, nearly tripping over some kind of obstruction. *A fishing net?* There was a raised runway above it, and bodies. *Too many bodies,* some of them in Clan uniforms. She took a step up onto the rough-cut planks, bringing her feet above the level of the netting.

"What happened here?"

"Rope trap, my lady. It's a partial doppelganger, if they'd had time to complete it they'd have locked us out, but we used the treason room instead—"

"I understand. Now take me to the duke. I'm meant to be guarding his life."

Her guide was already heading up the servants' stairs, two steps and a time, and all she could do was follow. Behind her another body popped out of the air and doubled over, retching. *It's not all over yet,* she realized.

The former guardroom was a mess—one wall blown in, furniture splintered and chopped apart by shrapnel, the bodies of two defenders shoved into a corner and ignored—but at least it was in friendly hands. Angbard's staff clustered around in groups, exchanging messages and orders, and—*Where's the duke*? Olga headed for the biggest knot, who seemed to be bending over a table or something—

"Your grace?" She gaped.

Angbard glared at her with one side of his face. The

other drooped, immobile. "G-get—" He struggled to speak.

"My lady, please! Leave him to us." A thick-set, fair-headed officer, one of the Clan Security hangers-on, Olga thought, struggling to recall his name, cradled the duke in his arms. "Where's the corpsman?" he rumbled.

"Your grace," Olga repeated, dumbly. The world seemed to be crumbling under her feet. *Sky Father, what are we going to do now?* The abrupt shift in perspective, to having to confront this mess without him, was far more frightening than the bullets and bombs outside. "Try to rest. We made it across, and we hold the keep."

"Corpsman!" the officer called. "Milady, please move aside." Olga stepped out of the way to let the medic through.

Eorl Hjorth, lurking nearby, looked at her guiltily. "He was like this when I got here," he mumbled. Olga stared at him. "I'm telling the truth!" He looked afraid. *As well you might,* she thought, looking away. *If this turns to be anything other than Sky Father calling his own home . . .*

A loud "Harrumph!" brought her attention back to the stocky officer who still supported Angbard's shoulder. He met Olga's gaze evenly. "I have operational command here, while his grace is incapacitated. Previously he had indicated that you have your own tasks to discharge, although I doubt you were expecting to discharge them here."

"That's true. You have the better of me, sir—"

"Carl, Eorl of Wu by Hjalmar. Captain of Security." He glanced at the communications team, who were still wrestling with their field radio and its portable generator. "You report directly to his grace, don't you? External Operations?"

"That is correct, yes."

"Well. We could do with a few more of your friends here, for sure." Carl grunted. "It looks like a mess here, but nothing we can't break out of in a few hours." A frown creased his face. "Although whether his grace lasts it out

is another matter. And I liked it better when we had no
enemy at the back door."

"He's—" Olga shut her mouth and looked back at the
medic who, with the assistance of a couple of guards, was
trying to make the duke comfortable. "He needs an
American hospital."

"Well, he's not getting one until we break out of here."
Carl's mustache twitched ferociously. A messenger
cleared his throat behind Olga. "Report!"

"Sir! We got them!" The man held up a handful of
yellow-sleeved wires.

"Yes, but did you get them *all?*"

"These were all the fuses first squad could find in the
cellars—"

A distant thud, like a giant door slamming shut outside,
took Olga's attention. "What was that?" she demanded.

"Don't know." Carl strode towards the nearest window.
"Shit."

"What is it?"

The security officer turned back to her. "That—"his
thumb aimed at a rising plume of dust"—unless I'm mistaken, is the culvert to the river."

"Oh."

"My compliments to Sergeant Heinz, and you can tell
him he did indeed find all the fuses in the cellar," Carl
told the messenger. "He's to hold until the heavy weapons
are in place, then proceed with task bravo." The messenger ran off. "Unfortunately he was in no position to check
the pump-house for charges," Carl continued, gruffly.
"Which is a problem. Because we're bottled up in here
under those guns, we have no water, our doppelganger location is besieged, and his grace is inconvenienced." He
didn't say *dying*, Olga noted. "So if you have any suggestions, before I go and attempt to retake the curtain wall in
the face of our own stolen machine guns, I'd like to hear
them."

Olga dry-swallowed, trying to work some juice into her
mouth.

"Have you radioed Eorl Riordan to warn him off the American trap?"

"Yes. But he has his own problems. He won't be able to relieve us in less than two days, and if the royal army is out there, that'll be too late."

"But he has a flying machine." Olga shook her head. Then she smiled. *Do I have to do all the plotting around here?* "With your permission, I should like to talk to Eorl Riordan immediately. And you might ready such of your men as are ready to world-walk again. I think we might be able to deal with the enemy without mounting a frontal attack on those guns: and in the process, inconvenience the pretender mightily. . . ."